BURNT SHADOWS

KAMILA SHAMSIE was born in 1973 in Karachi. She is the author of four previous novels: *In the City by the Sea*, *Kartography* (both shortlisted for the John Llewellyn Rhys Prize), *Salt and Saffron* and *Broken Verses*. Three of her novels have received awards from Pakistan's Academy of Letters.

BURNT SHADOWS

KAMILA SHAMSIE

BLOOMSBURY
LONDON · BERLIN · NEW YORK

First published 2009
This paperback edition published 2009

Copyright © 2009 by Kamila Shamsie

The moral right of the author has been asserted

Bloomsbury Publishing, London, New York and Berlin

36 Soho Square, London W1D 3QY

A CIP catalogue record for this book is available from the British Library

ISBN 978 1 4088 0701 9

10 9 8 7 6 5 4 3 2

Typeset by Hewer Text UK Ltd, Edinburgh

Printed in Great Britain by Clays Ltd, St Ives plc

FSC

Mixed Sources
Product group from well-managed
forests and other controlled sources

Cert no. SGS-COC-2061
www.fsc.org
© 1996 Forest Stewardship Council

www.bloomsbury.com/kamilashamsie

For Aisha Rahman and Deepak Sathe

. . . a time
                to recollect
every shadow, everything the earth was losing,

a time to think of everything the earth
and I had lost, of all

                that I would lose,
of all that I was losing.

                                        – Agha Shahid Ali,
                                    A Nostalgist's Map of America

In past wars only homes burnt, but this time
Don't be surprised if even loneliness ignites.
In past wars only bodies burnt, but this time
Don't be surprised if even shadows ignite.

                                – Sahir Ludhianvi, *Parchaiyaan*

Contents

Prologue

Once he is in the cell they unshackle him and instruct him to strip. He takes off the grey winter coat with brisk efficiency and then – as they watch, arms folded – his movements slow, fear turning his fingers clumsy on belt buckle, shirt buttons.

They wait until he is completely naked before they gather up his clothes and leave. When he is dressed again, he suspects, he will be wearing an orange jumpsuit

The cold gleam of the steel bench makes his body shrivel. As long as it's possible, he'll stand.

How did it come to this, he wonders.

The Yet Unknowing World

Nagasaki, 9 August 1945

L ater, the one who survives will remember that day as grey, but on the morning of 9 August itself both the man from Berlin, Konrad Weiss, and the schoolteacher, Hiroko Tanaka, step out of their houses and notice the perfect blueness of the sky, into which white smoke blooms from the chimneys of the munitions factories.

Konrad cannot see the chimneys themselves from his home in Minamiyamate, but for months now his thoughts have frequently wandered to the factory where Hiroko Tanaka spends her days measuring the thickness of steel with micrometers, images of classrooms swooping into her thoughts the way memories of flight might enter the minds of broken-winged birds. That morning, though, as Konrad slides open the doors that form the front and back of his small wooden caretaker's house and looks in the direction of the smoke he makes no attempt to imagine the scene unfolding wearily on the factory floor. Hiroko has a day off – a holiday, her supervisor called it, though everyone in the factory knows there is no steel left to measure. And still so many people in Nagasaki continue to think Japan will win the war. Konrad imagines conscripts sent out at night to net the clouds and release them in the morning through factory chimneys to create the illusion of industry.

He steps on to the back porch of the house. Green and brown leaves are scattered across the grass of the large property, as though the area is a battlefield in which the soldiers of warring armies have lain down, caring for nothing in death but proximity. He looks up

5

the slope towards Azalea Manor; in the weeks since the Kagawas departed, taking their household staff with them, everything has started to look run-down. One of the window shutters is partly ajar; when the wind picks up it takes to banging against the sill. He should secure the shutter, he knows, but it comforts him to have some sound of activity issuing from the house.

Azalea Manor. In '38 when he stepped for the first time through its sliding doors into a grand room of marble floor and Venetian fireplace it was the photographs along the wall that had captured his attention rather than the mad mixture of Japanese and European architectural styles: all taken in the grounds of Azalea Manor while some party was in progress, Europeans and Japanese mixing uncomplicatedly. He had believed the promise of the photographs and felt unaccustomedly grateful to his English brother-in-law James Burton who had told him weeks earlier that he was no longer welcome at the Burton home in Delhi with the words, 'There's a property in Nagasaki. Belonged to George – an eccentric bachelor uncle of mine who died there a few months ago. Some Jap keeps sending me telegrams asking what's to be done with it. Why don't you live there for a while? As long as you like.' Konrad knew nothing about Nagasaki – except, to its credit, that it was not Europe and it was not where James and Ilse lived – and when he sailed into the harbour of the purple-roofed city laid out like an amphitheatre he felt he was entering a world of enchantment. Seven years later much of the enchantment remains – the glassy loveliness of frost flowers in winter, seas of blue azaleas in summer, the graceful elegance of the Euro-Japanese buildings along the seafront – but war fractures every view. Or closes off the view completely. Earlier in the war those who went walking in the hills were warned against looking down towards the shipyard where the battleship Mushashi was being built under such secrecy that heavy curtains had been constructed to block its views from all passers-by.

Functional, Hiroko Tanaka thinks, as she stands on the porch of her house in Urakami and surveys the terraced slopes, the still morning alive with the whirring of cicadas. If there were an adjective to best describe how war has changed Nagasaki, she decides, that would be it. Everything distilled or distorted into its most functional form. She walked past the vegetable patches on the slopes a few days ago and saw the earth itself furrowing in mystification: why potatoes where once there were azaleas? What prompted this falling-off of love? How to explain to the earth that it was more functional as a vegetable patch than a flower garden, just as factories were more functional than schools and boys were more functional as weapons than as humans.

An old man walks past with skin so brittle Hiroko thinks of a paper lantern with the figure of a man drawn on to it. She wonders how she looks to him, or to anyone. To Konrad. Just a gaunt figure in the drabbest of clothes like everyone else, she guesses, recalling with a smile Konrad's admission that when he first saw her – dressed then, as now, in white shirt and grey monpe – he had wanted to paint her. Not paint a portrait of her, he added quickly. But the striking contrast she formed with the lush green of the Kagawas' well-tended garden across which she had walked towards him ten months ago made him wish for buckets of thick, vibrant paint to pour on to her, waterfalls of colour cascading from her shoulders (rivers of blue down her shirt, pools of orange at her feet, emerald and ruby rivulets intersecting along her arms).

'I wish you had,' she said, taking his hand. 'I would have seen the craziness beneath the veneer much sooner.' He slipped his hand out of hers with a glance that mixed apology and rebuke. The military police could come upon them at any moment.

The man with the brittle skin turns to look back at her, touching his own face as if trying to locate the young man beneath the wrinkles. He has seen this neighbourhood girl – the traitor's daughter – several times in the last few months and each time it seems that the hunger they are all inhabiting conspires to make her more beautiful: the roundness of her childhood face has melted away completely to reveal the exquisiteness of sharply angled cheekbones, a mole resting just atop one of them. But somehow she escapes all traces of harshness, particularly when, as now, her mouth curves up on one side, and a tiny crease appears just millimetres from the edge of the smile, as though marking a boundary which becomes visible only if you try to slip past it. The old man shakes his head, aware of the foolishness he is exhibiting in staring at the young woman who is entirely unaware of him, but grateful, too, for something in the world which can still prompt foolishness in him.

The metallic cries of the cicadas are upstaged by the sound of the air siren, as familiar now as the call of insects. The New Bomb! the old man thinks, and turns to hurry away to the nearest air-raid shelter, all foolishness forgotten. Hiroko, by contrast, makes a sharp sound of impatience. Already, the day is hot. In the crowded air-raid shelters of Urakami it will be unbearable – particularly under the padded air-raid hoods which she views with scepticism but has to wear if she wants to avoid lectures from the Chairman of the Neighbourhood Association about setting a poor example to the children. It is a false alarm – it is almost always a false alarm. The other cities of Japan may have suffered heavily in aerial raids, but not Nagasaki. A few weeks ago she repeated to Konrad the received wisdom that Nagasaki would be spared all serious damage because it was the most Christian of Japan's cities, and Konrad pointed out that there were more Christians in Dresden than in Nagasaki. She has started to take the air-raid sirens a little more seriously ever since. But really, it will be so hot in the shelter. Why shouldn't she just stay at home? It is almost certainly a false alarm.

Why risk it, Konrad thinks. He retrieves his air-raid hood from inside the house and starts to walk swiftly towards the shelter which the Kagawas had built in the back garden. Halfway across the garden he stops and looks at the wall which divides the property from the vacated lot next door. He hasn't checked on his birds, on the other side of the wall, since the last rain shower. Tossing the air-raid hood on the grass, he strides to the boundary wall and hoists himself over it, slinging his body low to reduce the chances of being seen by passers-by or the military police.

If anyone were to see him they would think he looked ridiculous – a gangling European tumbling over a wall, all arms and legs and hooded eyes, with hair and close-cropped beard of a colour so

8

unexpected in Nagasaki that Hiroko Tanaka had thought, the first time she saw him, that the hair of Europeans rusted rather than greyed as they aged. Later she discovered that he was only twenty-nine – eight years older than she was.

The dry grass crackles beneath his feet – he feels as though he is snapping the backs of tiny creatures – as he walks across to the giant camphor tree to which the birds are fastened, rotating slowly in the faint breeze. It is Hiroko who first referred to his purple notebooks as birds – the day they met; the only time she has been inside his house. She lifted a notebook off his desk, splayed, and glided it around his room. The animation of her touch made him acutely conscious of the lifelessness of his words: sentences thrown down on paper year after year simply so he could pretend there was some purpose to his being here, some excuse for cowering in a world from which he felt so separate that nothing in it could ever implicate him.

But ever since Germany's surrender shifted his status in Nagasaki from that of ally into some more ambiguous state which requires the military police to watch him closely the lifeless words have become potent enough to send him to prison. It says all there is to say about the paranoia of Imperial Japan: notebooks of research and observation about the cosmopolitan world that had briefly existed within a square mile of where he now lives are evidence of treason. Yoshi Watanabe made that clear to him when Germany's surrender started to seem imminent. *You write about a Nagasaki filled with foreigners. You write about it longingly. That's one step away from cheering on an American occupation.* And so, the night Germany surrendered, Konrad constructed a mobile of strong wire and hung each of his eight purple-leather notebooks from it. He climbed over the wall to the vacant property that adjoined his own, and attached the mobile to a tree. The wind twirled the purple-winged birds in the moonlight.

He remains certain that no one will think to enter the deserted garden to search for treachery amidst the leaves. The people who would willingly sift through every particle of dust in a house for signs of anti-state activity can always be deceived by a simple act of imagination.

Ducking beneath a low swooping branch, he reaches out a hand and finds the leather books dry and unmarked, though slightly faded. He looks gratefully up at the protective canopy of leaves before noticing the white streak on one of the leather covers: a real bird's comment on these purple impostors. His face breaks into one of those smiles which sometimes fool people into thinking him handsome. As he steps away from the tree his attention shifts to the slightly deranged tone that has crept into the mournful call of the air-raid siren. Not much point dropping a bomb here, Konrad thinks, making his way without haste back to Azalea Manor's air-raid shelter. The former Foreign Settlement where he lives is characterised now by absence, and always by waste. In Urakami ten families could live in this space! Hiroko said the first time they met, gesturing at Azalea Manor. And she followed it with: The rich! Ridiculous! before turning to ask him what he intended to pay her for the translation work he was requesting.

Weeks later, he accused her, laughingly, of driving up her price by playing on his guilt. Well, of course, she said, with characteristic frankness; scruples and starvation don't go well together. Then she spread her arms wide and scrunched her eyes shut as though concentrating hard on conjuring up another world: When the war's over, I'll be kind. Opening her eyes, she added quietly, Like my mother. He couldn't help thinking her mother would never have approved of starting up a romance with a German, or even walking alone with him through the hills of Nagasaki. It discomforted him to know his happiness was linked to the death of her mother, but then she took his hand and he doubted that anyone, even a revered mother, could have told Hiroko Tanaka what to do. Why should rules of conduct be the only things untouched by war, she once asked him? Everything from the past is passed.

Kicking the air-raid hood on the ground before him he enters the capacious shelter built into the slope of Azalea Manor's garden. The air musty and tinged with bitterness. Here, the deck of cards with which he and Yoshi Watanabe and Keiko Kagawa kept each other distracted, particularly useful during the early days of the air-raid sirens when there was more terror than boredom associated with the warnings; here, the oak chair from which Kagawa-san surveyed the behaviour of his neighbours and family and staff during those rare occasions when the air-raid sirens found him still at home; here, the hopscotch squares which Konrad had drawn in the dust for the younger Kagawa children; here, the hidden bottle of sake which the cook thought no one else knew about; here, the other hidden bottle of sake which the teenage Kagawas came in search of late at night when the shelter was empty. They knew Konrad could see them from his caretaker's house, but while their parents might still be uneasy after seven years about quite how to negotiate their relationship with the landlord who folded his lanky frame into the tiny house at the bottom of the garden the younger Kagawas knew him as an ally and would have happily welcomed him into their drinking parties if he had shown any inclination to join them.

Now all the Kagawas cross over to the other side of the road if they see him walking towards them. One round of questioning by the military police about the suspect loyalties of their landlord was all it had taken to move them out of Azalea Manor.

Konrad sits on Kagawa-san's oak chair, bouncing his air-raid hood on his knee. He is so immersed in what was that it takes him a moment to realise that the figure which appears in the entrance to the shelter, hood in hand, exists in present tense. It is Yoshi Watanabe.

As if asking for permission to enter a private party, Yoshi says, in English, 'May I come in? I'll understand if you say no.'

Konrad doesn't respond, but as Yoshi mutters a word of apology and starts to walk away, Konrad calls out, 'Don't be an idiot, Joshua. How'd you think I'd feel if a bomb landed on you?'

Yoshi steps inside, looping his spectacles over his ears and blinking rapidly.

'I'm not sure.'

Picking up the deck of cards, he kneels on the ground, shuffling the cards and then dealing ten each to himself and the empty space across from him.

Yoshi Watanabe is the 'Jap' whose telegrams James Burton had referred to when packing Konrad off to Nagasaki. His grandfather, Peter Fuller of Shropshire, had been George Burton's closest friend and neighbour. When Konrad arrived in Nagasaki it was Yoshi who was waiting at the harbour to welcome him, Yoshi who showed him around Azalea Manor, Yoshi who found him a Japanese tutor, Yoshi who produced the Kagawas as though they were a bouquet of flowers hiding within his sleeve within hours of hearing Konrad say he'd be far more comfortable living in the cosiness of the caretaker's house, Yoshi who regaled him with stories of Nagasaki's turn-of-the-century cosmopolitan world, unique in Japan – its English-language newspapers, its International Club, its liaisons and intermarriages between European men and Japanese women. And when Konrad said he needed someone to translate Japanese letters for the book he was planning to write about the cosmopolitan world, it was Yoshi who had introduced him to his nephew's German teacher, Hiroko Tanaka.

It was one of those friendships which quickly came to seem inevitable, and unbreakable. And then in a conversation of less than a minute, it ended.

They come increasingly to check on me, Konrad. My mother's family name was Fuller. You know what that means. I can't give them any other reason to think I have divided loyalties. Until the war ends, I'm staying away from all the Westerners in Nagasaki. But only until the war ends. After, after, Konrad, things will be as before.

If you had been in Germany, Joshua, you'd say to your Jewish friends: I'm sorry I can't hide you in my attic, but come over for dinner when the Nazi government falls.

'Why are you here?'

Yoshi looks up from the fan of cards in his hand.

'I was at home when the sirens started. This is the nearest shelter.' At Konrad's raised eyebrow he adds, 'I know. I've been going to the school house's shelter these last few weeks. But with this New Bomb . . . I didn't want to risk the extra minutes out in the open.'

'So there are risks in the world greater than being associated with a German? That's comforting. What New Bomb?'

12

Yoshi puts down his cards.

'You haven't heard? About Hiroshima? Three days ago?'

'Three days? No one's spoken to me in three days.'

In the shelter at Urakami, Hiroko is packed in so tightly between her neighbours she cannot even raise a hand to wipe the sweat damping her hairline. It hasn't been so crowded in here since the early days of the air-raid sirens. What could have provoked the Chairman of the Neighbourhood Association into such a frenzy about rounding up everyone in his path and ordering them to the shelter? She exhales through her mouth and turns her head slightly towards the Chairman's wife, who responds by turning quickly away from Hiroko. It is impossible to know if this is guilt or disdain.

The Chairman's wife had been a close friend of Hiroko's mother – she recalls the two of them giggling together over the newest edition of *Sutairu*, in the days before war brought an end to the magazine: no place in wartime Japan for a publication that advised women on the etiquette of wearing underwear with Western dresses. As she was dying, Hiroko's mother had called the Chairman's wife to her bedside with a single request: protect my husband against himself. There was even less place in wartime Japan for an iconoclastic artist than for magazines about modern girls. For a long time, the Chairman's wife had carried out her promise, persuading her husband to regard Matsui Tanaka's outbursts against the military and the Emperor as a symbol of a husband's mourning that was so profound it had unhinged him. But in the spring, Matsui Tanaka had been walking past a neighbourhood house and saw the cherry blossom festooning it to commemorate the sacrifice of the fifteen-year-old boy who had died in a kamikaze attack. Without saying a word to Hiroko who was walking silently beside him Matsui Tanaka darted forward, pulling out a book of matches from the pocket of his trousers, and set fire to the cherry blossom.

Seconds later he lay bloodied on the ground, the dead boy's father struggling against the neighbourhood men who had finally decided to restrain him, and Hiroko, bending down over her father, found herself pulled up by the Chairman's wife.

'Report him yourself,' said the woman who had been like an aunt to her. 'That advice is the only protection I can give you now.'

She hadn't listened, of course – the privations of wartime may have loosened up her scruples, but not her loyalty – and the next day three things happened: the military police came to take her father to prison, where he stayed for over two weeks; the principal of the school where she taught German told her she was dismissed, there was no room in his school for the child of a traitor and no need for the students to learn a foreign language anyway (the principal's body curling into itself as he spoke, as though he thought that if he occupied less space there wouldn't be so much of him to despise); and when she returned home, the Chairman was waiting to tell her she had been conscripted to work at one of the munitions factories.

She wants now to signal to the Chairman's wife that she knows the woman did her best, for so long; but in part she wants to signal this in order to shame her.

Someone new enters the shelter, and everyone else is squeezed back even further, though there is nothing but polite murmurs of apology to signal the indignity of being so closely pressed up to the armpits and groins of strangers. Hiroko finds herself moving back into a gap which has opened up from necessity rather than any physical possibility, and finds herself beside two boys. Thirteen, maybe fourteen years old. She knows them, these Nagasaki boys. Not these ones exactly, but she knows that look of them. She guesses the taller one with the arrogant tilt of the head is in the habit of wooing girls or catching the attention of young teachers with tales of the thoughts he knows he'll have on his one-way flight into the bridge of a US carrier (soon, very soon, the youngest of the pilots are not much older than him), all the while implying that the female towards whom he's leaning will be central to those final, heroic thoughts.

'You're lying,' the shorter boy whispers.

The taller one shakes his head.

'Those who were close, it stripped to the bone so they were just skeletons. The ones further away, it peeled off their skin, like

14

grapes. And now that they have this New Bomb the Americans won't stop until we're all skeletons or grapes.'

'Stop it,' Hiroko says, in her teacher's voice. 'Stop telling these lies.'

'They're not . . .' the boy starts to say, but her raised eyebrow silences him.

One of her former students – Joseph – really had piloted his Ohka into a US carrier. He told her once that on the final flight he would take with him two pictures – one of his parents standing beneath a cherry tree, and one of Myrna Loy. A picture of Myrna Loy, she said, as you destroy a US warship? But he couldn't see any irony in that. He was the neighbourhood boy whose death had propelled her father into burning the cherry blossom – perhaps he did it for her. The only way he knew of saying he understood her grief and fury, held inarticulate inside. She doesn't know which she is more surprised by – the possibility that this could be true, or the fact that it hasn't occurred to her earlier. Since her mother's death she has taken to interpreting the silence from her father as an absence of anything worth communicating rather than an inability to form a new configuration with his daughter now his beloved wife is no longer around to serve as the voice to his thoughts.

'Skeleton or grape?' the tall boy whispers. She can smell the fetidness of stale breath.

Outside are air and trees and mountains. It's worth any risk.

She shoulders her way forward, and all those who were polite in allowing more people in are outraged by her attempts to leave.

'What are you doing . . . there's no room . . . keep back, keep back . . .' An elbow collides with her ribs.

'My father,' she calls out. 'I must find my father.'

Some of the women in the shelter start to make room for her to exit, lifting their children up in their arms.

A voice says, 'Her father is Matsui Tanaka, the traitor,' and there's a ripple of unpleasantness around the shelter, more people making space for her but in a way that suggests they don't want her here.

She doesn't care. She is out now, gulping in the fresh air which almost seems cool by comparison.

15

She walks quickly to get away from the shelter, and then slows, aware of the emptiness around her. Under a pale-leafed tree she holds her arms up to be patterned with drifting spots of sun and shadow as the branches sway in a breeze that isn't perceptible at ground-level. She glimpses her hands as she holds them up – blistered from the combination of factory work and bamboo-spear drills. This was not how she imagined twenty-one. Instead, she imagined Tokyo – Hiroko Tanaka in the big city, wearing dresses, leaving lipstick marks on wine glasses in jazz clubs, her hair cut just below the ear – single-handedly resurrecting the lifestyle of the 'modern girl' of the twenties whose spirit had lived on in *Sutairu* through the thirties.

But that was childish dreaming. Or borrowed dreaming, really. She saw the way her mother sighed and laughed over stories of the modern girls and she imagined their world as the only mode of escape from a dutiful life. Though the older she got the more she was certain her mother – so devoted to husband and daughter and home – never really desired the escape, only enjoyed the idea that it existed in the world. That was where she and her daughter so sharply differed. For Hiroko, to know was to want. But that world glimpsed in magazines was known far less than the world she could reach out and grasp by the roots of its rust-coloured hair.

Now the childhood dreams are past. Now there is Konrad. As soon as the war ends, there will be her and Konrad. As soon as the war ends, there will be food and silk. She'll never wear grey again, never re-use tea leaves again, never lift a bamboo spear, or enter a factory or bomb shelter. As soon as the war ends there will be a ship to take her and Konrad far away into a world without duty. When will the war end? It cannot happen quickly enough.

He walks away from Azalea Manor, almost running.

He can hear Yoshi calling him to come back and wait for the all-clear, but all he can think is that if another New Bomb is to fall it will fall on Urakami: on the factories, on the people packed close together. The shelters won't keep it out, not the thing Yoshi described. And if it is to fall on Hiroko, let it fall on him, too.

16

He picks up his pace, runs through memories of her: the gate through which she walked in search of him as soon as Yoshi's nephew delivered the letter he had written, asking if she'd be interested in translating letters and diaries into German for a negotiable fee; the schoolyard where they used to meet every week for the first few months, the exchange of translations and money slipping further and further to the margins of their encounters; the road leading to the street-car, where she'd responded to his gloomy complaints about rationing by singing 'Yes, We Have No Bananas' and he discovered she spoke English as fluently as German; the Chinese quarter, where he made her laugh out loud for the first time, confessing the names he'd given to all the vegetables he didn't recognise: windswept cabbage, knots of earth, fossilised flower, lanky potato; Megane-Bashi, or Spectacles Bridge, where they had been standing, looking into the water, when a small silver fish leapt out of Konrad's reflected chest and dived into her reflection and she said, 'Oh,' and stepped back, almost losing her balance, so he had to put his arm around her waist to steady her. And here – he slows; the all-clear sounds; the threat has passed – the banks of the Oura, where he told her that his first winter in Nagasaki he had walked past the frozen river and seen splashes of colour beneath the surface.

'I went closer to look. And what do you think I saw? A woman's name. Hana. It had been written in red ink by someone – either a skilled artist or an obsessed lover – who knew how to paint on the water in the instant before the ice froze the characters into place.'

Instead of a shaking her head at him and offering up some entirely practical explanation for a name sealed in ice, as he had expected, she frowned.

'Your first winter here was '38. Why didn't we meet sooner? What a waste.'

It was the first indication he had that she – bizarrely, wonderfully – went at least part-way to reciprocating his feelings.

He sets off again, panic replaced by purposefulness. Ever since Germany's surrender he has told her it isn't safe for her – a traitor's daughter – to spend too much time with him. So they have been meeting only twice a week, for an hour at a time, always out in public, sometimes trailed by the military police – on those occasions they speak loudly, in Japanese, about the glorious history of Japan about which she pretends to instruct him. He has stopped his weekly practice of lending her books in German and English from his library, though it has formerly been one of his great pleasures to see the different expressions of delight with which she greets Yeats, Waugh, Mann; no matter the length or denseness she is done with the book – has sometimes read it twice – by the time the next week comes around. But now 'books' have joined the list of suspended intimacies between them. Each time they meet she complains that there's too much rationing in the world as it is, but he is unyielding. After the war, he always says. After the war. Now he sees how much of Yoshi's thinking has infected him.

Crossing into the valley, he looks up towards Urakami Cathedral with its stone figures that stand against the sky – on overcast days their greyness suggests each cloud is an incipient statue waiting for a sculptor to pull it down and hew it into solidity. And he, too, has been hewn into solidity – gone now those days of insubstantiality, not knowing what he's doing in Japan, a fugitive from a once-beloved country he long ago gave up on trying to fight for or against. He knows entirely why he's here, why here is the only place he can be.

Away from the river now, away from the Cathedral, he veers towards the slope she has described to him – with the denuded silver-barked tree painted black so that the moonlight doesn't make a steel tower of it and draw enemy fire (and on the topmost branches someone has painted stars). There, the purple rooftops of her neighbourhood which remind her of his note-books, so every day when she comes home from the factory she sees his birds, every night she falls asleep beneath their out-stretched wings.

'Konrad-san?' She stands on the verandah of her house, looking at him with concern. What could have brought him to Urakami, for all her neighbours to see?

He smiles and makes a gesture of mock-despair. Months ago he asked her to call him 'Konrad' and she said, 'It's a nice name, but on

18

its own it sounds naked.' Then she gave him her wickedest smile. 'One day, maybe that won't be a problem.'

'Is your father here?'

'Out walking in the hills. Come.'

She opens the sliding door and he fumbles to take off his shoes before joining her inside. She is walking up the stairs before he's in and he barely allows himself time to look around the small reception room, the focal point of which is an ink-and-brush painting of a Nagasaki seascape – her father's work, he guesses correctly, feeling strangely unsettled at the thought of her father. Hiroko once said she learnt how to question the world's rules from his example rather than his instruction, and Konrad can't help but suspect Matsui Tanaka's disengaged parenting will stop at the precise moment his daughter introduces him to the German she . . . what? . . . loves?

Upstairs, he enters a room in which a futon is rolled up, but hasn't yet been put away. He tries not to stare at her bedding.

Hiroko steps out on to the balcony and leans on the railing. This house is far up the slope and though it is hemmed in on three sides by other homes the balcony looks out on to nothing but trees and hills. And nothing but trees and hills look on to it.

'You never told me you live a single dive away from an ocean of liquid leaves,' he says.

She touches his sleeve.

'Are you all right? You look strange. And you're here. Why?'

As ever their conversation moves between German, English and Japanese. It feels to them like a secret language which no one else they know can fully decipher.

'I have to ask you something. I don't want to wait until the war ends to hear the answer.' In saying it he realises his purpose in coming here. 'Will you marry me?'

Her response is swift. She pulls herself to her full height, hands on her hips.

'How dare you?'

He steps back. How has he been so completely wrong?

'How dare you suggest there's a question attached to it? Last week when we talked about travelling around the world together

19

after the war – in what capacity did you think I was agreeing to go with you, if not as your wife?' The end of the sentence is muffled in his shirt as he pulls her to him.

Peace, she thinks. This is what peace feels like.

'Not Delhi,' he says.

They sit on the balcony, fingers tangling.

'But I want to meet Ilse. She's your sister; I have to meet her.'

'Half-sister,' he corrects. 'And it's been a long time since she was Ilse Weiss. Now it's just Elizabeth Burton. And you will meet her – just not on our honeymoon. Frankly the only person worth meeting at Bungle Oh! is Sajjad – if he's still there. Lovely Muslim boy who works for James. He's the one who told me that story of the spider in Islam, remember?'

She moves her head away from his shoulder.

'Bungalow?'

'Bungle Oh! It's a pun. Bungle Oh!, Civil Lines, Delhi. Maybe you're right – we should go. Who could resist an address like that?'

'You're not being serious,' she grumbles.

'That's a new complaint.' He kisses her head. 'Ilse won't want us there. I've told you how ashamed she is of what she refers to as her "German connections". That's what my father and I are reduced to. Connections. And that was before the war. Now, who even knows if she'll acknowledge she knows me? She probably tells everyone she sprang fully formed from her mother's Anglo-Saxon forehead.'

'OK,' she says. 'No Delhi. What about New York?'

He wonders if she's heard anything about this New Bomb. The thought of it makes him pull her even closer.

She decides not to point out that, despite the cloud cover, it's far too hot for such bodily contact. Her mind leaps ahead to the further kinds of bodily contact which will be made necessary by marriage. She wonders if his knowledge of what happens on wedding nights is less vague than hers. Her curiosity about this is entirely abstract.

'Your father will be back from his walk soon,' Konrad says. Regretfully he stands up, pulling her along with him. 'This is not how I want him to see his future son-in-law for the first time.'

'Come back for dinner then. I'll give you all you can eat of Urakami's best miso-flavoured water.'

'Sounds perfect.'

He's looking at her now in a way that makes her put her hand up to her mouth to brush off whatever he sees clinging there. He laughs softly, puts his arms around her waist and kisses her.

He has kissed her before, of course. Many times. But always in a hurried manner, quickly quickly before anyone sees. Now he is different. She feels something moist. It's his tongue. That should feel repellent, but it doesn't. Anything but. She is amazed by what her body seems to know to do in response, how this can feel both strange and yet familiar.

When he pulls away she says, 'Stay,' and leans back into him.

He shakes his head at her in a way that doesn't mean no, only not yet.

'Stay.'

But he steps back. He suspects she does not fully understand what is promised in that demand, what is already just a single breath away from being inevitable.

'I'll be back for dinner.' He steps backwards, his eyes never leaving her face.

In this manner he walks down the stairs, and she can't help laughing. He looks as if he's in a movie reel that has accidentally reversed itself.

'Where are you going?'

'I don't know . . . Urakami Cathedral!'

'Oh. Is that where we're going to get married?' Displeasure in her voice.

'Of course not. You're not even Catholic.'

'That's not the problem. I want to get married on a mountain, looking down at the sea.'

'I'll only be looking at you.' His grin manages to make the statement sexual rather than sentimental.

This side of him really is entirely new, and she is surprised by her own sense of anticipation even as she swats the air as though to dispatch his absurd comment.

He has reversed himself all the way to the verandah now.

21

'So why are you going to the Cathedral?'

'Father Asano said he'd lend me some books. I don't want the books, but since he's one of the few people still willing to associate with me I don't want to offend him.'

'We'll leave them all behind, Konrad. We'll find an island where only the two of us have to live.'

It is the first time she has said his name without the honorific. He steps forward, presses his mouth against hers again – uncaring that the neighbours might see.

When he is gone, Hiroko races up to the stairs to see if she can watch him from the window as he descends the slope, but the angles of her house don't allow it. She is suddenly, shockingly, aware of her own body. Such a mixture of heaviness and lightness – her limbs suffused with pleasure, exhausted by it, and yet it feels as though there are wings attached to her, on the verge of lifting her off the ground entirely.

In the corner of the room is a trunk in which her father keeps the most precious memories of his wife. She opens the trunk and reaches for the silk kimono which is folded beneath a seashell and an envelope filled with letters.

Hiroko removes the kimono from the trunk, and throws it up in the air. The silk shifts against itself and unfolds, so that what went up a square comes down a rectangle; again she throws it up, and it hits the ceiling lamp, catching on its shade before slithering down into her waiting arms. She closes her arms around the fabric that suggests being draped in a waterfall and thinks of holding Konrad, naked.

She undresses quickly, removing the hated grey monpe and the shirt that was once a gleaming white and is now just the colour of too many washes. Then she continues, removing every scrap of clothing. Something strange is happening inside her body which she doesn't understand, but she knows she wants it to go on happening. Without care for underclothes, she slips one arm into the sleeve of the kimono, the silk electric against her skin.

Konrad walks across Urakami Valley, his heart folding in and in on itself.

Hiroko steps out on to the verandah. Her body from neck down a silk column, white with three black cranes swooping across her back. She looks out towards the mountains, and everything is more beautiful to her than it was early this morning. Nagasaki is more beautiful to her than ever before. She turns her head and sees the spires of Urakami Cathedral, which Konrad is looking up at when he notices a gap open between the clouds. Sunlight streams through, pushing the clouds apart even further.

Hiroko.

And then the world goes white.

The light is physical. It throws Hiroko forward, sprawling. Dust enters her mouth, her nose, as she hits the ground, and it burns. Her first response is a fear that the fall has torn her mother's silk kimono. She raises herself off the ground, looks down. There is dirt on the kimono, but no tear. Yet something is wrong. She stands up. The air is suddenly hot and she can feel it on her skin. She can feel it on her back. She glides her hand over her shoulder, touches flesh where there should be silk. Moves her hand further down her back, touches what is neither flesh nor silk but both. She wonders if this has something to do with the burning she felt as she fell. Now there is no feeling. She taps the place that is neither flesh nor silk. There is no feeling at all.

Her neighbour comes out on to the verandah next door.

'What was that?' she says.

Hiroko can only think that her clothing is in shreds and she must go indoors to change. She hears the cry of her neighbour as she turns her back on the woman to enter the house. Hiroko runs her fingers along her back as she climbs the stairs down which, minutes earlier, she had followed Konrad. There is feeling, then no feeling, skin and something else. Where there is skin, there is feeling. Where there is something else there is none. Her fingers pluck at shreds embedded in the something else. Shreds of what – skin or silk? She shrugs off the kimono. It falls from her shoulders, but does not touch the ground. Something keeps it attached to her.

26

How strange, she thinks, as she idly knots the sleeves of the kimono around her body, just below her breasts.

She walks over to the window out of which she tried to catch a glimpse of Konrad as he walked away and looks down the slope, searching for clues. Houses, trees, people gathering outside, asking each other questions, people shaking their heads, sniffing at the air.

Then.

Hiroko leans out of the window, forgetting she is almost entirely naked. Something is wrong with her eyes. They see perfectly until the bottom of the slope and then they cannot see. Instead they are inventing sights. Fire and smoke and, through the smoke, nothing. Through the smoke, land that looks the way her back feels where it has no feeling. She touches the something else on her back. Her fingers can feel her back but her back cannot feel her fingers. Charred silk, seared flesh. How is this possible? Urakami Valley has become her flesh. Her flesh has become Urakami Valley. She runs her thumb over what was once skin. It is bumped and raw, lifeless.

So much to learn. The touch of dead flesh. The smell – she has just located where the acrid smell comes from – of dead flesh. The sound of fire – who knew fire roared so angrily, ran so quickly? It is running up the slopes now; soon if will catch her. Not just her back, all of her will be Urakami Valley. Diamond from carbon – she briefly imagines herself a diamond, all of Nagasaki a diamond cutting open the earth, falling through to hell. She is leaning further out, looking through the smoke for the spires of Urakami Cathedral, when she hears her neighbour's scream.

Hiroko looks down, sees a reptile crawling up the path towards her house. She understands now. The earth has already opened up, disgorged hell. Her neighbour's daughter is running towards the reptile with a bamboo spear in hand – her grip incorrect. The reptile raises its head and the girl drops the spear, calls out Hiroko's father's name. Why does she expect him to help? Hiroko wonders, as the girl keeps chanting, 'Tanaka-san, Tanaka-san,' hands gripping the sides of her face as she stares at the reptile.

The only light is from the fires. Her neighbour is calling her name, somewhere close. The neighbour is inside the house, her

27

footsteps on the stairs. Where is Urakami Cathedral? Hiroko bats at the air with her hands, trying to clear away whatever separates the spires from her sight. Where is the Cathedral? Where is Konrad?

Why is she falling?

'There. See? There.'
    'How can you be sure it's him?'
'No one else in Nagasaki could cast such a long shadow.'

Veiled Birds

Delhi, 1947

1

Sajjad Ali Ashraf had his eyes fixed on the sky as he cycled parallel to the Yamuna River, trying to locate the exact celestial point at which Dilli became Delhi. Dilli: his city, warren of 'by-lanes and alleys, insidious as a game of chess', the rhythmically beating heart of cultural India (he wasn't merely dismissive of opposing views, he was inclined to believe they were only made in jest), the place to which his ancestors had come from Turkey over seven centuries earlier to join the armies of the Mamluk King, Qutb-ud-din Aibak.

And then – Sajjad almost tipped over as his feet on the pedals turned recalcitrant, as they were apt to do when his attention was elsewhere – there was Delhi: city of the Raj, where every English-man's bungalow had lush gardens, lined with red flowerpots. That was the end of Sajjad's ruminations on British India. Flowerpots: it summed it all up. No trees growing in courtyards for the English, no rooms clustered around those courtyards; instead, separations and demarcations. Sajjad smiled. That was it. That would be the subject of today's discussion with James Burton. Not flowerpots, but separations. Of course, almost all the wisdom he polished and honed in his mind on his morning journey into Delhi remained unspoken. But even so, as James Burton said, the readiness was all.

On the matter of separations . . . Sajjad looked up again, but this time stopped the bicycle as he did so, and hopped off it. Yes, there, there was the boundary of Dilli and Delhi. There, where the sky emptied – no kites dipping towards each other, strings lined with glass; and only the occasional pigeon from amidst the flocks released to whirl in the air above the rooftops of the Old City where Sajjad's family had lived for generations.

I am like those occasional pigeons, Sajjad thought. At home in Dilli but breaking free of the rest of my flock to investigate the air of Delhi. He mounted the bicycle again, and wondered if there was a couplet to be written about pigeons and the Indians who worked for the English. Almost immediately he was impatient with the thought. He had no talent for verse, and it was only when in Delhi that he spoke fervently of the culture of poetry he had grown up with; in Dilli itself, while his brothers and sisters-in-law and aunts and cousins and mother traded couplets with each other, his mind would occupy itself with thoughts of the chess games which he and James Burton carried over from one day to the next as though they were stories of sultans and djinns. If he was to be honest, he missed the days when it was legal documents rather than chess games which occupied his thoughts each morning, but one day they would return to that – no doubt, no doubt. James Burton had promised him.

A few minutes later he was in the Burton property in Civil Lines, walking up the driveway lined with flowerpots. He paused by the Bentley to check his reflection in its window and when all he saw was the car's interior he moved undaunted to the bonnet, which reflected his image gleamingly back at him. He paid little attention to those aspects of his appearance that made his mother blow prayers over him to cast off the Evil Eye – the fine yet abundant hair, the perfectly proportioned features (except, at certain angles, the nose), the neat moustache, the fair skin of his Turkish ancestors, the confident air of a man of twenty-four who has never known failure – and instead fixed his attention on the beige cashmere jacket from Savile Row, running his hands along its length with sensuous pleasure.

'The peacock is here,' Elizabeth Burton said, watching from her bedroom window and believing it was the slimness of his torso rather than the softness of the fabric he was admiring. She saw Sajjad bring the sleeve of his jacket to his lips – so embarrassingly pink and fleshy – and her eyes flitted away from him impatiently.

'Say something?' James asked from the doorway.

'I wish you wouldn't give him your clothes,' Elizabeth said without turning towards James. 'He's started looking at everything you wear as if it's his property; did you see how upset he was yesterday when you spilt ink on your shirt?'

'Discarded clothes as metaphor for the end of Empire. That's an interesting one. I don't care how he looks at my shirt so long as he allows me to choose the moment at which it becomes his.'

Elizabeth leaned her cheek against the open window shutters, and James watched her for a moment – the copper hair falling sleekly just above her shoulders, the statuesque figure, the sensuous droop of her eyelids. At thirty-seven she wasn't fading, just sharpening her edges. Trying to remember the last time they made love, he recalled instead the furious passion that had consumed their nights in the aftermath of Konrad's death, and the relief he knew they had both felt when it ebbed away. ('So this must be what sex feels like for animals,' she had said one night during that crazed period while James was still inside her. He had been unable to meet her eye in daylight for the rest of the weekend.)

Elizabeth picked up her cup of tea from the windowsill and felt as though she'd posed herself for a portrait, *The Colonial Wife Looks upon her Garden*. It was worth looking upon, she conceded. The February sun had none of the antagonism that characterised it in later months, and the garden had responded to its benevolence with a burst of colour. Elizabeth made a mental checklist as she looked from one end of the front garden to the other: verbenas, dog flowers, larkspur, roses, sweet peas, phlox. And those were just the flowers at the far end, against the boundary wall. In colonial Delhi, gardens were to the wives what cricket was to the husbands – when conversation became tense, stilted, awkward, it would retreat to Bradman or gladioli. And February, when the chrysanthemums gave way to roses, was the very peak of the gardening year. All those interminable ladies' lunches!

Perhaps this would be the year she'd reveal that it wasn't the winter flowers for which she waited all year, it was the royal poinciana – or the gulmohar, as the Indians more romantically called it. She envisaged the indignation of the Delhi wives if she were to dismiss the winter flowers of Delhi – which were also the summer flowers of England – in favour of that most brazen of India's trees, with its red-gold flowers that flamed through the city in the summer, offering up resistance to the glare of the sun and, in so doing, unmasking the winter flowers as cowards.

'My imagined rebellions get more pathetic by the day,' she said.

She didn't expect James to still be there; they had long since fallen out of the habit of staying around to listen to each other's responses. Even so there was a moment in which she hoped to hear him ask her what she had meant. But James was already making his way slowly down the stairs – his leg still not fully recovered from the fall from a horse two months earlier.

Sajjad was waiting for him at the bottom of the stairs, and James smiled at the sight of the young man in his perfectly fitted jacket.

'Which of your poor sisters-in-law was up all night adjusting that to your size?' he said, hopping down the final two steps and allowing all his weight to fall on the stronger leg.

'Qudsia.' Sajjad held up a hand to steady James as he tipped forward on landing.

'Your younger brother's wife?'

Sajjad made a noise that sounded like confirmation. In fact, he was the youngest of the brothers but he saw no point in James Burton's occasional attempts to unfurl the tangle of consonants and relationships that made up his family.

The two men walked across the chequered-tile floor to the verandah where two tables were set up – one with a chessboard, its game already in progress, and the other bare.

On this second table Sajjad deposited the files he'd carried over, while his eyes scanned the back garden for anything feathered.

'There is a sunbird in your hollyhock, Mr Burton.'

'Sounds like a rude punchline. Go, wander' – he waved his hand in the direction of the garden – 'I'll look over the excuse for work they've sent me this week.'

Sajjad hopped down from the verandah to the grass, ignoring the steps. Elizabeth would see something pointed in that, James knew. She'd think the younger man was attempting to draw attention to the disparity between the elegance of his landing and James's earlier stumbling descent. But James was pleased with the carelessness with which the Indian felt he could hurl his body from one surface to the other; such a contrast from that studied formality which had marked his earliest interactions with James, eight years earlier.

It was Konrad who had first discovered Sajjad ('You say that as though he were a continent,' Elizabeth had remarked once on hearing him articulate the thought.) During his brief stay in Delhi he had come home to James and Elizabeth's one day, after a morning of taking in the sights, with an absurdly good-looking Indian boy following behind.

'Can't you find him a job?' Konrad had said, striding into the family room, where Henry, just learning to walk, was scrambling over James's knees. 'He speaks fine English – once you wrap your ear around the accent – and has no interest in his family's calligraphy trade.'

'Konrad, you can't simply pick up urchins off the street and bring them home,' James said impatiently, glancing at the boy who stood just inside the doorway, his eyes to the ground.

James saw the boy's head lift up for a moment, and the expression told him that the Indian's English was good enough to understand, and be offended by, 'urchin'. James looked him over more carefully. No, not an urchin – the dirt on his white-muslin clothes was that of someone who had thrown himself to the ground in a wrestling match rather than someone with only a single set of clothing, and the fact that Lala Buksh, James's bearer, was making no attempt to guide the boy out to wait in the corridor or in the driveway while the 'sahibs' discussed his fate was telling. In the year James had been in Delhi he'd learnt enough to know that Lala Buksh could be counted on to serve as divining rod for the hidden currents of social status among Indians.

He summoned the boy closer with a single gesture from his index finger.

'What can you do?'

Sajjad Ali Ashraf raised his eyes to James's.

'I can be priceless,' he said. At the sound of choked laughter coming from Elizabeth, he reddened. 'Invaluable,' he corrected himself. 'I can be invaluable.'

37

Who would have thought he'd one day come to see that declaration as understatement, James thought, watching the boy – a man now – pick his way quietly across the grass to the sunbird.

Sajjad lowered himself to a crouch near the ruby hollyhock from which the bird was feeding, the iridescent feathers at its throat winking from crimson to black to emerald as its head dipped and retracted. When he married, he sometimes fantasised, he would leave his family's home and buy a house, just for himself and his bride, and the central courtyard would be a garden, filled with flowers heavy with nectar and vibrant with colour to summon Delhi's birds.

The sunbird hovered between Sajjad and the hollyhock for a moment before darting out of sight. Sajjad stopped to wonder who his mother and aunts would pick to be his bride. They had chosen well for two of his brothers, but the third – Sajjad shook his head in contemplation of the sullen, slow-witted creature his brother Iqbal had married. Angling his back so that James Burton couldn't see what he was doing, Sajjad leaned forward and flicked his tongue into the hollyhock, trying to sample its nectar, but without any success. Well, whoever he was going to marry, Sajjad thought as he stood up and returned to the verandah, it would be soon. His father's illness and death two years earlier had terminated his mother's first round of searching, and the second round had proved itself an excessive waste of time – if his sister-in-law's cousin was going to elope why couldn't she have done it at the start of the marriage discussions, not when the final preparations were under way? The whole matter had sapped everyone's spirit, but in the last few weeks the women of his family had started to turn their attention once more to the matter of Sajjad's future.

Occasionally Sajjad imagined finding a wife for himself, but then he thought of the Burtons.

'Let's play chess,' James said, dismissing the contents of the file with a wave of his hand.

'The alleys of Dilli are "insidious as a game of chess".' Sajjad sat down opposite James, his hand sweeping over the lower half of his face to wipe off any pollen that might have attached itself to his skin. 'Don't you agree?'

'Rubbish.' James passed his handkerchief to Sajjad and gestured to the spot of pollen on the bridge of the other man's nose. 'Chess isn't insidious. It was my move, wasn't it?' This question incorporated a joke between the two men, referring back to a time when Sajjad was too conscious of the disparity of their social positions to contradict anything the Englishman said. Now, whenever they played and it was Sajjad's move first, James would claim the turn for himself.

'Yes, your move.' Sajjad brushed his fingers across his nose, and returned the handkerchief to James. He knew how important it was to James to enact these moments of camaraderie which undercut the rigidity of the barriers between them. That it was only in James's hands to choose when to undercut and when to affirm the barriers was something Sajjad accepted as inevitable and James never even considered.

James raised his eyebrows at Sajjad.

'No, it wasn't. It was yours.'

'Yes, Mr Burton.' With barely a glance at the board, Sajjad moved his knight into the path of James's pawn.

'What are you being so petulant for? Move that knight back, Sajjad, don't be ridiculous.'

'Why isn't chess insidious?'

'It's that damn book again, isn't it? You're quoting that damn book to me.'

The 'damn book' was Ahmed Ali's *Twilight in Delhi*, published during the war by Hogarth Press. James's mother had sent him a copy for Christmas and he'd read no more than two pages before deciding it an overblown piece of hyperbole and thrusting it in Sajjad's hands to show him the kind of nonsense that was being praised as an Indian masterpiece. 'Virginia Woolf and E. M. Forster at their patronising best. You could write a better book than this.' But Sajjad loved the novel, and had taken to peppering his conversation with quotations from it in the hope of revealing to James the beauty of its sentences.

Sajjad moved his knight back to its previous position, and pushed his pawn forward instead.

'Do you think an Englishman will ever write a masterpiece in Urdu?'

'No.' James shook his head. 'If there ever was a time we were interested in entering your world in that way, it's long past. And you wouldn't know what to do with us if we tried.'

It seemed to Sajjad these were the kinds of things said so often that repetition made fact of conjecture. He'd know what to do with an Urdu masterpiece written by an Englishman. He'd read it. Why pretend it was more complicated than that?

'Anyway, if it was going to happen it would have happened by now. The new Viceroy's arriving soon. To preside over the departure of the Raj from these shores.' He sat back, surveying both Sajjad and the garden beyond as though he were in equal parts responsible for both. 'Even the best innings must come to an end, I suppose.' Sajjad wondered how James Burton would have felt about the end of the Empire if he didn't have this cricketing phrase handy. James returned his attention to the board, smiling as he identified the trap Sajjad was laying for him. 'People who know about such things seem to think the creation of this Pakistan seems quite likely now. Ridiculous really.'

Sajjad twirled his fingers in the air in what James had learnt to recognise as an Indian gesture of indifference.

'Either way it won't matter to me. I will die in Dilli. Before that, I will live in Dilli. Whether it's in British India, Hindustan, Pakistan – that makes no difference to me.'

'So you keep saying. I think you're talking nonsense.'

'Why nonsense? The British have made little difference to the life of my moholla.' At James's look of confusion he translated 'neighbourhood', barely disguising his impatience at the Englishman's failure after all this time to understand that all-important Urdu word. 'It goes on as it has gone on. Yes, there are interruptions – 1857 was one, perhaps the departure of the British will be another – but believe me over the next century Dilli will continue to do what it's been doing for the last two centuries – fade at a very slow, and melancholically poetic, pace.'

James made a noise of disbelief at the assertion that the departure of the British would be nothing more than an interruption, but contented himself with saying, 'If that really is the case, then you're mistaken in thinking you'll live and die there. You're not cut out for a fading world.'

If Sajjad had the sort of relationship with James Burton of which he sometimes convinced himself while inventing speeches and subjects of discussion on the way from Dilli to Delhi he would have laughed and said, 'Is this what you call a flourishing life? Spending my days playing chess with you? Isn't it time for us to get back to the law offices, James Burton?' But instead he kept his eyes on the board and nodded his head slowly as though deeply reconsidering his relationship with his moholla.

'Don't believe me?' James said. When Sajjad merely smiled and shrugged, James put a hand on his arm. 'I don't know any man more capable.'

In moments such as these Sajjad loved James Burton. It was not so much for the compliment itself – Sajjad had no need of those from anyone – but for James's way of compressing a complicated matrix of emotion, one that encompassed the relationship of ruler–subject, employer–employee, father–son, chess-player–chess-player, into the word 'capable'.

There was the sound of the front door opening, and then Lala Buksh's voice said, 'Wait, please. I will tell Mrs Burton.' James and Sajjad heard his heavy tread go up the stairs.

'Wonder who that is?' James said, rising out of his chair. He walked into the hallway, Sajjad following.

There was a woman there, hands in her trouser pockets, looking at the portrait of James, Elizabeth and their son Henry which hung on the wall. In addition to the blue trousers, flared below the knee, she was wearing a cream pullover with sleeves pushed up to the elbows, and her dark hair was cut just below her ears. Even with her back turned to them she looked like no one James knew among the Delhi set.

'Are you here to see my wife?' he said.

She turned, and James said, 'Good Lord,' as he found himself looking at a Japanese woman.

'I'm Hiroko Tanaka. You must be James Burton.'

2

There were only three things Hiroko Tanaka knew about James Burton when she walked into his house. He was Konrad's brother-in-law. His uncle, George, had built Azalea Manor. He had a Muslim employee. So when Lala Buksh opened the front door for her and, amidst the black-and-white of walls and floor tiles, she saw the vibrant oil painting on the wall calculated to create a first impression of the Burton family for all visitors it was James more than Ilse who she stepped closer to examine. Who was this man about whom Konrad had nothing to say? But when she looked at the portrait – the man in his expensive suit, one hand on his wife's shoulder, the other resting on a cabinet which showcased sports trophies – she saw immediately what the painter had captured so perfectly: the complacency of James Burton. And then she understood why Konrad would have had nothing to say to, or about, him.

Standing before James, her extended hand unnoticed as he stared in confusion at her, she thought he looked like a discarded sketch that preceded the oil painting. The chestnut hair depicted in the painting was really light-brown, the slightly bronzed skin was pale and freckled, and the green eyes were set closer together than the painter had acknowledged. And yet, as good manners firmly but gracefully ushered the surprise off James's face and prompted him to take Hiroko's hand as though he'd been expecting her all along, she saw that the painting was a good likeness – here was a man at ease with ease.

'How do you know my name?' he said. And then, as if answering a question that would win him a bottle of champagne, he declared, stabbing the air in triumph, 'Konrad!'

Sajjad, standing unnoticed behind him, winced.

This is what Elizabeth heard: Lala Buksh's voice telling her there was a visitor from Japan, and then as she hurried along to the stairs James's cry of delight carrying up to her: *Konrad!* Her heart, if not her mind, had already leapt to its impossible conclusion when she rounded the curve of the stairs and saw the wholly unfamiliar figure standing beneath, back towards her.

Noticing James's eyes sweep from her towards the stairs, Hiroko turned her head. And discovered a new aspect to pain. It was Konrad become female, and beautiful. The ginger hair augmented to copper, the heavy eyes made sensual rather than sleepy, the lankiness transformed into slimness. Beside her, James was saying, 'My wife, Elizabeth. Darling, this is Miss . . . Tanker?' and a man's voice behind him corrected, 'Tanaka,' but Hiroko did nothing but stare at the figure walking down the stairs.

In the past eighteen months there had rarely been a day when she hadn't thought of Konrad walking backwards, refusing her invitation to 'stay', but at some point the memory had become associated with, rather than accompanied by, overwhelming emotions. Not so many months ago she had been dancing with an American GI in Tokyo when some shimmying movement of his recalled Konrad's departure, and she hadn't even lost a step as she saw the dance through to its end before excusing herself to the powder room, where she wept at her own callousness before returning for another dance. No, there was little Hiroko Tanaka hadn't learnt about the shameful resilience of the human heart. But seeing Elizabeth descend the stairs made it only yesterday that Konrad walked away from her to his death.

'Miss Tanaka,' Elizabeth said, extending her hand to the woman who was staring at her so disconcertingly. She intuited immediately that this was someone who had known Konrad well enough to be disturbed by his half-sister's resemblance to him. When there was no response from Hiroko, she reached out and caught the other woman's hand, which was hanging unthought of by her side, so for a moment they simply held hands before the unfamiliarity of Elizabeth's touch, the coolness of it, removed the ghost of Konrad

43

from between them and Hiroko adjusted her grip and shook the hand vigorously.

'Ilse,' she said. It occurred to her that she should be saying 'Mrs Burton' instead, but in conversations with Konrad it was always 'Ilse'.

'Elizabeth,' corrected the other, with an apologetic smile that suggested she was at fault for having discarded her childhood nickname. 'And what may I call you?'

'Hiroko.'

'Could we offer you a cup of tea, Miss Tanker?' James said. 'It's lovely out on the verandah.' Why couldn't Elizabeth be so affable with the wives of his clients? 'Lala Buksh, chai!' he called up to the henna-haired man on the upstairs landing. Then he extended one hand in the direction of the verandah, inviting both women to precede him there.

Hiroko waited for Elizabeth's response – she had pledged her allegiance in the household already, Sajjad thought – and only when she received a smile and nod of the head did she make her way down the hall, with Elizabeth following closely after. On the way to the verandah, she let her eyes linger on the Indian man who was standing to one side to allow the three foreigners to pass.

'Sajjad, find some way to occupy yourself. We'll get back to those files later.'

'Sajjad?' Hiroko stopped in front of the Indian.

'Yes?' He wanted to reach out and touch the black, raised spot on her cheekbone, to see if it was part of her or if it was a tiny beetle that had landed on her skin, tucked its wings under its body and decided never to leave. She struck him as a woman who would allow certain liberties – to beetles and to curious men – if the intentions weren't discourteous.

She was about to say that Konrad had spoken of him but before she could Sajjad gave Hiroko a look of warning and shook his head slightly. What are the rules of this place, she wondered, as she smiled uncertainly at him and walked on past James and Elizabeth's looks of curiosity. Had Konrad felt as lost when he first came to Nagasaki? If only she had his purple-covered books; if only there were that much of Konrad Weiss still in the world. But the tree on

44

which he'd hung his book mobile had burnt to a blackened stump on 9 August, though Konrad's neighbourhood was otherwise uncharred. Yoshi Watanabe had said the bomb couldn't possibly have been responsible – perhaps someone walking past the vacant plot had been lighting a cigarette when the flash of the bomb had startled him into dropping a match or the cigarette itself over the low wall. 'Even if that's true, the bomb is still responsible,' Hiroko had said.

The desire to sit down on the ground and weep was strong, but instead Hiroko stepped on to the verandah, and into another world. Everything was colour, and the twittering of birds. It was like walking into the imagination of someone who has no other form of escape. So beautiful, and yet so bounded in. She sat down on the chair James had pulled out for her, and said yes, she would love some tea.

'What brings you to Delhi? Have you been here long?' James crossed his legs at the knee and sat back, his elbows jutting out slightly from the arms of the chair.

Elizabeth watched him with interest as she settled herself less expansively. After eleven years of marriage she remained fascinated by James's way of directing people's perceptions of him. How casually he'd tossed the term 'darling' in her direction, minutes earlier. He did that often enough when they were in public, or hosting parties, but something about hearing it in the morning hours, with Sajjad standing near by glancing up in surprise, had made that travesty of endearment particularly striking.

'I just arrived. I didn't want to be in Japan any longer,' Hiroko said.

James nodded encouragingly, as though approving the opening of a play and indicating his willingness to stay and discover how events unfolded, but Elizabeth saw that Hiroko had reached the end of her answer.

'And you know Konrad?' she said. Hiroko nodded. 'He told you he had relatives in Delhi?' As she spoke she ran her palms along the fabric of her dress, smoothing what wasn't creased to begin with. As though she believed the flowers imprinted in the cotton had

45

fallen into her lap from the shrubs leaning into the verandah, Hiroko thought. That was a Konrad-thought.

'Bungle Oh!, Civil Lines, Delhi,' she said softly, speaking the memory out loud. 'He said who could resist such an address?'

James leaned forward slightly.

'Have you come from Nagasaki?' She seemed far too . . . whole to belong in any of those photographs that he still didn't see the point of publishing in magazines that people's children might get their hands on. As eight-year-old Henry had. *Daddy, did Uncle Konrad look like this when he died?* the boy had said, pointing to something barely recognisable as human in a magazine that Elizabeth had stupidly brought into the house.

'Tokyo. I've been working in Tokyo since soon after the war ended. As a translator. Someone I knew there told me about a friend of hers who was coming to India, to Bombay. We met, and I convinced him to let me travel with him. And from Bombay I took the train to Delhi.'

'What, alone?' James glanced over at Elizabeth. She's making this all up, his eyes signalled.

Hiroko didn't miss the unspoken communication – since the bomb she had started to watch the married with the keen interest of one who knows all her understanding of coupling must come from observation.

'Yes. Why? Can't women travel alone in India?'

Elizabeth almost laughed. So much for those demure Japanese women of all the stories she'd heard. Here was one who would squeeze the sun in her fist if she ever got the chance; yes, and tilt her head back to swallow its liquid light. At what point, Elizabeth wondered, had she started to believe there was virtue in living a constrained life? She clicked her heels against the floor in impatience at herself. Virtue really had nothing to do with it.

'Well, there's no law against it if that's what you mean.' James was oddly perturbed by this woman who he couldn't place. Indians, Germans, the English, even Americans . . . he knew how to look at people and understand the contexts from which they sprang. But this Japanese woman in trousers. What on earth was she all about? 'But there are rules, and there is common sense. I certainly wouldn't allow Elizabeth . . .' He faltered as Hiroko glanced towards Elizabeth to see her reaction to his choice of verb.

'You say you're a translator? Did you know Konrad in a professional capacity or . . .?' Elizabeth made a vague gesture that managed to capture her utter ignorance of Konrad's life in Japan.

'It's how we met. Through translations for his book. He was . . .' Hiroko paused. She had not spoken about Konrad to anyone but Yoshi Watanabe, and with Yoshi there was much that didn't need to be said. So now she had to take a second or two before giving words to the future she had lost. 'If our world hadn't ended he would have been my husband.'

Lala Buksh's arrival with the tea removed all necessity for an immediate response. James just sat back in his chair, not bothering to hide his disbelief. And Elizabeth thought, I did not know him at all! Nothing in the image she had of her half-brother – a man enclosed in his own mind who viewed other people as irritants distracting from the beauty of a leaf or an idea – allowed her to imagine him holding the attention of a woman as spirited as this. She wondered what marriage meant to the Japanese. Did it involve love? She really couldn't imagine it. Couldn't imagine Konrad and Hiroko Tanaka in love – and in early love, at that, when everything that matters in the world is distilled into two bodies. She was suddenly aware of James's physical presence in a way she hadn't been for a long time.

Who could resist such an address? James ran the odd sentence through his mind, while nodding at the Japanese woman – what was her name? – as though it was the news of her relationship to Konrad that he was taking in. Could it be that she had come here expecting to stay? Could she possibly imagine they would ask her to stay simply because she claimed to have been Konrad's fiancée? Although, she hadn't quite claimed that exactly. He glanced at her hands. No ring.

'Terrible about Konrad,' he said, realising Elizabeth was not going to be the first to speak. 'Just an awful business, the whole thing. We hadn't really been in touch with him for a while, Miss Tan . . .' He brought his teacup to his mouth to try and obscure his inability to recall the rest of her name. 'But, of course, we'd like

47

very much to know more about his life in Japan. You must come over for supper while you're here. Will you be staying in Delhi a while?'

James, you bastard. Elizabeth felt a rush of protectiveness towards the Japanese woman who had clearly come here because there was nowhere else for her to go. Which was a ridiculous thing to do, of course, but that hardly justified the cutting dismissal with which James had just directed her towards the door.

But other than a bright spot of red on her cheek, Hiroko showed no sign of perturbation.

'I have some money and no attachments. It means I don't need to make plans.' The truth was she had little money – the voyage from Tokyo had cut a swathe through her savings – but she had every confidence that her three languages and glowing references from the Americans would be sufficient to secure employment anywhere in the world. 'How long I stay depends on how Delhi and I get along.' She turned to Elizabeth, the slight repositioning of her shoulders dismissing James just as effectively as he'd dismissed her. 'Could you tell me where I can find a respectable boarding house? I have references from the Americans in Tokyo, and from Yoshi Watanabe, grandson of Peter Fuller from Shropshire.'

Whether it was simple curiosity, a feeling of sympathy, or a desire to offend James, Elizabeth didn't know, but she found herself saying, 'Why don't you stay here for a few days while we sort out further arrangements. Your luggage?'

'I left it with the man outside.' Hiroko tried to reconcile Konrad's bitter comments about Ilse, the sister who had made him feel so unwelcome in Delhi, with this woman of warmth and hospitality. 'But, please, I don't want to impose.'

'Elizabeth, a word.' James stood up, and moved indoors. After a pause long enough only to contain within it a glance of reassurance, Elizabeth followed.

Hiroko pressed her fingers just beneath her shoulder blade. From Tokyo to here she had found momentum in momentum. She had not thought of destination so much as departure, wheeling through the world with the awful freedom of someone with no one to answer to. She had become, in fact, a figure out of myth. The character who loses everything and is born anew in blood. In the stories these characters were always reduced to a single element: vengeance or justice. All other components of personality and past shrugged off.

Hiroko had once spent an entire afternoon looking at a picture of Harry Truman. She did not know how to want to hurt the bespectacled man, though she suspected she would feel a certain satisfaction if someone dropped a bomb on him; as for justice, it seemed an insult to the dead to think there could be any such thing. It was a fear of reduction rather than any kind of quest that had forced her away from Japan. Already she had started to feel that word 'hibakusha' start to consume her life. To the Japanese she was nothing beyond an explosion-affected person; that was her defining feature. And to the Americans . . . well, she was not interested in being anything to the Americans any more. She pushed herself up from the chair, her arms wrapped across her chest, and walked down into the garden. Some days she could feel the dead on her back, pressing down beneath her shoulder blades with demands she could make no sense of but knew she was failing to meet.

She ran her knuckles across the bark of a tree. The faint sound of skin on bark was oddly comforting. It reminded her of something . . . something from Nagasaki, but she couldn't remember what.

Sajjad walked out into the garden from James's study. The Burtons had started arguing outside the study door – they knew nothing about this woman (said James), they couldn't simply turn Konrad's intended on to the street (said Elizabeth), she was clearly lying about her relationship to Konrad (James), it would take little effort to telegram that friend of Konrad – Yoshi What's-his-name – and ask him about her, so why not just do that instead of being so unpleasant (Elizabeth), oh, I'm unpleasant, am I (James). Sajjad hated their arguments – not the fact of the arguments themselves but the sense both of the Burtons conveyed of restraining themselves, even at their most barbed, from saying what was most true and most hurtful until the unsaid words filled up the room and made Sajjad want to run away to his home, where even Allah was berated soundly and in ringing tones for all His shortcomings.

Surprisingly, the Burtons' voices did not carry into the garden. So the newcomer, he saw, was entirely unaware of them. Unaware of all the world, it seemed, as she rubbed the back of her hand determinedly against the tree-bark with its knots and nodules.

'Don't,' he said, suddenly appalled by how fragile she looked in the sunlight. She seemed not to hear him, so he ran across the grass to her, just as the blood started to well up beneath her broken skin, and pulled her hand away.

Lala Buksh walked out in time to see Sajjad's hand encircle Hiroko's wrist.

Trouble, he thought.

3

'I don't think it's going to work out with the girl we were considering as your bride,' Khadija Ashraf said, lowering herself on to the divan in the courtyard on which Sajjad was sitting, cross-legged, while sipping his morning cup of tea in the pre-dawn moments of in between.

Sajjad put an arm around his mother and whispered, 'While the others are still asleep, you can admit it. You don't think any of the girls in Dilli are good enough for you favourite son.'

Khadija Ashraf leaned back against the bolster-cushion after sweeping away the leaves that had fallen on it from the almond tree, and shook her head in exasperation at Sajjad's seeming indifference.

'This Muslim League nonsense about a new country is disrupting everything.'

'Back to that, again? Mohammed Ali Jinnah is starting to supplant Allah as the chief accused for all the problems of your life. There's a kind of devotion in that which exceeds even that of the most diehard Muslim League supporters.'

His mother straightened the lines of her gharara, and refused to smile. She'd taken a great deal of care in opening the formalities for the marriage negotiations between Sajjad and Mir Yousuf's daughter, Sheherbano, and all had seemed to be going well until Sheherbano's father had suddenly declared that of course this new nation would be a reality, and of course he would move there, and he would naturally expect his son-in-law to follow a similar course of action. Why the man didn't just leave the marriage talks to the women Khadija Ashraf couldn't understand, but the damage had been done. A new line of questioning had opened up, and it turned out the girl had herself declared that if there were pro-Pákistan processions in Delhi such as had been held in Lahore she would be proud to emulate the thirteen-year-old Fatima Sughra who had pulled down the Union Jack from the Punjab Secretariat building and replaced it with a green Muslim League flag, which she had stitched from her own dupatta. Whether the girl was wearing another dupatta at the time of this shameless act Khadija Ashraf didn't know, and was afraid to ask.

'Ammi Jaan—' Sajjad said, trying hard to find the words that would make his point without wounding his mother. 'Once I marry the girl she will enter our home; I will not become part of her household. Whether her father wants me to move somewhere else or not is irrelevant. And, as for the other matter . . . you've always said I'll need a wife with a strong will, otherwise I'll get bored.'

'I have a strong will. It doesn't make my dupatta fall off my head.'

'I want a modern wife.' It came out abruptly and unexpectedly, prompted by his imagination already falling in love with the girl who would dream of flying her dupatta in place of a Union Jack. Sajjad had no political allegiances, but many narrative preferences – in the stories of history two of his favourite characters were the Rani of Jhansi and Razia of the Mamluk Dynasty: powerful women who led troops and sat in council with men. And it was his mother who had told him their stories and made him fall in love with those images of womanhood.

'Modern?' His mother repeated the English word with disgust, and Sajjad tried not to imagine the Burtons laughing at her pronunciation: 'Maa-dern'. 'Do they tell you that's what they are, your English? Modern? These are words created only to cut you off from your people and your past.'

Sajjad shifted away from his mother. The idea that anything could cut him off from Dilli was not just absurd but insulting, and he knew his mother was aware of this.

'Modern India will start the day the English leave. Or perhaps it started the day we used their language to tell them to go home.'

Faintly, he wondered if he really believed this. 'No, modernism does not belong to the English. The opposite, in fact. They've reached the end of their history. They'll go back to their cold island and spend the next ten generations dreaming of everything they've lost.'

'They sound like the Muslims of India.'

Sajjad stood up, laughing.

'When I'm married, Ammi Jaan, you're still the one I want to have my morning cup of tea with.' He kissed her forehead, picked up his book and wiped away the ring of tea from its cover as he made his way to the vestibule.

Just as he was opening the heavy wooden door his brother Altamash came yawning out of one of the rooms off the courtyard and said, 'What's the little Englishman doing awake at this hour? Sunrise stroll with the Viceroy?'

Sajjad ignored the comment and stepped out, taking his bicycle with him. As though the soft *dhuk!* of the door closing were a signal, the muezzin of Jama Masjid began the call to prayer. Sajjad turned his head and glanced up towards the mosque, just a few minutes' walk away, its marble domes and minarets almost two-dimensional in appearance. He recalled sitting on his father's shoulder one Delhi night, at the base of the sandstone steps that led up to the mosque, his vision given over entirely to the mosque and the darkness of the sky behind it. His father had told him that the Emperor Shah Jahan had come here one night with scissors that had belonged to the Prophet, and cut through the sky; in the morning when the people of Dilli woke up, the Jama Masjid was in their midst, revealing a glimpse of heaven's architecture.

It had been weeks since Sajjad had last climbed those sandstone steps and walked across the pigeon-filled courtyard for Friday prayers. Pakistan was all anyone could talk about now, with the Imam and the most conservative members of the congregation arguing that you could not divide the Ummah, there was no place for nations in the brotherhood of Muslims; and the Muslim League supporters arguing back that it was already clear from the behaviour of the Hindus that they would not agree to share any power with the Muslims in a post-Raj India, and hadn't the descendants of the Mughals, the Lodhis, the Tughlaqs, fallen far enough already; and the Congress supporters insisting theirs was not a Hindu party but an Indian one, and what did the people of Dilli have in common with the feudals of the Punjab who would dominate this Pakistan? And so it went on and on, and in each group Sajjad found those who made complete sense and in each group also those whose opinions made him want to scatter seeds over the speakers so the pigeons would swoop down and stop their words with a tumult of feathers.

Someone in the distance called Sajjad's name – it was the retired Professor from Aligarh University who had taught his sister and him English during their childhood while his brothers preferred to learn calligraphy from their father – but though he usually went out of his way to greet the old man this time he pretended not to hear and started pedalling through the labyrinthine streets, all springing into wakefulness with the azan, eschewing the long route via the river to head straight through Kashmiri Gate into Civil Lines.

She had said, 'However early you arrive, I'll be awake.' He didn't really expect her to be dressed and ready at this hour, but the invitation – or was it a challenge? – seemed a good excuse to fulfil a long-held desire to see the Burton garden at dawn. He imagined himself sitting out on the verandah, watching the flowers emerge from the night's shadow while everyone in the house slept.

But Hiroko Tanaka was already sitting on the verandah as Sajjad was entering Delhi, pulling a shawl across her thin shoulders as she sipped a cup of jasmine tea, grateful to be regarding the world from a vertical position. It had not been so for most of these two weeks in Delhi. The first night in the Burton house she had slept in the guest room upstairs, too tired to wander out unassisted and find a place to live but determined that the next day she would leave this house where there was nothing of Konrad to be found except a notion, gleaned from a single day in the company of Elizabeth Burton, of what his features might have looked like if his life had been unhappy.

But the next day she had stepped out of bed feeling as though she were on a violently rocking boat and had barely made it down the stairs before collapsing on the floor. When she recovered consciousness she was in the bedroom on the ground floor, which was filled with the scent of James's aftershave.

The Burton family physician, Dr Agarkar, arrived within minutes and diagnosed an infection, probably picked up during her journey over to Delhi; nothing that rest and medication couldn't sort out.

'You'll be fine in, oh, a week or ten days,' he'd said and Hiroko, even in her enfeebled state, had whispered, 'Do you know somewhere I can go?'

'Don't be absurd.' Elizabeth's voice was both stern and kind. 'You'll stay here. There's no further conversation to be had about this.'

Later, as Dr Agarkar was leaving, Hiroko heard James talking to him in the hallway.

'Yes, a telegram came from that Watanabe fellow – Julian Fuller's cousin in Nagasaki. Did you know Julian – he was here in, oh, '34 or '35. Company man. Uncle married a Jap. Anyway, turns out there really was something between her and Konrad. And she's lost everyone, the telegram said. Everyone. Poor girl. I feel such a brute.'

'So she's staying with you while she's in Delhi?'

'I suppose, yes. At least until she gets better. After that, well, I don't know. We'll see how we get on. Might do Elizabeth some good to have someone to mother again. Did your wife get like this when Ravi went to Eton?'

Hiroko was asleep before the doctor answered. When she woke up, Elizabeth was sitting by her bed, her slumped shoulders suggesting she'd been there a while. Hiroko smiled, Elizabeth smiled back, and then Hiroko was asleep again.

Two days later, Hiroko was finally awake long enough to start feeling bored.

'I'll read to you,' Elizabeth said. 'Any preferences?'

'Evelyn Waugh.'

'Really? How strange.'

'That's what Konrad said. He said Waugh is for readers who know the English and understand what's being satirised. And I told

55

him that maybe the books are better when you don't know it's satire and just think it's comedy.'

Elizabeth considered this.

'You're probably right. I find him much too cruel. And almost unbearably sad.'

Hiroko's fingers moved just slightly so they were almost touching Elizabeth's hand as it rested on the coverlet. It was a gesture so astutely poised between discretion and sympathy that Elizabeth found herself imagining a life in which Konrad had brought Hiroko into this house as a sister-in-law.

'Perhaps after you've spent some time among us you'll see the satire.'

'Oh, I see it already,' Hiroko said, nodding, and then clapped her hand over her mouth.

But Elizabeth Burton was laughing as she hadn't laughed in a very long time. She took Hiroko's hand in hers and held on firmly.

'Forget this boarding-house nonsense. You're staying here. We're practically sisters, after all.'

James Burton, standing in the doorway, watched his wife's face glow with laughter, and nodded. Hiroko was far from convinced that living with the Burtons was an ideal situation but she was too weak to feel anything but gratitude for the continued offer of a bed to sleep in.

A couple of mornings ago she had woken feeling much stronger – a greater relief than she allowed anyone else to know; she had feared the radiation sickness which had so incapacitated her in '45 might have returned or simply reawoken from some state of dormancy, as the doctors had warned might happen. But as soon as she felt herself returning to strength she dismissed such thoughts with the briskness with which she had once dismissed Konrad's repeated suggestions that it wasn't prudent for her to continue meeting a German in Nagasaki, and decided it was time to start finding a way to fill her days. She had come to feel a greater affection towards the Burtons during her convalescence than she had imagined possible on her first day in Delhi but she knew she needed something beyond their company to occupy her.

She thought she had a perfect solution but her suggestion that someone in Delhi must have need of a translator who could speak English, German and Japanese met with little enthusiasm from the Burtons. Dr Agarkar was called in to inform her she was not yet well enough to go 'gadding around', though Hiroko half suspected he only said so as an act of friendship to the Burtons, who seemed to think their hospitality was being called into question if their guest found employment.

So Hiroko turned to the next option that announced itself to her.

'I'd like to learn the language they speak here,' she had said.

'It's not necessary. English serves you fine. The natives you'll meet are either the Oxbridge set and their wives or household staff like Lala Buksh, who can understand simple English if you just know a clutch of Urdu words to throw into the mix. Those Elizabeth can teach you,' James had said.

It was the oddest thing Hiroko had ever heard.

'Even so, I'd like to learn how to read and write,' she said. 'Is there anyone . . .?'

'Sajjad,' Elizabeth said. 'He used to teach Henry – my son.' Her upper lip didn't really stiffen, Hiroko thought, but there was some subtle shift around her mouth suggesting tamped-down pain at the mention of the child sent a year ago to boarding school in England, from where he wrote letters to his parents saying he wanted to be 'home, in India'.

'He doesn't have the time for that,' said James. 'You know I can't let him work half-days now. I don't have an office full of clerks any more.'

'You still have the office, James. You just choose to pretend your leg isn't healed well enough for you to go to it. And in any case, you and Sajjad do nothing but play chess all day.' Let the boy work for his salary again, Elizabeth thought to herself. She had been profoundly annoyed by Sajjad's acceptance of the raise James had given him at the start of the month; it seemed not just dishonest, but impudent.

Hiroko slipped off the sofa and went to look through the bookshelves, hoping by her movements to remind the Burtons she was in the room before they started one of their more unpleasant arguments, and wondered if Sajjad would mind being asked to play the role of teacher. She should have asked him first, she realised. Coming from the Burtons it would be a command rather than a request. But much to her relief, when James grudgingly broached the subject later that day, Sajjad seemed delighted.

'I will teach you the chaste Urdu of Ghalib and Mir so that you can read the poets of Delhi.' Seeing James's look of unhappiness, he added, 'And since you say you wake up early, Miss Tanaka, perhaps we could have our lessons before Mr Burton and I commence our day's business.'

James had smiled broadly and Elizabeth didn't know whether it was Sajjad, James or herself who she wanted to hit for the effortlessness with which the Indian could delight her husband.

Hiroko bent her face into the steam that rose from the teacup, its warmth a pleasant contrast to the chill of Delhi's winter-morning air, and hoped Sajjad wouldn't arrive soon. It was rare, and welcome, this feeling of being alone in the Burton house, no need to modulate her expressions so that nothing in them would give cause for concern or offence. When either James or Elizabeth was around she always had to look busily engaged with something to avoid provoking a panicked stir of conversation or activity; they behaved as though she had lost Nagasaki only yesterday, and their joint role in her world was to distract her from mourning. It was kind, but trying.

She rubbed her thumb along the interlacings of the green cane chair. And this world, too, was ending. A year or two, no more, James had told her, and then the British would go. It seemed the most extraordinary privilege – to have forewarning of a swerve in history, to prepare for how your life would curve around that bend. She had no idea what she planned to do beyond Delhi. Beyond next week. And why plan anyway? She had left such hubris behind. For the moment it was enough to be here, in the Burton garden, appreciative of a blanket of silence threaded with vibrant bird calls, knowing there was nothing here she couldn't leave without regret.

She was less than halfway through her cup of jasmine tea when she saw Sajjad enter the garden from around the side. He seemed surprised – almost disappointed – to see her there, but all that was just a flicker of the eyes before his polite smile settled into place and removed all expressiveness from his face. She wondered if her own face had revealed and concealed exactly as had his.

'There's a lot of dew this morning,' she said, watching his footprints turn the silver grass green.

'Yes.' He felt he should add something intelligent to that comment so he said, 'The spiders like it. On dewy mornings they build elaborate webs. Or perhaps the webs only become visible when dew is captured in their threads.'

'The spider is beloved of Muslims.'

'Yes.' He smiled, pleased beyond measure that she should know such a thing, as he stood beside the bridge table and waited for her to rise from her chair and join him there.

'Konrad told me that.' The day they stood together on Megane-Bashi and his heart had leapt into hers in a blur of silver. She couldn't recall the moment itself without an accompanying memory of remembering it as she lay on a hospital bed in the hours after Yoshi told her no one near Urakami Cathedral had survived the blast.

'Mr Konrad was—' Sajjad pulled his ear-lobe, trying to find a way to express himself. 'I liked him very much.'

Hiroko smiled as she sat down at the bridge table. It was so easy to see why Konrad had said this man was the only person in Delhi worth seeing.

'He mentioned you. He said you were lovely.'

'Lovely?'

'Yes.' She watched him take in the compliment as though it were a feast. 'Why didn't you want me to say anything to you in front of the Burtons the day I arrived?'

Sajjad set down the lined exercise book he had bought with his own money for the lesson, wiping his cuff against the remnant of a tea stain.

'I didn't know what you were going to say. But it didn't seem right.'

'What didn't?'

'I work for Mr Burton.' He quickly added, 'Not like Lala Buksh. I'm not a servant. I'm going to be a lawyer, one day.

59

Already I know all there is to know about . . .' He stopped, aware he was boasting. 'I'm not a servant,' he repeated firmly. 'But I'm . . . you're . . .'

'Yes?'

'You had just walked in. A link to her dead brother. It was not the time for you to stop and talk to me.' What he meant was, 'I could see that you were going to speak to me as an equal. They would have held it against both of us. You would not have been asked to stay.' 'I think we should start the lesson.' He opened the exercise book. 'To begin with, you will have to let go of the notion that writing starts on the left-hand side of the page and moves right.'

Hiroko started to laugh, wondered whether that would seem rude, but saw that Sajjad was unbothered – his head angled slightly to the side, his eyes curious, as though simply waiting for her to finish and explain herself rather than worrying that he had said something deserving of mockery. She turned the exercise book towards herself and wrote down its page.

'This is Japanese,' she said.

Sajjad's eyes opened wide.

'After Urdu you'll have to learn a diagonal script.'

She laughed again, and they both looked at each other and then dropped their eyes. They had both decided independently that it was merely the unfamiliarity of the other's features that gave rise to this desire to stare and stare which had been present since their first meeting.

'The first letter is alif,' Sajjad said, and the lesson commenced.

Within a few minutes Sajjad discovered what her German teacher at school and the priest who tutored her in English had earlier come to know: that for her language came so easily it seemed more as though she were retrieving forgotten knowledge than learning something new. Before he knew it they had progressed to the thirteenth letter of the alphabet.

'This is zal, the first of four letters in Urdu which replicate the sound of the English zed,' Sajjad said, drawing a curved shape with a dot on top. 'Zal, zay, zwad, zoy.'

'Why four letters for one sound?'

'Don't tell me you're one of those people who don't see the beauty in excess?' he cried – it was the first time she saw his deliberately ridiculous side.

'In other words, you don't know, Sensei.'

'What does that word mean?'

'Teacher.'

She was surprised by how red his skin could become. He picked up a pen, rolled it between his fingers, pressing a thumb against its nib and then examining intently the blue ink that spread across his skin.

'You call them Elizabeth and James. You mustn't call me anything other than Sajjad, Miss Tanaka.'

'You mustn't call me anything other than Hiroko, Sajjad.' The one thing she had liked most about the Americans was their informality with each other. No stifling honorifics to make every relationship so bounded in. She saw, in their company, how ridiculous she had been in referring to the man she loved as 'Konrad-san'. And she had even started to believe that if she'd said 'Konrad' instead he would have proposed earlier, and everything would have been different. Everything, except the bomb.

Sajjad saw that her mind was winging away from Delhi and everyone in it. He knew what the Burtons would do in such a situation – interrupt, hold her in the present. As far as he knew there was only one occasion on which Elizabeth had asked about her life before Delhi – Sajjad had been passing by the open door of her room when Elizabeth broached the question and he couldn't help but stay and listen. He had been struck by how matter-of-fact her response had been.

'After the bomb, I was sick,' she'd said. 'Radiation poisoning, though we didn't have a name for it at the time. Konrad's friend, Yoshi Watanabe, had a relative in Tokyo who was a doctor. Nagasaki's hospitals were overrun. So Yoshi-san accompanied me to Tokyo. He felt responsible, you see, because he felt he'd betrayed Konrad. Taking care of me was one way of making it up. He had me admitted to the hospital where his cousin worked, and then he went back to Nagasaki. Some American

61

Army doctors came to see me when we were there. I was such an object of curiosity. I spoke to them in English, and one of them asked if I was interested in working as a translator. Working for the Americans! After the bomb, you might wonder how I could agree to such a thing. But the man who asked me – he had such a gentle face. It was impossible to hold him responsible for what had been done. It was impossible, really, to hold anyone responsible – the bomb was so . . . it seemed beyond anything human. Anyway, I agreed.

'I worked as a translator for over a year. Made friends with one American nurse in particular, who took me to have my hair cut short like hers, and let me borrow her clothes when we went out to nightclubs together. I'd grown up in the war; these peacetime luxuries were all new to me. I didn't ever want to go back to Nagasaki, but I was content to be in Tokyo with the Americans. And then one day – near the end of '46 – the American with the gentle face said the bomb was a terrible thing, but it had to be done to save American lives. I knew straight away I couldn't keep working for them. The nurse came to find me when she heard I was leaving. What are you going to do, she said. The words just came out of my mouth – go far away. Not you as well, she said. That Canadian friend I keep telling you about is shipping out to India.

'India! She said it, and I knew immediately where I would go. I told her and she said that's crazy. But OK, let's see if we can find someone to keep you company. I love that about the Americans – the way they see certain kinds of craziness as signs of character. That night she and I took the Canadian to dinner and gave him lots of sake, and by the end of the evening we were drinking toasts to travelling companions. In case you're wondering if he had ulterior motives, Elizabeth, he was – what is that phrase you used about your cousin Willie? . . . of a Wildean persuasion.'

Later, when Elizabeth repeated all this to James, in Sajjad's hearing, he shook his head and said, 'I hope your curiosity is satisfied. But don't you think we should simply let her forget all that now?' And since then the Burtons had never asked a question about Japan, or allowed her a moment of contemplation that could lead to memory.

Sajjad considered all this as Hiroko's gaze turned inwards, then sat back in his chair, looking out at the garden, and let her be.

4

Hiroko watched the shadows thrown on to the ruins of Hauz Khas, around which an elaborate moonlit picnic was in progress. The ruins were just ruins, shadows just distorted impressions created by the interplay of light and dark. So even this had come to pass: a collapsing structure, the silhouette of a man falling upon it, did not impair her ability to turn with a polite smile to hear the question posed by the woman beside her.

'How are your Urdu lessons coming along?'

Hiroko couldn't recall the name of the Englishwoman who asked the question, though she knew her husband was on the Viceregal staff and that she had the finest jacaranda trees in New Delhi.

'Very well, thank you. It's been three weeks and we've finally accepted that I can only make a "k" sound using the roof of my mouth, not the back of it. It has drenched Sajjad in sorrow, but sorrow is inescapable with Urdu so he's not blaming me.'

'Sajjad? Oh, James's dogsbody. Is that what he said, "sorrow is inescapable with Urdu"? They make the oddest claims, don't they?'

Dogsbody? Hiroko bit into a piece of roast chicken to give her mouth something to do other than retort. She didn't know how to behave around these people – the rich and powerful, a number of whom had asked her about the samurai way of life and thought she was being charmingly self-effacing when she said the closest she had come to the warrior world was her days as a worker at the munitions factory. Two years after the war they could accept an ally of Hitler sooner than they could accept someone of a different

64

class, she thought, and wished she had entered India in a manner that would have allowed her into the houses of those who lived in Delhi's equivalent of Urakami. And yet, that was unfair to the Burtons and at least partially untrue. The soft sheets, the abundance of mealtimes, the dizzyingly coloured dresses Elizabeth had passed on to her, the vastness of the Burton library, the kindness of the Burtons themselves . . . she was more than grateful for all these things, and all too conscious that they were hers by generosity, not by right.

'Why are you wasting your time with Urdu?' Kamran Ali, one of the Indian Oxbridge set, lowered his bulky frame on to the picnic blanket beside Hiroko. 'Language of mercenaries and marauders. Do you know the word "Urdu" has the same root as "horde"? Now, Latin. That's a language worth learning.' He held up his empty glass and a liveried bearer stepped forward to fill it. 'Vini, vidi, vino,' Kamran Ali said, and the Englishwoman next to Hiroko laughed and drew him into the conversation about the odd utterances of one's Indian staff.

Hiroko felt someone touch her elbow and looked up to find Elizabeth there.

'Elizabeth, are you joining us?' the Lady of Jacaranda said without making any attempt to shift and make space.

'Thank you, no, Violet. The air's much too stifling here.' She paused for just a moment before adding, 'I mean, because of those—' She waved her hand in the direction of the six-foot-high sticks with flames billowing from their tips which lit up the picnic area.

Hiroko stood up with a mumbled excuse, caught between amusement and sadness at the acerbity of Elizabeth's interactions with these dull but harmless creatures. As the two women started to walk away from the gathering, James, watching them from a distance, saw the light shimmer off Elizabeth's emerald-studded necklace – he'd placed it around her throat for the first time in a world burnished so bright with love that the green gems had seemed dull by comparison. In a rare imaginative burst he saw Hiroko and Elizabeth as the twin slim gold chains of the necklace, progressing side by side except when some gleaming interruption (the Viceroy, the wife of one of James's clients, the Nawab of

Somewhere) prompted them to diverge for a while, assured that they would meet on the other side. James believed Elizabeth was solicitous of her foreign guest in establishing this pattern, never realising how much it counted for his wife finally to find herself a friend and ally.

Occasionally these last few weeks she had even found herself looking forward to going out when Hiroko agreed to accompany them to whatever social gathering was taking place that evening (there was never an evening without a social gathering).

'Sorry to wander off for so long. I wouldn't have heard the end of it from James if I hadn't spent some time discussing themes for the Easter Ball with the Harridan. Her husband looks poised to further justify James's chess-playing lifestyle.'

Hiroko had already learnt that it was best to keep quiet when either of the Burtons spoke about the other, but she determined right then to find a way past Sajjad's barrier of loyal silence in all matters related to James Burton and find out why exactly a solicitor could be allowed to sit on his verandah, drinking tea and occasionally moving chess pieces around a board, without anyone raising the slightest objection. The rich! Ridiculous! she found herself thinking and shook her head about all that didn't change no matter where in the world you went.

The truth of it was that since the very start of his legal career James's foremost, and unparalleled, ability had been the charm, social connections and air of command which combined to convince clients and – more importantly – prospective clients that James Burton was a man to rely on. He brought those in need of legal counsel to the offices of Burton, Hopkins and Price and once they were there he left all those with particularly thorny problems in the hands of his colleagues, who were able enough to ensure that the clients did not regret their choices. Since he'd broken his leg he had been unable to navigate the stairs up to the third-floor law offices but he'd been unflagging in his social obligations, making adept use of the sympathy his injury garnered to the betterment of his practice.

Once a week Sajjad went to the office and brought back work with which James could occupy himself, but everyone understood that was little more than a façade; though the leg was considerably healed no one had bothered to enquire when he could return to work, so it seemed foolish for James to broach the subject himself. Just as it had seemed foolish to broach the subject of returning to the upstairs bedroom when he found himself able to manage the stairs. The difference in the two situations was that he didn't particularly want to return to the office.

Only Hiroko's collapse on her second day in Delhi had finally restored James to the marital bed; she had to be moved to the downstairs room and Elizabeth had told Lala Buksh to transfer James's belongings 'upstairs'. The command was vague enough for James to wonder if she meant 'the upstairs guest bedroom' but Lala Buksh had not interpreted it that way, much to James's relief. On their first night in the same bed after a space of over two months it had seemed far too pointed to do anything other than make love, but it had been an awkward, unsatisfying business, the awfulness of the whole thing made worse by James patting Elizabeth on the head just before turning away to curl against his pillow as, long ago, he used to curl against his wife. In the middle of the night he'd woken up to find his body aching with demands; as silently as possible he'd taken care of his needs, thinking of Elizabeth as he did so, though she, lying awake yet immobile next to him, was convinced that wasn't so.

Elizabeth linked arms with Hiroko as they stepped away from the lanterns and torches. Earlier, when James's Bentley had approached the ruined complex of Hauz Khas, Elizabeth was appalled at her insensitivity in bringing Hiroko to such a place, reminding her that time and neglect should be the only cause of such devastation. We want to speed up everything in our modernity, she had thought, even destruction. But Hiroko had looked around the moonlit ruins in wonder, and stepped out from the Bentley towards the torchlight as though entering a fairy tale.

'Sometimes I forget the enchantments of Delhi,' Elizabeth said, sitting on the raised floor of a small stone structure, its pillars topped with a cupola. 'Then there's a night like this, and I almost believe I'll miss this place when all this is over.'

Hiroko sat down next to her.

'You don't mind, then? That the British have to leave?'

Elizabeth laughed softly.

'I'll tell you something that I've never told anyone, not even James. The British Empire makes me feel so . . .' She glanced at Hiroko as though considering how much she could be trusted, and then admitted, 'German.' She reached into the silver bag that hung off her wrist and pulled out a cigarette.

Hiroko accepted the cigarette with a wry smile. Elizabeth didn't smoke, but took a certain pleasure from seeing Hiroko doing so in front of James's stuffy clients, just as she took pleasure in the eyebrows of officialdom that raised themselves over the stylishly cut trousers Hiroko had brought with her from Tokyo.

Hiroko leaned back, her elbow resting on the stone floor, legs crossed at the ankles. Briefly in Tokyo she'd lived the life she had thought she'd wanted – that of the forties version of the 'modern girl'. Jazz clubs, and cigarettes, and no one but herself to support with the money she earned from translations. For a while she'd even enjoyed it. Now it was only to keep Elizabeth company that she sometimes acceded to coming out to these gatherings with their intricate rules of behaviour, which she knew she could only flout up to a point before embarrassing James Burton. She was much happier curled up on a sofa in Bungle Oh! working on Urdu exercises Sajjad set for her or reading a book from the Burton library.

'I always assumed I knew why Konrad was so obsessed with discovering all he could about the lives of the Europeans and Japanese in Nagasaki.' She could talk without constraint about Konrad to his sister now, though James hadn't entirely rid himself of the air of panic which suggested he was forseeing an oriental melodrama unfolding in his living room each time she mentioned his brother-in-law. 'So determined to see a pattern of people moving towards each other – that's why he kept researching his book instead of writing it, you know? He was waiting for the war to end and the foreigners to come back and give him his triumphant ending. He thought the war was an interruption, not the end of the story.' She looked once more towards the shadows flickering on rubble and exhaled a breath of smoke. 'I always thought his obsession grew from a need to believe in a world as separate as possible from a Germany of "laws for the protection of German blood and German honour".' She laughed without much humour. 'Imagine hoping to find that separate world in Japan.'

'And now? You think there was some other reason.'

'Yes, Ilse. You.'

'Oh.' Elizabeth shook her head, made an embarrassed gesture of disavowal. 'I was nothing in Konrad's life. His mother – my stepmother – had me sent away to boarding school in England before he was born. And most of my holidays were with my mother's family in London. Konrad and I were strangers.'

Hiroko nodded briefly. It would be too cruel to say that Konrad had been searching through Nagasaki for a world in which they didn't have to be strangers, a world in which he could have arrived in Delhi to see the sister he was finally old enough to know as an equal and not found that his Germanness, her Englishness, were all that mattered.

'I don't miss him at all,' Elizabeth said slowly. 'But even so, when you first came to our house, before I saw you, there was a moment when I thought it was Konrad. And it was . . .' She pressed her fingers against a spot just above her heart. 'A joy so deep I know nothing about its origins.' As she had known nothing about the origins of all that desperate passion in the aftermath of Konrad's death, when she had reached for James night after night, not mourning her brother but needing some assurance of her own body's existence – she was flesh, she was blood, not a shadow. But her only refuge was in orgasm, which felt like obliteration. Was that irony or just another of life's cruelties?

Hiroko looked from Elizabeth to the men and women lounging on picnic blankets while moths and Indian waiters flitted darkly between them, a wave of an uncalloused hand brushing one away, calling the other one near. And there was Kamran Ali speaking to a waiter in his broken, English-accented Urdu. Everything here was awful and – she glanced at Elizabeth – sad. And yet here she was with nowhere else to be. Did that make her awful, or merely sad? Either way she would have to do something – *something!* – to step out of the sense of temporariness that accompanied each moment, except the ones in which she and Sajjad sat on the Burton verandah and a new language ceded its secrets to her.

The bearer circled back to say Mr Burton was asking his wife to join him, and Elizabeth rolled her eyes and stood up.

'You would have liked Konrad,' Hiroko said. 'If I'd married him, I'd have made sure you liked each other.'

Elizabeth touched Hiroko's hair gently.

'I don't doubt you would. And I've never said this before – I should have. I'm so sorry for all you've lost.'

Together they walked back to the firelit gathering, neither remarking that from the moment Hiroko had mentioned Konrad they had started to speak in German, and that doing so felt like sharing the most intimate of secrets.

5

'And then my brother Sikandar's daughter said—'
'Which one? Rabia Bano or Shireen?'
'Shireen. She said—'

Elizabeth closed the wooden lattice doors that led from the sitting room to the verandah, blocking off the sound of Hiroko and Sajjad chattering in Urdu. Six weeks of daily classes should not have been enough to make Hiroko quite so conversational, she thought, allowing herself to feel aggrieved at the fixation with which Hiroko spent her days running her index finger along the curlicued script of the vocabulary lists and children's books that Henry had used for his lessons with Sajjad.

She sat back at her writing table, acknowledging with a grimace the foolishness of having shut out the breeze as she twisted the weight of her hair away from her neck. On the tabletop were two sheets of letter-writing paper, each with two words inked on it.

Dearest Henry –
Willie, Liebling –

She let her hair fall back into place with a fleeting thought of replicating Hiroko's haircut, picked up her pen and held it poised above the second letter. Willie – Cousin Wilhelm – was the only one of her German relatives who had ever truly felt like family to her. Perhaps in part it was because he understood – with his penchant for younger, beautifully dressed men – what it felt to be an outsider in the Weiss clan. She had thought him dead early in the war, rounded up with others of his 'Wildean persuasion' – his terminology, not hers. Only in '45 had she discovered he'd been working with the underground in Germany, helping Jews and homosexuals to escape the Nazis, and that at the end of the war he'd migrated to New York. And now he wrote to say it was the finest city in the world, and all it lacked was her presence.

The pen made a swooping motion as though leading up to some great burst of resolve, and then just before the nib touched the page it veered off to the other letter.

Dearest Henry . . .

She pressed the nib against the page and wrote firmly:

Of course you're coming home this summer. Yes, there's trouble in the Punjab but Delhi is perfectly safe, and Mussoorie as peaceful as ever. Your grandmother really shouldn't worry so much.

Your father has been boasting to everyone about your bowling average. We're both delighted to hear of your continued successes.

She stopped, and put down the pen. Why was it that the more Henry settled into boarding school the more formal his letters to her, and hers back to him, became? And why had she ever agreed to let James send him off to England? She batted away a fly with the hand holding the pen and a spray of ink appeared on the wall opposite her. The stigmata of the blue-blooded, she thought, moving the framed picture of Henry so that it covered the speckling.

It's the done thing. That's what James had said to begin and end every argument about Henry and boarding school. But in the end she'd had her own reasons for agreeing to send him away. The looming end of Empire meant they would all have to leave India before long; better to wean Henry away from it – summers in India, the rest of the year in England – than sever the tie in one abrupt motion. She glanced over at the latticed door. It still rankled that her boy had thrown his arms around Sajjad and wept, declaring, 'I'll miss you most,' when the time for his departure had come. Though it was ridiculous of James to insist it was jealousy about her son's affections that made her dislike Sajjad – she had disliked him from the start. Instinct, that was all.

'Is the lesson still going on?'

James's aftershave entered the room, followed by the man himself.

'Well, they're out there talking in Urdu. I don't know if it's a lesson or just chit-chat. You nicked yourself shaving.'

'Hmmmm . . .' James touched his finger to the cut on his jaw. 'They seem to start earlier and go on later each day.'

The combination of the dab of blood and the look of discontentment made him appear unusually vulnerable. Elizabeth pivoted out of her chair and walked over to him, feeling the word 'wife' slip around her shoulders with a feather-light touch.

'You're the one who employs him, you know. You have every right to tell him if you're unhappy with the way he's utilising his time.' She ran her finger along his jaw, wiping off the blood, and then absent-mindedly put the finger in her mouth.

'Vampire,' James said, smiling, the atmosphere in that moment light between them as it hadn't been in a long time.

Elizabeth looked at his jaw. There was still a spot of blood there. For a moment all she wanted to do was lean in and place her mouth against his skin, feel the tingle of aftershave against her lips and hear him sigh in satisfaction and relief as he used to do during their early married life when some expression of physical desire was Elizabeth's signal that whatever squabble had sprung up between them was now ended. But he was already wiping away what remained of the blood and stepping past her to glance at the letters on her writing desk.

Willie, Liebling –

James ran his fingers beneath the endearment, the paper darkening where he touched it with hands that had been less than thoroughly dried after his shave. 'Liebling' appeared underlined, and struck both of them as an accusation. She used to refer to him by that endearment – in the days when German was her language of intimacy. Which went first, he wondered? German or intimacy? How was it possible that he didn't know?

'Is Hiroko to stay with us indefinitely?' he said abruptly.

'Keep your voice down, James!'

'I don't mean I want her to go.' He picked up the pens in the penholder, one by one, and then replaced them again. He really should

73

write a letter to Henry, but Elizabeth's detailed weekly missives to their son left nothing for James to add. 'You clearly enjoy having her around.'

'You don't?'

'No, I do. The house doesn't feel quite so empty any more.'

James touched the blue dot on the wall, just behind Henry's photograph, and made a sharp noise of protest when the ink transferred itself to his hand. Honestly, Elizabeth. The wall had just been repainted. He could see by the perceptible shift in her stance that she was preparing for another fight, and the mere thought of it exhausted him.

'I'm just wondering what I should . . . we should be doing for Hiroko. Should we be introducing her to young men? British, or Indian? The whole Japanese thing makes it a little awkward. Should we find out if there are Japs in Delhi somewhere?'

'She doesn't seem much interested in that sort of thing. I broached the subject once – she said, "the bomb marked me for spinsterhood."'

'What's that supposed to mean?'

'Oh, James. Don't be so dense. Her head is still filled with dreams of Konrad. No one can compete with that.'

'More to Konrad than we thought, wasn't there?'

'Yes. I think there was much more to Konrad than we thought.' She sat down at her writing desk again, and James situated himself on the sofa that allowed him to look at her profile while she wrote, calling out for Lala Buksh as he did so.

His voice reached Sajjad and Hiroko outside.

'Time for chess?' Hiroko said, and Sajjad placed a finger over his lips and shook his head conspiratorially.

'We're in the middle of a game which he knows he's going to lose. I don't think he's in any hurry to continue with it,' he said, smiling. Hiroko tried to smile in return but it faltered almost on inception so that all Sajjad saw was a quiver of her lips. He looked at her in concern. Something was wrong today. He had been trying all morning to engage her with his stories but her responses had been at the very brink of politeness.

Hiroko glanced over at the closed doors leading into the house.

'It would have been Konrad's birthday today, Sajjad, and she doesn't even know that.'

Sajjad had never known how to bring up the subject of Nagasaki and Konrad with her, though the more time he spent in her company the more he wished simply to find a way of indicating that such sorrow should not come to anyone in the world, and particularly not to a woman so deserving of happiness.

'Can I tell you how I met him?' Sajjad said. 'Yes? It was in Dilli, in 1939. It was summer. And so hot. The sun is possessive of this city in the summer – it wants all its beauty to itself, so it chases everyone away. The rich to their hill stations, the rest of us to darkened rooms, or under trees where the shade marks the edges of the sun's territory. I was on my way to the calligraphy shop, where my brothers were waiting for me. And then I saw an Englishman. In Dilli, in my moholla. Not in Chandni Chowk, or at the Red Fort, but just walking through the streets lined with doorways.'

'Not an Englishman. Konrad!' Hiroko leaned forward, her cheek resting on her palm, seeing it so clearly.

'Yes. I had never spoken to an Englishman, never even considered it, but something in that one's face made me go up to him. He was standing by the side of the road, sniffing the air. It was summer, and the air was drenched in the scent of mangoes. "Sahib, are you lost?" I said. He didn't understand I was speaking English. So I repeated it. And he said, very slowly, as if he thought I might have as much trouble with his accent as he did with mine, "Can you explain this smell to me?" I didn't understand what he meant. It never occurred to me he wouldn't know the smell of mangoes. I decided he was looking for a story, the way my nephews and nieces do. So I said, "Some god has walked, sweating, through here." He held out his hand and shook mine, and said, "That's the best thing I've heard since I came to Delhi. I'm Konrad." Just like that. "I'm Konrad." And I never went to the calligraphy shop. We walked through Dilli, defying the sun for the rest of the morning, and at the end of it he brought me here and asked Mr Burton to give me a job. And this is my life now. I'm here now, in this place, talking to you because Konrad Weiss liked the way I explained the scent of mangoes.' He finished speaking and worried that the story had

75

been more about him than Konrad. But Hiroko was smiling at last, and that felt like victory.

'In just the few days we were here together he taught me how to look at things differently. How to notice the world. He was so conscious of beauty,' Sajjad said carefully, not wanting to overstep any limits or be presumptuous. 'I've wanted just to say that since he died. But there has never been an opportunity to say it to the Burtons.' He lowered his head and didn't look at her as he said, 'I'm glad you're here.' Quickly, he added, 'So I could say that to you. About Mr Konrad.'

Hiroko stood up and walked to the edge of the verandah, catching hold of a flowering shrub and pulling it towards herself, inhaling the sharp scent of its unripe berries. Sajjad could not bring himself to look away from her though he knew this was not a moment for him.

'Some nights I still wake up calculating,' she said, so softly he thought the words might have drifted in from far away on a breeze. 'The time he left me, the speed at which he was walking, the distance to the Cathedral. The conclusion is always the same. He would have been at the Cathedral, or very near it, when the bomb fell. Only melted rosaries remained, you know, of the people inside the Cathedral. It was less than five hundred metres from the epicentre. But I don't think Konrad was inside. I think he was still a minute or two away. There was a rock I found, with a shadow on it. Do you know about the shadows, Sajjad?' She didn't look back to see him nodding, or the ink blurring from words into patterns on the page at which he was looking.

He was remembering then how Konrad Weiss had walked him around this garden and told him the names of flowers, and explained which ones attracted birds with scent and which with colour.

'Those nearest the epicentre of the blast were eradicated completely, only the fat from their bodies sticking to the walls and rocks around them like shadows. I dreamt one night, soon after the blast, that I was with a parade of mourners walking through Urakami Valley, each of us trying to identify the shadows of our loved ones. The next morning, I went to the Valley; it was what the priest at Urakami had spoken of when he taught me from the Bible – the Valley of Death. But there was no sign of any God there, no scent of mangoes, Sajjad, just of burning. Days – no, weeks – after the bomb and everything still smelt of burning. I walked through it – those strangely angled trees above the melted stone, somehow that's what struck me the most – and I looked for Konrad's shadow. I found it. Or I found something that I believed was it. On a rock. Such a lanky shadow. I sent a message to Yoshi Watanabe and together we rolled that rock to the International Cemetery . . .' She pressed a hand against her spine at the memory. 'And buried it.'

She plucked the green berry off the tree and spun it between her fingers. She could not tell anyone, not even this man with the gentle eyes and an understanding of the scent of gods, how Yoshi had left her with the stone for a few minutes while he went in search of implements to dig with and she had lain down on Konrad's shadow, within Konrad's shadow, her mouth pressed against the darkness of his chest. 'Why didn't you stay?' she had whispered against the unyielding stone.

Why didn't you stay? She pressed the berry against her lips. *Why didn't I ask you just one more time to stay?*

Sajjad stood up quietly and walked over to her.

'There is a phrase I have heard in English: to leave someone alone with their grief. Urdu has no equivalent phrase. It only understands the concept of gathering around and becoming "ghum-khaur" – grief-eaters – who take in the mourner's sorrow. Would you like me to be in English or Urdu right now?'

There was a moment's hesitation, and then she said, 'This is an Urdu lesson, Sensei,' and returned to sit at the bridge table, pen poised to write the word 'ghum-khaur'.

6

Elizabeth looked across the dusty stretch of land towards the dizzyingly high Qutb Minar around which James and Hiroko were walking, inspecting the fluted sandstone of the tower's edifice. Elizabeth wished she hadn't declared the structure 'unsubtle' and insisted on waiting under a pillared corridor that stood among the ruins of the Qutb complex while the other two explored the tapering column. She wished even more fervently that Sajjad had not volunteered to 'wait with Mrs Burton'. He *would* be so impeccably polite about the fact that it was both unwise and improper for her to stand alone while wild dogs ran amidst the ruins, and strangers passed by. Though, frankly, with all the communal violence just next door in the Punjab, with occasional leaks into Delhi, who was to say that the presence of a Muslim man might not itself give rise to dangerous situations? She tensed, and looked around for places to hide, suddenly expecting to see armed Hindus or Sikhs charging towards Sajjad. But there was no one around, not even the dogs. Only those inescapable pigeons.

She ran her palm across her neck and it came away glistening. Soon it would be time to move to Mussoorie for the summer. It was hard to imagine Mussoorie without Henry – they had decided, after all, that it would be best for him to stay in England over the holidays given how uncertain things were in India. Her sense of dissatisfaction deepend. Why on earth were they here? Some plan which she'd only come to know of when James woke her up and said, 'We're going on an expedition. Get dressed; Sajjad will be here soon.' She'd been irritated at being excluded from the planning, and further irritated to come downstairs to find Hiroko sitting on a step leading to the garden, leaning against a flowerpot, which left a red mark on her dress, which was really Elizabeth's dress; how many times had she warned Hiroko against doing exactly that?

Liquid sprayed around her ankles and she looked up to see Sajjad sweeping his arm from side to side in front of her, a bottle in his hand and a thumb over the mouth of the bottle, covering all but a fraction of it.

'What in God's name do you think you're doing?'

'This will cool the air around you.'

'Oh.' The smell of the water hitting the earth was in itself a relief. 'Thank you.'

'You're welcome.' He continued to spray the ground.

'Why are we here, Sajjad? Winter is the time for the Qutb Minar, not April. And if Hiroko had a desire to go sightseeing surely there are places of cool interiors that would have made more sense.'

Sajjad knew he couldn't tell her the truth, particularly as it was obvious her husband hadn't chosen to do so. The previous day, as their lesson had drawn to a close, Hiroko had said, 'I'd like to see your Delhi, Sajjad. Would you take me there some day?'

If she had said it in Urdu, he didn't know – he couldn't now imagine – how he might have responded. But it was English, and James Burton had walked out on to the verandah in time to hear it, so there was nothing to be done but mumble something about it being time for chess, and hoping that was an end to the conversation.

But later James said, 'Qutb Minar. You once insisted you have some ancient familial link to the place, didn't you? Well, that's your Delhi then, isn't it? We'll take her there.'

To Elizabeth, Sajjad only said, 'I'm afraid it's my fault, Mrs Burton. I thought she might be interested to see what's left of my ancestors in Delhi.'

The Ilse Weiss who had grown up on her grandmother's stories of ghosts asserted her presence and looked around – both in terror and excitement – for the spirits of Sajjad's ancestors prowling through the ruins.

79

'I don't mean what is literally left of them,' Sajjad said, without mockery. 'My ancestors were soldiers in the armies of the Mamluks – I believe your English historians call them the Slave Kings. The Qutb Minar is the greatest remaining monument of those kings.'

'Slave Kings?' Against her will, she was intrigued. 'I assume they weren't really slaves.'

'Oh, yes. They were the first dynasty of the Delhi Sultanate. Thirteenth century, Christian calendar. Qutb-ud-din Aibak, after whom the Qutb Minar is named, was the first ruler – he was a slave who rose to the position of general. His son-in-law, Altamash, also a former slave, was the second ruler. He's buried there.' He waved his hands somewhere behind the ruins of the great mosque. It struck him as he did so that this was how things should be – he, an Indian, introducing the English to the history of India, which was his history and not theirs. It was a surprising thought, and something in it made him uneasy. He had thought the world would change around him but his own life would stay unaffected.

'India and all its invaders,' Elizabeth said. Her eyes followed a pale-winged butterfly which flew out between the stone pillars and then reeled back, staggered by the heat. 'How will all of us fit back into that little island now that you're casting us out? So small, England, so very small. In so many ways.'

Sajjad looked at Elizabeth, leaning against a pillar, her body angled towards the figures near the Qutb Minar. Was it James or Hiroko who she looked at with such sadness? Or was she also thinking of her son? He thought for a moment of Henry Burton and sighed. He hadn't realised how much he'd been looking forward to the boy's return until James had mentioned – off-handedly, as though it were not really a matter of concern to Sajjad – that Henry would stay in England this summer. It will have devastated her, he thought, continuing to look at Elizabeth Burton – and her phrasing of 'you're casting us out' conferred on him a sense of responsibility and authority which allowed him, for once, to address her in a moment when she clearly had her mind on other matters.

'In fact, the story of the Slave Dynasty which I most love is that of Altamash's daughter, Razia Sultana.'

'Some tragic love story?' Elizabeth's tone conveyed something of her gratitude at being drawn out of her musings on the symbolic significance of the wasteland that filled the space between her and James.

'Women do have roles in other kinds of stories,' he said, a fountain of lines springing out from the corner of his eyes as he smiled. She gestured to him to come and stand in the covered corridor with her, out of the sun, and he accepted with a nod of gratitude. This sudden cordiality was unexpected, but welcome. 'No, Razia Sultana was the most capable of Altamash's children, far more so than any of his sons. So he named her his heir. Of course, when Altamash died one of the sons seized the throne, but Razia soon defeated him. She was an amazing woman – a brilliant administrator, a glorious fighter.' Almost bashfully, he added, 'If I ever have a daughter I'll name her Razia.'

It was a moment of surprising intimacy. For the duration of a heartbeat Elizabeth allowed it to linger in the air between them, and then she gestured towards James and Hiroko.

'Let's join those two. You can give us all a history lesson about the tower.'

'Minaret.'

'That's lesson number one. Do you know I've been here at least a dozen times, but I've never known anything about who built it or why.'

'My history is your picnic ground,' he said, but there was no accusation in the comment, only a wryness which she responded to with a smile.

James watched Elizabeth and Sajjad walk towards him with a sense of relief. Hiroko was acting very strangely – he almost thought he'd done something to offend her in organising this surprise picnic and leading her ahead of the other two to point out personally the highlights of the Qutb complex. Here she was, not walking around the great tower so much as prowling. He'd thought of her as a wounded bird when she first came to stay, but now he saw something more feral in her.

I have to get away, I have to get away, Hiroko thought, circling the minaret. She was nothing in this world. It was clear now. Better even to be a hibakusha than nothing. Last evening, when James Burton had whispered, 'Tomorrow morning we're all going to see Sajjad's Delhi,' she had felt her face stretch into a smile that didn't seem possible. His world wasn't closed to outsiders! The Burtons weren't entirely resistant to entering an India outside the Raj! And she, Hiroko Tanaka, was the one to show both Sajjad and the Burtons that there was no need to imagine such walls between their worlds. Konrad had been right to say barriers were made of metal that could turn fluid when touched simultaneously by people on either side.

But when Sajjad had arrived on his bicycle, not quite looking at her, she knew he wasn't taking them to his moholla. And James Burton seemed entirely to have forgotten that this trip had anything to do with Sajjad as he walked her through the complex with its crumbling structures, pointing out the stretch of ground favoured by polo players, the metallurgical significance of an ancient iron pillar.

She could feel her mind twist away from the inescapable conclusion she knew she'd soon have to face: she had to return to Japan.

'James!' Elizabeth said, coming to stand beside her husband. 'Did you know Sajjad's family came here from Turkey seven centuries ago?'

'Young Turk, are you?' James smiled at Sajjad.

'No, Mr Burton,' Sajjad said, not understanding the reference. 'I'm Indian.' He glanced at Hiroko, who had her back to all three of them, looking up at the Arabic inscriptions on the minaret. She was offended, he knew, but what could he do about it? He looked at James, as though considering something that had never occurred to him before. 'Why have the English remained so English? Throughout India's history conquerors have come from elsewhere, and all of them – Turk, Arab, Hun, Mongol, Persian – have become Indian. If – when – this Pakistan happens, those Muslims who leave Delhi and Lucknow and Hyderabad to go there, they will be leaving their homes. But when the English leave, they'll be going home.'

Hiroko turned towards Sajjad, surprised and acutely self-conscious. She had been speaking to him of Konrad's interest in the foreigners who made their homes in Nagasaki, and now she saw her words filtering into his thoughts and becoming part of the way he saw the world.

'Henry thinks of India as home,' Elizabeth said, seeing how wounded James was by Sajjad's unexpected attack, and wanting to deflect it.

'Yes.' There was a tightening of Sajjad's voice. 'He does.' And you sent him away because of it, he wanted to say, the sense of offence which had started as an act to impress Hiroko no longer feigned. He recalled it very well, the day her opposition to the idea of boarding school ended. He had been playing cricket in the garden with Henry when Elizabeth came out and told her son he was 'such a young Englishman'. Henry had scowled, and backed up towards Sajjad. 'I'm Indian,' he'd said. The next day James Burton had told Sajjad how relieved he was that his wife had suddenly decided to withdraw all her 'sentimental' objections to sending Henry to boarding school.

'Something you want to say, Sajjad?'

'No, Mrs Burton. Only that I don't suppose he'll continue to think of India that way for much longer.'

'For the best,' Elizabeth said, looking around her, feeling something that was almost sorrow to think the descendants of the English would not come to the churches and monuments of British India seven centuries from now and say this is a reminder of when my family history and India's history entered the same stream irrevocably and for ever.

'Why is it for the best?' Sajjad's voice was as near angry as anyone had ever heard it. It was hard to say if Elizabeth or Sajjad was more surprised at his tone after eight years during which he used only excessive politeness as a weapon against her. But they were both aware that this would not have happened if Hiroko hadn't been standing there, disrupting all hierarchies.

'Steady on,' James said in a warning tone, and Sajjad turned very red and looked away with a mumbled apology.

Elizabeth wanted to catch Sajjad by the collar and shake him. *I was made to leave Berlin when I was just a little younger than him – I know the pain of it. What do you know of leaving, you whose family has lived in Delhi for centuries?* But beneath that anger there was something that felt a great deal like hurt. We were just starting to get on, that place beneath anger wanted to say.

'Sajjad.' Hiroko tugged at his sleeve. Her own rage was forgotten behind the need to stop the awfulness of the anger pulsing between these two people who had come to mean so much to her. 'Come, look. I found a word I recognise.' She pointed to some part of the Arabic inscription on the minaret, and Sajjad moved closer to her to better see where she was directing his attention, their two dark heads almost touching.

The ease of their proximity struck Elizabeth much as it had Lala Buksh on the day of Hiroko's arrival. She saw the quick glance Sajjad directed at Hiroko and understood more about what it meant than Sajjad did. She did not stop to think of how Hiroko might feel about it or to wonder how long it had been true – she only knew that at last she had found a way to get past that armour of charm and indifference that had allowed Sajjad Ali Ashraf to win over everyone else in her household while remaining impervious to all she ever said and did.

'Sajjad and I were just having a chat,' she said loudly, putting an arm around James's waist in an attempt at casualness which almost made him jump back in surprise. 'He was telling me the name he has in mind for his first daughter.'

James kissed the side of her head, allowing his lips to linger while he took in her scent. His fingers covered hers at his waist. She was almost distracted from her purpose, almost on the verge of turning to James and whispering that they should reacquaint themselves with the recessed archways built into the walls of the covered passageway, where, in happier times, they had sometimes slipped away during polo games on the adjoining fields to seek refuge from the sun and other onlookers. But then she heard Sajjad say something in Urdu which made Hiroko blush. What he'd said was, 'Before you know it I'll have to come to you for lessons in my language,' but Elizabeth only saw that Hiroko was drifting away from her towards Sajjad, as James and Henry had already done.

'So, Sajjad,' she said casually. 'How are your marital plans shaping up? James told me you said you'll need to take a few days off for your wedding before the end of the year.'

There was the briefest moment in which there was only anticipation of what might follow, and then Hiroko turned sharply on her heels and started to walk back towards the car.

'What . . .?' James said, surprised by the resoluteness with which she was striding away.

'The heat. It's not good for her.' Elizabeth's childhood self felt the ghosts of those attached to the world by remorse press their hot mouths against her skin in initiation. 'We should leave.'

'Oh, all right.' James looked regretfully towards the covered hallway. 'Sajjad, come along.'

'I'll find my own way home, thank you, Mr Burton.'

'Come on, James!'

James looked uncertainly at Sajjad, who waved him towards the car.

'I will walk among the ruins and compose great poems about my ancestors, Mr Burton. Please don't worry about me.'

Sajjad watched as the Bentley drove off, unsettling both pigeons and dust, and only when it was out of view did he lean back against the great minaret and look up to the whitening sky for some explanation of why his heart was racing so madly.

7

Civil Lines was aflame with gulmohar trees in bloom as Sajjad pedalled to work the next morning, each fiery flower-cluster reminding him of Hiroko stalking away across a barren tract of land with collapsing monuments strewn around, a smear of red on the back of her dress as though her heart had bled all the way through.

For an instant he had thought there could be only one explanation for her response to news of his wedding – but he quickly saw the vanity, the absurdity, of that thought. Of course she was angry with him; why wouldn't she be? She had spoken to him of the death of Konrad Weiss, and what had he told her of his own life in return? Nothing but superficialities. And so it fell to Elizabeth Burton casually to announce news that one friend had no reason to keep from another.

A woman friend. Sajjad shook his head in amazement to think such a thing had entered his life. A Japanese woman friend. The bicycle wheels whirred and the seat creaked as he pedalled faster, then slower, much slower, then faster again. Could he invite her to his wedding? What would his wife – whoever she might turn out to be – say to know there was a woman outside the family who he counted among his friends; a woman who wore trousers and low-cut necklines, and smoked cigarettes, and would never dream of allowing anyone else to choose her husband, and who was beautiful. No, perhaps it was better after all not to consider inviting her to his wedding.

And yet he could see her there. Could see her standing just a little apart from the women of his family, her eyes teasingly on him in that moment before he looked down into the mirror which would show him, for the first time, the face of the woman sitting beside him who he had just married.

No, no, she could not, must not, come to his wedding.

When he dismounted in the Burton driveway Lala Buksh was waiting for him. Sajjad nodded to him as he leaned his cycle against the wall. In all the years he'd been coming here he and Lala Buksh had barely spoken to each other beyond Sajjad conveying some request of James's to his bearer or wishing him a perfunctory *Eid Mubarak*. But in the last few weeks, as riots continued and the creation of a new state seemed increasingly likely, the two men had started to drink a cup of tea together in the morning while discussing what news the previous day had brought with it of death and politics and freedom.

Lala Buksh handed Sajjad a steaming cup, and they walked towards the kitchen entrance, where Sajjad sat on the step leading inside while Lala Buksh squatted on the ground as he would never do in the presence of the English.

'I am going,' Lala Buksh said bluntly. Sajjad looked at him quizzically, distracted by the thought that he would see Hiroko in a few minutes and had no idea of what he would say to her. 'To this country for Muslims. I will go.'

Sajjad leaned his head back against the screen door.

'The English are here for another year. Why don't you wait to see what the situation is in '48? Already things are much calmer than last month.'

Lala Buksh looked at his hands as they curled into fists, watching them as a scientist might watch some awful and brilliant weapon of his own creation begin to take form.

'By '48, I don't know what I'll have become.'

Unlike Sajjad, Lala Buksh lived in a neighbourhood that wasn't predominantly Muslim. He was there only on Fridays, when he had a day off from working for the Burtons, but he confessed to Sajjad that on those Fridays – when his family poured out a week's worth of stories from the Punjab, of Muslim men slaughtered, Muslim shops set on fire, Muslim women abducted – he had to force himself to stay at home because if he went out and saw a single

Hindu his eyes would reveal what was in his heart, and it would get him killed. Or else, a Hindu's eyes would reveal what was in *his* heart, and then . . .

Sajjad sipped his tea, not knowing how to respond to that. For years he'd watched Lala Buksh joke with the Burtons' cook, Vijay, and flirt with Henry's ayah, Rani, and sometimes he'd walk into the kitchen to find the three of them grumbling amiably about the Burtons. Now the only break Lala Buksh took from his duties was this one, with Sajjad. In talking to Lala Buksh, Sajjad realised that atrocities committed on Muslims touched him far more deeply than atrocities committed by Muslims – he knew this to be as wrong as it was true.

As Sajjad finished his tea in one large gulp and stood up, Lala Buksh said, 'You didn't come back with them from Qutb Minar yesterday.' Sajjad made a non-committal gesture. 'She was very upset about something.' He picked up Sajjad's cup and went into the kitchen.

Hiroko, on the verandah, heard the squeal of the kitchen's screen door and knew it meant Sajjad was about to walk around to the back garden. She wasn't sure she could look at him without revealing her envy.

She had tried so hard the previous night to bring Konrad's face to mind but he felt so far away. He felt like another life. In this life there was simply desire for more – more than a memory of his fingers tracing the veins of her wrist, more than a memory of his tongue surprising hers. But though Konrad grew more distant the harder she tried to summon him that thing that had started to happen in her body when she slipped on her mother's silk kimono had reawoken. Lying in the bath last night, she had slid her hand along her naked body (except it wasn't her hand, it wasn't her body – it was Sajjad's hand and his wife's body – even in fantasy she could not allow herself to believe her body could be the location of such caresses from any man) and as the hand moved lower her body had jerked, slamming her hip against the porcelain, and terrified her into pulling out the bath-plug and getting into bed, where she clenched her hands into fists and kept them resolutely away from the rest of her.

'Good morning,' Sajjad said, walking towards the verandah. 'I hope you're feeling better today.'

'Yes, thank you.' She looked at him and wondered how it must feel to watch Sajjad Ali Ashraf approach you and know that his body was yours to touch. The look she gave him was lightly accusing. 'Why didn't you tell me about her?'

'Who?'

'Your fiancée.'

'Oh.' Sajjad scrunched up his face. 'No, no. Nothing's settled yet. My mother and sisters-in-law have someone in mind, but I don't even know her name. It could all be nothing.' He placed his hand on the table, touching the spine of the book on which her fingers were resting.

She nodded, tried to ignore the strange feeling of hopefulness mingled with despair.

'You must be considered very eligible. Though . . . can I ask you something?'

'Of course. Anything.'

'You told me once that you're going to be a lawyer. But you spend your days playing chess with James Burton. I know you want more from the world.'

In all this time she had been the first person ever to say this to him.

'Without James Burton, I'd be working with my family, hating it. So as long as he wants me to play chess, I will. But he's said, he's promised, there will always be a place in his law firm for me. He said just the other day, when the British leave there'll be so many vacancies. I can wait. He lets me take law books from his libraries and read them at home. I'm not wasting my time. I'm learning. I'm getting ready.'

'I didn't mean to imply you were wasting your time. I think you'd make a wonderful lawyer.' She could see this was a compliment that truly mattered to him, though she couldn't help wondering whether it was really possible to be a lawyer without some kind of professional qualification.

'Can I ask you something now? Does it seem strange to you? That I'll marry someone I've never met? I know the Burtons think it very . . . backward.'

89

'I'm not the Burtons, Sajjad. It seems to me that I could find more in your world which resembles Japanese traditions than I can in this world of the English.' She said it almost accusingly, before smiling in acknowledgement of how little interest she had in tradition. 'Arranged marriages used to be quite common in Japan. I've always thought they must require more courage than I possess.'

Sajjad didn't feel very courageous.

'It's how things happen.' He traced the lettering on the book's spine and avoided looking at her. 'When you marry it'll be the English way?'

'I'll never marry.'

Sajjad flinched at his own insensitivity.

'I'm sorry. I know Mr Konrad . . . I'm sorry. This is none of my business.'

'I'll never marry,' she repeated. 'But it isn't because of Konrad.'

Sajjad nodded. And then shook his head.

'Then why?'

Hiroko did not stop to think if she wanted confirmation or denial from him of the truth she'd recognised in a Tokyo hospital when she heard the hardened doctor's horrified gasp as he looked at her lying on her stomach. Instead, she stood up and turned her back to him.

'Because of this.' She started to undo the buttons at the back of her blouse, exposing her bare flesh.

With a quick cry of shock, Sajjad turned his face away.

'Please. What are you doing?'

Hiroko tugged at the fabric that covered her back, parting the blouse as though it were stage curtains.

'This is just one more thing the bomb took away from me. Look at me.'

'No. Button your shirt.'

'Sajjad.'

The flatness of her voice made him turn towards her. Whatever he had been about to say remained for ever unsaid. She had stepped out of the shadow of the roof's overhang and into the harsh sunlight so there could be no mistaking the three charcoal-coloured bird-shaped burns on her back, the first below her shoulder blade, the second halfway down her spine, intersected by her bra, the third just above her waist.

She could not see the tears that collected in Sajjad's eyes as he looked at her charred and puckered skin, and so it was left to her to interpret his silence.

'You can read this diagonal script, can't you? Any man could. It says, "Stay away. This isn't what you want."'

Her pain shattered every defence he'd unknowingly constructed since that moment he'd looked at the mole beneath her eye and wanted to touch it. In a few quick steps he was next to her, his hands touching the space between the two lower burns, then pulling away as she shuddered.

'Does it hurt?' he whispered.

'No.' Her voice was even quieter than his.

He touched the grotesque darkness below her shoulder blade – tentatively, fearfully – as though it were a relic of hell, clamping his teeth together against the outrage of the lumps his fingers encountered. She couldn't feel his hand, but the warmth of his breath on her neck was enough to set off another shudder, one that rippled all the way inside her.

He closed his eyes and moved his hand to where the skin felt as skin should. This time when her body shook in a way that he knew was devoid of fear his own body responded; there was no space in this moment of intimacy for him to feel any mortification. He ran the back of his hand along her shoulders, down the curves of her to her waist, reminding her there was this, too, these parts of her also.

Seconds passed as she allowed herself the luxury of his touch, knowing this memory would join Konrad's kisses to form the entirety of her experience of physical intimacy.

'You don't have to be so kind,' she said at length, her hands fisting in the material on to which they still held. 'I know how ugly they are.'

'Ugly? No.' If his voice hadn't been so gentle she might have believed him. 'Birdback,' he said, resting his palm against the middle burn, his other hand swiftly wiping away his tears. 'Don't you know everything about you is beautiful?'

She swung to face him, anger bringing unfamiliarity to her face, forcing him to recognise how he had etched each of her everyday expressions into his mind to keep him company in the hours he was away from her.

'The bomb did nothing beautiful.' Her fist thumped against his chest as she spoke. 'Do you understand me? It did nothing beautiful.'

Elizabeth Burton, who had been woken at dawn by self-loathing, heard the shouts as she was about to sit down at her writing desk. Racing forward, she threw open the shutters to the verandah just in time to see Hiroko in a state of partial undress, yelling and pummelling Sajjad, whose trousers did nothing to hide his erection.

8

There was nowhere in the world more beautiful than Mussoorie, Elizabeth Burton thought, standing at the top of her garden slope, watching either mist or cloud cling to the white peaks of the Himalayas in the distance while the scent of pine forests drifted down from the top of the hill on which the Burton cottage nestled. What a pity beauty could be so meaningless.

Although, she conceded, walking towards the old oak tree, however bad things were here they would have been worse in Delhi with the stifling June heat – even worse than usual this year, she'd read in the paper this morning. And other than that heat, well, yes, other than that heat there was that matter of Sajjad. As much as she shared James's dismay about the just-announced British decision to pull out of India by mid-August instead of the following year – a decision which effectively put an end to any chance of a semblance of order to Partition – there was a part of her which hoped that by some miracle Sajjad would choose Pakistan and be gone from all their lives by the time they returned to Delhi in October. Even though they'd only be there long enough to pack up and leave India there was still so much that could happen – oh, why hide from the truth: the thought of seeing Sajjad again embarrassed her.

It still made her queasy to recall that morning in April when she'd stumbled on to that awful scene between Hiroko and Sajjad. She'd leapt to the worst possible conclusion – she would be the first to acknowledge it – and yelled such horrible things at Sajjad as she ordered him out of her house. She still had no memory of how

Hiroko had reacted, had only been slightly aware at the time that the girl was fumbling to button her blouse as Sajjad almost tripped over his feet in leaving.

Once he was gone, Elizabeth had tried to speak gently to Hiroko, but the younger woman had burst into tears and locked herself in her bathroom, from where she refused to respond to Elizabeth's requests – which soon became demands – that she open the door.

Elizabeth had finally gone upstairs to wake James, who had miraculously slept through all the shouting.

'If he's tried to do what I think you're not going to stop me from sending the police after him,' she'd said, shaking James awake. Her husband looked at her with a confusion that would have been comical under most circumstances. 'Sajjad. Your blue-eyed boy. I just found him downstairs with Hiroko.'

'The verandah's getting too hot for their lessons,' James said sleepily, pulling himself into a seated position. 'I should tell them to use my study.'

'She was practically naked, fighting to keep him off her. Stop blinking at me, James. He was quite visibly aroused. Do you want me to draw you a diagram?'

With a curse she'd never heard from him before, James was on his feet, reaching for his dressing gown and bellowing, 'Sajjad!'

'He's gone. I threw him out.'

'I'll chase him down in the car.' He slammed the flat of his hand against the door to push it open, the sound of flesh smacking wood violent and painful. Elizabeth's hands lifted in self-defence to shield her face.

Sajjad. He had practically lived in this house. And it had never once crossed her mind that he could be any kind of threat, not in that way. Before the thought was done she knew she'd made some terrible mistake.

'James!' she called out.

At the same moment James re-entered the room.

'Are you sure?' he said. 'Elizabeth, how is it possible?'

She went over and took his hand, reminded of the moment when they'd been told that Henry had thrown a rock at a native girl and blinded her in one eye. It turned out later to have been another

Henry – Henry Williams, a thuggish child even at five – and James and Elizabeth both believed they had passed some parenting test when they'd refused to accept their son was responsible.

Hand in hand they walked downstairs, where Hiroko was exiting her room to find them.

'I'm sorry. It was my fault. I undid my buttons. I made him look at me. He was only trying to be kind. Please. I tried to tell him things I wasn't ready to tell anyone. I'm sorry. I'll leave your house. Please don't punish him. I'm so sorry.'

There was much in there Elizabeth didn't understand, but she did understand enough to know what must be done.

'We'll all leave together. It's time to go to Mussoorie for the summer. Pack quickly, Hiroko. We'll leave by the next train. James, will you send Lala Buksh to Sajjad's house with his severance pay. Make sure he tells Sajjad that you'll give him a reference for whatever employment he finds next.'

And so here they were – in Mussoorie, most beautiful and romantic of India's hill stations. She stopped again to look at the extraordinary view; soon the monsoons would cause much of the vista to disappear amidst rain and mist, so while she could she intended to gaze and gaze at all the beauty on offer in this demi-paradise. She didn't know how she would have survived India without Mussoorie, where the official air of Delhi was cast off (or rather, sent off to Simla, the summer capital of the Raj) and the rides to Gun Hill, the picnics by waterfalls, the dances at the Savoy all made the world a kind of dream, even during the war years. She had expected – or perhaps just hoped – that Mussoorie would have the same revivifying effect on Hiroko as it always did on her, but if anything the joie de vivre and romance of the place seemed only to draw her further into whatever self-enclosed space she had entered that day in Delhi.

Elizabeth stood at the base of the oak tree, and looked up at Hiroko, curled on a branch with her back against the trunk, her white linen trousers ripped at the shin from a previous scramble up to this favoured spot. Elizabeth still didn't know which of their neighbours had subsequently hung this rope ladder from the branch on which Hiroko liked to sit, though she suspected it was Kamran Ali, who had the cottage next door.

'I'm coming up,' Elizabeth said, and began to ascend the rope ladder.

Hiroko felt the slight dip of the branch as Elizabeth pulled herself up from the final rung and dangled both legs off one side of the branch, but she said nothing, just continued to look out over the ridges of hills, carpeted with forests and flowers and cottages. On one of the few occasions she'd given in to Elizabeth's pleas to leave the Burton property she'd met a retired English general on the Mall, who said she must recognise so much of the flora here – Mussoorie was just south of the Sino-Japanese phytogeographical ('I mean, pertaining to floral life') region. That evening he'd sent his driver over to the Burton cottage with an abundance of flowers from the surrounding hills, and it was not just their familiarity that made her want to weep but the fact that she did not know their Japanese names, and there was no one she could turn to for that information.

Each day, sitting in this tree, eyes drifting over Mussoorie's trees and flowers, some as familiar as the texture of tatami beneath her feet, she strung together different memories of Nagasaki as though they were rosary beads: the faint sound of her father preparing paint on his ink stone, the deepening purple of a sky studded by clusters and constellations of light in an evening filled with the familiar tones of her neighbours' voices, the schoolchildren rising to their feet as she entered the classroom, the walks along the Oura with Konrad, dreaming of all that would be possible after the war . . .

Everyone in India was talking about the future – the English planning their return to England, Kamran Ali receiving daily telegrams from his cousins already in Karachi regarding property and prospects and family divisions, and Lala Buksh had just sent a message from Delhi to say he would be gone to Pakistan before the Burtons returned. Hiroko could not find a place for herself in any talk of tomorrow – so instead she found herself, for the first time in her life, looking back and further back. The Burtons' set seemed to have decided to make up for the shortfall of her imagination by proffering possible futures to her: travelling companion . . . governess . . . secretary . . . young wife to lonely widower. And

Elizabeth just said you'll come with us, of course, her voice revealing that she understood that sounded more like a threat than a promise. And beneath all this was the voice which said, Japan. In the end you will go back.

'Yes, I think it must have been Kamran Ali who you have to thank for the rope ladder,' Elizabeth said.

Hiroko kept her eyes turned away from Elizabeth. She owed the Burtons so much. How had she allowed herself to owe the Burtons so much?

Elizabeth's thin cotton dress provided little protection from the roughness of the bark she was sitting on, and there was an annoying branch tickling the top of her head, no mater how she angled her face.

'Enough,' she said. 'I've had enough of your moping.'

'Sorry,' Hiroko said dully.

'Say it. Just say it,' Elizabeth demanded.

'Say what?'

'Sajjad. You're angry with me about Sajjad.'

'Am I?' She thought about it. 'Yes, I suppose I am. More angry at myself for giving you the excuse you wanted to get rid of him.' The futility of her pleas for Sajjad to be absolved of any wrongdoing had taught her precisely her role in the Burton house.

'No good would have come of it. One day you'll see that.'

'Come of what?'

'You and Sajjad. How you felt about each other. It was impossible. His world is so alien to yours.'

Hiroko finally turned to look at Elizabeth, trying to make sense of her words. Light filtered through the leaves, everything so beautiful she recalled Konrad saying the Garden of Eden would never have had a story of its own if it hadn't contained a serpent. And then she understood.

'You think . . . you sent him away because you think he . . . that there is something inappropriate about our friendship.'

'Yes,' Elizabeth said, with a lift of her chin. 'One day you'll see that I acted in your best interests.' She caught hold of Hiroko's hand. 'His is a world you either grow up in or to which you remain for ever an outsider. And maybe he'd give up that world for you – if that's what it took to have you in his life – but when that first intensity of passion passed, he'd regret it, and he'd blame you. Women enter their husbands' lives, Hiroko – all around the world. It doesn't happen the other way round. We are the ones who adapt. Not them. They don't know how to do it. They don't see why they should do it.'

Hiroko could only stare at Elizabeth. 'Intensity of passion'? This Englishwoman was crazy.

But what if she wasn't?

Hiroko reached back to a place between burns where he had touched her. He had wanted her. Despite the birds. The blood rushed to her cheeks as she finally understood the strange lift of the fabric of his trousers. He had wanted her and she . . . she had wanted him to go on touching her. Everywhere. She covered her face with her hands, and Elizabeth saw that the woman beside her was just a child.

'Hiroko, it's impossible.'

Hiroko spread her fingers apart to glare through them at Elizabeth.

'Your marriage has just made you bitter. And resentful.'

It was a relief finally to be held accountable.

'Perhaps. It's certainly true that I'm jealous of Sajjad. I'm jealous of the fact that everyone I love loves him more than me, and I resent the fact that I'm the only person in the world whose love he's never been interested in. There, I've said it.'

Hiroko raised her eyebrows, unsure what to make of this.

'Is that a relief?'

'God, yes.' Elizabeth cupped her hands over her mouth and exhaled deeply. 'God in heaven, yes it is. Oh.' She crossed her hands over her chest. 'My goodness. What strange things we humans are.'

Hiroko couldn't help but laugh.

'Don't implicate all of us in this. Your strangeness is entirely your own.'

They were friends again now. Elizabeth moved closer to Hiroko on the branch.

'What I've said doesn't change the fact that you don't belong in his world.'

Hiroko was silent for a long time.

'I don't belong in your world either.' She tilted her head thoughtfully, and stopped being a girl. 'You just gave me something valuable. The belief that there are worthwhile things still to be found. All I've been doing all this while is thinking of losses. So much lost. I keep thinking of Nagasaki. You said to me once that Delhi must seem so strange and unfamiliar, but nothing in the world could ever be more unfamiliar than my home that day. That unspeakable day. Literally unspeakable. I don't know the words in any language . . . My father, Ilse. I saw him in the last seconds of his life, and I thought he was something unhuman. He was covered in scales. No skin, no hair, no clothes, just scales. No one, no one in the world should ever have to see their father covered in scales.'

Elizabeth gripped Hiroko's hand and brought it to her lips.

'And the thing is, I still don't understand. Why did they have to do it? Why a second bomb? Even the first is beyond anything I can . . . but a second. You do that, and see what you've done, and then you do it again. How is that . . .? Do you know they were going to bomb Kokura that day instead? But it was cloudy so they had to turn around to their second target – Nagasaki. And it was cloudy there, too. I remember the clouds that day so well. They almost gave up. So close to giving up, and then they saw a break in the cloud. And boom.' She said the 'boom' so softly it was little more than an exhalation.

'I always planned on leaving Nagasaki, you know. I was never sentimental about it. But until you see a place you've known your whole life reduced to ash you don't realise how much we crave familiarity. Do you see those flowers on that hillside, Ilse? I want to know their names in Japanese. I want to hear Japanese. I want tea that tastes the way tea should taste in my understanding of tea. I want to look like the people around me. I want people to disapprove when I break the rules and not simply to think that I don't know better. I want doors to slide open instead of swinging open. I want all those things that never meant anything, that still wouldn't mean anything if I hadn't lost them. You see, I know that. I know that but it doesn't stop my wanting them. I want to see Urakami Cathedral. I used to think it ruined the view, never liked it. But now I want to see Urakami Cathedral, I want to hear its bells ringing. I want to smell cherry blossom burning. I want to feel my body move with the motion of being on a street-car. I want to live between hills and sea. I want to eat kasutera.'

Want. Elizabeth heard the repetition of the word and knew what religious conversion must feel like. *Want.* She remembered that, dimly. Somewhere. *Want.* At what point had her life become an accumulation of things she didn't want? She didn't want Henry to be away. She didn't want to be married to a man she no longer knew how to talk to. She didn't want to keep hidden the fact that at times during the war – and especially when Berlin was firebombed – she had felt entirely German. She didn't want to agree that the British had come to the end of a good innings. She didn't want to go back to London and live under the shadow of her meddling mother-in-law. She didn't want to make James unhappy through her inability to be the woman he had thought she would turn into, given time and instruction. She didn't want to be un-desired. She didn't want her future to look anything like her present. She gripped the branch, feeling suddenly dizzy, and tried to concentrate on what Hiroko was saying.

'But should I tell you what I don't want? I don't want to go back to Nagasaki. Or to Japan. I don't want to hide these burns on my back, but I don't want people to judge me by them either. Hibakusha. I hate that word. It reduces you to the bomb. Every atom of you. So now I have to find something different to want, Elizabeth. And I'm sorry – you've been so kind, so incredibly generous – but moving to London with you and James, that's not it. That's not what I want.'

'What do you want?'

'I don't know. Maybe . . . Sajjad.' She said it as though testing the statement.

As gently as her voice would allow, and despite everything she had just been thinking about her own life, Elizabeth said, 'You must find a way to let go of that. His family . . .'

Those last two words sank into Hiroko's stomach with a terrible weight.

'I know. You're right. I know.' She closed her eyes and rested her head on her knees.

9

The morning after they buried Khadija Ashraf her four sons and son-in-law walked single file across the courtyard of the Jama Masjid, following behind an old man who drizzled water on to the ground from a bucket to cool the baking stones. The old man was an ascetic Sufi who for years now had been watering the sandstone for the recently bereaved who walked across the courtyard. Every evening he scraped the dead skin off his soles to ensure his own feet would not become hardened against the pain of the burning ground – he would have to endure, then overcome, suffering through purely spiritual paths. Khadija Ashraf had always disapproved of such thinking. 'It's the Christians who believe we were put on earth to suffer. But Muslims know that Allah – the Beneficent, the Merciful – forgave Adam and Eve their temptation.' And then she pointed an accusing finger at the sky. 'And so you should have – it was you, not the Snake, who tempted them by making a fruit forbidden.'

Who is this God of the Ascetics who wants to be reached through deprivation? Sajjad repeated his mother's words to himself, his lips moving soundlessly.

With her dying breath, Khadija Ashraf had whispered in his ear the ritual salutation from elder to younger – 'Keep on living' – and now the only way in which he could bear her loss was to believe some part of her soul had entered him with that breath and now nestled against his heart. That he didn't really believe such things in no way prevented him from taking comfort in the thought. In some way, he knew, she was within him – airing her opinions, chiding him, making him laugh.

Without a word, he turned away from the water-dappled path and veered towards the pillared corridor that ran along the perimeter of the courtyard. Stepping through an archway into the corridor, he received the coolness of the shaded stone with gratitude. He heard his eldest brother, Altamash, call out to him, but merely responded with a wave of his fingers to indicate they should go on alone, and wrapped his arm around a pillar, his fingers strumming its ridges as he looked towards the Red Fort. Dilli. My Dilli. But today it was absence, not belonging, that the Old City echoed back at him.

'Sajjad, come home with us.' It was his brother-in-law speaking. 'Your sister and I will be leaving this afternoon, and there are things we have to talk about before we go.'

'I'll be there soon,' he replied, not looking back at the men of his family who stood behind his back like a phalanx of guards.

'If there are things to talk about, talk about them now,' his brother Iqbal said. 'I'm going to say goodbye when we leave here. I'm engaged for the rest of the day.'

'I told your sister we'd talk about it when the whole family is gathered. Can't you delay your business, Iqbal?'

'No.'

Altamash made a noise of disgust. For years now it had been common knowledge in the mohalla that Iqbal had taken one of the Old City's courtesans as his mistress.

'You think we don't all know what your business is? You have no shame. The one promise you made to our mother was that you would always come home to your wife before midnight, and the first night she is gone from us you stay out until dawn.'

'She is threatening to go to Pakistan,' Iqbal said. They didn't need to ask who 'she' was. 'I told her last night I will do whatever I must to keep her here.'

Sajjad turned around.

'You threatened this woman you claim to love?'

'I didn't threaten her. I promised to marry her.'

With a curse, Altamash caught his brother by the arm.

'Did you forget you have a wife?'

'I'm allowed a second wife.'

'Yes, if you treat them both as equals and receive your first wife's permission.' Sikandar, the quietest and most devout of the brothers, spoke up. 'We all know neither of these things will happen.'

'Even the Prophet had a favourite wife,' Iqbal said, pulling away from Altamash. 'And if my wife doesn't give me permission to marry again I will happily divorce her.'

Altamash caught hold of Iqbal again.

'You have one wife and she will remain a sister to all your brothers no matter how badly you behave. We will never accept this other woman. We will never accept any children you have by her. You will not be welcome in our home with her. And we will no longer pay any of the debts she has made you accumulate. How long before she returns to the only life she has ever known when she discovers her husband is a pauper with no ability beyond that of extravagance?'

Iqbal turned to his brother-in-law.

'You won't be so unkind to me, will you, brother? You'll let us come and live with you in Lucknow?'

'No, I can't. Don't look at me with those eyes, Iqbal. I don't approve of what you want to do. And besides—' He looked away from the brothers.

'Besides what? You planning to move to Pakistan, too?' Altamash didn't even look at his brother-in-law as he said it, his eyes focused on conveying contempt to Iqbal.

'Yes.'

Sajjad let out a huge sigh and sat down on the low barrier that ran between pillars. Bending forward, he covered his ears with his hands to try and shut out the shouting. Everything was collapsing now.

Less than three months ago he had touched Hiroko's skin – a moment he now recognised as one of pure exaltation. But exaltation was always the bugle cry that awoke lamentation – hadn't he read enough poetry to know that? That his hand touching her back was the greatest moment of physical intimacy that would ever exist between them he would have borne without bitterness; though it stopped far short of his desire, he knew that was both necessary and inevitable. Even now he couldn't imagine a circumstance in which there would have been another outcome. The unexpected pain and resentment didn't come from Hiroko but from the Burtons' dismissal of him. When Lala Buksh came to Sajjad with money and an offer of a reference he understood that Hiroko had told them that he was not an 'animal', a 'rapist'. Even as some part of him wanted to fall to its knees in relief, another part looked at the too generous severance pay and understood it meant he would never receive any form of apology beyond this. That it was Elizabeth not James who owed him the apology was not something he stopped to consider – despite their differences the Burtons still functioned in many ways as a unit, and if one half of the unit could not acknowledge the injustice done to him then it fell to the other half to do so.

'I am done with the English,' he had said, and started to consider what he might want to make of his life now that he had been lifted from the sense of obligation that had kept him tied to James Burton long past the point when he saw there would be no advancement in that position. Altamash asked him to help with the calligraphy business for a few weeks, just until he found someone to replace the Nazir brothers who had worked with the family for years and were now on their way to Karachi with dreams of establishing themselves as the finest artisans of language in that British cantonment town with its own dreams about its future in the still-unconfirmed state of Pakistan. His mother urged him to take on the financial side of the business, so Sajjad agreed 'for a period of six weeks only'. But at the end of the six weeks came the British announcement of 15 August – just over two months away – as the date for the British withdrawal and the creation of the independent states of India and Pakistan. It was hardly a time to consider a future career; everything was turmoil, every day brought news of further atrocities, and relationships that had seemed to be cast in steel disintegrated under the acid question: Are you for India or Pakistan? Even Sajjad couldn't pretend it no longer touched his life as he felt his nails bite into his palms at tales of the atrocities, and heard his heart beat a farewell tattoo for all those Dilliwallas who said they could not stay.

And then his mother fell ill, and everything else in the world became backdrop.

Hands still covering his ears, he looked up at the other men, all yelling and gesticulating now. He loved them all, but – he only just realised this – he did not care too much about disappointing any of them. He looked from one brother to the other in turn, weighing the character of each, and using that assessment to forecast the future: Iqbal would never marry this woman of his if Altamash withheld financial support – but he would drift away from their lives, replacing one mistress with another, and becoming a stranger to his children. Ali Zaman – his brother-in-law, who never committed himself to anything less than wholeheartedly – would move to Pakistan and become a zealous patriot, which would make things tiresome when he'd visit Dilli. Sikandar, whose increased devoutness had taken on an internal, meditative form, would withdraw increasingly into his own world, happiest when the fluidity of his pen shaped Quranic verses into unfurling roses to express the harmony he found in the Holy Book. And Altamash, already equal parts patriarch and poet, would ossify into both these roles, handing out dictums in verse to all those who lived in his household, and accepting everything from his family save disobedience.

He could not see himself in the household. Not without his mother. She had tempered Iqbal's excesses, drawn Sikandar out into the world of life and laughter, served as the primary reason why her adoring daughter came from Lucknow to visit twice a year, and with a single glance could reduce Altamash from potentate to child. And for Sajjad, she had been the certainty that no matter how often he circled Delhi he would always return to the world of Dilli.

But that world itself was departing. Perhaps even his mother wouldn't have been enough to hold its remnants together. How could he stay amidst the shards? Equally, how could he walk away, alone, when solitude for him had never been more than the anticipation of stepping back into the world of companionship?

Sajjad stood up, the abruptness of the movement silencing his brothers.

'I am going to ask a Japanese woman to be my wife. If she says yes, we will live in New Delhi, and all of you will be welcome into our home. But I will never go anywhere she is not accepted.' Extending both arms in front of him, he pushed his brothers aside with a swimmer's action and walked out into the courtyard, one step, two, and then his heart leapt up inside him and he started running so fast a merchant taking his shoe off at the gate thought the courtyard must be hotter than ever before and so wedged his foot back into the shoe and turned away.

The merchant was less than halfway down the steps when he was overtaken by the running man, who had paused only long enough to slip on his own shoes and was now charging past stalls and children and venerable old men, disrupting pigeons everywhere he went so they rose up in the sky as he approached, creating a grey-winged trail anyone could have followed from Jama Masjid right up to the Ashraf house.

And there the man stopped.

It would be a betrayal of his mother to do what he was contemplating, he knew. But she had told him to keep on living and perhaps if death freed her from convention she would understand that was precisely what he was doing. This place, this moholla, was past already. Soon the ghosts would outnumber the corporeal presences among his intimates. And there was something else. There was a girl who had trusted him enough to undress in front of him and show him the marks of the deepest pain he had ever encountered.

His hand was on the door, ready to push it open and repeat to the women what he had already told their husbands. But some movement at the corner of his eye – a ginger cat streaking past, calling to mind the colour of Elizabeth Burton's dress the last time he'd seen her – made him pause.

What if Hiroko said yes, and they moved to a house constructed without brothers and sisters-in-law and nephews and nieces in mind, and then what happened to the Burtons happened to them?

They had not been unhappy together when he first entered their lives. Yes, their arguments were frequent, but there had been a lightness to them. Henry had been a shared joy, not territory to

107

argue over. And from time to time the most casual of gestures – his hand on her wrist, her fingers straightening his tie – would suggest a world of physicality which made Sajjad want to get up and leave the room to escape the complex mix of emotion it engendered. And gradually, so gradually it was a form of torture to watch it, he'd seen everything between them fragment.

There was no one moment at which things went wrong, just a steady accumulation of hurt and misunderstanding. There were arguments about how to raise Henry, about James's professional life, about Elizabeth's manner of inhabiting the social role of 'Mrs Burton', about the food she served at parties, about when to leave for Mussoorie, about whether or not to send Henry to boarding school, about how far from the boundary wall to plant a certain tree – and all these could have been minor arguments, but weren't. Time moved them apart from each other; that was the best explanation Sajjad had.

So what was to prevent time doing the same to him and Hiroko, leaving them in a house without other allies to turn to, other relatives to fill up the silence with laughter?

When his brothers returned home, several minutes later, they found Sajjad standing in front of the doorway, his fingers tracing bird shapes into the wood.

'Of us all you loved our mother most,' Altamash said, putting an arm around his brother's shoulder. 'It's no wonder her death has made you feel so adrift. Come. Cling on to your family.' He rapped sharply on the door and when it opened he led an unprotesting Sajjad inside, assured the crisis had passed and need never be mentioned again.

10

'Ilse! You can't kill that spider. It's beloved by the Muslims. Konrad told me the story one day on Megane-Bashi – Spectacles Bridge. It's called that because when the tide is high the two archways of the bridge are reflected in the water, creating an image of a pair of glasses.'

'That's where the silver fish leapt from his heart into yours.'

'Yes. Oh, I've told you that already. Have I told you about the spider? How it wove its web – quick as lightning – over the mouth of the cave where Mohammed and his friend were hiding when they fled from Mecca, and so convinced their pursuers that no one had entered the cave in a long time.'

'What a charming little story. Where did Konrad pick that up?'

There was a pause, and then Hiroko said, her voice strange, 'From Sajjad.'

James had been about to enter the family room of the cottage – had hesitated outside the doorway only because the two women were talking in German and it sometimes seemed rude to force the conversation back into English just by the fact of his presence – but when he heard the word 'Sajjad' he turned and let himself out of the front door, grabbing his raincoat on the way.

Outside, there was a break in the monsoon rain for the first time in days, but that did nothing to improve the visibility. Mist shrouded Mussoorie, making it impossible to know if the mass at the end of the garden was a tree or just a particularly intense gathering of condensation. Thick enough to chew on, James thought, recalling his Scottish grandmother's description of highland mist around her childhood home. He imagined himself as an old man, living in the Highlands in a futile attempt to recapture the Mussoorie summers.

Now it was only weeks away, their departure from India. He supposed Hiroko would come with them to England. He prodded the wet grass with his shoe. That seemed to be the assumption under which everyone was operating. Well, why not? She could make Elizabeth laugh, which was a talent that he had once possessed without knowing it was a talent.

James walked around the house, shoes leaving imprints in the sodden garden, until he was near the window that looked into the family room. What would Elizabeth see of him if she looked out? The man she had married, or an intense gathering of condensation? No one would ever imagine he could think of himself in these terms, he knew, not even Elizabeth. Well, the truth of it was he rarely did. But since Sajjad had gone – been sent away, brought it on himself, of course, but even so – well, he'd just been feeling wrong about the world.

He would never see Sajjad again. This thought kept coming back to him, its insistence an irritation. He kept telling himself that it was the way things had ended which caused him these feelings of regret. Remorse, even. But in moments of real honesty when he heard his wife and Hiroko laughing together, something more than language acting as a barrier between him and them, he knew simply that he missed Sajjad's company. And that was ridiculous, of course it was.

'James Burton.'

And now I'm hearing voices, James thought.

'James Burton!'

James turned. Walking through the mist towards him was Sajjad, dressed as he had been the first time James saw him, and never since, in white-muslin kurta pyjama. A large umbrella was tucked under his arm, leaving a wet imprint down one side of his body.

'My dear fellow.' James stepped forward, extending his hand. Sajjad looked at it in confusion, and James laughed and clasped the other man's shoulder. 'Didn't bring a chessboard with you, I suppose.'

Sajjad pulled away.

'I'm not here to return to my duties.'

'No, of course not.' James's hand was suspended mid-air in the posture of gripping Sajjad's shoulder, and he looked at it curiously as if not sure what to do with it. Sajjad regarded him in pity, unable to keep up the attacking attitude he had talked himself into, and placed his own hand over the Englishman's to push it back down.

'I just read *A Passage to India*,' James said. 'Ridiculous book. What a disgrace of an ending. The Englishman and the Indian want to embrace, but the earth and the sky and the horses don't want it, so they are kept apart.'

'Yes. I've read the book.'

'It's not about the earth and the sky and the horses, is it, Sajjad?'

'No, Mr Burton.'

'I don't mind "James", you know.' Sajjad rolled his shoulders forward, in one of his ways of indicating he'd heard a comment without actually responding to it. 'I'm sorry for what Elizabeth said to you. And so is she. You must know we both realised she had been wrong even before Hiroko told us what happened.'

'No, sir, I didn't know that. And you have not communicated with me these last months to tell me so.'

'I thought you would have understood that from the message we had Lala Buksh deliver.'

'I understood that the English might acknowledge their mistakes in order to maintain the illusion of their fairness and sense of justice, but they will not actually apologise for those mistakes when they are perpetrated on an Indian.'

James stepped back.

'When did you and I become the Englishman and the Indian rather than James and Sajjad?'

'You're right. It's not a question of nation. It's one of class. You would have apologised if I'd been to Oxford.'

'I was embarrassed, Sajjad, don't you understand that? So was she. And dammit, man, you should have known better than to stand watching a woman while she undresses. You're not without blame in this situation, whatever Hiroko might say. How could I have asked you back into the house with her still living there? And

111

how could I apologise in any meaningful way if I wasn't willing to ask you back? God dammit.' He swiped his hands viciously at a climbing plant, and his fingers made painful contact with the brick wall behind it.

Sajjad flinched as if he'd been wounded, a gesture that escaped neither man.

'Why are you here, if not to play chess?' James said quietly, trying to ignore the throbbing of his fingertips.

'My mother is dead.'

'I'm so sorry. Sajjad, truly.'

'It changes everything.'

'You can't mean Hiroko?'

'Will you prevent me from seeing her?'

'No, of course not.'

'Then I would like to see her.'

'I'm here.' The words were spoken in Urdu. James looked over Sajjad's shoulder to see Elizabeth and Hiroko standing there.

'We've been here since E. M. Forster,' Elizabeth said, walking up to James. 'You're really not very observant. Come on – let's do something about your hand.' She tugged on his sleeve, and led him inside, stopping only to give Sajjad a look of unfettered apology, which he received with a nod that said the matter was closed, though not forgotten, between them.

When the door shut behind the couple, Hiroko walked up to Sajjad, her eyes as intent upon his face as his were upon hers. She took his wrist between her thumb and finger, as he had taken hers the day she arrived in Delhi.

'How did she die?'

'One illness paved the way to another. The final one was pneumonia.' His hand rested on hers, as she continued to hold his wrist. 'The last time we met . . . I never meant to suggest the bomb wasn't a terrible thing.'

'No, of course you didn't.' She let go of his wrist and walked away a few steps before turning to face him again. 'So you're here to see me. Because your mother is dead.'

'I'm here to see you. My mother . . . yes, it's true. I wouldn't have come if she'd been alive.'

She had imagined him coming for her, countless times these last few weeks, even though she believed it impossible. But never like this.

'What's the matter? Did her death disrupt your marriage plans? Have you rushed here in search of the first available woman to make your tea for you in the morning and massage your head with oil at night?'

'I wouldn't have to come all the way from Dilli to Mussoorie to find the first available woman.'

'You're impossibly vain,' she said, turning away from him and walking towards the oak tree at the end of the garden.

'Stay, please. Please. Stay.'

She stopped, her back still towards him, and waited for him to walk up to her.

'I grew up believing in continuity, Hiroko.' His voice was more sombre than she'd ever heard. 'I grew up honouring it.'

'Don't be ridiculous. The calligraphy trade would have been continuity for you. Not a life of playing chess with an Englishman.'

'I have uncles and cousins who work for the English. It's what we do during the day. It's employment. And then we come home, and take off our shirts and trousers, replace them with kurta pyjama and become men of our moholla again. That's our true world.'

'I see. So I've never seen you in your true world?'

'No, you haven't.' He lifted a hand into the space between them. 'And I've never seen you in yours.'

'Mine doesn't exist any more.'

'Neither does mine. I don't only mean because of my mother. This Pakistan, it's taking my friends, my sister, it's taking the familiarity from the streets of Dilli. Thousands are leaving, thousands more will leave. What am I holding on to? Just kite-strings attached to air at either end.'

'And so?'

'I have to learn how to live in a new world. With new rules. As you have had to do. No, as you are doing. Perhaps it would be less lonely for both of us to have a companion. Some constancy is comforting during change.'

113

The wet grass had seeped up through her shoes. She was cold and irritated and there was too much in him she didn't understand.

'I could never live the life your sisters-in-law accept.'

That was her version of goodbye. But Sajjad saw in it an offer. 'Yes,' he said, smiling with a delight she couldn't understand. 'There are other options, of course. There's New Delhi. Both a world apart from the Old City and just a few minutes away by bicycle. A great city must always present you with options, and Dilli-Delhi is the greatest of cities. I've been thinking of moving there, you know.'

'Have you?' She was very confused now.

'Yes, I'm going to buy a house, just a small house. One of those modern ones. And I'm going to work with a law firm. I went there just a few days ago, to speak to a solicitor I know. I can start whenever I want.' The solicitor, an Indian, had formerly worked at James's law firm, and when he left to join another practice he told Sajjad to come and see him if he ever needed employment. Time we stopped letting the English take the credit for all the work we do, he said when Sajjad went to his office earlier in the week. You're not actually qualified, but we'll find a way to take care of that. You know more about the law than any of these fresh-faced boys with their newly inked law degrees. It's a disgrace how James Burton has squandered your talents.

'Congratulations, Sajjad.' She found she was genuinely happy for him. 'I'm pleased for you.'

'There's just one problem.' He looked very grave. 'Perhaps you can help me with this. Who will make my tea in the morning?'

'Oh.' She blinked at him. 'I hate the tea in India.'

'Ah.' He had done what he could. In his heart, he hadn't ever truly believed she would say yes. 'Well. I wish you the very best.' He extended his hand. She took it, and then neither of them let go.

They stood there for what seemed a very long time, fingers immobile in each other's grip. Then she took a deep breath, as if preparing to submerge herself in an underwater world.

'Come with me. I want to tell you something.' Still holding on to his hand she led him to a bench in the middle of a covered pavilion on a slope near the Burton property. On most days the pavilion commanded a clear view of the Himalayas but today it just felt like the last stop before the edge of the world.

And there, for the first time since it happened, Hiroko talked about what had happened to her when the bomb fell.

The mist gave way to rain as she spoke – not a gentle rain that whispered of harvest and bounty but a harsh, hammering rain. It fell like sheets of liquid steel, pounding all the life out of the tiny creatures in its path. Monstrous watery shapes formed and disintegrated before Sajjad's eyes as his tears splintered the rain. If he let go of Hiroko she would slip away in fluid form. Everything about her so precarious.

When she finished speaking, she was lying on the bench, her head in Sajjad's lap while his hands ran lightly through her hair as though afraid it would fall out if he touched it too roughly.

'So you see, I can't in fairness agree to be anyone's wife,' she said, sitting up. 'No one knows the long-term effects of this thing. They don't know if it will affect my ability to have children. They don't know that it won't kill me in another five years.'

He leaned forward, so their foreheads were nearly touching.

'I like being with you. I would like to go on being with you. I almost put that aside myself in fear of a possible tomorrow, but if these days teach us anything it's that all we can do in preparation for tomorrow is nothing. So let's talk about today.'

She smiled. Optimism. That was Sajjad's gift. She opened her mouth and breathed it in.

'Can I ask, have you ever kissed a woman?'

'A gentleman doesn't answer such questions.'

'I just want to make sure you know how to do it. My decision may hinge on the matter.'

'I see I shall have to demonstrate.'

11

'Where do you think they are?' James asked, for the seventeenth time that day (Elizabeth was keeping count, and noting that the spaces between each repetition were getting increasingly narrow). He looked out of the window of the family room to see nothing but the evening approach.

'Really what you want to know is, what are they doing?' Elizabeth replied, curling herself on the sofa and picking up the book which she had been pretending to read ever since she and James had returned to the cottage and left Hiroko and Sajjad outside. 'If what we used to do in all our private moments at a time in our life when we looked at each other in that way is anything to go by . . .'

'For heaven's sake, Elizabeth.'

'It embarrasses you to remember it,' she said flatly.

'No, it doesn't.' He sat down on an armchair next to her. 'I just don't think it's the same situation at all. He can't possibly be thinking of marrying her.'

'Why not? Because it'll make things socially awkward for us to invite him to our farewell party in Delhi with the "smart set"? Or because Hiroko might think that the "our home is your home" offer continues to apply, and what if she should arrive with him in London and expect to be put up in our house? What will your mother say? What will the neighbours say?' At James's look of irritation (once, he would have laughed and thrown a cushion at her for the acuity of her response) she added, 'His mother is dead. That changes everything. He wouldn't have come here if he was going to offer anything less than marriage. That will give her two options – him or us. Which would you choose?'

'You could at least try talking to her.'

'She won't listen,' she said.

'So you disapprove, too?' He leaned forward, but only slightly.

'It makes me nervous to be unable to imagine the life she'll lead as Sajjad's wife. We really know nothing about Delhi beyond our narrow circle.'

'He's a good man.'

'Good men don't necessarily mean good marriages.'

They looked at each other, and James came to sit beside her on the sofa.

'New start when we get back to London?'

Across the room was a sealed envelope containing the letter Elizabeth had finally written to Cousin Wilhelm. In German it said:

Dear Willie,

You make New York sound so appealing. Yes! I will come there. But not with James. I am leaving him. Please, please say nothing of this to anyone. Even he doesn't know yet. I will go back to England with him and settle him into his life there. And then I will come to New York and see if there's anything of your cousin Ilse left to be salvaged from the lonely, bitter (but still well groomed, you'll be glad to know) wreck that is Mrs Burton. Dearest, why didn't I simply listen to you when you said it would kill me to be the Good Wife? I will write to you from London when my plans are more assured.

With love, I.

Elizabeth touched his cheek gently.

'New start, James.'

James patted her hand and stood up quickly so that she wouldn't see the tears coming to his eyes. In doing that, he ended any thoughts she had of tearing up the letter.

'On the matter of London, I think we should leave sooner than we'd planned. I think we should leave as soon as possible.'

'I thought we wanted one last Mussoorie season.'

'I don't know what's going to happen in this country the day British rule ends.' He started to pace. 'They haven't even settled the boundaries yet. Millions of people with no idea which country they'll find themselves in less than a month from now. It's madness waiting to happen. And Delhi . . . so many Muslims, so many Hindus. If the violence reaches there, it'll be carnage.'

'But James. How can we leave Hiroko in that? After all she's already had to suffer?'

'Well, you tell her not to marry him then.'

But it was already too late for that. If Kamran Ali in the cottage next door had gone out to his garage he would have seen that the MG in which he'd been giving Hiroko driving lessons was gone.

'Where are we going?' Sajjad had said, earlier in the day, getting into the passenger seat after he'd pushed the car far enough away from the cottages for Hiroko to turn on the engine without being heard. 'And to repeat my question yet again, if he doesn't mind you using his car why couldn't you start it up in the garage?'

'We're going to get married,' Hiroko replied, which successfully removed the other question from Sajjad's mind. 'What do we need? A mosque?'

'We'll have to have a civil ceremony,' he said, since pulling her into his arms didn't seem a wise option while she was so intent on pushing knobs and levers on the dashboard. 'By Muslim law, I can't marry out of my religion unless you're a Jew or a Christian. You aren't, are you?'

'No.' She finally found the switch she wanted and turned on the headlights. The more brightly coloured flowers were starting to splash colour in the mist, but it was still far from clear on the road ahead. 'How does one become a Muslim?'

'One repeats the Kalma – la ilaha ilallah Muhammadur rasool Allah – three times.'

'Say that slower.' As the car headed down the hill, speeding up, the flowers appeared increasingly blurred in their frenzy to burst out of the surrounding greyness.

'Why?'

'So I can repeat it three times.'

Sajjad was silent for a while. 'Don't you at least want to know what it means?' he said at last.

'No. I'm not saying it because I believe it. I'm saying it because I see no reason to make things more difficult for you with your family than is necessary.'

Again he was silent, and this time she began to worry.

'Have I offended your beliefs?'

'I'm just surprised by your practicality.' He touched her arm. 'And grateful for it.'

By the time they found a mosque she was a Muslim.

And by the time James had asked for the seventh time, 'Where do you think they are?' Hiroko was taking her husband's hand and leading him into a secluded grove with springy turf squelching beneath their bare feet, a blanket over Sajjad's shoulder. (Hiroko's remarkable practicality had made her stop to procure it on the way from the mosque, though her reason for doing so had only just made itself known to Sajjad.)

By the eighth time James asked the question, Sajjad and Hiroko's clothes were hanging from a tree branch, the breeze scattering tiny yellow flowers over them.

By the ninth, Sajjad was trying to recover his voice to explain to Hiroko that certain parts of the male anatomy were best left unsqueezed.

By the tenth, Hiroko's head was tucked under Sajjad's chin, her quick breath ruffling his chest hair as his hands traced the outline of her burns.

By the eleventh, they were lying on the blanket, and Hiroko was about to give up her search for a word in any of four languages to describe the pleasure of sliding rainwater off a leaf into Sajjad's belly button and then curling her tongue into the dip. ('The pleasure is nectarous,' Sajjad said, and though she couldn't feel it she knew he touched one of her birds as he said it, and the words and gesture together made her kiss his mouth.)

By the twelfth, she was beginning to think the pain meant he didn't know what he was doing, and was on the verge of telling him so.

By the thirteenth, a silver fox came to investigate the sounds, and then streaked away, running through a narrow beam of sunlight as it departed, convincing Sajjad that at that moment of climax he had seen a burst of starlight.

By the fourteenth, Hiroko, who had seen the fox for what it really was, rested her head on Sajjad's arm and told him the Japanese word for fox was 'kitsune' – a figure prominent in myth. The oldest and wisest of the kitsune are kyubi – nine-tailed – and the colour of their fur is silver or gold. With a flick of just one of their tails they can start a monsoon shower, she said. So let's presume the break in the rainfall is a sign of our kyubi's favour. Our kyubi, he asked? Yes, I think we've found ourselves a guide and guardian.

By the fifteenth, she demanded to know why he had shifted down to rest his head on her thigh, thereby depriving her of his arm as pillow. So he showed her, and she stopped complaining.

By the sixteenth, they discovered the branch on which they'd hung their clothes was wet, and it only made them laugh.

By the seventeenth, they were on their way to the Burton cottage, where they had decided Hiroko would stay while Sajjad returned to Delhi and found a place for them to live. The mist had lifted entirely and Sajjad, who had never seen mountains before, believed the Himalayan peaks were surrounded by quick-flowing rivers of snow until Hiroko said, 'Don't be silly, husband, they're clouds.'

Lamentation will not follow, Sajjad thought, putting his arm around Hiroko's shoulders. The exaltation is too great. No sorrow could ever match this joy.

12

Sajjad stood on the banks of the Bosporus, and wondered how he could have ever thought the mosques of Istanbul beautiful. Now it was clear: the buildings were too squat, their minarets too narrow. The Bosporus itself was a strait, not a river; it should have been a river. And the written language – in Roman script! How could a nation choose to discard the grace of Arabic lettering (generations of Ashraf calligraphers wept in their graves at the thought). No, nothing here conformed to his aesthetic; even the crumbling decay of this once grand city did not have the right tempo, the right texture, the right quality of sighing.

James Burton. It was all his fault they were here.

He had been so convincing that evening when Sajjad and Hiroko walked into the Burton cottage, Sajjad desperately self-conscious because of the wet patches on his clothes, and said they were married. It was obvious the Burtons had expected the news, if not the timing of it. Elizabeth had at least pretended some happiness, but James had taken Sajjad by the arm and walked him outside.

'You can't take her to Delhi,' he'd said. And then he'd begun to speak in his lawyer's tones, as Sajjad hadn't heard him do for a very long time. Here were the reasons, he said. He talked about the likely increase of violence leading up to, and leading on from, Partition. The communal make-up of Delhi he laid out in great detail. His own thoughts on the nature of violence and its effects on the most seemingly rational of human beings. The actions that desperation or rage or self-defence could provoke. He asked Sajjad questions starting with 'What would you do if . . .', asking the younger man to consider his possible responses to a range of violations – personal, religious, communal, familial. And when Sajjad was crouching on the ground, head in his hands, he had bent down, hand on Sajjad's shoulder, and delivered his coup de grâce: 'And after all Hiroko has had to endure, do you want to add to her suffering?'

Sajjad looked up, a supplicant before a man of wisdom.

'But what other option do I have?'

James held out his hand and pulled Sajjad to his feet. This last act he would perform before leaving this place, these people. This final act of benevolent rule, against the tide of the Empire's blood-soaked departure from India.

'There's an old general in Mussoorie who wants to give you a wedding present.'

It had been Elizabeth's idea. There was no point telling Hiroko not to marry Sajjad, she'd told James; instead a way must be found to keep them away from Delhi 'until all the Partition nonsense clears up'. She'd joined him in pacing for a while, and then cried out 'Istanbul!' and reached for the telephone. She placed a call to the General who had stopped Hiroko on the Mall to talk about flowers. His first wife, who had died many years earlier, had been Japanese and Elizabeth saw no reason to do anything other than take advantage of the old man's sentimentality in regard to the figure of his lost love.

'He has a home in Istanbul. His second wife was Turkish. But he hasn't been there since her death in '43. There's a caretaker, though, and the General's forever making drunken offers to any-one who'll listen to go and stay in his yali by the Bosporus. And now he's made an entirely sober offer for you and Hiroko to spend an extended honeymoon there.'

Honeymoons were for the English. Even if Sajjad had considered one, he couldn't afford it. Hiroko would understand that. All his savings would have to go towards their new home in New Delhi. But he had heard the talk in the Old City about defence and revenge and infidels and justice, and he knew that James Burton was right when he said that Hiroko could not be allowed to witness further brutality. He would find a way to borrow money for the house when they returned to Delhi.

It had all seemed so inevitable, so sensible.

Sajjad turned his back on the indisputable beauty of the Blue Mosque, and trudged towards the ferry which would take him to the General's yali and Hiroko. She would be sitting by the window looking at the light sparkling off the Bosporus, he imagined, finding a glimpse of calm in the image.

In fact, right then she was standing on a table, her palm pressing against the damp, sagging ceiling, trying to determine whether there was any immediate danger of the roof caving in. The yali, which had clearly once been glorious, was entirely in a state of disrepair. Its wood was rotting, the deep-red paint of its exterior peeling, and most of the windows had broken panes, or no panes at all. Even so, she had come to love the place in the months she and Sajjad had been here. They only used one room – the recessed one that overhung the Bosporus, and which Sajjad insisted had tipped forward several degrees since they started living there – but that was quite enough for both of them.

Hiroko stepped from the table to a chair and from there to the floor, and returned to the recessed room in which she thought she could detect the faint scent of this morning's lovemaking. As she walked past the rosewood cabinet she touched the top drawer as though it were a talisman. Inside was Elizabeth's wedding present to her.

'This belonged to Konrad,' Elizabeth had said minutes after James took Sajjad by the arm and marched him outside the cottage. She unlocked a cupboard and took out a velvet box. 'It was given to him by our grandmother, for his bride. He would want you to have it.'

Hiroko opened the box and, seeing the diamond set inside, she thrust it back at Elizabeth.

'Let's leave the grand gestures to the men,' Elizabeth said. 'You are the only person in the world with any claim to this. I'm not saying it in reproach to you for marrying someone else. I might hardly have known him, but I still know enough to be certain Konrad would only want your happiness. Take it.'

'Save it for your son's bride,' Hiroko said. She felt no guilt about Konrad – could almost see a beautiful shape to the way he had

123

brought both her and Sajjad to Bungle Oh! and to each other – but she wouldn't claim things to which she knew she had no right. 'What occasion will I have to wear it anyway?'

'Sometimes you can be quite obtuse. I'm giving it to you. It's yours. What you choose to do with it is your business. If you're not going to wear it, well then . . .' She shrugged, and as clearly as though the words had been spoken aloud Hiroko heard, Sell it!

Hiroko held out a hand to take the box. For an instant Elizabeth felt herself start to draw back – James had given her this diamond set on their wedding night, placing the necklace at her throat, the bracelet on her wrist, the earrings on her lobes while she lay naked on their bed – but then she released it into Hiroko's hand.

Hiroko moved away from the cabinet and made herself comfortable amidst the many cushions on the window seat. Soon they would be back in Delhi and Sajjad would sell Elizabeth's gift to a jeweller he could trust and use the money to buy their house. He had, at first, strongly resisted the idea of being so indebted to Elizabeth Burton – much of August had been spent in fighting about the matter – but as his own savings dwindled and each day brought further evidence that Hiroko was entirely unsuited to life within the joint family system his resistance had worn away. The relief of coming to a resolution about the matter so overwhelmed them both that they had spent the last few weeks in a state of total harmony, both careful to be generous with the other, willing – almost grateful – to give ground on minor disagreements. That was what was meant by the honeymoon period, Hiroko had thought the night before when Sajjad brushed her hair for her and said no, of course he didn't wish it were longer, never mind that no woman in his moholla had hair as short as a boy's. She wondered what would follow when the honeymoon ended.

She leaned out of the window, taking in the cool air that came off the Bosporus. Delhi in October! Sajjad had said they could wait a little longer before going back so that they'd arrive closer to winter, but she knew he said it hoping she'd refuse, and so she did. She had seen how it had agonised him to be away from his home in September when the Partition riots had overtaken Delhi, and the Old City had become a virtual siege town.

'It's not that I want to be there,' he had said one night, lying on his stomach with the comforting weight of her resting on top of him, their fingers loosely linked. 'What would I do? Join the men with machine guns guarding every entrance to my old neighbourhood? Refuse to join them, and cower inside my family home instead? That's where we'd be, you know – Muslim homes in New Delhi are being destroyed. Women pulled out of their beds at night . . .' He turned his face, and the moonlight showed Hiroko the unusual introspection of his expression. 'Everything James Burton said about violence is true. It is the most contagious of all the madnesses. I don't want to know which of my childhood friends have become murderers in the time we've been away. I don't want to know what Iqbal might have done in all his frustrated passion. No, I don't want to be there. But it feels like a betrayal, all the same.' He had not then, or at any time, told her he'd left for her sake.

But that was September. Now the violence had ended, and though Sajjad said he knew it would be a different Delhi he'd be returning to, nothing could change the essential Dilliness of the place. He said it emphasising the 'dil' (it was in their first lesson that he'd told her 'dil' meant heart. She'd seen him blush as he said it, and she'd blushed in response. Remembering all the blushing of that initial lesson made her want to laugh. What strangers they'd been to each other and to themselves.)

She heard the door open. At last he was home. How ridiculous that he'd had to go to the Indian Consulate to get paperwork processed before they could return to Delhi.

He entered the room and the look of him made her breath stop. Without saying a word, he walked across to her – his steps so slow, so dragging, everything about him defeated.

'What's wrong? What happened?' she said as he sat down beside her, carefully, as though his bones were brittle.

'They said I chose to leave.' He said the words slowly, carefully, as though they were a foreign language whose meaning he was trying to grasp. 'They said I'm one of the Muslims who chose to leave India. It can't be unchosen. They said, Hiroko, they said I can't go back to Dilli. I can't go back home.'

Hiroko could only watch as her husband drew up his legs and curled over on the mattress. She said his name, repeated endearments in English, Urdu, Japanese – but he couldn't hear her above the fluttering of pigeons and the call of the muezzin of Jama Masjid and the cacophony of his brothers' arguments and the hubbub of merchants and buyers in Chandni Chowk and the rustling of palm leaves in the monsoons and the laughter of his nephews and nieces and the shouts of kite-fliers and the burble of fountains in courtyards and the husky voice of the never-seen neighbour singing ghazals before sunrise and his heartbeat, his frantic heartbeat . . .

Part-Angel Warriors

Pakistan, 1982–3

13

Hiroko Ashraf watched the patch of brightness slide across the dining table towards her son, Raza, whose attention was firmly fixed on the crossword his mother had set for him. The sunlight bumped up against Raza's arm, which was curled around the crossword in the defensive posture of the smartest boy in class who is accustomed to everyone around trying to copy answers from his exam papers. Its gentle nudging failing to convince Raza to move his arm, the sunlight crept up on to his shoulders from where it could peep down at the grid with its Japanese and Urdu clues and German and English solutions.

Hiroko blinked once, twice, and the image was gone. In place of the young boy whose two chief delights were multilingual crosswords and stories told by his mother in which everything familiar – birds, furniture, sunlight, crumbs, everything – acquired character and role there was a sixteen-year-old tracing his finger over pictures from glossy magazines advertising the various electronic gadgets his cousin in the Gulf claimed to own. ('Doesn't he own a camera?' Sajjad had said. 'Why can't he send you photographs of his fancy VCR and his fancy answering machine and his fancy car instead of clippings from magazines you can buy in Urdu Bazaar? God knows if he's even left the country – he's Iqbal's son, after all.')

Strange, Hiroko thought, that through more than five decades she had never allowed nostalgia to take up more than the most fleeting of residencies in her life, despite all that glittered in her memory – the walks through Nagasaki with Konrad, the ease of life in the Burton household, the Istanbul days of discovering love with

Sajjad – but since adolescence had suctioned Raza away from his younger self she'd learnt the desire to walk behind time. A demure Japanese woman at the end of the day, she thought to herself, and then smiled, with a touch of self-satisfaction, at the ridiculousness of the idea.

Raza looked up, found his mother watching him and realised that the glossy pictures he'd pasted inside his textbook when his father first insisted he had to spend at least six hours a day studying for his exams were clearly visible to her. He hid his embarrassment in a noise of discontentment before walking out into the court-yard.

These days it was impossible to know from moment to moment who would emerge from the form of her son: a sweet, loving boy or a glowering creature of silences and outbursts. She could recall it quite clearly, the moment when the latter had announced his presence – three years ago, when she'd asked her thirteen-year-old son why none of his friends had come to visit in the last few weeks. 'I can't ask any of my friends home,' he had yelled, the sound so unexpected Sajjad had run into the room. 'With you walking around, showing your legs. Why can't you be more Pakistani?' Afterwards, she and Sajjad hadn't known whether to howl with laughter or with tears to think that their son's teenage rebellion was asserting itself through nationalism. For a while, though, she had packed away her dresses and taken to wearing shalwar ka-meezes at home, though previously they were garments she reserved for funerals and other ceremonies with a religious com-ponent; Sajjad said nothing, only gave her the slightly wounded look of a man who realises his wife is willing to make concessions for her son which she would never have made for him. But a few months later, when Raza said her kameezes were too tight, she returned to the dresses.

Hiroko put down her newspaper, and was about to call out a reminder to Raza that it was Chota's day off and he needed to clear up after himself when she was distracted by the sudden chittering of the sparrows which had been feeding from the earthenware seed-filled plate that hung from the neem tree in the courtyard. She looked out of the window and saw Raza standing beneath the tree, looking up at the sky while lazily brushing his teeth with the twig he'd just snapped off. Hiroko smiled. There was a freshness to April's early-morning breeze, her son was almost done with his exams and could soon return to the world of cricket and dreaming which gave him such pleasure, and tomorrow she would have lunch with a friend from the Japan Cultural Centre and perhaps hear of some translation work, which would allow her to buy that painting of Old Delhi for Sajjad's sixtieth birthday.

She turned her eyes from the courtyard to the wall across the room from her, just above the dining table. Most houses in the neighbourhood had living-room walls covered in framed photographs, paintings, vast reproductions of beautiful landscapes or (among the more devout) scenes of worshippers at the Ka'aba. But Hiroko had always insisted that a room could only have one work of art as its focal point. For twenty-five years that focal point in this room had been a sumi-e painting of two foxes nestling together which Sajjad had commissioned for the price of an ice-cream soda and a brightly coloured hairbrush, from the fifteen-year-old daughter of one of Hiroko's friends at the Cultural Centre; it had been his tenth-anniversary gift to her. She wrinkled her nose affectionately at the foxes – she would move them into the bedroom if the Delhi painting arrived.

Thirty-five years of married life! And her husband about to turn sixty. She wasn't so far behind herself. She tried out the word 'old' in her various languages, but they only made her giggle. No, she didn't feel old at all – and certainly didn't think of Sajjad that way. And yet, something separated both of them by an incalculable distance from the young couple who had arrived in Karachi at the end of '47 so uncertain of tomorrow. Time hasn't aged us, it has contented us, she thought, nodding to herself. Contentment – at twenty, she would have scorned the word. What was it she dreamed of then? A world full of silk clothes, and no duties. She considered the gap between the words 'duties' and 'dutiful' – nearly four decades after Nagasaki she still had no time for the latter, but the former had become entwined with the word 'family', the word 'love'.

The door to the adjoining room rattled open. Sajjad came yawning into the living room, and bent down to pick up the newspaper his wife had discarded, brushing his thumb across the mole on her cheek as he did so. The action was ritual, one that had started the first morning they had woken up together – in a ship on its way from Bombay to Istanbul. 'Just checking that the beetle hasn't flown away,' he'd said when she asked him what he was doing.

'Isn't Raza awake yet?' he said, walking over to the dining table, where he poured milky tea into his cup from a thermos and used the sleeve of his kurta to soak up the drops that spilled on to the plastic table-covering, drawing a half-hearted sound of exasperation from Hiroko. That sound – like Sajjad's shake of the head as he unscrewed the thermos cap – was a remnant of once passionate fights. For Hiroko, fastidiousness was synonymous with good manners. For Sajjad, a steaming-hot cup of tea brought to a man first thing in the morning by a woman of the family was a basic component of the intricate system of courtesies that made up the life of a household.

Sometimes when Hiroko looked back on the first years of marriage what she saw most clearly was a series of negotiations – between his notion of a home as a social space and her idea of it as a private retreat; between his belief that she would be welcomed by the people they lived among if she wore their clothes, celebrated their religious holidays, and her insistence that they would see it as false and had to learn to accept her on her own terms; between his determination that a man should provide for his wife and her determination to teach; between his desire for ease and her instinct towards rebellion. It was clear to her that the success of their marriage was based on their mutual ability to abide by the results of those negotiations with no bitterness over who had lost more ground in individual encounters. And also, Sajjad added, taking her hand, when she once told him this, it helped that they found each other better company than anyone else in the world. Other things helped, too, Hiroko whispered back, late at night.

'Yes, he's awake.' She sat down beside Sajjad, and touched his arm. 'Now, don't give him a lecture about taking his foot off the pedal before the finishing line. You know it'll just upset him.'

132

'I promised you already, didn't I? When do I break my promises to you?' He dipped a tissue in water and ran it along her hairline. Since Hiroko's hair had started to turn white it was always possible to know if she'd read the morning papers or not by glancing at her roots. Smudges of newsprint attested to her habit of running her fingers along her hairline while reading.

'You shouldn't do it for me. You should do it for him,' she said quietly.

Sajjad sat back and sipped his tea. He sometimes wondered how different his relationship with his son might have been if the boy had been born earlier. He would have been well into adulthood by now, settled and earning a good income, and Sajjad would be spared his attacks of panic about both Raza and Hiroko's financial future each time he felt the slightest twinge in his chest or woke up with a pain that hadn't been there the night before. But after her miscarriage in 1948 Hiroko learnt fear in imagining what her radiation-exposed body would do to any children she tried to bear, and nothing Sajjad could say would change her mind about it. But at the age of forty-one she found herself pregnant. And Sajjad suddenly found himself counting the years towards his retirement with mounting panic, though until then he had viewed his finances with the careless air of a man of property (the house they lived in was paid for with Elizabeth Burton's diamonds), with no children, a reasonable pension plan and a wife who earned a useful supplementary income from teaching.

Strange and unpredictable, the alleyways that open up into alleyways as a man makes his way through the world, Sajjad thought, dipping a piece of bread into his tea and chewing thoughtfully on the sodden mass. At the start of 1947, he had believed that by the year's end he'd be married to a woman who he would learn to appreciate after signing a marriage contract that bound his life to hers; this woman, he knew, would be chosen for him in large part for her ability to meld into the world in which he had grown up. And that world, the world of his moholla, would be the world of the rest of his life, and his children's lives and their children's lives afterwards.

If he had known then that he and Dilli would be lost to each other by the autumn – because of a woman he had chosen against his family's wishes – he would have wept, recited Ghalib's verses lamenting the great poet's departure from Delhi, cursed the injustice and foolishness of passion, and made lists of all the sights and sounds and daily texture of Dilli life that he was certain would haunt him for ever, making every other place in the world a wilderness of loss. He would not ever have believed that he would come to think of Karachi as home, and that his bitterest regret about his separation from Dilli would be the absence of safety nets that the joint-family system had once provided.

But now even that regret was easing. Raza was sixteen and already sitting for his Inter exams, a year younger than all the other neighbourhood boys – Sajjad glanced appreciatively at his wife, who he had always credited as being directly responsible for Raza's quick mind – and soon now he would enter law college, just a few steps away from an assured income, a bright future, of which any father would be proud. And then, Sajjad promised himself, he would stop being so demanding of his son – insistent on results and achievements, impatient with his more frivolous side – and allow himself the luxury of simply relaxing into Raza's company.

'There he is,' Sajjad said, standing up, as Raza re-entered the living area, his grey trousers and white shirt perfectly ironed and his hair slicked back in recognition that this was the final day on which he'd wear his school uniform. Usually the hair fell over his eyes, and kept his face hidden from the world. Now the surprise of his mother's eyes and cheekbones ceding ground to his father's nose and mouth was plainly evident, beautifully so. 'I had forgotten how nice you look when you clean yourself up.' At Hiroko's sound of exasperation he said, 'What? That's a compliment.'

'I should go,' Raza said. 'I don't want to be late for the exam.'

'Wait, wait. Are you going out celebrating with your friends tonight?'

Raza shook his head.

'Most of them still have one or two papers left. We'll go out on Friday.'

'Then tonight I'm taking us out for Chinese,' Sajjad said expansively, looking at Hiroko to catch her smile of pleasure. 'And you can wear this – here, I don't want to wait until tonight to give it to you.' He gestured his son over to the steel trunk which doubled as a table, carefully removed the flower-patterned cloth that covered it, and opened it to release a smell of mothballs into the room. 'Should have aired it,' Sajjad muttered as he took out something wrapped in thin tissue, and gestured for his son to come closer. 'Here.' He stood up, holding out a beige cashmere jacket to Raza. 'It's from Savile Row.'

'Is that in Delhi?' Raza asked, touching the sleeve of the jacket. 'London.'

Hiroko saw Raza's hands lift away from the jacket. He checked his palms for dirt, holding them up against the sunlight before allowing his fingers to drift back down on to the cashmere in slow, gentle caresses.

Hiroko smiled to see Sajjad help their son into the jacket he'd been wearing the first time she had seen him.

'My lords,' she said, with a trace of amusement, 'I hate to be the one to say this, but winter is over.'

'Oh, practical Ashraf! The restaurant will be air-conditioned. Raza can put it on when he gets inside.' Sajjad brushed nothing off Raza's lapel, feeling the need for an excuse to touch his son. It was in Hiroko's company that he felt his love for Raza most powerfully – it was indivisible from his love for his wife. Those first years of married life which Hiroko recalled as 'negotiations' – he was still startled sometimes by the language of practicality which she could bring to situations of intimacy – he remembered quite differently. Always, in the beginning, the fear of losing her. She was a woman who had learnt that she could leave everything behind, and survive. And some nights he'd wake to find her looking steadily at him, and believe that she was imagining – practising – life without him. For him, the loss of home had a quite different effect – it made him believe he only survived it because he had her. Would survive anything if he had her; would lose everything if he lost her. All those 'negotiations' – he would have given in to her on each one if he didn't know she would disdain him for it. So behind every negotiation was his own calculation of where to give in, where to hold his ground in order to keep her love and respect.

His fear of her leaving subsided over the years, but didn't disappear entirely until the day Raza was born and he entered the hospital room to see his wife holding their child in her arms with a look of terror which said she had been handed something she could never leave behind, never survive the loss of. And then she looked at Sajjad, differently from ever before, and he knew she was tethered to their marriage by the tiny, wailing creature.

When, years later, he'd confessed all this, she'd teased him. 'So if we'd had a child right away, you'd have been a tyrannical husband instead of the generous, accommodating man I've lived with all these years?' But she never denied she used to imagine a life without him or – when he elaborated on his fears – that the new life would have been in the company of Elizabeth Burton, now Ilse Weiss, whose every letter in the first years implored Hiroko to come and stay with her in New York, while never mentioning Sajjad.

'You'll let me wear this tonight? Raza said, his hands gently stroking the arms of the jacket, wondering if his cousin in Dubai had anything this fine.

Sajjad kissed his son's forehead.

'It's yours. A present for my young lawyer. You make me proud.'

Raza took off the jacket, and carefully folded it.

'I'm not a lawyer yet,' he said.

'Only time stands between you and that.' Sajjad looked unchar-acteristically thoughtful. 'This is the right way. You go to school, you go to college, you pass every exam, you prove what you are capable of and what you know. Then no one can take it away from you.'

'Yes, Aba,' Raza said automatically. Every father in this neigh-bourhood of migrants, each with stories of all they had lost and all they had started to rebuild after Partition, made a similar speech to his son. Perhaps he should be grateful that it was law, not medicine or engineering, that he was expected to spend his life pursuing, but that seemed a difficult thing to be grateful for when there existed a world beyond among the sand dunes where boys like his cousin

Altamash who had never even passed his Matric exam could work in hotels with escalators and lifts and marble floors in the employee quarters, and earn a salary sufficient to buy everything new and gleaming while still having enough left over to send home for their families.

All those years in which he insisted he was perfectly happy working as general manager in a soap factory, Hiroko thought, looking at her husband, and from the day Raza was born suddenly he couldn't stop using the word 'lawyer'. He'd made only one attempt, when they first came to Karachi, to re-enter the legal profession in which he'd always imagined he would one day distinguish himself. The lawyer on whose office door he knocked said he could start the next day – on a clerk's salary, a pittance of an amount. When Sajjad listed all he could do, all he knew about the law, the man said, 'You have no qualifications whatsoever.' Sajjad sat up straight, took the name of the solicitor in Delhi who had offered him a job, and was told that man was dead – no, not Partition riots, a hunting accident. Sajjad spent a single evening holding his head in despair and the following day went to find the newly migrated and well-connected Kamran Ali, in whose car he and Hiroko had driven into their wedding mist in Mussoorie, and came home, proudly beaming, saying, 'General manager! With a factory of over a hundred workers to oversee!' as though that was all he had ever wanted from the world.

And it was true, Hiroko knew, that he was content to be in a position of authority, respected and well liked, able to provide for his wife and son, and also in large part for the family of his dissolute brother Iqbal in Lahore. But all those other dreams – for a career that would bring more than mere contentment – had come to rest on Raza's shoulders now. And if only Raza had admitted he wanted something else, she would have found a way to show Sajjad the damage he was doing. But Raza only ever laughed when she directly confronted him and said, 'Habeus corpus! A priori! We'll add Latin to the list of my languages, Ami.'

'Why must you be so adored,' Hiroko grumbled to her husband as she picked up the jacket with its overwhelming mothball smell and took it into the courtyard to air out.

'More adoring than adored,' he called after her. He rested his hand on Raza's back and gave him a gentle push. 'Go, my prince. Go, conquer.'

Raza slung his satchel over his shoulder – inside was the textbook from which he planned to study during the lunch hour between his history and Islamic-studies exam – and kissed his mother on the cheek before heading out on the short walk from his quiet residential street to the commercial road where three other boys from the neighbourhood were already waiting for the bus. It was still early enough for most of the shops to be closed, though the advertisements painted on to steel shutters ensured there was always some kind of commercial life in process. Across the street men were unloading crates of squawking chickens from a van and carrying them into the butcher's shop, which was located right next to a flower-seller, who carried on a roaring trade despite the stench of blood from next door. If your business is weddings and funerals, the flower-seller liked to say, nothing can stand between you and success – except another flower-seller.

'Junior!' one of the boys, Bilal, greeted Raza, his arm looping over his shoulder to bowl an apple core at high velocity between Raza's legs.

Raza, ready for him, had already taken his textbook out of his satchel, and used it gracefully to flick the apple core on to the dusty pavement, where a crow swooped down and pecked at it.

'Such a hero our Junior has become,' Bilal said, affectionately grabbing Raza in a headlock. 'Look, at him, all slicked-back and ironed.' The nickname 'Junior' had followed Raza around since he was ten and his teachers had decided he should skip a class year and take his place among the eleven-year-olds.

'Bilal, I ironed that shirt. If you crease it, I'm going to get very angry.'

At the sound of Hiroko's voice, the boys turned, smiling, standing up straight, all the childhood that was still in their seventeen-year-old faces suddenly apparent. While every other mother in the neighbourhood was 'aunty', Hiroko was Mrs Ashraf – their former, and beloved, schoolteacher who only had to threaten disapproval to give rise to both consternation and obedience. When she and Sajjad had moved to this newly constructed neighbourhood in the early fifties and she had taken up a teaching position at the school near their house it was her students who were her first allies – recognising in her a woman who could never be fooled or flattered, but whose smiles of approval or encouragement could transform a day into glory. Through the children she won over the mothers, whose initial reaction towards the Japanese woman with the dresses cinched at the waist was suspicion. And once the mothers had made up their minds, the neighbourhood had made up its mind.

'You didn't take money to buy lunch,' she said to Raza, handing him a five-rupee note. 'And share with your friends. Now quick, quick, the bus.'

The brightly coloured bus was hurtling down the quiet early-morning street towards them, slowing rather than stopping as it came alongside the boys, who jumped on with cries of accomplishment.

'Sayonara,' they all called out to Hiroko as the bus picked up speed again. Or at least, all of them except Raza called it out. He only spoke Japanese within the privacy of his home, not even breaking that rule when his friends delighted in showing off to his mother the one or two Japanese words they'd found in some book, some movie. Why allow the world to know his mind contained words from a country he'd never visited? Weren't his eyes and his bone structure and his bare-legged mother distancing factors enough? All those years ago when he'd entered a class of older boys, at an age when a year was a significant age gap, his teacher had remarked on how easily he fitted in. He saw no reason to tell her it wasn't ease that made it possible but a studied awareness – one he'd had from a very young age – of how to downplay his manifest difference.

14

Hiroko exited the sanctuary of the bookshop with its thick walls and slowly whirring fans into the chaos and furnace-like heat of Saddar. This used to be her favourite part of Karachi in the early days, when almost every one of the yellow-brick colonial buildings housed a café or bookstore, before it became a thoroughfare for buses with their noxious exhaust fumes and the impassioned university students disappeared into a new campus built far away, while the migrants who had crowded in refugee camps within walking distance of here went wheeling into distant satellite towns. Now every time she came here another several bookstores or cafés had disappeared, often replaced by the electronic shops through which her son loved to wander.

The one she most missed was Jimmy's Coffee Shop with the art deco stairs leading up to the 'family section' with lurid green walls where, for years, she used to meet a group of Japanese women on the first Saturday of each month at 5 p.m. Those monthly meetings had started in early '48 when she and Sajjad were still living in the refugee camps, not so far from here, and he had come running to find her one evening and said he'd met a Japanese woman, her husband worked at the Embassy, she was sitting in one of the cafés waiting for Sajjad to bring Hiroko to meet her. Through her, Hiroko met the other Japanese wives in Karachi, and entered their weekly gatherings at Jimmy's – it had meant a lot, more than she would have guessed, to have the promise of an evening every week to sit and laugh in Japanese. She never told any of them about the birds on her back, though. Considering it now, she decided the day she knew her life had tilted into feeling 'at home' in Karachi was when she found she was able to tell her neighbourhood friends that she had lived through the bombing of Nagasaki, while still insisting to the Japanese women that, although she grew up there, she was in Tokyo when the bomb fell.

The ripple ice cream at that café – she closed her eyes to remember it – was particularly wonderful. But really, the heart went out of those meetings when the capital shifted to Islamabad in 1960, taking the Japanese Embassy with it. The café stopped reserving the entire family section for them, though the meetings continued – Hiroko's participation becoming more sporadic after Raza was born – until the demolition of the café a few years ago brought an end to the weekly gatherings altogether. She found herself mourning the loss, even though in the last years prior to Jimmy's closing she had attended the meetings mainly from a sense of obligation – she had become the fount of wisdom about all things Karachi-related for the group.

She wondered sometimes near the end if she seemed as foreign to the newer members of the group as they did to her – so Japanese! she sometimes caught herself thinking. The only person she could really talk to about this was the one Pakistani member of the group – Rehana, who had spent twenty years in Tokyo before her Japanese husband had come to Karachi to set up an automobile plant. Rehana had grown up in the hills of Abbottabad, and said Karachi might be part of the same country as her childhood home but it was still as foreign to her as Tokyo, 'but I'm at home in the idea of foreignness.' When Hiroko heard her say that she knew she'd found a friend. But now Rehana was back in Abbottabad – she had moved there two years ago when her husband died – and months could go by without Hiroko going to the Japan Cultural Centre and meeting other past members of the group, though there were several for whom she retained an affection.

As she retained an affection for Saddar, despite the electronics shops and the loss of Jimmy's, she thought, looking around. There was one world at street-level – frenzied, jostling, entirely in the now: pavement vendors, large glass display windows, neon signs, gaping manholes, rapid-fire bargaining, brakes and horns and throaty engine sounds, the rush, the thrum of urban life – and then, overhead, if you stood still, shoulders squared against the passers-by, and looked at the arched windows, the cupolas, the intricate carvings, there was another world of buildings constructed in the belief that life moved at a different pace, more elegant, more pompous.

She was entirely happy for the pomposity to be displaced, but there was something else seeping into the atmosphere, worse than electronic shops, which made her uneasy. A few minutes earlier she'd picked up a copy of *War and Peace* to replace her battered copy, shaking her head in fond exasperation at the memory of her son telling her time and again that eventually he'd learn Russian and then he'd read it, when a man standing beside her – the air of ordinariness about him – said, 'You mustn't read their books. They are the enemies of Islam.'

After the man left, the bookseller apologised.

'Strange times we're in,' he said. 'The other day a group of young men with fresh beards came in and started to pull all the books off their shelves, looking at the covers for which were unIslamic.'

'What makes a cover unIslamic?' Hiroko asked.

'Portraiture,' the man replied. 'Particularly of women. Fortu-nately, there was a policeman walking past who saw what they were doing and came and stopped them. But I don't know what's happening in this country.'

'It won't last,' Hiroko assured him. When any of her friends in the staff room complained of this new wave of aggressive religion which was beginning to surface in some of their students she always told them that compared to the boys she'd first taught who dreamt of kamikaze flights these Karachi boys with their strange fervour for a world of rigidity were just posturing youths. And in any case, nothing could supplant cricket as their true system of worship.

Ignoring the crippled beggar who had dashed crazily across the street in his wheeled crate to get to the foreigner in whom he saw the possibility of compassion long since erased from locals, she looked around for her son. He was late, which was unlike him, but everything in Raza had been a little bit strange these last weeks

142

since he finished his exams. She couldn't explain to Sajjad exactly what disturbed her, beyond saying there was a falseness about their boy as he threw himself into enjoying the time before college, talking loudly and excitedly about the law, boasting that when the exam results came out his name would be at the top of the list – he who'd always been so circumspect about his successes. She found herself thinking that she shouldn't have agreed when the teachers suggested he skip a class – intellectually he was ready for it, but there was so much growing up to be done in the year between sixteen and seventeen and she wondered if he was yet ready for the next stage of life.

'Ma!' Raza pulled up in Sajjad's car, extending his torso through the window to take the heavy bag of books out of her hands, impervious to the car horns behind him.

'Wait,' she said. 'I forgot my other shopping inside. Go round the block and come back.' Without waiting for a response she darted back into the shop.

Raza continued sitting where he was, taking a strangely masochistic pleasure in the humid stillness which made sweat stains bloom on his shirt. As the beeping of horns grew more insistent he gestured to the cars behind to go round, even though there was no room for them to manoeuvre. The crippled beggar raised a hand in supplication towards the open car window but Raza's indifferent 'Forgive me' – the words a matter of custom, rather than meaning – convinced him that nothing would be gained by staying here. As the man wheeled away, Raza's hand rested briefly on the afternoon newspaper on the dashboard, its reflection in the windscreen revealing columns of names – the exam results. Grimacing, he picked up the newspaper and slid it beneath the mat on which his feet were resting. Almost immediately, he changed his mind and returned it to the dashboard.

At least it had finally happened. No more lying, no more pretence. By the time he arrived home he knew all the boys in the neighbourhood would have seen the newspaper. Who would be the first of them, he wondered, to stop scanning the lists of candidates who had 'passed' and realise that it wasn't just an error that prevented him from finding Raza's name where it should be?

And when they asked him what had happened, urged him to appeal to the Board because obviously it was a mistake, it couldn't be anything else, right, Junior, right, even total idiots got the 33 per cent required to pass – what would he say then? How could he explain to anyone – when he didn't understand himself – what had happened the final day of the exams when he sat down to the Islamic-studies paper?

The initial moment of panic when he looked at the questions was nothing new. For years he'd been familiar with this sickening sense of free fall as his eyes jumped from one question to the next, unable to finish reading one before darting forward, individual words and phrases from different questions clumping together in his mind to create an unintelligible mass. But then he'd steady himself, force his mind into quietness and read more slowly – and meaning would attach to the words, answers flying from his pen to the paper as quickly as he could write. There had been times, through these Inter exams, when the moment of panic had lasted longer than normal, and it took three or four attempts of reading through the questions before everything fell into place. But that afternoon, that final exam of his school-going days, nothing fell into place. The jumble of words only grew more jumbled, bright spots of light appeared before his eyes as he tried to read, and nonsensical answers to questions he didn't even understand kept coming to mind in Japanese. He knew he had to calm down, that panic only bred panic, but then he remembered that this was a compulsory paper, failing it would mean failing everything, and how would he ever look his father in the eyes again? As soon as he thought of Sajjad Ashraf – pictured his trusting, expectant face – everything emptied from his mind. And then, the examiner was collecting the papers. Just like that. And his was blank. He picked up his pen, wrote firmly on the page, 'There are no intermediaries in Islam. Allah knows what is in my heart,' and handed in the paper.

When he emerged from the examination hall, there was a group of his friends clapping him on the shoulder. 'All done, hero! We really can't call you Junior any more, college boy.' One of them – Ali – slung an arm around Raza's shoulder and called out to a group of girls walking past, 'Who wants to go for a scooter drive with my

144

friend, the college boy? Top marks this one will get.' He dropped the keys to his Vespa into Raza's hand, and pushed him towards the group of girls, two of whom were smiling directly at Raza, no coyness, no pretence, in the way that college girls smiled at college boys. Right then Raza knew he wouldn't tell anyone what had happened. For a few more weeks he could still be Raza the Brilliant, Raza the Aspiring, Raza the Son Who Would Fulfil His Father's Dreams.

When his mother sat down in the passenger seat he handed her the newspaper and pulled away from the pavement, his voice strangely calm as he said, 'I didn't pass. I left the final paper blank.'

A small noise of shock and disappointment escaped her mouth before she stopped herself and said, 'What happened?'

'I don't know.' He wished she would shout at him so he could be petulant or resentful in return. 'I couldn't understand the words on the exam paper. And then time was up.'

She had been a teacher long enough to know things like this sometimes happened to the best of students.

'This was your Islamic-studies paper?' When he nodded, she allowed herself a long, luxurious expression of disgust, though it wasn't directed at him. Devotion as public event, as national requirement. It made her think of Japan and the Emperor, during the war. 'And why do you need that to study the law? Ridiculous!' She stroked the back of his head. 'Why didn't you tell me this earlier, Raza-chan?'

The childhood endearment brought tears to his eyes.

'I don't want to be the new neighbourhood Donkey.' Abbas, who used to live down the road from him, had acquired that nickname when he was eight and had to repeat a class year after failing his exams. For three years he barely scraped through, coming at the bottom of the class, and then he failed again. After that, no one called him anything but Donkey. Failure was the ultimate embarrassment in the neighbourhood, a disgrace to the whole family, and the children picked up on this early, distancing themselves quickly from it through insults and jeers.

'Raza! No one will think of you that way. It was only one paper. You'll retake it in a few months. Everything will be fine.'

'But how will I tell Aba?'

'I'll tell him,' she said firmly. 'And if he says one word in anger to you I will make him regret it.' At his smile of relief, she said, 'In return you have to do one thing for me. Tell me what you really want from your life. I know it isn't the law.'

Raza shrugged and gestured to the electronic shops. 'I want to have everything that's in there,' he said grandly.

'I'm not asking what you want to possess. I'm asking what you want to do.'

They were stopped at a traffic light, behind a rickshaw that had a pair of sultry eyes painted on it, beneath which was emblazoned, in Urdu, *LOOK – BUT WITH LOVE*. Raza's mind found itself instantly translating the words into Japanese, German, English, Pashto – a reflexive response to any piece of writing he glimpsed as he drove through the city's streets.

'I want words in every language,' he said. His hands briefly left the driving wheel in a gesture of hopelessness. 'I think I would be happy living in a cold, bare room if I could just spend my days burrowing into new languages.'

Hiroko rested her hand on Raza's, not knowing what to say to that unexpected moment of raw honesty. To her, acquiring language was a talent, to her son it was passion. But it was a passion that could have no fulfilment, not here. Somewhere in the world perhaps there were institutions where you could dive from vocabulary to vocabulary and make that your life. But not here. 'Polyglot' was not any kind of practical career choice. She was overwhelmed by a feeling of sorrow for her boy, for that look in his eyes which told her he knew and had always known that he would have to take that most exceptional part of himself and put it to one side. She knew what Sajjad would say if she tried to discuss it with him: 'If the greatest loss of his life is the loss of a dream he's always known to be a dream, then he's among the fortunate ones.' He'd be right, of course, but that didn't stop this pulling at her heart. There was something she had learnt to recognise after Nagasaki, after Partition: those who could step out from loss, and those who would remain mired in it. Raza was the miring sort, despite the inheritance he should have had from both his parents, two of the world's great forward-movers.

When they arrived home she went inside first, leaving Raza outside, leaning against the car, until she talked things over with Sajjad.

First, he was disbelieving, convinced she was playing a ridiculous joke on him. Then he raised his voice, bellowed that the boy didn't study enough. But when she told him which exam he'd failed, and what had happened, Sajjad just shook his head in disbelief and sat down, his anger unable to sustain itself, as always.

'He'll take the exam again in the autumn,' Hiroko said, sitting next to him and clasping his hand. 'The results will be in before college starts, and they'll hold a place for him pending that one result. It's happened with our students before.'

For a few moments Sajjad was silent, but finally he nodded and brought her hand to his lips.

'All right, I won't be angry with him. It might not hurt him to miss a rung on a ladder. Next time, he'll leap right over it.'

He went outside to find his son, to tell him – Hiroko instructed him to use these words – 'These things happen'. On his way out he cursed under his breath the government which kept trying to force religion into everything public. His mother, with her most intimate relationship with Allah, would have personally knocked on the door of Army House and told the President he should have more shame than to ask all citizens to conduct their love affairs with the Almighty out in the open.

What Sajjad saw as he stepped outside was this: Bilal and Ali, his son's closest friends, driving down the street on a Vespa, Bilal waving the exam results in the air like a victory flag, while Raza hunched down behind Sajjad's car, hiding out of their sight.

15

Flying into Karachi at night, the American, Harry – formerly Henry – Burton, looked down on to the brightly lit sprawl of one of the fastest-growing cities in the world and felt the surge of homecoming that accompanies the world's urban tribes as they enter unfamiliar landscapes of chaos and possibility. This is more like it, he thought, exiting the airport to a pell-mell of cars using their horns in a complicated and unrelenting exchange of messages about power, intention and mistrust. Even the beggar tossing a twenty-five-paisa coin back at him with a sneer made Harry smile.

God, it was good to be away from Islamabad – the bubble in the hills, a town barely two decades old, characterised by government and not history, where everything had the antiseptic air of diplomacy with germs rife beneath the surface. 'Dull, but pretty', they'd described it to him beforehand. But pretty wasn't enough for a man who'd spent his childhood summers in Mussoorie. Harry wanted chaos of his cities and nothing less than beauty of his hill towns. Only on the one occasion he'd driven out of Islamabad into the hill station of Murree, and stood at Kashmir Point looking at snow-capped mountains in the distance with the smell of pine trees all around him, had he felt the gnarly stuff of space and time which separated him from his childhood thin to cobwebs.

Karachi, Karachi, he almost sang out loud as the car with the diplomatic licence plate sped its way through the city. A truck driving on the wrong side of the road veered away from Harry's car at the last possible moment and he cheered with delight. Six months in Islamabad, without reprieve. How had he managed it?

The sacrifices a man makes for his country, Harry thought, saluting his reflection in the tinted window.

But the next afternoon he was somewhat less buoyant – at least mentally so, though physically he couldn't keep from bouncing up and down on the springless seat of a wedge-shaped auto-rickshaw, while fumes from exhaust pipes entered his pores and traffic crowded so close he could see each bristle on the moustache of the President-General whose face decorated the back of the truck that the rickshaw was stuck behind in the slow crawl through the commercial heart of Karachi. Although it was December the afternoon sun was still hot, and the sea breeze which had been so refreshing just a couple of miles back seemed unable to force its way through the thick fumes. Harry distracted himself with architecture, admiring the loveliness of an enclosed balcony jutting out from a yellow-stone colonial building, its lower half fashioned from delicate woodwork, its upper half coloured glass.

But eventually the rickshaw left behind all colonial remnants, left behind the spacious homes of the elite in which he'd spent all his time on his previous visit to Karachi, and snaked through the streets of a city which had grown too fast for urban planning, everywhere concrete and cement and almost no greenery, thorny acacias overtaking all empty plots of land, except where they'd been cut down to make space for the makeshift jute homes of the poor; and the further from familiarity the rickshaw travelled the more Harry began to fear the circumstances in which he might find the man he sought out.

'What's Nazimabad like?' he'd said two nights earlier, in Islamabad, to a businessman at a party, who he found trying to catch fish with his bare hands in their host's pond while the armed guards employed to shoot predatory birds looked on uncertainly.

The man had barely glanced up.

'Muhajir depot,' he replied. 'Never been there. Very middle class.'

One of the more perplexing things about Pakistan, Harry had found, was the tendency of the elite to say 'middle class' as though it were the most damning of insults. He wasn't quite sure what to make of 'Muhajir depot'. He knew 'muhajir' was the Urdu word for 'migrant' – and, as such, was a word Harry himself identified with, though he also knew that in Pakistan it was used specifically for those who had come to Pakistan from what was now India at Partition. But though he knew the word he wasn't sure what its connotations were for this businessman of whose ethnic background Harry was utterly unaware. The fact was, Harry had been briefed extensively about the different groups within Afghanistan, could expound at length on the tensions, enmities and alliances between Pashtuns, Uzbeks, Tajiks and Hazaras, but knew little about any groups in Pakistan other than the Inter-Services Intelligence agency.

What he did know was that Karachi was nothing like Islamabad, though it was clear people in Islamabad were mixed in their feelings about how positive a comment this was on the port city.

The businessman by the fish pond had been far from complimentary about it.

'Nothing but a city of failed aspirations,' he said.

But a woman standing near by with hair like black water had disagreed.

'It's got life,' she said simply. 'People wouldn't be migrating there from every part of the country if all aspirations failed as they approached the sea.'

It was for this comment as much as for her hair that Harry had gone to bed with her; afterwards, there was no pillow talk, and no mention of phone numbers or last names. In truth, there was barely any afterwards. She was dressed and out of his house just minutes after he'd pulled out of her. Harry had never known sex to so intensify his feelings of loneliness.

It was loneliness, he knew, that had brought him here, in search of a past that was as irretrievable as his parents' marriage or his own childhood. For months now he had ignored his desire to fly to Karachi and knock on the door of a particular house in Nazimabad and now it was the desire to put that desire to rest more than any kind of hope that had finally persuaded him to seek out the first person he'd ever been conscious of loving.

The rickshaw turned into a quiet street of a residential neighbourhood: a more communal area than the parts of Karachi Harry knew – no dividing boundary walls, no gardens and driveways buffering the space between one house and another; instead, there was a long row of homes abutting each other, a single step leading from each doorway to the street. Harry released a breath he didn't know he'd been holding – it wasn't grand, but there was no whiff of failure or disappointment about the street.

The rickshaw driver turned to look at him as he exhaled heavily and Harry shook his head to say he'd meant nothing. The man quoted the fare to Harry, whose raised eyebrows received the response: 'If I don't overcharge an American, everyone will know I work with the CIA.' Though there was clearly no one else around to see how much he was charging, the cheek of the remark amused Harry enough to pay the full amount.

'I could be a while.' He pointed to a tree growing at the front of a house, its roots creasing the road. 'It might be better if you park in the shade.'

The man nodded.

'Your Urdu is very good.'

Harry eased himself out of the rickshaw – there was an unpleasant sucking sound as the sweating bald patch on his head detached from the vinyl canopy – and nodded towards house number 17.

'My first teacher is in there. I'll tell him you said so.'

The group of boys playing cricket further down the street stopped to watch Harry as he strode across to the door and rang the bell. He looked back at them, amused by the cricket sweaters some of them were wearing in the balmy afternoon.

There was a sound of footsteps on the other side of the door, and Harry stepped back as it swung open to reveal a young man – little more than a boy – in jeans and a faded red T-shirt and with facial features Harry immediately identified as belonging to the descendants of the Mongol tribes – Hazara, probably. Maybe Tajik. Uzbek, even. The intensity of his disappointment startled him. Had he really expected to find the man he was looking for at an address last known to be accurate over twenty years ago? But perhaps – oh clutch those straws, Burton – the present occupants might know where he could be found.

'Hello,' he said. 'I'm looking for Sajjad Ashraf. He used to live here.'

Raza just stared at the tall, green-eyed redhead, whose shiny bald spot and thickening waist did nothing to dissipate the glamour that attached itself to his *Starsky and Hutch* accent.

Harry repeated the question in Urdu, wondering which language the boy spoke, and what he was doing here.

'I speak English,' the boy said, his tone offended. 'And Japanese and German.' For the first time in months he had reason to boast, and that made boasting necessary. 'And Urdu, of course. Pashto, also. What do you speak?'

Harry Burton couldn't remember the last time he'd been so taken aback.

'English and German and Urdu. And a little Farsi.'

'I beat you,' Raza said in German. There was no arrogance in the statement, just a muted pride which was unsure of its own right to exist.

'Conclusively,' Harry replied in English, feeling a ridiculous urge to pull the boy into an embrace. Then, switching to German, 'I'm Harry. You must be Sajjad and Hiroko's son.'

'Yes.' The boy smiled. 'I'm Raza. How do you do?' He extended his hand with the tentative air of someone executing a move he'd only ever practised in front of the mirror, and Harry shook it vigorously. 'Come,' the boy said, taking Harry's arm with the physical familiarity of Pakistani men to which the American hadn't yet become accustomed, and pulling him indoors. 'I'll tell Aba.'

Harry stepped through the vestibule and into a smaller version of the Ashraf home as he recalled it from his childhood: low-roofed rooms built around an open-air courtyard which was dominated by a large tree. But the flowerpots filled with marigolds, snapdragons and phlox which were clustered near the tree brought to mind another Delhi world.

A grey-haired man dressed in a white kurta pyjama was pouring water into the flowerpots, and Harry almost laughed out loud with joy at the sight. Of course it would happen this way. In this city, where tree roots cracked cement, and broad tree-trunks were canvases for graffiti, and branches became part of the urban

152

architecture as sidewalk vendors draped cloth over them to create makeshift roofs, of course he would find Sajjad Ashraf in a sun-dappled courtyard, surrounded by flowers and leaf-patterned shadows.

'Aba, Uncle Harry is here to see you,' Raza said, unsure what to make of the expression with which this foreign stranger was staring at his father.

The grey-haired man straightened – instantly recognisable as the Sajjad of old, the laughter which always suggested its presence beneath the surface now inscribed on his face in fine lines around his eyes and mouth – and looked at the newcomer with no trace of recognition. It was Hiroko, stepping out from the bedroom, who saw in his red hair and the slight droop of his eyelids something familiar but before she could excavate Konrad's features from her memory the man said, 'I'm Henry Burton. James and Ilse's son.'

Sajjad took a step forward, and then another one.

'But you were a child,' he said. 'Really? Henry . . . Henry Baba!'

'Just Harry now. I've been working in Islamabad for the last six months at the American Embassy. I'm a consular officer – you know, visas and things. And I couldn't be in Pakistan without coming to see you.'

The American stepped forward and held his hand out to Sajjad, who laughed and said, 'I used to carry you on my shoulders. Can't we do more than shake hands?' He clasped one hand against the small of Harry's back and leaned his head forward so his chin was just above Harry's shoulder, his ear inches away from Harry's ear. Then he moved his head so that it was Harry's other shoulder, his other ear framing part of Sajjad's face. It was all too quick for Harry to respond before Sajjad was standing back, smiling. 'Don't you remember? You made me teach you how to gala-milao when you came to condole with my family at my father's death. You walked into the courtyard, took your shoes off, stood up on a divan and embraced each of my brothers like that. They all thought you were the finest Englishman in India. You must have been about nine.'

'Seven. I was seven. It's one of my clearest memories of child-hood. My first time in a home that wasn't English. Why was I there without my parents? I don't remember that part.'

Sajjad could barely contain his delight at hearing the Urdu sentences trip so lightly off the tongue of his former student. Unable to think of anything to say that wouldn't strike a false note with this stranger who was not a stranger, he took off his glasses and cleaned the lenses with the sleeve of his kurta. When he put them back on he nodded as though he now had a better view of the events of 1944.

'You wanted to come. You said, I wish to condole with your family on behalf of my family.' Sajjad smiled and nodded at Raza as though imparting a lesson. 'I was so proud of my Henry Baba that day.'

The tips of Harry's ears reddened to be provided with such a good account of his younger self. He was spared having to think of a response by Sajjad holding out his hand to gesture to the woman who was walking up to them.

'My wife. Hiroko.'

'Hiroko-san.' Harry bowed. He was not a man used to bowing and was conscious he looked as though he had been attacked by a back spasm.

Hiroko took Harry's hands in her own.

'Just Hiroko. It's very good to meet you. Harry.' Her smile recognised – and dismissed – Harry's startled awareness of the associations she must have with that name. 'There is a piece of my heart reserved for members of the Weiss family.' She turned to her son. 'Raza, this is Konrad's nephew.'

'Oh.' The boy regarded Harry with new interest. 'My middle name is Konrad.'

Harry nodded, as though there were only delight, not surprise, to be garnered from this revelation. In the months leading up to their daughter's birth, still unaware of her gender, Harry and his ex-wife had searched the world around them for names that they could both commit themselves to for the rest of their lives (they already knew by then that their commitment to each other would crumble, but that only gave extra impetus to this desire to find a mutually loved syllable or two to which they could hold on long after they'd let each other go). His ex had been the one to suggest 'Konrad' for a boy after a weekend visiting Ilse in New York, but

Harry had waved his hands at her in distress and taught her the Urdu word 'manhoos', meaning 'bad-omened'. And yet here was Sajjad, who had taught him that word, smiling as his son claimed the name of the man Hiroko had loved first, who had been eradicated from the earth's surface before he turned thirty.

'So are you at school or university, Raza Konrad?' Harry turned back to the boy – something about the discovery of his middle name allowed Harry to feel avuncular.

Raza's head dipped forward, hair tumbling over his eyes.

'My father never went to university. Why should I have to?' He spoke in German, and Harry was aware of a strange tension in the air, and of Sajjad looking sideways at Hiroko for a translation that was not forthcoming.

'No reason,' Harry replied in German while casting Sajjad a glance meant to convey that there was no conspiracy here. 'If you read the world in five languages you're probably better off without classrooms boxing in your thoughts to fit the latest fashionable mode of thinking.'

Sajjad watched his son straighten, smile and widen his stance into something that was almost a swagger and, recalling the ease of his early relationship with Henry as contrasted to that of the Burton father and son, wondered at life's ironies and reversals.

'How is your father, Henry?'

'Dad? He's . . . unyielding – even to death. He had a scare with his heart some months ago, no way he should have survived. Not at his age. But he's still around – going to lots of parties. He had the sense after my mother left him to marry a woman who loves that sort of thing. Don't know that she much likes Dad, but she likes his lifestyle. And that's enough for him. He has his Gentlemen's Club for companionship.'

Harry could feel displeasure settle around the courtyard. Of course. He couldn't say a word against his father, not even among people who were entirely aware of James Burton's shortcomings – such were the rules of Indian courtesy (he still considered Sajjad an Indian though he'd been in Pakistan long enough to know he should never voice such a thought). 'My mother's doing well,' he said, nodding to Hiroko in acknowledgement of the friendship

155

between the two women, which had continued via letters for over a decade after Partition, before the anarchy of international mail ended it. 'She'll be overjoyed to hear I've found you. She still has a photograph of you and her together, up on her mantel.'

Raza hardly knew what to do with himself as Harry took the proffered chair and the offer of tea, and made it clear there was nothing he'd rather do with his evening than spend it with the Ashrafs. Almost more astonishing than the presence of the American was the attitude of Sajjad and Hiroko, who seemed to think it perfectly natural to have him in their courtyard, talking about 'the Delhi days'. Raza was completely transfixed by everything about Harry Burton – the expansiveness of his gestures, the way he had of suggesting that whatever mundane things Sajjad and Hiroko had to say about their lives were more interesting than anything he could bring to the conversation, the way he pronounced words in both Urdu and English. ('Naw-shus, Tom-aytoe, Skedule', Raza repeated to himself as though it were a mantra.)

When Harry asked if he might have a glass of water, Raza jumped up to get it, and was rewarded as he was entering the kitchen by the American's voice drifting across the courtyard, saying, 'He's a great kid. Do you have a parenting handbook I can borrow?'

But almost instantly the exaltation left him. Next he would ask, 'Which class is he in at school? What does he like to study?' and then his parents would tell him, or, worse, they would feel the need to lie.

Raza covered his face with his hands and leaned against the kitchen wall. It came upon him with no warning now, this swooping down of complete hopelessness, of despair.

He had failed the exam again. The second time it was even worse than the first. Even before he walked into the exam hall he'd lost the ability to make sense of words – in the bus on the way to the exam he'd looked at billboards and graffiti and the words all smudged and blurred in front of him. When the examiner said it was time to start he could already feel his heart pounding so hard it seemed impossible it wouldn't tear out of his chest. And nothing made sense. His hand couldn't hold his pen. He walked out after five minutes and came straight home, unable to look directly at his parents as they saw him walk in and knew it was too early, much too early, for him to have finished.

He saw tears in his father's eyes that day, and for the first time Sajjad Ali Ashraf looked old as he begged his son, 'Why? Why can't you do this one little thing? Please, my son. Do this for me.'

All the neighbourhood boys who had laughed off his first failure and said it was 'just a drama, all good heroes need a drama, and it's only that one paper, you'll retake it and everything will be fine', this second time round they didn't know what to say to him. Conversations stopped when he entered a room. They were just days away from university now, and it was all they dreamt and talked about. He couldn't bear the kindness with which they tried so hard to speak of other things around him – strained silences entering the space between him and them – and so he stayed mostly at home, and though they occasionally coaxed him out he could tell that it was always a relief – to everyone, including himself – when he left their company.

He poured water into a tall glass and looked out of the kitchen window, trying to see if the set of Harry Burton's shoulders revealed he'd just discovered that the 'great kid' was the new neighbourhood Donkey.

There was another exam in a few months. His father was determined he take it. But he knew he would only fail again and insisted no. Something inside him had stopped working, it was as simple as that. He placed the glass carefully down on a tray, wiping away his smudged thumbprint from its surface, and thought, Just this easily everything worthwhile in a life can be erased.

157

16

'Not the port. The fish harbour!'

The rickshaw driver – Sher Mohammed – swerved at the sound of Harry's barked instructions from the back seat.

'Sorry, sorry. Forgot. Too early. My brain is still asleep.'

Not the most reassuring statement to hear from the man in the driver's seat, but then again Harry had already decided that Sher Mohammed navigated the streets with a mixture of intuition and Providence. In the crush of midday he at least acknowledged certain traffic rules, but in the early morning he drove through the almost deserted streets with the air of a man who does not conceive the possibility of other vehicles impeding his progress, treating 'right of way' as an unassailable personal liberty which he carried with him through every intersection and traffic light.

Harry pulled his shawl tight around himself as the rickshaw hurtled onwards, wind whistling through it. So Karachi actually could get cold, he thought, watching his breath steam in the dawn air.

When they arrived at the entrance to the fish harbour, Sajjad and Raza were already there in Sajjad's car, Raza slumped against his father's shoulder, asleep.

'Wake up, my prince.' Sajjad rubbed his knuckles on the top of Raza's head, and his son's eyes flickered open, closed, and he mumbled 'Fish' before falling asleep again. Carefully – as once Harry had seen him handle an egg that had fallen out of a nest miraculously intact – Sajjad eased his son off his shoulder and positioned him as comfortably as possible against the passenger-side door. 'We'll wake him for breakfast,' he said, stepping out of the car, looking out of place in a thick woollen sweater and open-toed shoes. 'This gives us a chance to talk, Henry Baba.' He looked down at Harry's shoes, shook his head, climbed back into the car and emerged holding up the rubber-soled shoes he'd taken off Raza's feet. 'Wear these,' he said.

Harry's toes curled over the edge of Raza's shoes, reminding him incongruously of Billy, his cat – from his early days in America – who used to perch on the very edge of the stoop waiting for him to return from school. He wriggled his toes, and the cat batted the air with its paw.

'Believe me, you'll be glad you're wearing them,' Sajjad said, taking Harry's arm and leading him towards the harbour.

Perhaps it was the memory of the cat, which regarded all forms of insect life as prey, that did it – when Harry walked through the rusty gates and the harbour came into view all he could think was that the swarm of wooden sailing boats with their riggings painting chaos against the sky looked like grasshoppers lying on their backs, waving their insect limbs in the breeze. There were hundreds of them – in peeling paint of blues and whites and greens – lined all the way along the dock and stacked against each other four, five, six ships deep.

'Breathe through your mouth until we get to the market,' Sajjad recommended, walking swiftly towards the boats.

'Why?' Harry said, and then he caught a whiff of a smell so overpowering it made him imagine a fish-monster the size of a house, sliced open to rot for years in the baking sun.

'Come, come.' Sajjad caught his arm and pulled him along, in through another gate. 'Now you can use your nose again.'

They had entered a bazaar of seafood, all wares too fresh for any unpleasant odour. All along the cement ground, beds of ice with fish laid out on them. Men with wheelbarrows were tipping ice-chips on to the ground to replace what was melting, while other men pushed past holding baskets of fish listing with the weight of their contents. And water everywhere you stepped – not the overflow of the sea as Harry had first thought, but liquefied ice. It was barely dawn, but the activity was already frenzied. Harry caught hold of Sajjad's elbow, as the latter moved forward along the aisle between the two rows of fish. Snapper and salmon and cauldrons of flounder. Sharks. Eels. Huge great whiskered things with dinosaur-era jaws.

Sajjad stopped to haggle with a fish-seller who jokingly tried to steer him away from the tuna and towards a fish the size of a man.

'What am I going to do with that? Sleep with it?' Sajjad laughed.

A man approached Harry, holding a little shark in his hand, his fingers waggling the fin.

'For sex,' he said, in English.

'Not necessary,' Harry replied in Urdu, and everyone around him laughed approvingly.

'Where are you from?' the man with the shark asked.

'America. You? Karachi?'

'No, Mianwali.' The man gestured around him. 'People here are from every nation within Pakistan. Baloch, Pathan, Sindhi. Hindu, Sikh even. Everyone. Even an American can come and sell fish here if he wants.'

'Thanks.' Harry grinned. He loved the way every Pakistani became a tour guide at the sight of a foreigner. 'I'll keep it in mind.'

Sajjad, overhearing the conversation, caught hold of a fisherboy and directed Harry's attention to him, taking control of the tour.

'But these are the original inhabitants of Karachi. The Makranis. They're descended from African slaves. See?' He pointed to the boy's hair and features in a way that made the American deeply uncomfortable but clearly didn't bother the boy in the least. 'This coastline was along the slave route – not your slave route, of course. The Eastern one.'

'I wouldn't call it *my* slave route.'

'Of course you wouldn't,' Sajjad said dismissively, letting go of the boy with a pat on the head. 'What I'm saying is, this is a city of comings and goings – even before Partition. These days it's the Afghans. Why sit in refugee camps when you can come to Karachi?' He bent over a beautifully arranged circular pile of pink-hued fish and prodded one's flesh. 'What are you laughing at, Henry Burton?'

'You, Sajjad. You used to talk about Delhi as if it were the only city worth belonging to – and now listen to you, speaking with such pride about a place you would have mocked once for its lack of history and aesthetics and poetic heritage.'

Sajjad stopped smiling, picked up a pebble of ice and wiped his finger on it.

'Dilli is Dilli,' he said. He stepped slightly to one side, in between a display of barracuda and a crate filled with crabs, so that he was slightly apart from the press of buyers and sellers. 'My first love. I would never have left it willingly. But those bastards didn't let me go home.'

'I'm sorry,' Harry said miserably, though he wasn't entirely sure why he felt so culpable. 'What happened to all your brothers? Did they stay there?'

'My oldest brother, Altamash, was killed in the Partition riots,' Sajjad said, nodding as he spoke as though confirming to himself, all these years later, that such a thing really was true. 'I was in Istanbul; no one told me. They were waiting for me to come home. And my brother Iqbal left for Lahore. He said he couldn't stay in the city that had murdered Altamash. He left behind his wife and his children – they tried to follow him but they were on one of those trains. The ones that arrived with the dead as their cargo.'

'Christ, Sajjad. I had no idea. There was one more brother, wasn't there?'

'Yes, Sikandar. He stayed. But because two of us were in Pakistan, our house was declared evacuee property. Maybe Sikandar could have fought to retain a portion of it, but he was never a man for practicalities. So he moved out – with his family and Altamash's family, and they live in such sad conditions I can't bear to visit them. So I almost never go.' He said this so cheerfully it was almost heartless, but Harry knew enough migrants to recognise a survival strategy when he heard it. 'You know, for a long time I blamed your father.'

'For what?'

'Everything.' Sajjad smiled.

'Yeah. I do that myself. Something about him makes it so easy. You don't blame him any more?'

'Now I say this is my life, I must live it.'

161

'Muslim fatalism?'

'No, no. Pakistani resignation. It's a completely different thing.' He made a gesture of enquiry at the man whose catch he'd been inspecting and the bargaining started again. Harry caught the eye of a fisherman smoking a cigarette, and the fisherman inclined his head in Harry's direction in a knowing fashion. Harry wasn't sure if something beyond a greeting was being signalled. How many of the men in this harbour, he wondered, were involved in smuggling arms bought by the CIA and transported by the ISI from the Karachi docks to the training camps along the border?

There was a certain freedom about being in Karachi, and knowing no local assets other than Sher Mohammed. A certain freedom, also, in being known to no one – though, of course, every Pakistani assumed that all Americans in their country were CIA operatives. Harry looked at Sajjad, who now had two blue polythene bags dangling off his wrists, fish squashed inside the packaging, one glassy eye pressed against the thin blue material, reminding Harry of an early-winter frost and a garden pond with fish frozen beneath a skin of ice. He wondered if the reason none of the Ashrafs had asked him any details about his position as consular officer at the Embassy was that they suspected it was a CIA cover. Absurdly, it bothered him to think he might be suspected of lying by the family with whom he had spent part of each of the last three weekends. He was already beginning to regret the spring thaw in Afghanistan when things would pick up pace in America's proxy war and there would be few opportunities for casual leave.

'Now for the crab,' Sajjad said, handing one of his bags to Harry. 'So that there'll be something at dinner that I can eat. Have you ever eaten raw fish, Henry Baba?'

'Sushi? I love sushi.'

'Really? Thirty-five years of marriage and she still hasn't convinced me to put it in my mouth. All her other Japanese food I've learnt to appreciate. I say to her, whatever you cook, I'll eat. But it must be cooked.'

Harry stepped round a boy who had dropped a fish on the floor and was trying to pick it up only to have it slither out of his grasp at every attempt.

'The two of you – you know, when I was growing up, falling in love for the first time, listening to the kind of music guaranteed to make you feel sadder than any of the circumstances of your life merit, I used to think of the two of you as the greatest of all romantic couples.'

'Oh, no no. We were just young and foolish. What did we know about each other? Almost nothing. It was luck, pure luck, that we discovered after marriage that our natures were so sympathetic to each other. And also' – he stopped, twirled the polythene bag so it braided itself all the way up to his wrist – 'we both had too much loss in our lives, too early. It made us understand those parts of the other which were composed of absence.' He wrinkled his nose – it was a tic he'd picked up from his wife. 'If she heard that she'd say it's the melodramatic Dilli poet inside me. Look, oysters. I think we'll take some. You can't go wrong with an oyster. Open it up and you'll either find a pearl or an aphrodisiac. You're smiling, Henry Baba. I didn't think you'd know the Urdu term for "aphrodisiac". Quick, tell me why you know it. There must be a story behind this.'

How was it possible, Harry thought, to have such a man as this as your father and grow up as uncertain of your place in the world as Raza appeared to be. If you were Sajjad Ashraf's son, how could you fail to regard the world as your oyster, regardless of whether you saw yourself as gemstone or mollusc?

At that moment, though, Raza didn't see himself as either gemstone or mollusc but merely a boy whose shoes had been stolen from his feet as he slept. He didn't see Harry's shoes with socks stuffed into them in the driver-seat area as he rubbed his eyes to ensure he was properly awake before rolling up his shalwar to shin-height and stepping tentatively out of the car, cursing in German as his feet touched the cold, filthy road. No sign of any thief, just a truck parked a few feet away. Near fifteen feet above the ground a Pathan man was perched like a gargoyle on the frame of the truck's container portion, watching the early-morning ocean traffic.

'Anything exciting going on out there?' Raza called up in Pashto – it was the only one of his languages that Hiroko hadn't taught him; he'd learnt it instead during all the years he'd gone to and from school in a van driven by a sweet-natured Pathan who had insisted Raza sit up front with him ever since the boy, at the age of six, first expressed an interest in learning the driver's first language. For nearly a decade of Raza's life the van driver remained the finest of all his teachers.

The man shaded his hands with his eyes, almost saluting.

'Are you Afghan?'

Raza touched his cheekbones reflexively. Until the Soviets invaded Afghanistan he'd never heard that question; but in the last four years, as increasing numbers of refugees made their way into Pakistan, it had become something less than unusual for Raza to be identified as an Afghan from one of the Mongol tribes.

'Yes,' he said, and felt the rightness of the lie press against his spine, straightening his back.

The man swung down from the container to look more closely at Raza.

'Who are your people?'

'Hazara,' Raza said confidently. He knew that was what Harry Burton had assumed him to be.

'Come, meet someone,' the man said, hopping down on to the ground and placing his arm around Raza's shoulder. 'Abdullah! Wake up!'

The carved wooden driver's-side door was kicked open by a pale foot, and a few seconds later a boy – no more than fourteen – jumped out of the cab. His wide, upturned mouth and the childish chubbiness of his cheeks did nothing to undercut the adult gaze he directed at Raza through his hazel eyes.

'You have a brother here from Afghanistan,' the man said. 'A Hazara.'

The boy ignored Raza and twisted his features at the older man.

'What does Pakistan do to people's brains? Is it something in the air? Am I going to get stupider if I spend more time here? Since when are Hazaras and Pashtuns brothers?'

Pashtun, not Pathan, Raza noted.

The older man smiled as if recognising the insult as a form of love, and it was Raza who answered, just to assure himself that he wasn't intimidated by a boy six inches shorter than him.

164

'Since the Soviets marched into our house and we both had to escape through the window, that's since when Hazaras and Pashtuns are brothers.'

The boy frowned.

'How long have you been away from Afghanistan? You speak Pashto like this Pakistani here.' He indicated the older man, who looked offended this time. 'Is Dari your language?'

'Raza!' It was his father, walking towards the car, waving bags of fish at him while Harry pointed at Raza's feet and made a gesture of distress before pointing to his own feet.

'I have to go,' Raza said.

'Is that man American?' Abdullah asked.

Raza smiled.

'I have to go,' he said again.

The boy nodded, his eyes still on Harry.

'Where do you live? I haven't seen you in Sohrab Goth.'

Raza had been about to walk away, but at mention of Sohrab Goth he paused, weighing up the possibility that his lies would expose him to humiliation against the usefulness of knowing someone in Sohrab Goth, where, one of the neighbourhood boys swore, it was possible to buy cassette-players and televisions and telephones with loudspeakers at a fraction of the lowest price anywhere else in the city. This boy, it was obvious, could bargain down an Afghan trader to a price Raza couldn't demand without his voice conveying his own suspicion that he was insulting the seller.

'I might be there soon,' he said. 'How can I find you?' He didn't even bother making up an answer to Abdullah's query about where he lived. He had realised already that the boy didn't ask questions for the purpose of being answered, but merely to maintain an interrogatory style that asserted control.

'There's a truck yard next to Bara Market. Just tell anyone there you want Abdullah – the one who drives the truck with the dead Soviet.'

Raza took a step back, alarmed, and then saw the boy pointing to the side of his truck, its wood panelling decorated with brightly painted birds and mountains and flowers and – Raza looked in the

165

direction of the pointing finger – a miniature portrait of a man in Soviet Army uniform lying on the ground with blood gushing from his body as though it were a multispouted fountain.

The boy laughed.

'Everyone knows me, and my truck.' The older man made a noise deep in his throat and the boy said, 'It's actually this Afridi's truck. But I'm the one who asked for the Soviet to be put there.'

Raza nodded.

'Next time I'm there, I'll ask for you,' he said.

'If I'm around,' the boy said. 'You never know. One day Karachi, one day Sargodha, one day Peshawar. I've seen everything in this country.' He glanced over towards Harry, who had taken off his shoes and was walking, barefoot, towards Raza, holding them in front of him like an offering. 'But I never thought I'd see that.'

Harry reached Raza, apologising profusely even as he went down on one knee and placed the shoes on the ground for Raza to step into. In normal circumstances, Raza would have objected, insisted Harry wear the shoes, brightened with embarrassment to be treated with such deference by anyone older than himself. But as he saw the look of awe in Abdullah's eyes – a look not dissimilar to the ones his classmates used to direct at him when he scored full marks in the most difficult of exams – he just winked at the younger boy and slipped his feet into the rubber shoes, his hand touching the air above the American's head as though in benediction.

17

The fifteen-year-old American girl held out the pirated video to the man behind the counter, who was about to place it in a brown paper bag when he noticed the title, and frowned.

'Not appropriate,' he said, whisking the video into a cubbyhole beneath his desk. He offered her another video. 'Why don't you take this?' The girl read the scrawled title and made a whistling sound of disgust through the little gap in her front teeth, her green, almond-shaped eyes looking squarely at him in a manner he found both unfamiliar and embarrassing.

'If there's a law against me taking that other movie, fine. But "appropriateness" is not something you get to decide about.'

He almost laughed at this strange hierarchy which placed the law above advice by an elder but something in those clear green eyes suggested this might not be a wise course of behaviour.

'If your father says OK, then I will give it to you,' he said in the manner of one who has found a compromise and expects gratitude for it.

The girl made a sound which was unfamiliar but clearly meant to convey disgust and walked out of his store, leaving him to wonder about this odd creature with her metal-studded leather jacket, her black lipstick, and her short, copper-coloured hair, from which one long strand extended like a rat's tail curling beneath her shoulders.

'Daddy Warbucks!' Kim Burton called out to her father as she walked out of the shop. 'He wants me to watch *Annie*. What kind of place is this?'

Harry held up a hand to his daughter to gesture she should go back into the video shop and wait for him, and continued talking to the man selling nuts and dried fruit from a wooden cart on wheels. Ignoring his directive, she walked closer to him, almost managing to be unbothered by the stares of passers-by in the busy commercial square – it was the women who stared more, she'd noticed in her four days in Islamabad, and several had actually come up to her and taken hold of the long, gelled strands of her hair using the word 'chooha', which her father had enthusiastically translated as 'mouse'.

He carried on speaking to the other man in Urdu as she stopped next to him, slinging his arm across her shoulder to acknowledge he knew she was there. She felt such a rush of warmth and safety to be pulled in against him that it made her step away, scowling. He was different here. Looser somehow. He preferred it here, that's what it was. Gran had said he would.

Later, when they were driving down a wide, tree-lined bou-levard towards the vast mosque under construction at one end of it, a video of *Tootsie* in her lap (at the last moment she'd lost the nerve to tell him it was *Porky's* she wanted), she said, 'Why do you keep saying you hate Islamabad when you're obviously so much happier here than even New York, never mind DC or Berlin?'

Harry Burton glanced in surprise at his daughter. Like her adored grandmother she had the ability to see things in him which he was sure no one else would guess. It made him nervous. Ilse Weiss was one thing – she'd known him his whole life – but to this girl he'd been a fleeting presence since she was four years old and divorce had ended familial life in DC, unshackling her parents from each other and from the city they both disliked, but which had proved a compromise between one's insistence on raising her child in America, the other's insistence on staying with his chosen career. He was a failed parent, he knew this, and so when Kim came to visit – formerly in Berlin, now here – or when he stopped for a few days in New York to see her he accepted her sulks and tantrums as his just deserts; but these moments of insight in which she showed him glimpses of the woman she could grow into once adolescence

168

passed made him uneasy. There was too much he didn't want her ever to know about him.

'I do hate Islamabad,' he said firmly.

He stopped at a traffic light, and the man on a bicycle who stopped beside him leaned slightly towards Harry's open window, his head nodding in appreciation of the music from the car stereo. Harry ejected the cassette and handed it to the man – prompting a gasp of outrage from Kim, even though she had the master cassette at home and this was just the copy she'd made for the stereo, which was in the habit of chewing up tape. The man took the cassette, his tentativeness suggesting he couldn't believe it was really meant for him, and directed the question 'Amrcekan?' at Harry. When Harry nodded, the man stuck his pinky finger into one of the holes around which the tape spooled and held it up with an expression of amazement, turning his hand this way and that as if admiring an engagement ring. Then he removed a bagful of apples from his handlebar and passed it over to Harry before driving off, ringing his cycle bell, the cassette still wedged on to his finger.

'I do hate the place,' Harry said. 'But I love the people. Not the ones in officialdom – the real people.'

'Huh,' Kim said, swallowing this piece of information. 'That's funny. I used to think the rule which said you can't be President of America if you're born somewhere else was really stupid because of course people who migrate in are going to be more loyal citizens than the ones who take it for granted. I thought that because of you – and how England means nothing to you. But I guess England's not really the country you left behind, is it?'

'England was a way station,' Harry said, feeling some satisfaction in imagining Kim repeating this to her grandfather. James Burton would choke on the information. Ilse Weiss, on the other hand, would delight in it.

The story of Harry's childhood was one Kim knew well – it was also one of the few stories Harry could be trusted to tell without any evasion, belonging, as it did, to that time in his life before secrecy and lies became necessary.

The only thing worse than leaving India was arriving in England. Harry would always start the story with that line. The war was still everywhere, the sun was nowhere, and all the boys at school laughed at his 'Indian expressions' (both verbal and physical) and wanted to know what his father had done in the war. And then the final horror: the only other boy who had just arrived from India, and who Harry had considered an ally, said, 'His mother's German.' So, much of the first year was abject misery. Things only improved near Easter when one of the boys threw a cricket ball his way with the words, 'Hey, Maharaja Fritz. Know how to bowl?' Then the skills taught to him by Sajjad – he always looked somewhat wistful when he mentioned that name – turned him into something of a school hero.

Two years later, when his father announced over Easter break that his mother's 'short trip to New York', which had commenced three months earlier, was going to be permanent, and Harry was to go there to join her, the eleven-year-old was torn. He wanted to be near his mother, but he knew his cricketing skills would get him nowhere in New York City. And what else did he have, after all? Nothing but another foreign accent. By now, India had left his speech, and what remained was 'Marmite and sardines', as his mother put it.

There was only one thing to be done, Harry decided. He would go to New York at the start of the summer, not the end of it as had been planned, and prepare. 'Teach me to speak American,' he said on his first day in New York to the beautifully dressed young man who had let him in to Uncle Willie's Upper East Side flat. ('It's an apartment. That's your first lesson.') He resisted all attempts by his mother to introduce him to boys who would be his classmates ('Don't say "mate" ') in the autumn ("fall"). He learnt the rules of baseball, the stats of all the Yankees players over the last twenty years, and found himself weeping as he stood in front of the recently unveiled Babe Ruth monument.

Even so, on the first day of school his foreignness overwhelmed him to the point of muteness. He mumbled his way through the first hours, keeping his head down and paying attention to no one but the teachers. It was only during recess, as he sat alone on a stone step listening to the boys around him, that he realised he was surrounded by a group of immigrants. German, Polish, Russian.

They were all, like him, bound by class in this exclusive public ('Private, Henry, private') school, and bound also by the fact that their parents, for one reason or another, wanted no more to do with Europe after the war.

Harry looked at the group, and then looked towards the boys lounging beneath a tree, no whiff of the Old World about them.

Standing up, he paused, realising he was about to take the first real risk of his life, then walked up to the second group of boys and said, 'Hi, I'm Harry.'

That winter, in London, James Burton would tell his son that confidence gets you far in life – and that if Harry had been less insecure when he first arrived at boarding school in England he would have met with a friendly reception there, too. But Harry watched not only himself but also the other sons of immigrants as they made their way through the school year, and understood that America allowed – no, insisted on – migrants as part of its national fabric in a way no other country had ever done. All you had to do was show yourself willing to be American – and in 1949, what else in the world would you want to be? ('And do all the Negro students at your school agree with this assessment, Henry?' 'I never said it's a perfect country, Dad, just the best there is.')

'Huge sacrifice you've made,' Kim said, closing her eyes to take in the fragrance of jasmine flowers which had leapt through the window in a rush. 'Living outside the world's best country in order to serve it.'

Harry glanced sideways at her, and sighed.

'I do miss you, you know. And if there was any need for consular officers in New York, believe me, I'd be there in a heartbeat.'

'Drop the consular-officer crap, Dad,' Kim said, her eyes still closed.

There was a squealing sound as Harry swerved on to the side of the road and braked sharply.

'Apologise,' he said.

Kim opened her mouth to issue something other than an apology but then the thought came to her that his car might be bugged; someone who shouldn't know the truth might learn it from her and that could hurt him.

171

She leaned sideways and wrapped her arms around Harry, startling him.

'Sorry, Daddy. Sorry. I'm just mouthing off.'

Harry kissed the top of her head fiercely. It was the first glimpse he'd had of his child through the prickliness of adolescence since she'd arrived in Islamabad for her Christmas holidays. He wanted to say he wished he'd chosen differently but he had a horror of her recognising the lie. Right now, more than ever, he knew he was doing with his life precisely what most excited him. When had the shift occurred, he wondered, as Kim sat back in her seat, arms crossed, looking mortified at her outburst. When had it become about excitement rather than idealism? He felt himself only tenuously connected to the young man who in '64 had stepped away from the path of academia and applied for another line of work entirely, explaining to the men who interviewed him that he wanted to join them because he believed fervently that Communism had to be crushed so that the US could be the world's only superpower. It was not the notion of power itself that interested Harry, but the idea of it concentrated in a nation of migrants. Dreamers and poets could not come up with a wiser system of world politics: a single democratic country in power, whose citizens were connected to every nation in the world. How could anything but justice be the most abiding characteristic of that country's dealings with the world? That was the future Harry Burton saw, the future of which he determined to be a part. And he would not be one of those men to stay out of a war while claiming to care passionately about its outcome.

Well, he cared just as passionately now, but it had been a long time since he'd thought about it in relation to justice, let alone dreamers and poets.

He pulled up next to the vast mosque, which had been under construction for twelve years now against the verdant backdrop of the Margalla Hills, and watched his daughter smile at the construction site as she smiled at nothing else in Islamabad.

'What's that thing shaped like an armadillo's shell ringed in by four spears?' she'd asked the first evening he'd taken her driving around Islamabad. It was the first sentence she'd spoken that didn't contain the word 'boring'.

Now he watched her shrug off the leather jacket and tuck the eyebrow-raising tail of hair into her T-shirt while wiping a tissue vigorously across the lips – and suddenly all the bristling attitude had gone out of her appearance, and she was just a young girl, eyes bright as she approached the contractor, who had become the one person in Islamabad in whom she showed any interest. Harry wondered which version – bristling or not – would have manifested itself in front of the Ashrafs if he had taken Kim to Karachi. Hiroko and Sajjad had both expressed a desire to meet her, but Harry had only to conjure a mental image of the differences between the considerate, polite boy the Ashrafs had raised and his own hellion offspring to know such a meeting might go disastrously wrong. And yet, in this moment, he wished he'd chosen differently – not least because he missed the Ashrafs, and saw how Christmas in their company might feel like a real family Christmas. Never mind – he would see them in a couple of weeks. Kim was leaving, and he'd arranged to get the keys to a beach hut in Karachi from a colleague at the Consulate there. He smiled, imagining how delighted Raza would be by the outing he'd organised. Then he glanced at Kim, and sighed. It was easy enough to delight someone else's teenage child.

'Can you tell him as we were driving up I saw how the roof is a tent, and not an armadillo's shell,' she said, indicating the contractor who was walking up to them with a smile. 'Though the four minarets still look like spears.'

Harry translated partially, leaving out the part about the spears, which he suspected might not go down too well, even though he had a feeling the contractor knew enough English to understand a good part of what Kim had said. The contractor nodded, smiled, and ushered them inside the vast mosque; Harry's hand hovered protectively above Kim's head in the absence of any hard hats, but his daughter was too excited to react with the irritation she would otherwise have exhibited.

'Wow,' Kim kept saying, as the contractor walked them around – the first time he'd agreed to let them see the interior – and showed how the unusually shaped roof was supported on giant girders.

The tale of generations, Harry thought. James Burton watched with dismay the collapse of Empire; Harry Burton was working for the collapse of Communism; and Kim Burton only wanted to know how to build, one edifice at a time, the construction process being all that mattered, not whether the outcome was mosque or art gallery or prison. Of all of them, Harry thought with one of his sudden rushes of sentimentality, she alone could be counted on to engage with the world without doing any harm.

18

From a distance, it looked as if they were praying.

Harry Burton and Hiroko Ashraf knelt on either side of a rock pool, hands on their knees, neither looking left towards seagulls gliding above the water's surface nor right towards the beach life on the sand: families sitting on shawls, eating oranges to counter the salty air; a group of boys rolling a tennis ball towards a group of girls, a piece of paper taped to the ball with something written on it which made the girls giggle and cluster together; camels with heavily mirror-worked seats eliciting screams from young passengers as they dipped forward and back in the see-saw of standing; Raza constructing an elaborate sand fort, because that's what Harry said he used to enjoy doing at the beach in his youth, while Sajjad inscribed Urdu verses on the fort's walls with the sharp end of a cuttlebone.

'Sometimes you only know the salamanders are there because they stir up the mud. Their camouflage is slightly more effective than yours.' Hiroko waved a hand in the direction of Harry's hennaed hair, several shades brighter than its natural colour.

Harry laughed.

'Don't mock. Even the Pathans think I'm Pathan when I'm wearing a shalwar kameez. I tell them my name is Lala Buksh, and then my inability to say very much more in Pashto gives me away. Any idea what happened to him? The real Lala Buksh?'

Hiroko shook her head. Turning her face towards the sea, she closed her eyes and smiled.

'It's such a pleasure to be here. We live so far inland I sometimes forget this is also a coastal city.'

'Also?'

'Like Nagasaki.'

She looked towards the three wooden fishing boats progressing in a line towards the horizon, no sails, and at this distance no sound of motors, so that they seemed to be propelled by the will of the sea. Nagasaki to Bombay. Bombay to Istanbul. Istanbul to Karachi. All that sea-travel in a single year, made more extraordinary by the fact that in the years preceding she'd never left Japan, and in the years that followed she had never left Pakistan. Rarely left Karachi, in fact – Sajjad sometimes took Raza to Lahore to see his brother Iqbal, or to Peshawar to see his sister, and once a decade or so they'd cross the border to visit the family that remained in Delhi, though those were always dispiriting trips. But Hiroko didn't accompany them on these family trips, and Sajjad had long ago recognised that his Japanese wife would always be an outsider to his family, her presence reason for discomfort on every side, and he'd finally stopped asking her to come along. So every so often she would have these days alone in Karachi, and always there'd be a secret thrill of imagining she might dip into their savings and board a flight to somewhere – Egypt, Hong Kong, New York – returning in time to welcome her husband and son home.

'Do you still think about it a lot? About Nagasaki?' It was not the kind of question he would usually ask of someone he had first met only a couple of months earlier, but already Hiroko seemed like someone who had been in his life a very long time.

She touched her back, just above the waist.

'It's always there.'

Harry nodded, and looked down into the clear water of the rock pool, seeing his face with sea plants growing out of it.

'How did you explain it to Raza? With Kim – the first time she asked about Konrad, I made an excuse and left the room. My mother told her something – I still don't know what, except that it made her look terrifyingly grown-up when she walked out of the room. She was eight.'

Hiroko glanced over to Raza, his concentration intent upon his fort. In this moment, he was a child.

'Fairy tales,' she said. 'I made up fairy tales.'

Harry shook his head, not understanding.

She took a deep breath.

'I'll tell you,' she said, and he knew by her voice that he was going to hear something that she would speak of to almost no one else. 'There was the one about the girl whose dying father slithers towards her in the shape of a lizard; she is so horrified by his grotesqueness it takes her years to understand that his final act was to come towards her, after a lifetime of walking away. The one about the boy shaken out of his life and told that was a dream, and so was everyone he loved in it – this charred world, this prison, this aloneness is reality. The one about the purple-backed bookcreatures with broken spines who immolate themselves rather than exist in a world in which everything written in them is shown to be fantasy. The woman who loses all feeling, fire entering from her back and searing her heart, so it's possible for her to see a baby's corpse and think only, There's another one. The men and women who walk through shadow-worlds in search of the ones they loved. Monsters who spread their wings and land on human skin, resting there, biding their time. The army of fire demons, dropped from the sky, who kill with an embrace. The schoolteacher in a world where textbooks come to life; she cannot escape from the anatomy text, its illustrations following her everywhere – bodies without skin, bodies with organs on display, bodies that reveal what happens to bodies when nothing in them works any more.'

'God. Hiroko.'

When he had applied to work at the CIA's Directorate of Operations he had anticipated running into trouble over his foreign birth and the question of divided allegiances; but the India and England years rated little mention in his interview, and the only sticky moment occurred when he was asked his views on the dropping of the bombs on Hiroshima and Nagasaki. Acutely aware of the polygraph machine attached to him, he had said, 'Like President Eisenhower, I believe we should not have done that.'

Now Pakistan was developing its nuclear programme. The CIA knew. And as far as Harry could make out all they were doing in response was gathering information that confirmed this was so and then funnelling more money into the country, making possible the huge expenditure that such a programme required. Harry had no memory of Konrad, but that hadn't prevented him from dreaming of mushroom clouds on a regular basis since the day in 1945 when he found the magazine his mother had brought home with its pictures of atomic-bomb victims – he had looked from the photographs of burnt lumps of humanity to the picture of Uncle Konrad as a young boy, just a little older than Harry was himself, smiling at the camera with Harry's own smile.

It was Ilse Weiss, not any of the CIA psychologists, who had suggested that at the very root of Harry's determination to join the CIA at the height of the Cold War was the terror of nuclear war, the threat of which could only be eliminated by conclusively ending the battle between America and Russia. Harry had laughed dismissively – he always refused to acknowledge to his mother that he worked for the CIA, though she had somehow managed to work it out while he was still in training at the Farm; but ever since he had read a colleague's report to Langley about the Pakistan nuclear project there had been times, while sitting across from the ISI officials, when Harry felt a rage that went beyond the usual mistrust and annoyances and anger that accompanied every step of the ISI–CIA alliance, and then he couldn't help wondering if his mother might have had a point.

'But I never told Raza the fairy tales,' Hiroko said. 'Not any of them. I kept thinking, One day he'll be old enough. But why should I ever let my child imagine all that?' She cupped water in her hand and drizzled it on Harry's scalp, which was beginning to turn red in the sun. 'He knows there was a bomb. He knows it was terrible, and that my father died, and the man I was engaged to died. He once received a history book for a birthday present which had a full page about Hiroshima, with a paragraph appended about Nagasaki. It showed a picture of an old Japanese man looking sad, and holding a bandage against his bloodied head. It looked as if he'd scraped it falling off the low branch of a tree. Raza showed it to me, nodded his head, and never said anything about it again.'

'And the burns on your back?'

He was unprepared for the anger streaking across her face, the bite in her voice as she said, 'Your mother had no business telling you about that.'

'I'm so sorry.' He found he was actually frightened of her displeasure, shaken by the unfamiliarity of her features without their customary good humour.

She brushed a hand over her face, as though wiping away the unpleasantness that had settled there, and reached out to pat Harry's wrist.

'Forgive my vanity. Sajjad is the one person in the world who I allow . . .' She stopped, smiled in a way that told Harry that to continue would reveal details of intimacy between husband and wife, and added, 'Actually, Raza's never seen them.'

'He hasn't seen them?' Impossible to keep the shock out of his voice.

'Oh, he knows they're there. He knows there are places without feeling. When he was a child he liked to sneak up behind me and tap against my back with a fork or a pencil, laughing when I carried on doing whatever I was doing, unaware. It made Sajjad so angry, but I was grateful he could approach it with such lightness.' She looked amused by Harry's continued expression of amazement. 'This is not a world in which young boys see their mother's bare backs, you know. I never made a conscious choice for him not to see it – I simply didn't think I needed to go out of my way to show him what was done to me. And yes, Harry Burton, they're ugly. And I am vain.'

He wanted – strangely, wildly – to apologise to her, to beg her forgiveness. The only thing that stopped him was the certainty that whatever he said would be inadequate, and embarrassing to her.

'But I don't want you to think my life is haunted by the past,' Hiroko continued. 'I'm told most hibakusha have survivor's guilt. Believe me, I don't. Here I am, breathing in the sea air, watching for salamanders and hermit crabs with a Weiss while my husband and son build forts on the sand. Yesterday, I picked up the ringing telephone and heard my old friend Ilse's voice for the first time in thirty-five years.' She smiled with a deep pleasure. It had been extraordinary, the way the intervening years had compressed into nothing, and they had talked without constraint for over an hour, Ilse's voice happy in a way it had never been during the days of her marriage to James. 'And tomorrow morning I will walk into the schoolyard with my neighbour and friend, Bilqees, who teaches with me, and my students will crowd around to tell me about their school trip to the zoo, so many of them chattering at the same time that I won't understand a word any of them is saying. Yes, I know everything can disappear in a flash of light. That doesn't make it any less valuable.'

She leaned back and sank her feet into the rock pool. She didn't know how to tell him – without making him uncomfortable – that he had become part of all that was valuable in her life. The way he had entered their house in Nazimabad, entered their daily lives – there was something simply amazing in it. Earlier, watching Harry play cricket on the sand with Raza and a group of young boys, she realised that while Konrad would have determinedly wandered into parts of town which his sister stayed far from he would have done it self-consciously, aware of his own transgression. And Ilse, for all her years in New York, mingling with 'people of all kinds', as she put it, would still not be able to enter Sajjad's presence without remembering he had been only one rung up from a servant – this much was obvious in the only stilted moment of their conversation, when Ilse said, 'And how is your husband?' But Harry's attitude was simply one of gratitude for being welcomed.

Americans! she thought, watching Harry remove a tube of sunblock from the pocket of his shorts and apply some to the top of his head. In Tokyo, thirty-five years ago, she had decided their snobbery was not of class but of nation ('The bomb saved American lives!' Even now, even now, she could feel her face burning at the memory). But around Harry Burton she felt herself relent. He was a consular officer – Konrad's nephew, a consular officer. It seemed entirely right. He was the gatekeeper between one nation and the next, and all she had seen of him these last weeks led her to believe he swung the gate open, wide.

'Partition and the bomb,' Harry said, interrupting her. 'The two of you are proof that humans can overcome everything.'

Overcome. Such an American word. What really did it mean? But she knew he meant it generously, so it seemed discourteous to throw the word back in his face with stories of a 'not right' foetus which her body had rejected, or the tears Sajjad wept after his first visit to his collapsed world in Delhi.

Instead she said, 'Sometimes I look at my son and think perhaps the less we have to "overcome" the more we feel aggrieved.'

The drifting sense of hopelessness that had taken over Raza's life after his second failed attempt at his exam had sharpened into self-pity these last weeks in which Sajjad had started taking him each morning to work at the soap factory where he was general manager, while all Raza's friends took the bus to their universities.

'At least let him work in the office building,' Hiroko had said, after the first day, when Raza came home filthy with machinery grime, and refused to wash his hands because the smell of soap made him sick.

'I've told him he will work in the factory until the day he decides to take his exam again. Don't you understand I want him to hate the work enough that he chooses the only way out? You just let him mope at home all day. Give him time, you said. Well, he's had time. Now please allow me to try my way. The exam is only a few weeks away.'

Hiroko was sufficiently worried about her son's state of torpor that she acceded, shaking her head against Raza's pleas to intervene with Sajjad on his behalf even as she made sure there was always a pile of ash and lemon-wedges next to the sink for Raza to scrub with in place of soap when he returned from the factory. She remembered acutely the stench of the munitions factory, how she carried it in her nostrils all through the day.

'I don't understand,' Harry said. 'He's incredibly smart. What's the problem?'

She tried to explain to him, as much as she understood from Raza's muttered comments, about words disappearing into bursts of light, fingers unable to hold on to a pen, and – worst of all – the brief flashes of clarity when the answers appeared in his mind, one fact leading inevitably to the other, so all he needed was to catch hold of the first one and the rest would follow like a row of dancers with arms interlocked – and somewhere in the journey from his mind to the pen the facts scattered, whirling apart from each other without discernible pattern.

'Is that it?' Harry said. He stood up, scrubbing at his knee where it was imprinted with the pattern of the rocks. 'If you'll excuse me, I need a word with your son.'

Hiroko watched Harry walk across to Raza and Sajjad, and then take Raza by the shoulder and draw him aside. She wished she believed in heaven so that she could know Konrad was watching this. Her eyes moved from her family members to the other Karachiwallas at ease on the beach. There was that wretched group of children who had danced around Raza earlier, tugging at the skin around their eyes while chanting, 'Chinese, Japanese, money, please . . .' until Harry had bellowed and sent them running. The children didn't bother her so much as Raza's inability to see their taunts as childish ignorance, without malevolence. She wondered if his acute sensitivity was the result of her anxiety during pregnancy communicating itself to him as he grew inside her.

Her eyes moved away from the children to the various women sitting on the beach. So many sleeves all the way to wrists instead of just part-way down the upper arm, and covered heads here and there. It made no sense to her. 'Islamisation' was a word everyone recognised as a political tool of a dictator and yet they still allowed their lives to be changed by it. She didn't worry for herself but Raza was still so unformed that it troubled her to think what the confusion of a still-forming nation might do to him.

'Will you walk into the sunset with your husband?' Sajjad said, coming up to her, and she took the hand he was holding out to her, grateful for the distraction, and stepped off the rocks just as Harry and Raza started to walk in the opposite direction, towards the water's edge.

'I haven't had a chance to give this to you yet,' Harry said, opening his shoulder bag and reaching inside. 'Though I still don't know why you want it.' He pulled out a transparent bag, which he placed in Raza's hands. Raza looked down at the cotton-wool-like objects squashed against each other and poked the bag tentatively with his finger.

'These are marshmallows?' A wave crashed a few metres away from him, but he barely registered the spray of cold water except to hold a hand protectively over the bag.

'Uh huh. Now are you going to tell me why I asked my daughter to carry them all the way from New York – in her hand luggage, by the way, so they wouldn't get completely squashed.' He'd told Kim they were for the young daughter of one of the consular staff, not wanting to see her reaction to the idea of a sixteen-year-old Pakistani who wanted marshmallows above all else from America.

'I've just always wondered what they were.' He turned the bag this way and that. 'They're in American comics a lot. Thank you, Uncle Harry.'

Harry watched the boy's face, so vibrant with hero worship it was almost an abstraction. No one had ever called him 'Uncle Harry' before, and until he met Raza he hadn't been conscious of regarding that as a loss.

'You going to share them with your girlfriend?'

Raza grinned, and it transformed him from a burdened boy to a quick, bright spark, filled with charm. The one ray of light these last few weeks – other than Uncle Harry, and that look of awe in the truck boy Abdullah's eyes – was the telephone romance he'd started up with Bilal's sister, Salma. He'd told no one about it until he whispered it in Uncle Harry's ear earlier in the day.

'You know who was asking me if you had a girlfriend?' Harry said conversationally, picking up a pebble and skimming it across the water. 'My daughter, Kim.' He watched Raza blush, and tried to imagine Kim with her black lipstick and her ripped T-shirts having

183

anything to say to this boy who had worn his cricketing whites to the beach. It's true, she had asked if he had a girlfriend, but it was a question that anticipated the no which followed and used that as a way to deflect Harry's praise of Raza – his intelligence, his fine manners.

'How is she? Is she well?' Raza said, as Harry knew he would, with the fine manners which would have Kim screaming with laughter. She'd be running through the waves now if she were here, dismissing with a toss of her head all these people who came to the beach for the sand and the air and didn't know what to do with their limbs in water. He missed her terribly, even though their recent interaction had consisted of little other than shouting matches and sulky silences.

His ex-wife's smug phone calls from Paris, where she was on holiday with her fiancé, had done nothing to brighten the situation either. 'One of us has to deal with real conflict every day, Harry, while the other one is playing boy's games in exotic locations of the world,' she said. 'I've earned my break from it.' As if he didn't know that his own mother did all the real parenting while his ex flitted from work to social engagements. Sometimes he wondered if she had moved to New York after the divorce simply because of the convenience of having Ilse there as permanent babysitter, with Uncle Willie as backup.

'Yeah, Kim's doing great,' he said to Raza. 'There was a while there, though, when I was really worried about her. Early adolescence, you know. Some girls get pimples, some get breasts.' He watched in some amusement as Raza blushed again. 'Kim got test anxiety.' Raza looked quizzically at him. 'It was the damnedest thing. She explained it to me once. She knew the answers to all the questions, right until the moment she sat down to take the exam. Luckily there was a teacher there who understood what was happening. Mrs O'Neill. Kim's personal angel. She taught Kim certain strategies for overcoming it.' He was only slightly twisting the truth – Kim didn't really have test anxiety, but Harry's colleague in Islamabad, Steve, had once spent a drunken evening toasting his ninth-grade teacher Mrs O'Neill and explaining in great and boring length the ways in which she'd helped him overcome his habit of failure – instilling in him the belief that any problem could be defeated if you only had the right strategy.

Test anxiety. It was a real thing with a real name. And Uncle Harry's daughter had it, too. Raza caught the other man's arm.

'Do you remember them? Any of the strategies?'

Harry nodded.

'I'll teach you,' he said. He'd have to call Steve later. 'Tomorrow. We'll get your mother to help you. And once you've crossed that hurdle, the world opens up to you, Raza Konrad Ashraf. America is full of universities who'd love to add a bright, inquisitive Pakistani to their student body. You do well in their entrance exams and they'll want you enough to pay for you to go there. I'll help you out with all the application stuff. How does that sound?' For a moment he wondered if he should have discussed this with Hiroko and Sajjad first, but he couldn't imagine they'd be anything but grateful for the suggestion, given the high premium placed on an American-university education in the middle-class homes of Pakistan.

Raza nodded, trying to appear composed.

'Cool,' he said.

'Cool.' Harry raised his palm so Raza could slap a high five on it. 'And then you and Kim can meet.'

'Kim.' Raza had never said her name out loud before but the test anxiety created a bond between them. 'It's a good name.'

'Yeah,' said Harry. Long before the CIA there had been Kipling and a boy astride a cannon. 'I don't know how you and Kim will get along but I'm pretty sure you and America will like each other. Forget like. Love at first sight – that's how it was for America and me. I was twelve when I went there, and I knew right away that I'd found home.'

'Aba says you loved Delhi.'

'I did. I truly did. But in India I would always have been an Englishman. I didn't see that when I was growing up, but it's true. In America, everyone can be American. That's the beauty of the place.'

'Not me,' Raza said. 'You look like Clint Eastwood and John Fitzgerald Kennedy. So of course you can be American. I look like not this and not that.'

185

'Everyone,' Harry said firmly, knowing it would hurt Raza if he laughed at the incongruous comparisons. 'Everyone can be American. Even you. I swear it.'

'America.' Raza rolled the word off his tongue.

Harry looked across at the dreamy-eyed young man with a gift for language, an ache for something to believe in, and features that would go unnoticed in many Central Asian states and parts of Afghanistan, too, and a thought flickered across his mind.

Just for an instant, and then he brushed it away.

19

He called three times before she was the one to answer the phone instead of her mother.

'Hello, Fatima?' she said when she picked up. 'I have those notes for you. Wait, let me pick up the extension in the other room.' He held on a few seconds, grinning to himself while running his hands over the unopened marshmallow packet. When she spoke again, her voice was throaty and sarcastic, nothing like the earlier tone of ordinariness. 'How nice of you to interrupt your busy life and call me, Raza.'

'Salma,' he said, with that melting tone of adoration which he knew she loved. 'Don't be like that. I was at the beach with Uncle Harry – I only just got home.'

'Oh, well, if you'd rather be with your American,' she said, but he could tell she was impressed.

'I asked him to bring you a present from New York.' He pressed a yielding marshmallow through the packaging, and wondered if Salma's breasts would feel anything like this.

'You didn't!' she said, sounding a little faint. And then her voice changed. 'You told him about me?'

'Of course not. I said it was for me. Do you want it? If you do, you'll have to meet me. Properly.'

'What does "properly" mean?'

He hesitated a moment. This was delicate. But any American university would be proud to have him! Kim Burton also had test anxiety! His worth glimmered unexpectedly through the room.

'It means . . . you know. I'm tired of you ignoring me every time I come to your house.' Which was seldom, these days, but his mood was such he didn't allow himself to be pulled down by that.

'And what do you think my brother would do if he knew his friend was meeting me to . . . you know?'

'I don't mean "you know" like that, Salma. We've been talking every day for over a month now. How can you doubt that I respect you?'

This line met with no further success than it had on every previous occasion he'd tried it. Clearly another tack was necessary.

'You know, you'll regret this attitude when I'm gone.'

'Gone where? To the soap factory?'

It was the first time she'd ever mentioned she knew where he went with his father each morning, and on any other day it would have devastated him. But now he just smiled.

'I'm going to university there. In America. Uncle Harry says he'll help me with the admissions, and make sure they even pay me to go. That's the kind of thing they do there.'

'I don't believe you.'

'It's true. Meet me and I'll tell you all about it.'

'Why are you keeping on with this? I'm not going to meet you. What would happen to my reputation if someone found out?'

'What do I have to do, send my mother over with a proposal? I'll do it. You know I will. Come on, Salma, marry me and we'll go to America together.' He only meant it as a way of indicating he would never behave dishonourably with her, didn't think her fast, but in the silence that followed he realised, sickeningly, that she was taking him far more seriously than he'd intended.

'Raza, my parents will never let me marry you,' she said finally, while he was trying to think of a way to extricate himself from the position he'd talked himself into.

He smiled, relieved, extending his arm along the sofa-back with an air of well-being which could have rivalled that of James Burton in his Delhi home.

'I don't know why age difference is such a big deal. You're only two years older than me. But how can we fight against tradition?'

'It's not about age. It's your mother. Everyone knows about your mother.'

'What about her?'

'Nagasaki. The bomb. No one will give their daughter to you in marriage unless they're desperate, Raza. You could be deformed. How do we know you're not?'

Raza sat forward, gripping the phone tightly.

'Deformed? I'm not. Salma, your father is my doctor. I'm not deformed.'

'Maybe not in any way we can see. But there's no guarantee. You might have something you can pass on to your children. I've seen the pictures. Of babies born in Nagasaki after the bomb.'

'I've never even been to Nagasaki. I was born twenty years after the bomb. Please. You don't want to talk to me any more, OK, say that. But don't say this. Don't say you think I'm deformed.'

'You need to know. This is how people think about you. Go to America, darling.' The endearment – in English – came out clumsily. 'And don't tell anyone there the truth. Goodbye, Raza. Please don't call again.'

The curved receiver of the telephone gripped Raza beneath the chin as the tone of disconnection pulsed against his ear. Twilight cast the shadows of branches across the window, distorting the symmetry of the iron grille with its curlicues inspired by treble clefs.

As he placed the receiver carefully on its cradle, first pausing to wipe off the tears that had run down to the mouthpiece, he realised he had been waiting a long time for confirmation that he was . . . not an outsider, no, not quite that. Not when he'd lived in this moholla his whole life, had scraped and scabbed his knees on every street within a one-mile radius. Not an outsider, just a tangent. In contact with the world of his moholla, but not intersecting it. After all, intersections were created from shared stories and common histories, from marriages and the possibility of marriages between neighbouring families – from this intersecting world Raza Konrad Ashraf was cast out.

He walked out into the courtyard, deeply inhaling the sharp evening breeze, and shook his head at his father's invitation to sit, sit, listen to Sikandar's letter from Delhi, before heading out into the street, deserted except for a feral tomcat, which squatted on its haunches and hissed at him until he turned and walked in the opposite direction, nodding as if to indicate the cat was a guide, not a threat.

She'd marry Sikandar's son if he proposed.

The thought – though absurd and untrue – came to mind as a statement of fact. Yes, Salma's parents would let her marry his cousin Altamash, Sikandar's youngest son, named for the eldest of the Ashraf brothers. They'd let her marry Altamash even though he was Indian and poor and they knew nothing about him worth knowing except that he was Sajjad Ashraf's nephew, Raza's cousin. Raza hunched over, arms crossed around his body, causing a woman watching from her balcony to wonder if the strangely arresting young man had a stomach ache.

In the neighbourhood, people still asked about Altamash, though it was five years since he had come to Karachi, accompanying his mother, who hoped the middle-class neighbourhood in which Sajjad lived would net her a wife with a sizeable dowry for Altamash's eldest unmarried brother. Altamash was the only one of the Delhi cousins near Raza in age, and the two boys had fallen upon each other in a rough-and-tumble fight of instant adoration when they met. But when they went out together it was Altamash, not Raza, who everyone took for Sajjad's son.

And then there was that Friday afternoon, a group of boys making their way from mosque to cricket ground, when Altamash had turned angrily on Bilal after he hailed down a rickshaw and, pointing at the two cousins, asked the driver to play the 'guess which one of these two boys is not Pakistani' game which had so entertained him over the past few days. It's not funny, Altamash explained. In India when they want to insult Muslims they call us Pakistani. Bilal had laughed out loud. In Pakistan when they want to insult Muhajirs they call us Indian, he replied. The two boys had slapped each other on the shoulder while Raza stood awkwardly beside them, sliding the skullcap off his head and trying to understand why such injustice should be seen as humour.

He'd never known until now what it was in Bilal's game that had upset him so much, just as he'd never really interrogated his need to keep hidden his Japanese vocabulary. But in that moment, unable to duck the knowledge that more than anything else Salma pitied him, it was inescapable: he didn't fit this neighbourhood. A failure, a soap-factory worker, a bomb-marked mongrel. He spat the words out, over and over: Raza Konrad Ashraf. Konrad. His lips drew back from his teeth as he said it. He wanted to reach into his own name and rip out the man whose death was a foreign body wedged beneath the two Pakistani wings of his name.

Hands clenched, he turned on to a street lined with compact shopfronts, and saw the familiar sight of young boys playing tape-ball cricket in the middle of the road, cries of 'O-ho, Khalifa!' greeting the captain, who had just promoted himself up the order. A car came zipping down the road, swerving away from the boys and the wickets, windows down and the sound of the beautiful teenage girl singing the new hit 'Boom! Boom!' spilling out on to the street. A few months ago he and his class-fellows would have been part of that cricket match, or one near by . . . as he thought that he saw two of those former class-fellows strolling towards him, pulling the paper wrapping away from kabab rolls. They were both studying to be engineers and from the gesticulations of their hands he knew they were discussing something they had learnt that day, using kabab rolls to stand in for – what? Aeroplanes? Currents? Railway tracks? He knew nothing of the language in which their days were now steeped. One of the boys glanced in his direction, and Raza backed into the shadows. You could be a bomb-marked mongrel or a failure but not both. Not for a second, both.

And then he thought a single word. America.

He exhaled slowly, unclenching his hands. Yes, he would go there. Uncle Harry would make it happen. None of the rest of this mattered while he had the promise of America.

20

Raza stood in the doorway of his parents' room, listening to his father's groans of pain with a mixture of concern and guilt.

'Oh Allah – the Beneficent, the Merciful – it is this you tried to spare us!'

Raza didn't know what Allah had to do with throwing Harry Burton out of the house the previous night, but he did know that he was the reason his father had acted so against his own hospitable nature that he was suffering physical agony over it.

He still couldn't believe how things had turned out. The evening had started magnificently – it was dinner in the courtyard to celebrate Raza's decision to retake his exams, armed with Uncle Harry's strategies for test anxiety. Raza had taken advantage of the cool February breeze to put on his cashmere jacket, which he felt compelled, halfway through dinner, to offer to 'return' to Harry. Uncle Harry said no, of course – and, winking, added, 'Just because I stole your shoes that once doesn't mean I'm going to run off with your entire wardrobe.'

Everyone was so happy, so filled with laughter – and his parents both extended their hospitality so far as to drink large quantities from the bottle Uncle Harry had brought for Hiroko, even though it was clear to Raza from a single sniff that the liquid was badly fermented. Failure was a world away on a night like this, bombs an entire universe apart.

But after dinner Raza asked if it was true that in New York the city lights were so bright you couldn't see the stars, because if so he'd take a picture of Karachi's night sky with him to university and pin it on to the ceiling of his room.

Then he'd turned casually to his parents, who were looking askance at him, and said, 'Oh yes, I forgot to tell you. Uncle Harry's going to get an American university to pay for me to go there.'

That's when things started to fall apart. Uncle Harry said well no, that wasn't what he'd said at all – though there was no reason Raza shouldn't get into university if he managed to do well in his exams. Of course, funding wouldn't be easy – but he'd be sure to get Raza one of those books which detailed all the American universities and their admission and financial-aid policies and procedures.

It took Raza a few moments to realise he wasn't joking.

'But you said . . .?' He turned to his father. 'He said!'

'Come on, Raza.' Harry leaned forward, frowning. 'I said I'd teach you strategies to combat test anxiety. That was the only promise I made and I've delivered on that, haven't I? Well, haven't I?'

'Those stupid exercises won't do any good,' Raza sulked.

'There's a difference between stupid and simple. Grow up. Christ, it's ridiculous the way this country makes you believe that if you know the right people everything is possible. Do you really think I can snap my fingers and get you into university?'

'You said, "I'll help you out with all the application stuff." Those were your words.' He had worn them on his heart these last few weeks.

'Well, of course I'll help you figure out the admissions process. Of course I'll do that. And I'll give you any information the Embassy has about standardised tests.' He spread his hands generously. 'I'll even look over your personal statement. There's nothing more than that I can do. If I'd meant anything more – if I'd given any kind of guarantee – I'd have told you there's no need to retake the Islamic-studies exam. American universities won't need that. But no, you need to retake it in case you have to fall back on higher education here. I never told you to rely on getting to America.'

Raza was horrified by the tears that started to leak from his eyes, and further horrified when Sajjad slammed down his glass on the table and turned on Harry.

'You Burtons! You're just like your father, Henry, with your implied promises that are only designed to bind us to you. He used

193

to tell me there was no one more capable than me – I didn't understand that meant I was the most willing and uncomplaining servant he'd known.' Some long-buried outrage, brought to the surface by the crushing disappointment on his son's face, made him stand up and point towards the door. 'We Ashrafs don't need any more Burtons in our lives. Please leave my family alone.'

Now Raza watched his father lying in bed with his hands pressed to either side of his head as though he thought he might be able to squeeze out the memory of yesterday, and wondered why it was so much easier for him to make things worse than better. On a sudden inspiration he bounded from the room into the living room, unplugged Sajjad's most beloved possession – his tape recorder – and brought it into his parents' room along with a cassette of sarangi music which he had bought for his father yesterday with his wage from the soap factory. He had thought he would present it to his father after dinner last night, but Harry Burton's departure had destroyed the necessary mood of festivity.

Raza plugged in the tape recorder, inserted the cassette and pressed play, mouth already forming into a smile in anticipation of Sajjad's delighted response. But at the first sound of the stringed instrument, Sajjad cried out, 'Turn it off!' and Raza, startled, slapped down on the stop button, the force of his hand unbalancing the tape recorder from its precarious position at the edge of the bedside table and toppling it on to the floor with a sickening crash.

Sajjad turned his head, saw the pieces of the tape recorder on the floor and looked at his son only long enough to say, 'Raza . . .' in a tone of total despair before turning on his side, his back towards the boy.

Hiroko, entering the room with a piece of toast, saw the broken machine and made a noise of grief.

'It's broken,' she said. 'Oh, Raza. Your father's tape recorder.'

Raza backed out of the room.

'I'm sorry,' he said, but Hiroko was already bending over her husband and telling him to eat some toast.

'I'm dying,' Sajjad said. 'I'm dead already. I'm in hell.'

'If this is hell why am I here?' Hiroko demanded, a hand on her hip.

Sajjad opened one eye.

'You've come to rescue me?' he said hopefully.

'Yes,' she said. 'With toast. Eat it and stop complaining, you silly drunkard.'

But Raza didn't hear any part of this conversation. He was in his room, stuffing the entire wad of his earnings from the soap factory into the pocket of his kurta, an expression of resoluteness on his face.

An hour later he was elbowing his way off a 'yellow devil' minibus and heading for the truck-stand by Sohrab Goth's Bara Market.

Before the Soviet invasion of Afghanistan, Raza knew from the Pathan school-van driver, Sohrab Goth was a village on the outskirts of Karachi, where nomadic Afghans lived in makeshift homes during the winter months when their lands in Afghanistan yielded nothing but barrenness and the perennial nature of Karachi's demands – for labour, for goods – beckoned men from their mountains and plains towards the sea. But now Sohrab Goth had sprawled into Karachi, a rapidly expanding part of the city's 'informal sector', serving everyone from the policemen whose meagre salaries left them dependent on bribes to factory-owners looking for cheap labour to smugglers who needed markets and middlemen for shiny new technologies that reflected the gleaming eyes of teenagers searching for some way to make things up to their fathers.

Raza kept one hand jammed into the pocket of his kurta as he walked through Sohrab Goth, clutching the bundle of money, wondering whether he should simply go back to the factory next week instead of wasting his time over another attempt at the exam. The belief that Harry's strategies for dealing with test anxiety would work now seemed as foolish as the belief that any American university would pay for him to study there. Perhaps he just needed to accept his fate. Failure. Bomb-marked mongrel. No talisman to replace the 'America' wrenched from his grasp and stamped beneath Uncle Harry's heel.

There was no one at the truck-stand beside Bara Market, but in the adjoining plot a child picking through the garbage and slinging what could be recycled into a cloth bag on his back nodded when

195

Raza asked for 'Abdullah with the dead Soviet on his truck' and directed him towards a squatter settlement on the other side of Bara Market.

Raza had never walked through slums before, and the fastidiousness that was his Tanaka inheritance almost turned him around as he made his way gingerly through the narrow unpaved lanes and the stench of a rivulet of water announced itself as sewage. But he pushed forward, wondering how he was supposed to find Abdullah in this densely populated gathering of refugee homes. Bare wires looped dangerously low, attached by hooks to the electricity lines beside which this tenement had sprung up. From a distance they had looked like fissures in the sky, revealing the darkness beyond. Raza tried not to think about sanitation as a man walked past him with two buckets filled with brackish water.

'Abdullah . . . the truck with the dead Soviet,' he kept repeating to the men who walked past (the women, covered-up, he felt it best to ignore). Some shrugged, others ignored him, but there were enough men who knew who he meant to direct him through the maze of homes – the sturdier ones of mud, the rest flimsy constructions of jute and sackcloth – until he came to a mud hut with a rope bed outside it on which Abdullah was seated next to a very young girl, his finger moving slowly over the words in a picture book, his mouth making encouraging sounds as she slowly read out the syllables and pieced them into words.

'Abdullah?'

The boy looked up and smiled.

'Raza Hazara!' he said without any hesitation, as if he'd revisited the memory of their meeting so often that he'd kept Raza's image sharp in his mind through the intervening weeks. That look in his eyes – the gleam of awe that replicated the one with which he'd watched Harry Burton kneel in front of Raza – made Raza stand up straighter, reshape his expression from that of a boy who needed help with bargaining to that of a man condescending to stop by and greet a young acquaintance.

Abdullah touched the girl's arm and whispered something and she slid off the bed and ran into the mud house.

'Your sister?' Raza said.

196

'Yes, but not by blood. I live with her family here. We're from the same village.'

Raza nodded, wondering where Abdullah's real family was.

'I didn't know if I'd find you here. I'm glad I did.'

The boy seemed genuinely pleased by that.

'I'm glad, too. Afridi's taken the truck to Peshawar but I had to stay here to look after the women. My brother, whose house this is, has gone away for a few days. Sit.'

Raza picked up the picture book as he sat. There had been something intriguing in the concentration of the girl's face as she translated shapes into sound; he had always slipped into syntax and vocabulary with such ease that he was unable to see it as any kind of accomplishment.

'Did you go to school?' Abdullah asked.

'What? Today?'

'Don't be funny.' Abdullah took the book from Raza's hand and placed it reverently aside. 'Ever. Before this.'

It had never occurred to Raza that someone might imagine him uneducated. He wondered if it were because in this boy's world education was never assumed, or if something in the lexicon of the van driver who had taught him Pashto revealed itself as unlettered.

'Yes,' he said, finding this was not something he was prepared to lie about. 'Before this.'

'I used to come first in class,' Abdullah said, leaning back against the mud wall. 'You lived in the north?'

The young girl pushed aside the cloth which acted as doorway and Raza had a brief glimpse of movement – which he understood to be female, and various – within the house, before he quickly looked away. The girl handed him a cup of green tea, smiled shyly at his words of thanks and ran back inside.

Raza swallowed hard.

'I don't want to offend you, but I can't tell you anything about my life before I came here. I made an oath. When the Soviets killed my father.' Abdullah said nothing, placing a hand on Raza's shoulder. His kindness was shaming, but it was too late to stop. 'I don't even speak my own language any more, only this borrowed tongue. I will not speak the language of my father, I will not speak

197

my father's name, or the name of my village, or claim my kinship to any other Hazara until the day the last Soviet leaves Afghanistan. And I will be the one to drive out that last Soviet.'

In the silence that followed, Raza wondered if Abdullah had watched the television show that had gripped him a few months earlier, with Kashmiris and Indians in place of Hazaras and Soviets; and if yes, what was the price of lying in this place where codes filled the vacuum where there should have been laws?

Abdullah tightened his grip on Raza's shoulder.

'We may fight over which one of us gets to drive out that last Soviet. But until that fight, we're brothers.'

Raza grinned.

'Brother Abdullah, will you help me buy something? I have a feeling the traders here know they can't cheat you.'

Abdullah crossed his arms.

'Does "something" come from the poppy fields?'

'What? No. No!'

Abdullah smiled at Raza's vehemence.

'Oh. The other "something". Wait here.' He called out, 'I'm coming in,' and went into the hut.

Raza traced the outline of the bundle of ten-rupee notes in his pocket as he looked around. Hardly anyone had looked twice at him since he'd stepped off the bus. It was a curious feeling, almost disappointing. He had seen one boy with features that looked as though they could have been cast from the same mould as his and had wanted to cry out, 'Impostor.' He ran his hand over his face. Raza Hazara. He ran the name backwards and forwards in his mind. Razahazara. Arazahazar. There was a balance to the name. More balance certainly than in Raza Konrad Ashraf. He took another sip of tea and felt glad he was wearing his oldest, most worn kurta shalwar.

'Here.' Abdullah came out cradling something, a piece of cloth covering it. 'Hold out your arms.' Raza complied, worried there was something alive under there.

It was cold metal and smooth wood, heavier than he'd expected from the ease with which Abdullah carried it. He ran his fingers along its straight lines, leaned forward and felt the curve of the magazine jut against his stomach. Abdullah plucked the cloth off, like a magician, and the AK-47 gleamed – polished steel and plywood.

'You haven't held one before,' Abdullah said.

Raza shook his head, careful not to let his wandering hands approach the trigger.

'You can't drive out the last Soviet without knowing how to use this,' Abdullah said, lifting the semi-automatic from Raza's hand, and bracing it against his shoulder. He looked heroic. Smiling jauntily, he held it out to Raza.

Raza Konrad Ashraf wiped his hands on his shalwar and stood up. But it was Raza Hazara who took the AK-47 in his arms and learnt how everything about a man could change with that simple act. He hoisted the semi-automatic in the air, feeling the thud of it against his shoulder as he imitated Abdullah's stance, and Abdullah cheered, and Raza knew, he *knew*, how it felt to be Amitabh Bachchan or Clint Eastwood A group of children ran on to the path, as if Raza's handling of the AK-47 had set off a beacon, and Raza pivoted, pointed the gun at them and laughed as they ran off, squealing in terrified delight.

Abdullah allowed him to pose and pivot for a while, then took the gun from him and within seconds had it dismantled.

'I'll show you how to put it back together, if you tell me what you were doing with the American.'

Raza picked up the magazine section of the gun, and tried to twirl it casually but ended up dropping it on to the ground. Abdullah swatted him on the leg, picked up the magazine and ran the cloth over it in slow, gliding motions.

'I can't tell you what I was doing with the American,' Raza said, in an attempt to recover some ground. 'But there are ways of driving out Soviets without directly handing Kalashnikovs. If you see what I mean.' He settled back on the rope bed, leaning on his elbows, pleased with Abdullah's look of near reverence.

'Does he speak Pashto? Your American?'

'A little. Mostly we speak in English.'

'You speak English?'

Raza shrugged, as though it were nothing.

'Will you teach me?'

Languages had always come easily to Raza, but that didn't mean he was unaware of the weight attached to language lessons. His mother would never have met Konrad Weiss (the German man she wanted to marry! The thought didn't get any less strange over the years) if she hadn't taught German to Yoshi Watanabe's nephew. And she would not have gone to India to find the Burtons if not for Konrad Weiss. In India, it was language lessons that brought Sajjad and Hiroko to the same table, overturning the separateness that would otherwise have defined their relationship. And all the tenderest of his recollections of childhood were bound up in his mother's gift of languages to him – those crosswords she set for him late each night when he was growing up, the secrets they could share without lowering their voices, the ideas they could express to each other in words particular to specific languages ('no wabi-sabi' they would sometimes say to each other, when rejecting a poem or a painting lacking in harmony that Sajjad held up for praise, and it would amaze Raza how his father still hadn't quite been able to understand the concepts of wabi and sabi which seemed as natural to Raza as an understanding of why being udaas in Urdu was something quite different to feeling melancholic in English).

'Walnut,' he said to Abdullah.

Abdullah repeated the English word slowly.

'What does it mean?'

Raza told him and Abdullah threw back his head, laughing.

'I've never understood why they call us that.'

'Because a walnut looks like a little brain, you witless Pashtun.'

Abdullah smiled broadly.

'If you weren't my brother I'd kill you for saying that.'

'I am your brother. And your teacher. Bring me a pencil and paper. We'll start with the alphabet.'

Abdullah stood up, gathering the pieces of the AK-47 in his arms as he did so.

'You teach me, and I'll give you one of these free of charge. No one notices if one or two go missing. The next shipment, I'll get you one.'

Raza held back his questions, and his objections. How could you tell a boy who had promised you an AK-47 that all you wanted from him were the bargaining skills needed to procure a cheap but top-quality cassette-player so that Sajjad Ali Ashraf could listen to the sound of the sarangi reverberating through the house, encapsulating the principles of wabi-sabi and evoking udaas?

21

Harry Burton tilted his whisky glass towards his mouth and wondered, not for the first time since his arrival in Pakistan, if the paper napkins wrapped around the glasses were designed to prevent condensation forming and turning fingers clammy or to keep the contents of glasses masked in the capital of the Islamic Republic of Pakistan. He unwrapped the glass and used the napkin to wipe the drip of sweat which was meandering from his temples down to his cheek with the sluggishness that seemed to infect everything in this stultifying heat.

He looked briefly towards the glass doors which separated him from the bulk of the party crowded into the air-conditioned living room of whichever influential businessman's home this was – somewhere in the course of the evening he had shaken hands with someone who declared himself 'your host', but all he could recall of the man was the awkwardly soft plumpness of his palm. The air-conditioning inside was tempting, but the press of people was not. He was happier, on balance, out in the garden with the smell of kababs and smoke drifting over from the driveway, which was lined with buffet tables and perspiring men cooking meat on skewers. He could close his eyes, concentrate on the smell, and remember accompanying Sajjad to the Old City in his childhood.

Sajjad. Harry sighed deeply. It had been four months since that dinner in the Ashraf courtyard when Sajjad had asked him to leave and Hiroko had walked him to the front door, and pressed his hands tightly in hers.

'Raza's still a child in many ways – he gets too caught up in the stories he makes up about his life. And as for Sajjad – his anger doesn't know how to last beyond a few minutes. Call us next time you're coming to Karachi. And don't bring any more sake.' She kissed him on the cheek before he walked out into the emptiness of the street.

He'd had no intention then of staying away so long, but there had been no opportunity of late even to consider his personal life. On the subject of which – there, walking out into the garden, was a beautiful woman, who held his gaze just long enough to signal interest.

'Look away, Burton,' said a voice at his elbow. 'She's on the payroll of the I-Shall-Interfere.'

The woman looked over her shoulder at Harry, who immediately turned his back to her, though not without a curse that contained an irritation more professional than personal.

'I prefer It's-Sorta-Islamic,' he said to the stocky blond man standing next to him.

His colleague Steve raised a glass to the comment. One of Steve's pleasures in life was to come up with alternative names for the Inter-Services Intelligence agency.

'What do you think?' Steve said. 'Does the ISI do a better job of spying on us than we do on them? You think they know yet they might soon have Israel to thank for supplying arms to their Holy Warriors?'

In Harry's mind, there was a map of the world with countries appearing as mere outlines, waiting to be shaded in with stripes of red, white and blue as they were drawn into the strictly territorial battle of the Afghans versus the Soviets in which no one else claimed a part. When he arrived in Islamabad, it had been a three-way affair: Egypt provided the Soviet-made arms, America provided financing, training and technological assistance, and Pakistan provided the base for training camps. But now, the war was truly international. Arms from Egypt, China and – soon – Israel. Recruits from all over the Muslim world. Training camps in Scotland! There was even a rumour that India might be willing to sell on some of the arms they had bought from their Russian friends – even though it might prove to be little more than a rumour Harry couldn't help enjoying the idea of Pakistan, India and Israel working together in America's war.

Here was internationalism, powered by capitalism. Different worlds moving from their separate spheres into a new kind of geometry. With a mix of satisfaction, irony and despair he raised his glass to the ghost of Konrad Weiss.

Across the country in Karachi, Hiroko Ashraf was also thinking of Konrad as she lay in bed, reading a letter from Yoshi Watanabe which said he was retiring as principal of the school housed in what was once Azalea Manor. After the war, Konrad's former tenant, Kagawa-san, had claimed the property as his own – hadn't he been living there for years just prior to the bombing? Whose house was it if not his own? And though Yoshi had written to Ilse to inform her of what was happening, no Weiss or Burton family member attempted to contest Kagawa-san's claim. But when the Kagawa children had inherited the property in 1955 they had asked Yoshi, who became a teacher after the war, to run the International School they were establishing on the premises in memory of Konrad Weiss. It was the only indication they ever gave of any guilt about those final months of Konrad's life when they crossed the street to avoid him.

I hope the new principal will continue the tradition of taking the schoolchildren to the International Cemetery where Konrad's rock is buried.

Hiroko set down the letter, pressing her hand against her back. One day perhaps she would take Raza to Nagasaki. And Sajjad, too. She glanced at the sleeping form of her husband beside her as she picked up the photograph Yoshi had sent of himself standing in the grounds of Azalea Manor with a group of schoolchildren kneeling in front of him. This was the group about to set off to America for an exchange visit with a school near Los Alamos. She wondered how Raza would interact with a group of Japanese schoolchildren of near his own age. It didn't bother her in the least to know she would always be a foreigner in Pakistan – she had no interest in belonging to anything as contradictorily insubstantial and damaging as a nation – but this didn't stop her from recognising how Raza flinched every time a Pakistani asked him where he was from

Sometimes Konrad entered her mind as an abstraction, and she wondered what their lives would have been if he'd lived. Would they have visited James and Ilse in Delhi, and would she and Sajjad have met and felt a glimmer of the life that might otherwise have been . . . ? No, of course not. Of course not. Nothing was inevitable in that way, no relationship, no confluence of events – some things just ended up seeming that way. She rested her fingers on Sajjad's mouth, one fingertip lightly scratching at the softness of his silver-grey moustache.

No, nothing was inevitable, everything could have been different. Their daughter might have lived. The one she miscarried in the fifth month, the one the bomb killed (the doctor never told her precisely what was so wrong with the foetus, she only said some miscarriages were acts of mercy). She would have been thirty-five now. As the years went on the deaths of Konrad and her father had receded from her heart, but the child who she had known only as a stirring within, a series of hiccups and kicks – her loss still remained, occasionally rising up in a great wave of anger which Hiroko never knew how to express, where to place; only the company of her son would allow it to pass. If the first had been born – Hiroko thought of her as Hana after the bright-red name Konrad had seen frozen beneath the ice – there would have been no Raza. Somehow she knew that to be true.

The front door opened, setting up a cross-breeze which rustled the leaves in the courtyard, and Hiroko smiled at the perfect timing.

'Where are you coming from, my prince?' she said, meeting her son halfway across the courtyard.

Raza touched his hand to her cheek.

'I told you I'd be late. You haven't been worrying, have you?'

Something in him had opened up these last few weeks, releasing the sweetness of his boyhood. Sajjad thought it was merely the relief of sitting for his exams once more and finding that Harry Burton's strategies for combating test anxiety really did allow his pen to fly across the page with an ease that bordered on disdain, but Hiroko had seen the openness begin well before last month's exams, and suspected that it, rather than Harry Burton's advice, had

205

allowed Raza to walk into the exam hall with confidence and walk out in triumph.

'I've been looking at that book of American universities,' she said. Sher Mohammed the rickshaw driver had delivered the book to them just days after Sajjad had told Harry to leave their house; Hiroko had insisted Raza write Harry a note of thanks – he had, spending more time over the letter than any of the love notes he had written to Salma during the course of their romance, and was so relieved it was almost embarrassing when Uncle Harry called from Islamabad to say he hoped the book helped and that they'd talk more about university the next time he was in Karachi.

Raza waved a hand in dismissal.

'It's so complicated, all that applying and tests and recommendations.' He wouldn't fool himself again into thinking an American university was a possibility for him – particularly not after he'd looked at the financial-aid forms and realised just how much money he'd need to ask for.

'All right.' Hiroko was more relieved than she'd admit to know he wasn't planning to leave the country. 'So you'll go to university here. Good. Later on, postgraduate, if you want to go abroad then maybe we can find a way.'

Raza hesitated, then put his arms around her.

'I'll make you proud,' he said, his hand resting by habit on what he knew to be the space between her burns.

'And what does that mean?' she said, pulling back. 'You smile and laugh these days, Raza Konrad Ashraf, and never get angry, and this is starting to worry me very much. Where do you go every day? I met Bilal this morning. He says he hasn't seen you in weeks.'

Raza's arms dropped away from her.

'If you want me to get angry, this is the right way to go about it. Bilal and all the others are busy with their university lives and I've made new friends. I'm happy. Don't spoil it.' He stepped back, bowed – which always made her smile, and didn't fail this time – and turned to walk into his room, leaping up as he went, his fingers straining towards the star-printed sky.

22

For months now, Raza had been living two lives. In one, he was plain Raza Ashraf, getting plainer each day as his friends' lives marched forward into university and he remained the failed student, the former factory worker, the boy marked by the bomb. In the other, he was Raza Hazara, the man who would not speak his language – or speak of his family or past, not even to other Hazaras – until he had driven the last Soviet out of Afghanistan, the man for whom an American took off his own shoes, which could only signal that somehow, in some way – though Raza would only look mysterious when questioned about it – he was of significance to the CIA (every American in Pakistan was CIA, of course).

While Raza Ashraf's greatest pride came from the joy with which his father turned on his new cassette-player from Sohrab Goth every evening after work, Raza Hazara learnt to measure pride in the decreasing number of seconds it took him to take down and reassemble an AK-47. Raza Ashraf spent more and more time alone, locked in a world of books and dreams, while Raza Hazara was greeted with cries of delight each time he entered the slums of Sohrab Goth to teach English to an ever-expanding group of students. Raza Hazara never had to duck his head forward so his hair would hide his features.

It was exhilarating, it was thrilling – it was wearying.

As he spent an increasing amount of time with the Afghans in Sohrab Goth, Raza found, surprisingly, that he missed his own life. He missed a world free of guns and war and occupied homelands. He missed being able to answer any question about his life without thinking twice about how best to construct a lie. He missed a world less fraught about honour and family than this world of men who recited poetry about mountains. He missed women, though he'd hardly ever thought of them as being a significant presence in his life.

So some days, weeks even, he stayed in Nazimabad, played cricket with the neighbourhood boys, studied for his exam. And found that each time he started to worry about what would happen in the examination hall he needed only to bring to mind the memory of assembling an AK-47, that satisfying *click* as the piece came together, and all his anxieties would dissipate. Then he would be restless to return to the life of the Hazara once more, and he'd take the now familiar bus route to Sohrab Goth to find Abdullah – and in his absence, any one of the Afghans who now welcomed him as a respected teacher – and if queried about his long absence he'd give that same mysterious smile which he directed at all enquiries about the American who gave him the shoes off his feet.

But he knew there was no living in two worlds, not for any length of time. And the day he walked out of the examination hall, knowing he'd performed to excellence, it was entirely obvious which world he was going to give up. Who chooses borrowed dreams over the dreams they've grown up with? The dream Raza had thought he'd lost – of excelling academically, of feeling knowledge propel him forward through the world – had become possible once more. The Intermediate exams had demanded little more than exercises in memorisation – but beyond was another world, of following clues and making connections, of analysis and argument. He didn't need America! He would be a lawyer, as his father had always wanted. All those months of thinking he would never get into law college had made the prospect of studying law exciting for the first time.

He didn't see quite how much his newly acquired confidence and the re-emergence of his love for learning owed to the hours he had spent in the shady patch in Sohrab Goth where he conducted his English classes, with Afghan boys of different ages sitting cross-legged on the ground before him, riveted by every word he said as though it were a promise of a previously unimagined future; but even so, he felt, as he sauntered from the examination hall, a great burst of affection towards Abdullah, who had made possible the life of Raza Hazara, and then the thought that he was planning to simply vanish from the life of the young Afghan without explanation or words of farewell struck him as a travesty in a way that his daily lies to Abdullah were not.

Thinking all this, he was unusually preoccupied – unusually for Raza Hazara, that is – as he sat with Abdullah at a kerbside eating place favoured by truck drivers, eating chapli kababs. He recalled Uncle Harry pointing out a similarly constructed 'restaurant' as Harry had called it (and though Raza knew that a restaurant was grand, and that this was merely a 'hotel', he had picked up the American's usage, never considering the possibility that he knew the names of things in Karachi better than Harry did) – Harry had said he loved the way the absence of an outer wall made it possible to imagine passers-by might trip over their own feet on the narrow bustling pavement, fall into a chair inside the restaurant, and simply stay on for a meal with whoever was already sitting around the table. But as Raza sat across from Abdullah he wished he didn't have to look at the world jostling around, which only served to remind him that his presence in it was a lie. Today the exam results had been announced. Raza had done as well as he'd expected. And the time for choosing one life over the other suddenly seemed to be at hand.

Afridi, the truck driver, walked up to their table – he'd been involved in a protracted conversation with a group of men outside – took hold of Raza's chair-back and jerked it down a few inches, laughing at Raza's cry of fright before righting it again.

'Stop fighting now. Talk to each other,' he said, smacking Abdullah on the back of the head before wandering out again.

Both Abdullah and Raza looked up in surprise at each other. Each had been too caught up in his own silence to notice the other's lack of conversation.

'What's wrong?' they said in tandem.

'Nothing,' Raza said. 'You're so quiet I thought maybe I've offended you.'

Abdullah's hazel eyes crinkled.

'How could you offend me, Raza Hazara?' Very slowly, in English, he said, 'You only can call me "walnut".'

Raza looked guiltily down at his plate. He had never known such generosity as Abdullah extended him with an air that suggested Raza was the one doing him the favour in being pulled in so completely, so unreservedly, into his life. A few weeks ago Raza had arrived in Sohrab Goth after an eight-day absence, and there was no recrimination from Abdullah, only a broad smile of delight at Raza's return. It was Afridi who told him, accusingly, that Abdullah had to be forcibly dragged out of the environs of Sohrab Goth on the days Raza was absent – 'Otherwise he just stays, waiting for his teacher to arrive.' Raza hadn't missed a day since then.

'Why are you so quiet then?' Raza asked.

'I'm fourteen now,' Abdullah said, leaning back vertiginously in his plastic chair. 'My brothers promised when I was fourteen I could go to one of the training camps.' Abdullah's surviving brothers were all mujahideen, as had been the brother who died near the start of the war – the rest of his family was in a refugee camp outside Peshawar but Abdullah, at twelve, had left the camp on the back of a truck to Karachi, where a family from his village had taken him in, and the truck driver in whose company he'd travelled to Karachi had said, 'Come and work with me,' and so Abdullah had become a gun-runner between Karachi and Peshawar.

'Really? When was your birthday?' In Abdullah's company Raza's Pashto had become increasingly the Pashto of Kandahar, not of Peshawar.

Abdullah shrugged.

'I don't know exactly. Some time near the beginning of summer.' He ripped a piece off his naan and made a complicated gesture that Raza couldn't make any sense of. 'Afridi's going to Peshawar next week. My brother Ismail said I should go with him, and he'll meet me and take me to the camp. But I don't know. You said once, there are other ways to fight the Soviets. Maybe I'd be more useful here, with Afridi. You can't underestimate the importance of the supply line from Karachi.' He looked imploringly at Raza. 'Isn't that so?'

Raza chewed slowly on a large mouthful of kabab and naan. Ever since he'd started to spend time with Abdullah he'd hankered to travel as the younger boy did, heading all the way north through Pakistan in a truck, lying at night in the open-top container watching the stars, stopping along the way for chai and parathas and kababs, no parents to say what was and wasn't allowed, just the open road, the shifting landscape, the thrilling knowledge of gun-running.

Peshawar. Sajjad's sister and brother-in-law lived there – Raza had last been to visit them years ago with his father. His uncle had promised to take him to the fort on his final day there, but rain had interfered with the plan. 'Next time you're here, we'll go, I promise,' his uncle had said – but that next time hadn't come again; the Ashraf siblings of Pakistan gathered each year in Lahore instead, and mentions of return trips to Peshawar remained un-fulfilled ideas.

'Raza?' Abdullah said. 'I should tell my brother I'm needed to help with the supply line, shouldn't I?'

Here it was, Raza thought. The chance to bring the friendship of Raza Hazara and Abdullah to a close in a manner that it deserved, in a burst of adventure and camaraderie.

He grinned.

'What's the matter, little boy? Scared?'

Abdullah stood up, knocking the kabab out of Raza's hand.

'When was the last time you slit the throat of a Soviet?'

The men at tables near by turned to watch, and Raza heard someone call out to Afridi.

'Sit down,' Raza said, reaching across to Abdullah's plate and taking his kabab. The younger boy had reacted precisely as he'd known he would. He gestured to Afridi to say everything was OK. 'Next week, you and I will go to Peshawar together.'

Abdullah stared at him.

'You'll come to the training camps with me?'

'Why not?' Raza said. 'A true Afghan doesn't waste time with the CIA. He attacks the Soviets directly. I've learnt this from you.'

Abdullah smiled his broad, joyful smile.

'You and me together. The Soviets won't stand a chance!' He caught Raza in a wrestling hold and the two boys tumbled, laughing, to the pavement outside, where the men gathered around reached out hands to break their fall.

'Walnut!' Raza said, sitting up and brushing down his clothes. 'I could have choked on the kabab.'

Abdullah rested his weight on his elbows, unmindful of the pavement dirt, and continued smiling at Raza.

'There'll still be time for our lessons, won't there? When we're in the camp. You'll still teach me?'

'If you teach me how you can wrestle people twice your size and win.'

Abdullah jumped up and pulled Raza to his feet.

'This will be so much fun.'

And so it was that a little over a week later, Raza was in a truck heading from Karachi to Peshawar. There was much he learnt in that three-day drive: he learnt that nothing in the manic quality of Karachi traffic could prepare you for truck drivers on narrow mountain roads; he learnt that when you're in a truck filled with guns you can travel the length of the country without harassment from the military at checkpoints; he learnt to recognise cigarette burns on truckers' palms and the backs of their hands as badges of their profession – testament to the nights they drove their vehicles and their bodies to the brink of what was possible, burning their own hands to ward off sleep; he learnt not to ask Abdullah or Afridi or anyone at the stops along the way if they knew anything about the ancient rock carvings they passed because he'd only hear that they were the work of infidels; learnt the beauty in bleakness as the mountains compelled him, by the sheer force of their presence, to look beyond barrenness; learnt that the closer he got to the Afghanistan border the less people gave him a second glance; learnt, through absence, the luxuries he'd taken for granted; learnt of the existence of muscles he'd never considered until hour after hour on the thin seat of a speeding truck awoke them, screaming in agony; he learnt most of all that he would miss Abdullah's friendship.

The Afghan seemed to have forgotten by now his earlier hesitation about joining the mujahideen – he spoke of it now with such fervour that Raza would find himself getting entirely caught up in the idea of the training and the brotherhood in the vast, thrilling playground of the north where the terrain seemed designed for boys to execute grand adventures. And then he'd remind himself of his plan, clear to him that night in the highway restaurant: to accompany Abdullah to Peshawar and then vanish.

Really he'd just slip away and make his way to his aunt's house. But to Abdullah it would seem like a vanishing. He wondered what the Afghan would make of his disappearance – would he suspect a failure of courage on Raza's part, or would he think that, somewhere in Peshawar, that hub of espionage and jihad, Raza's CIA affiliation had caught up with him. Raza hoped for the latter. Largely, though, he didn't think of what would happen once he left Abdullah and Afridi – it saddened him too much. He didn't know who he'd miss more – Abdullah or Raza Hazara, but he knew that there had been a richness to his life these last weeks which it had never known before.

There were even moments, contemplating that richness, when he thought maybe he'd go with Abdullah to the camps for a while, maybe there'd be no harm in that. But that idea never lasted long. It was too much now, this sundering of his self, he told himself as explanation for why he couldn't consider the camps for more than a few moments. Three days in the truck with Abdullah, three days on the road with his Afghan brother, and then enough. He squeezed his eyes tightly at the memory of how his students had lined up on his last day in Sohrab Goth, just before he and Abdullah climbed into the truck, each one of them presenting him with a memento – some handwritten notes in English, a tiny Quran, a pair of woollen socks, a clump of soil from Afghanistan, a decorative porcelain shoe. The voice that told him he was betraying them warred with the voice that said he had given them months of education which they would never have received if not for his charade, and those months were his gift to them, and not a commitment.

'Wake up.' Abdullah shook him.

Raza sat up, rubbing the side of his face where it had been resting against the truck door as he slept.

'Are we in Peshawar?' he said, looking out of the windscreen and seeing only mud and pebbles – a path of mud and pebbles cut into mountains of mud and pebbles with a mud-and-pebble drop to the mud-and-pebble valley beneath. Somehow, it managed to be majestic. If you're big enough, Raza thought, looking up at the mountains, it doesn't matter what you're made of.

Abdullah laughed and half pushed Raza out of the door, on to the side of the road. The dust kicked up by the wheels of the truck was settling slowly, almost regretfully, in the stillness of the early-morning air. Raza swept his arm side to side and felt the stuff of mountains drift on to his skin. This clearly wasn't Peshawar. Just another bathroom stop.

He stepped on to the side of the road, untying his shalwar. There was so much nothingness around him. Beyond, he knew, were peaks of white and behind fertile plains but knowing this didn't stop him from feeling he was on a barren planet where any mythological creature might be lurking – a Japanese tengu would be less out of place here than a boy from Karachi.

When he turned back towards the truck, he saw Afridi leaning out from the driver's seat, clasping Abdullah's hand.

Then the older man raised a hand in Raza's direction.

'Look after each other. And don't fight over that last Soviet.'

'What? No, wait.'

But his voice was lost beneath the roar of the engine, and then the truck was pulling away, leaving Raza and Abdullah in the middle of a vast emptiness.

'Where did he go?'

Abdullah looked at him in surprise.

'To Peshawar, of course. My brother's going to meet us near here. Come, we have to walk a little.'

His words echoed strangely in the mountain pass. Raza looked down at his feet. There seemed to be heavy weights attached to them. It was clear he couldn't move.

'Come on, Raza.'

Raza took a deep breath. It was OK. Somewhere during the few seconds when he'd considered joining Abdullah in the camps he had thought of an idea to get himself out. When he was ready to

214

leave, he'd decided, he'd come to Abdullah with a look of anguish and say he'd just had a phone call from home, his grandfather was dying. This grandfather had been an early and, it now transpired, inspired invention: the sole surviving relative with whom Raza lived, in a little shack near the railway lines, away from other Afghan refugees, who the grandfather could not look at without weeping for the lost mountains of his forefathers.

Of course he'd have no option but to leave the camp and return to his grandfather, promising to come back as soon as the old man was buried. It was his duty, after all, to lower his grandfather's body into the ground and close his eyes while the mauvli by the graveside prayed for his soul.

Yes, Raza thought, considering that plan again. Yes, that would work. And maybe – maybe he'd spend a day or two in the camps first. Listen to the mujahideen stories, learn to fire a rocket-launcher. He moved his feet forward towards Abdullah.

They walked along the narrowing dirt road through nothingness for what seemed hours, the mountains providing no shadow at this time of day to protect against the harsh sun; then, as they rounded a corner, Abdullah pointed to something rising from the plains beyond – a range of low mountains, stretching on for ever. No – Raza looked again. Tents. A city of refugees.

'It doubles in size every time I come back,' Abdullah said, his voice quieter, more grave than Raza had ever heard it before.

They kept walking towards the tent city but, just when Raza thought they were going to start to descend to the plain on which it stood, Abdullah sat down by the side of the path, which had widened again, his back to the tents, and said, 'Now we wait.'

'I want to see it,' Raza said, nodding in the direction of the refugee camp. At this distance, all he could tell was that it was vast.

'What do you want to see?' Abdullah said sharply. 'People living like animals? These places are the enemies of dignity. It's good. It's good that we should live there, like that.'

'How is that good?'

Abdullah looked over his shoulder towards the camp.

'I was forgetting, Raza.' He said it as though confessing the worst of crimes. 'I went to Karachi, I saw its lights and its promise, even all

215

the way at the edges in Sohrab Goth – and I was forgetting this. I haven't been to the refugee camps in a year. Afridi always offers to stop when we travel up to Peshawar, but I tell him no, I don't want to see it. I was forgetting why there is no option for me except to join the mujahideen. The boys growing up in the camps, they won't forget. They'll look around and know, if this is the better option that must mean our homeland now is the doorway to hell. And we must restore it to Paradise.' He turned to Raza, his expression as adult as the tone of his voice. 'Thank you, brother.'

Raza looked from the camps to Abdullah, and for the first time saw the smallness of his own heart, the total self-absorption.

'You were right,' he said. 'Before. When you said there were other things you could do. The supply line. Abdullah, that's so important. All the boys down there' – he waved his hands towards the tents – 'they'll all go to the training camps. Who'll be left to look after the supply line? How will Afridi manage without you? The camps are no good without guns for the mujahideen to fight with.'

Abdullah looked curiously at Raza.

'Why are you saying all this now?'

'I just didn't see before.' Raza stepped closer to Abdullah and put a hand on his arm. 'You have the number of that friend in Peshawar who Afridi is staying with. You should call him as soon as we get to the training camp. Tell Afridi to come back and pick us up.'

Abdullah looked at Raza as though he didn't recognise him, but before he could say anything a jeep turned the corner, headed for them, and the boys held their hands against their eyes to guard against the pebbles ricocheting from beneath the wheels.

'They've come to take us to the training camp. And, Raza, don't be such a city boy. There are no phones there.'

23

The morning of Raza's departure from Karachi, Hiroko woke with the dawn azan as was her practice. She loved to hear the echoes of Arabic dropping gently into the courtyard like a lover stealthily entering a home, undaunted by the knowledge that today again his beloved will turn him away – her rejection of him so oft repeated, so tenderly repeated, it becomes an expression of stead-fastness equal to his. But that morning, as she listened to – and felt – Sajjad's gentle snores against her shoulder, some quality of stillness about the house had her lifting her husband's arm from her waist and slipping out of bed.

Raza's bedroom door was open. Nothing unexpected there. It was hot enough now for the need for cross-ventilation to override any desire for privacy that a seventeen-year-old boy might have. Even so, she quickened her pace across the courtyard.

When she saw the note on his pillow, written in Japanese, she knew something was very wrong. What could he be doing that required him to leave the house before dawn and of which he knew his father would so strongly disapprove that it was necessary to leave it to Hiroko to find a way to deliver the news to him?

She read the note, and seconds later she was shaking Sajjad awake, translating the Japanese for him without any thought to softening its blow.

Please don't worry about me. I have gone away for a few days with my friend, Abdullah. We are going to travel through Pakistan. There is so much of this country I haven't seen and Abdullah has friends

everywhere who will look after us. I will bring back presents for both
of you. Soon I will be a serious university student and there will be no
time for such holidays, so don't be angry with me. Raza.

To her amazement, Sajjad seemed entirely unconcerned. If anything, he was mildly amused.

'You don't know what it's like to be a seventeen-year-old boy,' he
said, yawning as he reached for the mole just above her cheekbone,
clicking his tongue in irritation when she moved back and
wouldn't let him touch her. 'You know if he'd told us he was
going you would have asked a million questions. Where will you
go, who will you stay with, who is Abdullah, what does he do, why
don't you ask him to come over for dinner first, what is his family's
phone number, what are the phone numbers of his friends you'll
be staying with, which clothes are you taking with you –' He sat up
in bed and pulled his wife down next to him. 'In the meantime,
you overlook the fact that, for the first time in many years, you and
I are living alone together.' He kissed the mole lightly. 'It'll be like
when we were first married.'

'You are as silly and irresponsible as your son,' she said, half-
heartedly trying to disengage the arms around her waist. 'Who is
Abdullah?'

'There was some boy called Abdullah at school with him, wasn't
there? There must have been. Abdullah – everyone knows an
Abdullah.'

'Everyone knows an Abdullah,' she echoed, shaking her head
in disgust. 'Who knows what company your son is keeping,
where he's going, and all you can say is everyone knows an
Abdullah.'

'Don't you trust your son?'

'I trust my son. I don't trust Abdullah.'

'But you don't know Abdullah.'

'Exactly. So why should I trust him?'

Sajjad covered his ears with his hands.

'Nagasaki, Dilli, Karachi. No matter where you women grow up
as soon as you become mothers you all start using the same logic. If
it makes you happy, ask some of his old schoolfriends. Ask Bilal.' As

she stood up briskly, he caught her arm. 'Not now. It's just sunrise. You can't wake people up at this hour.' But she shook him off with a look he knew there was no point in arguing against.

Just a few minutes later, she had let herself in through the side gate of Bilal's house and was tapping on the kitchen window, where she knew Bilal's mother, Qaisra, would be making her morning cup of tea following the dawn prayers. Over the years, the friendship between their sons had extended into a friendship between the mothers.

'Bilal's not here,' Qaisra said, when Hiroko told her why she had come calling so early. 'He stayed at the hostel overnight, working on some project with two other college boys. Or at least that's what he told me. God knows what they do now they're out of school and think they're grown men.' She handed Hiroko a cup of tea. 'But he's never talked about an Abdullah. And, you know, our boys, they don't see each other so much any more.'

'He would have told us where he was going unless he knew we would disapprove,' Hiroko said, putting the teacup down and busying herself removing the dead leaves from the potted plant in the kitchen window.

'They want to be grown men as much as we want them to be little boys, but really they're neither. Doesn't that sound wise? You said it to me last year when Bilal took the car without permission. Listen, stop worrying. And stop attacking my plant. He'll be back soon, and wherever he is he won't do anything stupid. You've raised a good son.' She lowered her voice. 'Which is more than can be said for some people. Have you heard? About Iffat's son getting divorced? Isn't it terrible?'

'Not for his wife, it isn't,' Hiroko said, and Qaisra threw back her head and laughed.

'Only you would say that.'

For years Hiroko and Qaisra had taken turns being the worried parent, the consoling parent, and now, as always before, Hiroko felt considerably reassured as she said goodbye to her friend, whose final words were a reminder that Raza would never do anything of which his parents might seriously disapprove.

But as Hiroko was exiting the side gate she heard a voice say, 'Mrs Ashraf!' and Qaisra's daughter Salma, one of her former students, followed her out into the street.

'He's gone somewhere near Peshawar,' she said, speaking very low. 'This Abdullah is some Afghan boy with a truck. Raza met him at the fish harbour a few months ago. He's gone with him to one of those training camps. For mujahideen.'

'Don't talk nonsense,' Hiroko said. 'What does Raza want with training camps?'

'I saw him yesterday when I was at the bus stop. We started talking. He told me. He said in two weeks at these camps they teach you as much as the Army will teach in cadet colleges in two years. He was making it sound like some kind of holiday.'

It wasn't at the bus stop that he'd said any of this to her. They hadn't spoken in months when he called her the previous night to say triumphantly, 'Thank you for your advice. You were right. People like me better when I don't tell them who I really am.' He obviously had some secret he was itching to share, and she understood as soon as he started speaking that she was the only one in Raza Ashraf's life to hear about Abdullah the Afghan who was going to vie with Raza Hazara to drive the last Soviet out of Afghanistan.

'Am I supposed to be impressed by how good you are at lying to stupid Pathans?' she'd said, when he got to the part where he convinced Abdullah to go to the training camp. It was this response that made him veer away from the truth into declaring that he was going to join Abdullah at the camp 'for a couple of weeks or so'. She had been impressed then – and made it obvious by telling him to be careful and to call her from there, to which he'd said, 'Maybe,' and hung up. It had occurred to her that she should say something to someone – Bilal, her parents, Raza's parents – but then they would ask why he had told her, of all people. And how would she answer that? So she told herself that he was inventing stories – just as he had invented that story about the man from New York who would convince a university in America to pay for his education.

Hiroko did not stay to ask why Raza had revealed his plans to Salma when the girl finished telling her everything Raza had said.

Instead, she turned and set off instantly towards home, trying to run, convincingly scissoring her arms through the air but finding her legs had trouble understanding how to move at a pace brisker than a walk; Sajjad, setting off for work in his car, had slammed on the brakes to see his wife running in slow motion towards him as though in a parody of a scene from a movie in which a wife races home to tell her husband something terrible has happened to their son.

When she told him what Salma had said his first instinct was to laugh. The stories a boy told to try and impress a girl! And Salma was certainly the kind of girl a boy would want to impress. Older than Raza, but even so. He'd have to tell the boy off soundly when he came back from wherever he was, of course – unacceptable to worry Hiroko so much. But he felt vindicated – years ago he'd told Hiroko there was more than a touch of his brother Iqbal in Raza and this certainly proved him right. Hiroko had disagreed sharply, calling him an ungenerous father, refusing to accept that of all his brothers he loved Iqbal the most despite knowing him to be the most flawed of all the Ashrafs.

But then – as Hiroko seized him by the back of his head, shocking him into thinking his wife was about to kiss him here, on the street, in public – everything in Raza's behaviour which had mildly puzzled him the last few weeks coalesced into a single explanation. All the interest in Afghanistan! He'd bought a map of the country, asked Sajjad questions about the war there, paid close attention to every news item about it, though previously cricket had been the only current event that interested him. The truth didn't just seem inescapable, it also seemed so obvious Sajjad marvelled at how it was possible he hadn't realised earlier that his son had been making plans that delighted him in the way that only very foolish plans could delight a young man of Raza's temperament.

Very gently, Sajjad disengaged his wife's grip on his skull.

'I'll find him,' he said.

'How? He could be anywhere.'

Sajjad touched the mole on her cheek in a promise, and stepped back into his car.

221

'I'm going to the fish harbour. Someone there must know this boy. I'll find a way to call you from there. See if Salma knows anything else.'

Hiroko watched him drive away and then felt a hand on her arm.

'That's all I know,' Salma said. 'I'm sorry. I think I'm responsible for this.'

It was impossible to be angry with Salma when she revealed all she had said to Raza in the conversation about marriage. Impossible even to be angry at Qaisra, her dear friend, from whom Salma must have picked up those comments about Raza being 'deformed'. All Hiroko could think was: the bomb. In the first years after Nagasaki she had dreams in which she awoke to find the tattoos gone from her skin, and knew the birds were inside her now, their beaks dripping venom into her bloodstream, their charred wings engulfing her organs.

But then her daughter died, and the dreams stopped. The birds had their prey.

They had returned though when she was pregnant with Raza – dreams angrier, more frightening than ever before, and she'd wake from them to feel a fluttering in her womb. But then Raza was born, ten-fingered and ten-toed, all limbs intact and functioning, and she had thought he'd been spared, the birds were done with her.

She had not imagined the birds could fly outwards and enter the mind of this girl, and from her mind enter Raza's heart. She had never truly understood her son's need for belonging, the anger with which he twisted away from comments about his foreign looks – in truth, she had thought that anger little more than an affectation in a boy so hungry to possess the languages of different tribes, different nations – but she knew intimately the stigma of being defined by the bomb. Hibakusha. It remained the most hated word in her vocabulary. And the most powerful. To escape the word she had boarded a ship to India. India! To enter the home of a couple she'd never met, a world of which she knew nothing.

She waved off Salma's words, whatever they were – why didn't the silly girl just stop talking – and walked down the street towards her home. He was her son. Her son. Like her, so intent on escape that nothing seemed impossible except staying put. She pushed open the door of her house, stepped into the vestibule and paused at the entry into the courtyard. The shadows of the neem tree fell exactly where she knew they would fall at this time of the morning; the emptied flowerbed surrounding the tree told her Sajjad had cleared away the remnants of the spring flowers and was preparing to plant zinnias – and so summer had truly begun. And the zinnias would bring butterflies. Somewhere during the course of the decades she had settled into this place, learnt to anticipate – not merely to react to – its lengthening days, its shifting shadows.

She walked swiftly across the baking courtyard into Raza's room, and lay down with her head on his pillow. How often had Raza heard the story of his mother's great adventure – from Tokyo to Bombay! Bombay to Delhi! She never told him what an act of desperation that voyage was, had always wanted to seem fearless, above all. Fearless and transmutable, able to slip from skin to skin, city to city. Why tell him of the momentum of a bomb blast that threw her into a world in which everything was unfamiliar, Nagasaki itself become more unknown than Delhi? Nothing in the world more unrecognisable than her father as he died. But she had always wanted Raza to know as little of all this as possible. So the story of Hiroko Ashraf's youth was not the story of the bomb, but of the voyage after it.

'Weren't you scared?' Raza had asked once of her arrival in India.

She'd smiled and said, 'No,' laughing at the look of wonder on her son's face. It was true enough. She hadn't been afraid. But only because she didn't allow herself to think of anything beyond the next stage of the journey.

And now her son was proving himself her son, and nothing could keep her from seeing everything that might happen next, and next, and next.

She lay with her arms around his pillow until she drifted to sleep. In her dream, Raza was speaking to an Afghan boy but the boy, although an Afghan boy, was also her ex-student, Joseph, the kamikaze pilot. 'Maybe I won't join the Air Force,' Joseph, who was also the Afghan boy, said. Raza sneered. 'Scared, little boy?' Joseph stood up taller, unfurling his black wings, and when he opened his mouth desiccated cherry blossom cascaded out, blanketing the dry soil of Afghanistan.

24

The camp was more than an hour's drive from wherever they were before, on a mountain plateau which could only be reached via a dirt road that snaked from Pakistan into Afghanistan and back again. The single point of entry made it easy to guard against such inconveniences as occurred at the camp where Abdullah's eldest brother had trained – a group of tribesmen taking a short cut stumbled upon the camp, which had to be moved to a new location the next day.

The driver of the jeep – a man whose face was all beard and nose – pointed in the direction of a narrow path winding along the mountain and said one of the Arab training camps was along there. He spat out the word 'Arab' as if it were a curse.

'But don't worry,' he said, turning to Raza with a smile that was unexpectedly boyish. 'Where we're going, it's all Pashtun. You might be treated a little roughly at first – there are men in there who aren't happy about a Hazara entering our camp. But don't worry – you're an Afghan and a Muslim and a friend of Abdullah's. You'll earn their trust.' He cuffed Abdullah, who smiled in return, and Raza understood only then that this was Abdullah's brother.

Raza heard the camp before he saw it. At first he thought he was listening to the sea – he recalled illustrated geography books with pictures of fossilised fishbones discovered on icy summits – but then the roaring got louder and became gunfire.

'How are you supposed to keep this location secret?' he yelled above the noise.

Abdullah's brother Ismail shrugged.

'The echoes make it impossible to know where it's coming from.' He parked the jeep and pointed to a winding pathway. 'Follow that down. I'll be back later.' He reached into the back seat, picked up two grey-brown pieces of cloth and tossed one each at Abdullah and Raza. 'That's half your essential supply. The other half – your guns – they'll give you when you get there.'

'What's this for?' Raza said to Abdullah as the jeep reversed at great speed down the track. He held the square of cloth by a corner and it unfolded into a rectangle the height of a tall man.

'For everything,' Abdullah replied. 'Don't Hazaras have pattusis?' He walked towards the mountain path, a rapid motion of his hand urging Raza along. 'It's your blanket to sleep under, your shawl to keep you warm, your camouflage in the mountains and desert, your stretcher when you're wounded, your blindfold to tie over the eyes of the untrustworthy, your tourniquet, your prayer mat. If you're killed in battle you'll be buried in your bloodied pattusi – the mujahideen don't need their bodies washed and purified before burial. We are already guaranteed heaven.' He smiled at Raza over his shoulder. 'But heaven will wait for us. No need to rush towards it, brother, so don't step so close to the edge of the path.'

Raza hopped back and pressed himself against the mountain. He hadn't realised how close he had strayed to the edge of the path in his intent perusal of the scene on the plateau below – the cluster of tents, the unexpected livestock, the men with light shining from their bodies. The creatures of this planet are part angel, he found himself thinking, before a closer view revealed each one of the men carried a Kalashnikov which reflected the sun's rays.

By the time they reached the plateau – as hot and still as an oven – Raza thought he might faint. It was not just the exertion of mountain-walking and the intensity of the sun which made his lips turn white and set his brain rotating. How could a man escape such a place? Even if he climbed back up the path undetected, where would he go from there? What had he been thinking? He had been so buoyed by months of living a lie that he thought he could control everything, and suddenly his own stupidity and arrogance was breathing hot on his face. He sat down – collapsed, really – on a rock, paying little attention to the men who came to welcome Abdullah and look questioningly at him.

He wanted his parents. He wanted his bed, and the familiarity of the streets in which he'd grown up. For no reason he could explain, he wanted a mango.

One of the men prodded him with his foot.

'Practising blending in with the scenery, my rock?' he said in a tone that was not unkind, just amused.

Raza looked up at the man's green eyes, which were examining him with interest, and all the stories he'd heard in his Muhajir neighbourhood about the proclivities of Afghan men for delicate-featured boys rushed back at him and immobilised him further.

'Doesn't he speak Pashto?' the man said, turning to Abdullah.

Abdullah slapped the back of Raza's head.

'Pashto is the only Afghan language he'll speak.' He related the tale of Raza Hazara and the vow he had made to put a warrior's mission between himself and his mother tongue. Raza, listening, tried to remember how to become the Hazara – he pictured himself raising a Kalashnikov to his shoulder, but in the midst of these men for whom a Kalashnikov was something familiar enough to be casual with he saw his own posturing for what it was.

Abdullah bent down, a hand gripping Raza's shoulder.

'If you cry, I'll kill you,' he whispered.

Raza looked up at Abdullah, at the green-eyed man, at the mountains and the sky. Everything was shifting. He pressed his hands against the ground, felt sharp-edged stones cut into his skin as he propelled his body into a prone position, head pillowed against the rock on which he'd been sitting. His vision grew white at the edges and only the quickness of his breath kept him from throwing up. He had never known anything like this heat, this terror.

The voices around him were coming and going, staccato. Perhaps he wasn't here but in his room at home where the ceiling fan whirred and then juddered on each of its rotations, the juddering breaking up the flow of sounds that came in from the courtyard, causing approximately every third syllable of his parents' conversation to be lost.

Warm water splashed on his face and his eyes flickered open to see the green-eyed man pouring something out of a bottle into his palm and gently tilting his hand so the water slipped from it towards Raza. Abdullah kicked him again and the green-eyed man said something that Raza didn't understand because the ceiling fan was on again. And everything was slipping from his vision except those green eyes.

Uncle Harry, Raza thought, and then the green eyes closed and there was only darkness.

When he regained consciousness, he found he'd been moved; his pattusi was a pillow and the mountain itself a provider of shade. There was a bottle of water next to him and he drank greedily, propped up on one elbow, before lying down and falling asleep, every emotion pushed to the side by exhaustion; his body finally registered the toll of days of sleeping in the cramped cab of the truck or on a bed of Kalashnikovs in the container portion, woken up by sharp braking or breakneck turns before he could reach the point of dreaming.

Later, much later, there was a sandal knocking against his ribs. Abdullah seemed to have decided that the only way to separate himself from the shame of this fainting creature was to treat Raza as though he were an animal.

Raza was awoken by the first kick but kept his eyes closed. When the second kick landed, his hand grabbed Abdullah's foot and, twisting it, knocked the younger boy to the ground. Abdullah scrambled to his feet, but it was too late by then – three muja-hideen sitting near by, chewing their niswaar and entering a pleasant intoxication, were already laughing at him.

'Your friend has given you a bonus lesson for the day,' one of the men said. 'Never assume a man is incapable of striking back simply because his eyes are closed.'

Abdullah walked away without responding, and now it was something other than exhaustion that made Raza curl himself up and retreat into the safety of sleep again.

The next time, it was the green-eyed man who woke him up, shaking him by the shoulders and pointing towards the setting sun. Raza sat up, not understanding.

'You've slept through two prayer times already,' the man said. 'Come, stand up. You may not be a Pashtun, but you're still a man. Enough of this.'

Raza clambered to his feet, which was not easy to do with all the heaviness that seemed to weigh on each limb and on his heart. He watched the man pick up a fistful of dirt and rub it over his hands and arms before scrubbing his face with it. Camouflage, Raza thought.

'We're like the first Muslims, in the deserts of Arabia,' the man said, running his hands through his hair, and Raza saw he was performing his ablutions.

Nodding, Raza mimicked the man's actions, trying not to think of his mother putting aside a pile of ash for him each day when he had worked in the soap factory. He had not realised, until now, that it was a gesture of love. No, he couldn't think of Hiroko. Or of Sajjad. To do so was to feel loneliness rise within him, stronger than terror.

When Raza had finished scrubbing his feet, the green-eyed man gestured him towards the prayer space – next to one leafless tree with branches the colour of the men's pattusis – where all the occupants of the camp were lining up in rows. Guns hung, like metallic fruit, from the tree's branches. Raza saw that most of the men were younger than he was, some younger than Abdullah even. The setting sun dulled all the sharp edges of the world, everything aglow or in shadows. It was cooler now, and silent. All at once, Raza saw the beauty in the moment and it was with a true sense of reverence, such as he had never felt before, that he laid his pattusi on the ground and stepped on to it. Abdullah turned to look at him and the two boys nodded and smiled shyly at each other as though they were both on their way to meet their future brides and recognised something of their own emotions – the tangle of exhilaration and fear – in each other's eyes. Raza Hazara woke up, looked upon the world, and found it extraordinary.

The man leading the prayer recited 'Bismillah' in a voice that carried across the mountains. Even the sky here was different to anything Raza had seen before, stained in unusual hues of violet.

He felt the words of prayer enter his mouth from a place of pure faith. He had occasionally felt this before, but never so intensely. More often, prayer came to him from his mind, as memorised words with little meaning attached. But in that moment, though he still didn't know the literal translation of what he was saying, he found meaning in every muttered syllable of Arabic: *Lord, Allah, let me escape this place, deliver me, deliver me.*

And following that thought was this one: *Give these men Your blessing.*

After the prayer ended, Abdullah came to him and slung an arm around his shoulder.

'You made me angry,' he said. 'Maybe I said something I shouldn't have.'

'You didn't say anything,' Raza said. 'You only kicked.' He tapped his toes against Abdullah's ankle to signal forgiveness.

'No, not to you. To him.' He pointed in the direction of a very tall man, who was looking at Raza with his arms crossed over his chest. 'That's the Commander. You have to go and talk to him.'

'About what?'

But Abdullah was walking away, not looking at Raza.

'Just go and talk to him.'

The Commander jerked his head sharply and Raza found there was no option but to walk over to him.

The Commander said nothing, just grabbed him by the neck and pushed him into a tent. Once more Raza recalled all the stories about Pathans and their proclivities, and then he saw there was another man in the tent, not a Pathan at all. A small man, darker than anyone else in the camp, with a clipped moustache, who was fastidiously wiping his hands with a pink tissue.

'That's him?' he said in unconvincingly accented Pashto to the Commander, who nodded and stepped out of the tent, leaving Raza alone with the other man.

'Name?'

'Raza.'

'Father's name?'

Raza Hazara hadn't mentioned his father's name in years. He would not utter it until the last Soviet had been driven out of Afghanistan.

'Sajjad Ali Ashraf,' he said.

'He's Hazara?'

'No. His family is from Delhi. My mother's Japanese.'

The man raised an eyebrow and sat back.

'The name of the American you were with at the harbour?' he asked, switching from Pashto to Urdu.

'Harry Burton.'

The man shook his head in disgust.

'How can we work together with such little trust?' he said.

'I trust you,' Raza blurted out, and the man laughed unpleasantly.

'Who are you? What do I care if you trust me or not? Harry Burton, Harry Burton.' He shook his head again. 'I've never met him, but I know the story. Do you know the story? When he coloured his hair, wrapped a chador around him and thought this meant he could enter one of our camps without word getting back to us that the CIA had been where their own government has forbidden them to go.'

Uncle Harry?

'Give him a piece of advice from me. Say the CIA needs to give its agents lessons in walking. Americans walk differently to everyone else. I can spot one as far away as the horizon.' He held out the tissue, and Raza automatically stepped forward, holding out his hand to take it. This seemed to please the man. 'So why have they sent you? You seem completely incompetent.'

'No one sent me.'

'You only make things worse by lying,' the man said mildly. 'You've already admitted you work for the CIA. Now what's the point of saying they didn't send you here?'

'I can leave if you want,' Raza said, and then wanted to hit himself for the idiocy of the statement.

The man's laughter seemed more genuine this time.

'Yes, I want. Go back to your Mr Burton and tell him we can't afford to be spying on each other. It's enough that I have to spend

231

all my time mediating between Afghan commanders and politicians whose hatred for the Soviets is eclipsed by their hatred for each other – and their hatred for each other eclipsed by their hatred for our Arab brothers who have come to fight in this jihad. It's too much. I've had an upset stomach for months now because of it.'

'I'm really sorry,' Raza said.

This time the man's laugh was unmistakably filled with humour.

'I don't know what the CIA thinks it's doing with someone like you. Do you have any money?'

Raza reached into the pocket of his kameez and pulled out a fistful of rupee notes.

'Here, sir.'

'Now I know you're just playing the idiot.' The man smiled. 'You're coming with me. This minute. I'm taking you to a train station. That money should be enough for a ticket back to Karachi. And, Raza Ali Ashraf, if ever again you try something like this you won't find me so forgiving. Tell Harry Burton there are limits to what every friendship can endure.'

'Yes, sir, I will,' Raza said. As he followed the man out of the tent and up the mountain road towards the jeep that would carry him to a train heading home he kept looking up into the sky, overcome with gratitude for the unparalleled blessing of an answered prayer.

But he was only halfway up the road when he heard his name and Abdullah came running after him.

'Where are you going?' he said.

Before Raza could answer the man turned towards Abdullah and held up a hand of command.

'He's coming with me. Go back down.'

But Abdullah didn't move.

'Is this because of what I said?' His eyes opened in horror and he reached out and caught Raza's sleeve. 'No, I didn't mean it. He's not with the CIA. He's come to fight with us. He's an Afghan, he wants to be a mujahideen. That's all he wants. I was angry, so I said some lies about him.'

'Go back down,' the man repeated, the tone of his voice making Raza shiver. But still Abdullah didn't move.

'You can't send him away. He's come here to fight with us. That's the only reason he's here. I lied. I'm telling you, I lied.'

The man looked placidly at Raza.

'Move,' he said mildly.

Raza gently detached Abdullah's hand from his sleeve, unable to bring himself to look at the younger boy, who had fat tears running down his cheeks.

'I'm sorry,' Abdullah whispered. 'Raza Hazara, brother . . .'

Raza shook his head and walked away, each step that put distance between him and Abdullah intensifying the physical pain of grief and loneliness.

'They really are a bunch of walnuts,' the man said as he pushed Raza ahead of him towards the jeep.

25

By sunset on the fourth day of Raza's absence from Karachi, Sajjad Ali Ashraf had almost resigned himself to another wasted day of back and forth between the port and the fish harbour, asking the fishermen and the truckers if they knew anything of Abdullah the Afghan boy. His only success had been on his second day when he found a trucker at the harbour who remembered the Afghan boy Abdullah, and said he worked with another Pathan – Sajjad remembered them faintly, the boy and man who Raza had been talking to when he and Harry exited the fish harbour all those months ago; but the trucker didn't know how to find Abdullah or the other Pathan. 'I see them now and then either here or at West Wharf. Eventually, they'll show up.'

'He won't show up,' Hiroko had said that evening when Sajjad finally gave up for the day and returned home. 'He's gone to a camp near the Afghan border. What are you hoping to find at the harbour, Sajjad?'

'Maybe his friend, the other Pathan, will be there. He might know something more. What do you want me to do, Hiroko? Sit at home playing cards while my son thinks he's in some movie but everyone else around him is carrying real AK-47s and God knows what else is going on? What will they do when they find out he's lying? Hazara! What is he . . . is he mad? Is he on drugs? These Afghans and their drugs. I'm telling you this Abdullah has put him on drugs.'

So before dawn each day, Sajjad went down to the coast to wait for the Pathan truck driver – not even knowing if he'd recognise him again based on just that one glimpse and other truckers' descriptions, but knowing he couldn't go to work in the morning as if everything was all right. All day and into the night he traversed the space between the fish harbour and West Wharf, his car besieged at both stops by the street urchins to whom he paid a daily sum of money to keep an eye out for the Pathan, though the effect of the much larger amount he'd promised to whoever found the man first resulted in half a dozen false sightings a day and nothing beyond. He couldn't keep this up much longer, he knew. The managing director of the soap factory – a relative of Kamran Ali, in whose car Hiroko and Sajjad had driven through Mussoorie, lifetimes ago – had been sympathetic when Sajjad had called to explain why he needed some time off, but sympathy only translated into a limited number of days away from the office.

But late on the fourth evening – while Raza watched the grimy train window reflecting a face which he looked at with honest distaste – Sajjad walked on to the docks at West Wharf. Ships of all sizes were moored in the harbour, the smell of oil more pungent than anything the sea could naturally produce. The bent giant arms of cranes at rest hovered menacingly above the docks. But Sajjad only noticed that – finally, finally – he had seen someone he recognised. It was Sher Mohammed, Harry's rickshaw driver, shaking his head at a wiry man who was gesticulating in anger.

Sajjad had spent four days in prayer. Religion had never been more than a constant background hum in his life, but he discovered praying was something to do, some ritual in which to pass the time as he drove back and forth, saw one street urchin after another shake his or her head, no, no, maybe yes but really no, and waited, just waited for deliverance to announce itself. His lips moved constantly, body rocking forward as he recited the 'Ayat-ul-Kursi', having discovered he had none of his mother's talent for finding comfort through conversing with God as though He were a recalcitrant lover. He could not yell familiarly, familialy, at the Almighty and so he prayed to Him in a language he didn't understand, and felt the rightness of incomprehension when dealing with a power which showed no mercy when Altamash was killed, when Iqbal's wife and children were massacred, when

Sajjad entered the Consulate in Istanbul, and yet had the mercy to give him a son he hadn't known he'd wanted so desperately until . . . until now, if he were honest. He had loved Raza from the moment he'd first taken the wriggling infant in his arms, but he had also soon grown to take him for granted as Sajjad had always taken the blessings of his life, other than Hiroko, for granted.

But as his brain recognised familiarity in the shape of Sher Mohammed and he remembered that the rickshaw driver had been parked outside the fish harbour when Raza first met the Afghan boy he was overcome by a feeling of gratitude so overwhelming he staggered back with the force of it. For a few seconds he could do nothing but stare at Sher Mohammed, thinking that it was unlikely the answer to a prayer had ever taken a more unexpected form than this little man with only a scattering of teeth still attached to his gums, and an ear-lobe in tatters. He had complete certainty that Sher Mohammed would help him find Raza; it was impossible for his presence here to be anything but an act of Providence.

He would have liked to lower himself on to his knees in gratitude, but there was a puddle of oil-slicked water on the ground and Hiroko would have something to say about it if he came home with a ruined shalwar. So instead he allowed himself a moment to watch the fiery pupil that was the sun staring out at him from the dark eye of oil. I will be a better father after this, he promised. Whatever he wants to do with his life, I will accept.

He was certain there was no one but himself to blame for what had happened. Hiroko had barely spoken these last few days – refused to see any of her friends when they came to call – and when she did say anything it was to ask, 'What did we do that was so wrong?' She didn't just mean how could he have done something so foolish, but also, how could he have convinced an Afghan boy to go to one of those camps just because he saw it as occasion for his own adventure. Sajjad couldn't bring himself to care about the Afghan boy. He just wanted his son back. He wanted a chance to be a different father – Hiroko had done everything a mother could do, was in no way to blame for what had happened. Any faults in Raza were signs of his flaws as a parent. Law school! It seemed so irrelevant now. What did it matter if the boy passed an exam or not, became a lawyer or not? Let him be here, be well. Nothing else mattered.

Rainbows bubbled at the edges of the puddle. He wished he could sift them out into his palms and take them home to Hiroko. He'd walk into the courtyard, toss the rainbows up so they'd catch in the limbs of the neem tree and call Hiroko out to sit under the canopy of colour while he told her how he'd found their son through the man with the tattered ear-lobe.

Their first weeks in Karachi together, living in refugee tents, he used to wake up every morning thinking, Will this be the day she decides to go back to the Burtons with their expanse of book-shelves and feather pillows and gardens? So every day became a day to find something of beauty in their strange new home that he could point her towards to say, Look, there's loveliness here, really there is. One day a seashell with an ocean roaring behind its pursed lips, one day a cactus flower in bloom, one day a Dilli poet who wrote verses on leaves because he couldn't afford paper (he gave an armful of leaves to Sajjad, and Sajjad pasted them directly on to the inside of their tent, just above the bedroll). In his desperation to make Karachi a place where Hiroko could imagine her life he learnt reasons to fall in love with the city, realising only much later that Hiroko had known what he was doing and had let him do it because she knew he was the one who needed to find ways to imagine a future in this place so removed in its architecture and its air and its pace of life from the city he had wanted to live and die in.

Sajjad touched his heart briefly, and stepped over the puddle. 'Sher Mohammed!' he called out, quickening his pace. 'Sher Mohammed!'

The rickshaw driver was deep in argument with one of the ships' captains responsible for transporting arms to Karachi for transit to the mujahideen. The ISI had been to see the captain, demanding to know why his supply didn't match up to the CIA inventory and though he had given them a line they seemed to accept because it was so often true – that the discrepancy must have occurred somewhere earlier in the supply line – the encounter had both shaken and angered him. So he now rounded on the man responsible for the discrepancy – Sher Mohammed, one of the CIA's local assets who had previously used the occasion of driving the captain to a CIA rendezvous to convince him no one would notice if a few guns went missing.

'Don't panic. If the ISI didn't believe you you'd be having your fingers broken with a hammer right now,' Sher Mohammed said, as the man paused to draw a breath. 'Is this an attempt to get more money from me? Don't play these games.'

And that's when he heard his name called out in this place where he had never revealed his name.

He turned towards the voice, saw the man with whom Harry Burton was on the most intimate of terms, his 'first teacher', Harry had once called him – which Sher Mohammed had taken to mean that the unassuming Muhajir in Nazimabad was involved in training CIA agents.

The man was walking towards him with the stride of an executioner, utterly purposeful.

Sajjad saw Sher Mohammed reach into the back of his shalwar and pull out a gun.

What's he doing with that? he wondered.

26

H iroko shook her head reprovingly at the cracked skin of
   Sajjad's heel, the dirt of the harbour that had lodged itself
within each groove.

'General manager of a soap factory!' she scolded him, lifting his
foot as he lay on the divan, and rubbing a wet cloth vigorously
along the length of it before attending to the fissures at the heel.
'And look at me, washing my husband's feet. This is wrong, Sajjad
Ali Ashraf. This is wrong.' The last word was whispered, as though
her voice itself had gone into retreat, unable to be present at this
scene.

She placed the foot gently down on the divan, which had been
moved into the centre of the room to make it easier for her to walk
around it and wash her husband's corpse. And now it was done.
There remained only one last thing she could do for him – wind
around his body the white sheet on which he was lying before
calling in the mourners for one final look at him before the men
took him away to be buried.

But Sajjad hated the constriction of sheets, insisted they could
only rest lightly upon him as he slept; if he started to feel his feet
tangle with the bed coverings he would kick and flail. How often
had she been woken up by his kicking and flailing?

There was too much, too much that had been such a part of her
life with him that it had become indistinguishable from the mere
process of living. She had thought Nagasaki had taught her everything to know about loss but in truth it was only horror with which
she had become completely familiar. At twenty-one it had been

impossible for her to learn all the facets of loss. She couldn't have known then what it was to lose the man you had loved for thirty-six years.

Sitting on the divan, she touched a finger to the bullet wound in his chest. It seemed so small, so incapable of creating the exodus of blood which had drenched his clothes and skin as he lay in the hospital, waiting for her to claim him. Death had been instantaneous, they said, as if there were relief in that. She did not want death to have been instantaneous; she wanted to have at least held his hand as he lay dying and said goodbye to him in terms other than the, 'Why are you going again? You'll find nothing. Stay. Oh all right, go,' that had been her farewell to him that morning.

Stay. Stay. Stay. She should have repeated it like a madwoman, banged her head against the wall in a frenzy, hit him and wept. She should have said it just one more time, just a little more forcefully. She should have taken his dear, sweet head in her hands and kissed his eyes and forehead. *Stay.*

His skin so cold, so unyielding, after a night in the hospital morgue. Sweat was running down her back despite the fan which was on full speed right above her head, but he who had always perspired so much more heavily than she was utterly dry. Bone-dry. She was repulsed by the expression.

She could not bear to touch his belly, which had always had such a comfortable softness to it. Instead, she wrapped her hand around his penis, but the hardness there was even more unbearable than anywhere else. So she moved her hand up to his hair, the only part of him which still felt alive. She closed her eyes, ran her fingers through his hair, whispered endearments in Japanese – the only words of Japanese she ever taught him were words of love.

Neither the closed door and shuttered windows nor her engulfing sorrow could keep out the clamour of the world. Her brother-in-law Iqbal, who flew down from Lahore last night after Hiroko said yes, she'd reimburse him for the ticket, had found an extension cord and taken the phone out of this room into the courtyard and she could hear him shouting into it, at Sikandar in Dilli: 'What do you mean you can't get a visa? He's dead. You're my only brother left. What am I supposed to do without Sajjad?'

It was Iqbal who would climb into the grave with Sajjad and close his eyes, not Raza.

She could not think of Raza without being overwhelmed by rage.

Then there was another voice in the courtyard, and she raised herself off the divan. Harry Burton was here. Harry, whose driver Sher Mohammed shot Sajjad – the crane-operator who brought Sajjad to the hospital described the whole scene of the killing to Hiroko: Sajjad calling the man's name, the gunshot, the man with the tattered ear-lobes yelling, 'He's CIA,' to the ship's captain before turning to run, both men probably halfway across the ocean by now, the police informed Hiroko.

She wrapped a sheet – loosely – over Sajjad's lower body and opened the door, and there was Harry, with the lost expression of a little boy. All the gathered mourners stood up as they saw her – the men in the centre of the courtyard, the women sitting under the overhang of the roof where there was shade. Hiroko looked only at Harry, beckoned him inside, then stepped across the room to look at the painting of the two foxes while Harry walked over to Sajjad's body and whispered things she didn't try to hear.

'Thank you for coming,' she said, when she heard him walk over to stand behind her.

Harry wanted to embrace her, but didn't. After Hiroko's phone call woke him up early this morning he made call after call to his ISI contacts and the CIA station chief in Karachi, and well before his plane took off from Islamabad he had pieced together, almost precisely, what happened at West Wharf.

'How exactly is it your fault that an irresponsible kid ran off and a thieving son of a bitch panicked and pulled a trigger?' Steve had asked as he drove Harry to the airport, and Harry saw that his colleague was unable to recognise that it was grief, pure grief, not guilt at all, that had unmoored him so completely from his everyday aspect.

'You think because he was Pakistani I couldn't have loved him?' he bellowed, and Steve said, 'Hell,' and nothing more for the rest of the journey.

But Steve wasn't entirely wrong, he realised now. It was guilt that kept his hands from reaching out to Hiroko, though it made no sense to him that he should feel guilt for this when he hadn't for so

241

many other things which by the standards of ordinary, little-picture morality should have had him sobbing in a bar or some other secular confessional.

'Why did your driver shoot him?' Hiroko asked, turning towards him. 'Why would anyone shoot Sajjad?'

'I don't know.' It was not any act of friendship that had prompted Steve to drive him to the airport, but a professional need to reiterate the importance of giving away nothing that needed to be concealed.

'He thought Sajjad was CIA.' She touched the mole beneath her eye, which had been untouched all day. 'Because of you, I suppose,' and Harry found he wanted her to guess the truth, but she was drifting off. 'Sajjad and I used to joke about that sometimes. We'd joke you were a CIA agent. It's what everyone assumes of Americans here, you know.' She put a hand to her mouth. 'Do you think Sajjad could have joked about that with Sher Mohammed? And maybe because of it . . . ?' Her voice disappeared again and she shook her head and looked at the corpse, which Harry was deliberately keeping his back towards.

'Maybe,' he heard himself saying. 'Maybe that's got something to do with it.'

In the courtyard the sound of men talking and women muttering prayers stopped, and then a different quality of noise started up. Hiroko paid no attention to it.

It was Raza. He pushed open the front door to feel the word 'home' embrace him for the first time, and then saw the gathering and knew, instantly, that there was no home any more.

His uncle Iqbal was the one who folded him in his arms and whispered in his ear, 'Your father's gone,' and then there was a press of people around him, explaining in words that were disjointed because no one truly understood yet. But Raza heard, 'And then he shouted, "He's CIA," ' and he knew this was Harry Burton's doing.

He pushed aside the mourners, and entered the room where his father's body lay.

At first he wanted to laugh. It was a joke. Death couldn't look so exactly like sleep. But when he shook Sajjad by the shoulder, the body was ice, and there was a puncture above his heart.

'Raza,' Harry said, because Hiroko seemed incapable of stepping forward and taking her weeping son in her arms.

Raza was kneeling at the divan, clutching his father's cold shoulder, but at Harry's voice he stood, turned and raced forward, fists flying. Harry had him pinned on the floor in seconds.

'You did this!' Raza shouted. 'You killed my father.'

'Raza Konrad Ashraf!' Hiroko pushed Harry away and dragged her son to his feet. 'What bad manners are these?'

'Ma, you don't know.' He caught hold of Harry's shirt. 'They told me all about you at the camps. He's CIA. He's been lying to us all along. Aba's dead because of him.'

Harry took Raza's fist which was gripping his shirt and squeezed it.

'He's dead, you idiot, because he went to the harbour looking for you.'

Raza reeled back. Somewhere in the explanation out in the courtyard, this detail missed him. He looked to his mother, and Hiroko saw that he would be haunted now, by this, for the rest of his life. He was too young for such pain, just a boy, her little boy. She held open her arms and he rushed into them.

Harry said, 'Hiroko,' and she shook her head, turning away so that even his shadow was out of her sight. He allowed himself to look at Sajjad for a moment – one long moment in which he saw the best part of his childhood and himself lying dead – and then he left.

Hiroko's hands stroked Raza's back and hair, her eyes resting on Sajjad. It was nearly sunset. Soon they would take him away. She had only these minutes left now to remember every detail – the swoop of his collarbone, the tiny scar on his knuckle, the veins at his wrist.

The Speed Necessary to Replace Loss

New York, Afghanistan, 2001–2

27

Kim Burton pushed the tip of her tongue between the gap in her front teeth. Manhattan's downtown skyline gaped back at her. She scraped her tongue along the sharp edge of a tooth. Jagged metal debris, eight storeys high. Three months on, everything was still reminder or testimonial. Thirty storeys above Mercer Street, it was possible now to stand at this window in her grandmother's apartment, twelve feet across and four feet high, and look straight ahead without any human construction encroaching on the view. Instead, so much sky outside it could have been Montana.

She cranked open the small side window – smoker's window, her father called it – and dipped her head so she was looking down at the street, watching the thin stream of human traffic: graveyard shift workers returning home to lovers for a few precious minutes of shared sleep; NYU students bouncing with whatever stimulant was carrying them through the sleepless nights of finals week; a man carrying two buckets overflowing with flowers, their scent making him weep for a faraway country; a pair of transvestites, arms looped around each other's waist, their stiletto heels keeping perfect time just as their boots had done in their former lives as military men.

From this far up, it was possible to overlay any story on to the tiny figures below. Kim liked to think her stories revealed a certain largeness of spirit, though she suspected each one could be traced back to something she'd seen on television in the preceding week.

Her eyes shifted their focus from the world outside to the window, and she grimaced at the angular face captured in the glass.

Green eyes dulled with exhaustion, jet-black hair being overtaken by the copper roots long enough that she felt she should start calling them stalks, skin so pale and circles under her eyes so dark she was beginning to look less human than lunar. Red-eye flights, coffee and dreams of collapsing buildings weren't the best of combinations for a glowing complexion.

Looking away, she reached into the space behind the radiator, and extracted a packet of cigarettes and a little silver skull which opened its jaws and blew out a steady flame when she depressed its occipital bone. She had carried this lighter through her life for nearly twenty years now, since one of the Marine guards at the Embassy in Islamabad with whom she'd conducted a minor flirtation to irritate her father had given it to her as a farewell present. Once she had the lighter it was necessary to take up smoking. Later that year, Grandpa James had found her lighting up in the back garden of his house in London and said, 'I suppose your grandmother encouraged you to do that just to annoy me.' It seemed to give him a measure of satisfaction to think he was still significant enough to Elizabeth – he never called her Ilse – to prompt her into such behaviour, though they hadn't met since Kim's parents' wedding.

She took a drag on her cigarette and found herself wondering what Grandpa James would make of the world if he were still alive. Would his air of condescension about all things American other than Lauren Bacall and his granddaughter have diminished or augmented over the last few months? Would he still look with dismay at Harry's life and wonder which of its wrong turns he could have forestalled, which of its failures bore the stamp of DNA? And what would he make of Gran's flatmate, whose late husband's name had only to be mentioned to cause him to change the subject with an air of guilt that was otherwise quite absent from his life?

'Spare cigarette?'

Kim's body jerked; a spark landed on her black T-shirt and burnt away, unnoticed.

'Since when do you smoke?'

'Since 1945. Thanks to an American in a Tokyo bar.'

Laughing, Kim handed Hiroko her cigarette.

'Take this. I've quit. Who was the American?'

'Just a GI.' Hiroko lowered herself on to the sofa, and saluted smartly. 'When did your flight get in? I thought you weren't leaving Seattle until this afternoon.' She dragged on her cigarette and exhaled very slowly in the careful manner of someone having her only smoke of the year.

'Meeting got moved up to today so I took the red-eye,' Kim said, carefully watching the other woman.

There was a certain frailty about Hiroko that hadn't existed three and a half years earlier when she first entered this apartment with a manner that suggested she knew she was late – by about half a century – but that she would be forgiven for it. Surely it was ridiculous, Kim told herself, not to accept a certain brittleness of someone Hiroko's age. And yet it was hard to give credence to such a thought – there was something so youthful in her posture, legs tucked under her body, elbow resting on sofa-back while her hand propped up her chin and a cigarette glowed between two fingers. The shadows in her corner of the unlit apartment conspired to make it seem just a short-circuiting of the mind to think this woman in silk pyjamas with stylishly short hair was seventy-seven years old.

Kim switched on a lamp and shallow lines etched themselves all across Hiroko Ashraf's face. The mole which used to rest above her cheekbone had slipped, just slightly. But the single green streak in her ivory hair attested to that which hadn't changed at all: her continued willingness to enter into new experiences without too much concern for whether anyone else might consider it either foolishness or frivolity.

'What's the meeting about? I thought you'd negotiated every-thing about moving to the New York office?'

'Oh, there's always something else to iron out,' Kim said, stretching her lean body, trying to get rid of the kinks that remained from the flight. 'But it suits me fine to be here. The run-up to Christmas is the time for exes to get in touch and suggest giving things one last try and God knows I don't need another one of those conversations with Gary. You do know I'm staying on until after Christmas, right?

'Just because you're terrible at communicating with everyone you've ever lived with doesn't mean your grandmother and I have the same problem.' Hiroko smiled. 'Of course I know. And I'm delighted.' She gestured towards the early-edition newspaper splayed on the coffee table next to Kim's half-empty mug. 'What's going on out in the world?'

'The last fire has almost burnt out.' Kim pointed in the direction of the looming emptiness outside before coming to sit down on the sofa.

'That's not the world, it's just the neighbourhood,' Hiroko said sharply.

Kim's eyebrows rose.

'Right,' she said, voice heavy with irony. 'Just a neighbourhood fire.'

Hiroko raised a hand in apology.

'Sorry, I didn't mean it that way.'

Kim took hold of her hand and squeezed it lightly.

'What's the matter, Roko?'

It seemed impossible sometimes, Kim Burton's blindness. And yet more impossible to hold anything against a woman of such genuine warmth and charm, all the most appealing parts of Konrad, Ilse and Harry right there in the pressure of her fingertips, the concern in her open, guileless face, her desire to know what exactly it was she'd got wrong this time. Hiroko had quite fallen in love with her within minutes of their meeting.

'Stupid posturing men, that's the matter. As ever,' Ilse Weiss said, walking out of her bedroom. She stopped beside the antique globe which rested on the drinks cabinet, and spun it slightly so the continents slid westwards and the unpartitioned mass of India was beneath her fingertips, *HINDOOSTAN* stamped across it. Very faint, the border which Harry had inked in when he was a young boy, to whom an outdated globe was a useless artefact.

'You're looking well, Gran.'

Ilse snorted, and came to sit between Hiroko and Kim, slapping down the leg Kim was resting on the coffee table.

'At ninety-one the best you can hope for is to be well preserved. Which is just a synonym for looking pickled.'

True enough, Hiroko thought, not unkindly. But despite the gauntness that had once been a striking angularity, and the mass of wrinkles which called to mind the topographical map of a particularly varied terrain, Ilse's aspect carried such a powerful memory of beauty with it that people still stopped to stare, and to imagine what might be revealed if you could only peel layers of time from her face.

'I thought you said you were going to be dead by morning.'

Ilse smiled, turning to Hiroko.

'It's not quite morning yet.'

Hiroko caught Ilse's wrist, pressed down against its veins.

'Well, you have no pulse that I can detect. Perhaps we both died, and this is the what comes after. And Kim's come visiting!'

'Nonsense. I'll get there before you. Like Delhi, like here.' She removed the cigarette from between Hiroko's fingers and took one short drag, before blowing out a strand of smoke with a schoolgirl's smile of transgression. 'But, you know, last night I really did feel that I'd be dead by morning.'

'You feel that at least twice a week,' Hiroko grumbled, retrieving her cigarette.

'Well. Eventually I'm bound to be right.' She tapped a finger on her granddaughter's knee. 'Don't tell her about fires burning out as though that's the world's most significant event. She thinks Pakistan and India are about to launch themselves into nuclear war.'

'Shit,' Kim said. 'Sorry, Hiroko.'

'And don't say "shit", Kim. If you must swear, say "fuck". It has a certain savage elegance to it.'

She said it primarily to amuse Hiroko enough to distract her but Hiroko only exhaled smoke, watching the cloud amass in front of her.

Ilse knew that look in her friend's eyes. It had been there, lurking beneath the thrill of arrival, when Hiroko had come to New York in 1998. 'Both times you've entered my home it's been nuclear-related. Once was acceptable; twice just seems like lazy plotting,' Ilse had said, with mock asperity, but that look of Hiroko's – the one that was back again – had told her that the bomb remained the one thing in the world she would not laugh about.

Hiroko extinguished the half-smoked cigarette, and traced wings of ash on the ashtray with its tip.

'Any news from Harry? Raza hasn't been in touch in a few days.'

In the decade the two men had been working together she'd been grateful to have an alternate conduit of information about Raza's life through Ilse, and Harry himself. Prior to that, in those first few years after Sajjad's death, months would sometimes go by without any word about him. She had assumed at first he was angry with her or had just grown uncaring, but whenever they did speak or meet he was as devoted as ever – so she saw that it wasn't lack of love that made him stay away, but something else, some guilt she brought out in him. Guilt about his father's death. Guilt, perhaps, about his own life, she sometimes wondered, but what was there to be guilty about?

Perhaps she wasn't enthusiastic enough about his profession, and he thought there was a judgement in there. It wasn't a matter of judgement – she just wished she could understand why two men as intelligent as Harry and Raza would choose to work in 'the administrative side of private security' – how much satisfaction could there be in overseeing the surveillance systems of banks and assigning bodyguards to people of influence? At one point she had thought it was just another cover for working with the CIA, and the thought of Harry pulling Raza into that world had so incensed her she made both men swear on Sajjad's grave that it wasn't true. They had both looked so ashen as they swore, she'd known they weren't lying. Then Ilse had firmly said, 'Harry's no longer with the CIA. I'd know if he was lying about that' – and there was no question of asking Ilse to swear on anyone's grave. She always said total honesty was one of the gifts of old age.

If only he was happy. That was all she had ever wanted for him. Perhaps that was an aspiration he felt he could never live up to. She pressed her hand against her heart – sometimes just thinking about him made her feel a crushing sense of devastation, quite out of proportion to the circumstances of his life.

Kim said, 'I can't even remember the last time Dad called me.' She did remember it, of course. She always remembered. 31 October.

He'd been in one of his nostalgic moods, recalling the Halloween she dressed up as World Peace – sticking maps of the world on to her clothes and a peace sign over each map. Except, she missed the third prong of the peace sign so instead she was, as Harry pointed out, World Mercedes-Benz. He laughed about it over the phone and Kim, wishing she could just laugh, so glad to hear his voice, found herself saying, 'You only pointed it out months later when you saw the pictures. You weren't there when it happened. As always.' Too often around her father, she couldn't stop being a teenager either in adulation or sullenness. And so she ensured he wouldn't call again for a very long time. Though perhaps he wasn't calling because she had a fairly certain idea of where he and Raza were, and he didn't want her to know, but he could never lie to her without getting caught out.

'I spoke to Harry yesterday,' Ilse said. She gave her granddaughter a slightly disapproving look. 'It does work to call him, you know. You shouldn't always wait for him to make the effort.' When there was no response to this other than a shrug she addressed herself to Hiroko. 'They're both fine. He didn't say where they are, but there's no need for you to start thinking they're in India or Pakistan. They could very well be on their way back to Miami.' That was where their company's head office was, but a few weeks ago they'd both said they were travelling on a year-end junket to see various clients in different parts of the globe, and satellite phones would be the only way to contact them until further notice. Only Hiroko had believed this line.

Hiroko's nod lacked all conviction.

'I've tried calling Sajjad to ask him what's going on along the border, but I can't get through to him.'

'Perhaps you need a better medium. Sajjad's been dead for years. Oh Hiroko, you can't go senile before me. You promised.'

I wish I were old, Kim thought, watching the two women. Really old. Old enough to have left everything troublesome behind – careers, lovers, regrets. Fathers. Mothers. Were you ever old enough for that?

Hiroko patted Ilse's arm.

'I don't mean my Sajjad. His nephew – Iqbal's youngest son.'

'Iqbal? Oh yes. The dissolute brother. I saw him once – he came to Bungle Oh! to tell Sajjad their father had died. It was winter – he wore a fabulous cloak. I suppose you've told me a dozen times who his son is, but you'll have to repeat it.'

Sometimes when presented with the increasing acuity of Ilse's recollection of the past Hiroko wondered if her own memory would undergo a slow dissolve, executed with perfect linearity, so that she would recede backwards through her life until there was nothing after the bomb in her remembrances – nothing of survival except the evidence of her body, so incredibly intact other than the charred tattoos between her shoulders and waist.

She made a quick gesture of impatience with her fingers.

'He's the one in the Army.'

'Oh yes. Indian Army?'

'Pakistan Army, Ilse. Sikandar's the one who stayed in India, not Iqbal.'

'Well, I'm just glad you're here, not there.'

Hiroko didn't answer. Today she felt acutely her initial unease about living in this luxurious apartment – if you were this high up, you should be in the hills. Abbottabad, that hill station with its echoes of Mussoorie, had become home in the years after Sajjad's death. Within a year of his funeral she had sold the house, taken early retirement from the school, and accepted the offer from her old friend Rehana – who had lived in Tokyo and Karachi before widowhood returned her to her childhood home – to come and live with her in the hills of Abbottabad, away from the chaos of a city which was so emptied of joy without Sajjad and Raza that to live in it was to live in regret.

In Abbottabad, she had discovered she was a woman of hills and greenery, a woman content to walk for hours through stretches of silent valleys, with only a German shepherd – she called him Kyubi – for company and protection. But then India tested its nuclear bomb, and around her almost everyone said Pakistan must do the same, there was no real option (the only voices of exception came from a retired general who lived down the road from her, the journalist who always asked her to edit his columns, and the woman who came twice a week to cook and clean who said non-violence was the only solution). So she picked up the phone to call Ilse Weiss in New York, and said she was going to stay with Raza, now in Miami, and perhaps she'd stop in New York along the way. Somehow that stop had extended into three years, through a combination of Ilse's insistence and Raza's lack thereof.

'Raza did email yesterday,' Hiroko said abruptly. 'Not to say where he was. Just to cancel his visit. It doesn't fit his schedule.' She caught and held Kim's look of sympathy. They both knew what it was to be an easily erased entry in the cluttered schedule of a beloved relative. Though how it had happened with her and her boy she still didn't know. Somewhere she had failed, terribly.

'What a pity,' Ilse said unconvincingly.

'I've told you before. You don't have to pretend. I know you don't like my son any more than you liked his father.'

'Oh, I'm sure I was a little in love with Sajjad. Don't you think? He was terribly good-looking, and I was always quite shallow about that sort of thing.'

Hiroko, laughing, clasped Ilse's hand in hers.

'I'm so glad you're my friend, Ilse Weiss.'

I really, really wish I were old, Kim thought, watching the two of them.

28

'K on! Kon-man! Hey, Razor!'

Raza Konrad swivelled sharply in the direction of the voice, prepared for a challenge. But all he saw was a smiling young American tanning on a beach towel, his body an assortment of puffed-up muscles bisected by black shorts so tiny they could have been inked in by an underzealous censor. The American could hardly have presented a sharper contrast to Raza with his slight frame concealing its wiriness beneath button-down shirt and trousers, and his guarded expression.

'Throw me a can of beer from the icebox,' the man said, running the flat of his palm over his close-cropped hair, and wiping the sweat on the edge of the towel. 'And have one yourself.'

Raza paused a moment to test the sentence for insults – was it merely a friendly offer, or did it presume that Raza needed permission from this boy to take what he wanted from the icebox? The tanning man continued to smile; Raza shrugged and reached into the icebox, which was only a few steps away from him. The chill against his fingers was welcoming, and he plucked out a nugget of ice, sliding it along his throat and face. By the time he was close enough to the tanning man to toss the can of beer at him the ice had melted.

'This time next year this place will be a five-star resort,' the man said, gesturing expansively around the mud compound with its high walls and gun towers. He tapped the side of his head. 'I've got a plan. You want in?'

Raza shook his head and continued to walk in the direction of the armoured juggernaut which he wasn't supposed to take out of the compound without clearance. Well, there was no one here for him to get clearance from – everyone out hunting down terror, other than the tanning boy, whose sprained ankle was keeping him away from active duty, and the cooks, cleaners and other assortment of Third Country Nationals (a group from which Raza had always been exempted by virtue of payscale rather than passport). He would have preferred the jeep – open-aired and therefore less of a challenge to men with guns – but he didn't want to commandeer the only vehicle available to the TCNs. Though around here he didn't know where they might want to drive to. Perhaps 'away' was destination enough, he considered, as he drove the Humvee out with a roar into the dusty plains of Afghanistan.

That was how he had felt – what was it? Nearly nineteen years ago – after his father died. Simply to be out of the spaces which Sajjad Ali Ashraf had filled with his laughter and his embraces. So when his cousin Hussein – Iqbal's eldest son – called from Dubai to condole over Sajjad's death and mentioned that should Raza need a job there was an opening at the hotel in which he worked there was no hesitation in Raza as he said yes.

Hiroko had been furious. University, she told her son. You will go to university as your father wanted.

I have to provide for us now, Raza said, trying to play the part of the son who puts aside his own desires for the sake of his responsibilities as head of the family.

Hiroko wasn't fooled, but she saw that it wasn't just the memory of his father that he wanted to escape but also the presence of her own grief, which sharpened his guilt with its every expression. That made it impossible for her to demand that he stay.

Was that the moment he walked in one direction and his conscience in another, Raza wondered, or was it earlier when he urged a boy towards a training camp filled with militants?

He lowered the tinted-glass windows of the Humvee – though this was expressly against company rules – and ejected the rap CD from the player, replacing it with Nusrat Fateh Ali Khan. *Sometimes the walls shake, sometimes the doors tremble* . . . Raza looked out at the landscape speeding past in which it was impossible to separate rock from rubble. Something metal glinted at him from the rubble and he imagined a watch, still keeping time on a wrist without a pulse.

In his decade in Dubai, prior to Harry re-entering his life, he sought out as many nationalities as possible, acquiring language with the zeal of a collector – Bengali and Tamil from the hotel staff; Arabic from the receptionists; Swahili from the in-house jazz band; French from Claudia – the most consistent of his many lovers; Farsi from the couple who ran the restaurant at the corner of his street; Russian from the two hookers who lived in the apartment next door to his studio and knew they could use their spare key to slip into his bed after their clients had left, seeking comfort or laughter or platonic embraces; and beyond this, a smattering of words from all over the globe. The more languages you learned, he discovered, the more you found overlap: 'Qah-weh' in Arabic, 'gehve' in Farsi, 'café' in French, 'coffee' in English, 'kohi' in Japanese . . .

But he stayed away from the Afghans. To take even a word from them seemed an act of theft.

He raised the window and everything became mercifully unreal. No brilliant blueness of the sky forcing him to recall Abdullah who said the winter sky over Afghanistan was different from anything 'those Karachiwallas' could believe possible.

Hours later, Raza jumped down from his Humvee, blinking away the darkness of the tinted-glass enclosure. He was in a broad pass through the great mud-and-pebble mountains which had once stirred mythic creatures in his imagination. But instead of gunfire echoing through the silence there was the noise of commerce instead. Tea shacks and taxis, donkey carts piled high with wares of one kind or another, boys selling bottles of mineral water and cheap plastic sunglasses. Raza watched a van unload a group of men who walked forward about twenty feet, got into another van and drove off. Somewhere in that twenty-foot expanse Afghanistan became Pakistan. The Pakistani soldiers on the far side of the expanse didn't seem particularly interested in checking the papers of any of the Pathans who went back and forth, but as Raza approached one of them put up a hand, palm pressed almost against Raza's face.

'So you let Afghans into Pakistan without any trouble, but you stop a Pakistani who's coming home,' Raza said in Urdu. 'Strange world this has become. Go, tell Captain Ashraf his brother's here.'

He walked back to the Afghan side and sipped a cup of tea as he sat on his haunches with the other men, feeling slightly foolish for being the only man out of uniform who was wearing trousers rather than a shalwar. Within a few minutes he saw Captain Sajjad Ashraf approach – he was the youngest by far of Iqbal's sons, and as Raza watched him strut forward, beating the air around him with a stick, he wondered if Hussein in Dubai really thought it was worth it: all those years of working in hotel kitchens so that this Sajjad could be given the education his brothers never had, and with it prospects they could only dream about in all the years their father was whoring and gambling away all the family money.

Raza stepped forward to meet his cousin, but when Sajjad stopped he did too. Raza was the elder – by almost a decade – he should be the one who was approached.

His cousin smiled across the distance between them.

'If I come towards you the Pakistan Army will have invaded Afghanistan.'

Raza rolled his eyes, and walked forward.

'Welcome home,' Sajjad said, embracing him perfunctorily. 'You look well. The American military must be looking after you.'

'I'm not with . . .' He stopped, and shrugged away the rest of the sentence. The line between working for the American military and working for a private military company contracted to the American military was so fine he knew he would only look foolish for trying to delineate it. 'How are things with you? How's Hussein? Everyone else?'

'Fine, everyone's fine. Hussein and Altamash have expanded their business – they're opening a third supermarket next month.'

Raza smiled at that. His life in Dubai had grown very separate to that of Hussein and their other cousin Altamash from Delhi, as his language skills and unPakistani looks had moved him swiftly from the kitchens where his cousins worked (so much for all Hussein's letters about his high-flying life among the sand dunes) on a path upward to the 'gold-star reception desk' at a five-star hotel, but any guilt he felt about that separateness was put to rest the day he gave his cousins the initial down payment for their first tiny store with his sign-on bonus from Arkwright and Glenn.

'I've just sent my wife and children to Dubai to stay with them,' Sajjad continued. 'Safest option with the way things are now. Bastard Indians.' He swiped the air with his stick. 'They never miss an opportunity. Well, let them try to take us on.'

'What'll happen when they try,' Raza mocked. 'You going to scare them away with your big stick?'

Sajjad scowled – his face instantly transforming into that of the youngest member of a family who spends his life bullied and teased by those older than him. 'We've got better weapons than sticks, Raza bhai.'

'The nuclear option?' Raza said steadily. 'My mother has been worrying about that. I told her no one's that crazy.'

Sajjad looked thoughtful.

'Here is our problem. India is so big. How can we ever destroy their missile launchers, the nuclear installations in the south, in the east? Our planes would be shot down before they got that far, our missiles can't travel that distance. India, on the other hand, can take out our launchers, no problem. And then we're left with nuclear weapons and no way to deliver them.'

Deliver. It sounded so polite.

'So where does that leave us?'

'With only one option. The instant the war starts, before the bastards have time to take out our launchers, we must launch our missiles. Our biggest missiles. Right into the mouth of their government in Dilli. Cause such havoc that they turn around and run, and never ever think of even looking us in the eye again.'

'Dilli?'

'Yes. Dilli.'

The earth shook beneath Raza's feet and for a moment he believed Sajjad Ali Ashraf would rise out of it and pull the man who shared his name down into the grave with him – but it was only the rumbling of a van making its way along the mountain pass. Suddenly able to see the absurdity of it all, Raza started to laugh.

'And you're sharing this classified strategic information with a man who works with the United States military.'

'You're my cousin,' said Sajjad, looking wounded. 'What? What are you smiling at?'

'This strategy of yours. Ours. We're crazier than you are. We could push that button at the slightest provocation so don't even slightly provoke us.' He switched to English. 'Not MAD, but madder. Are you hoping I'll pass this on to the Indians via the Pentagon?'

'I don't know what you're talking about,' Sajjad said. 'And if you take this attitude I won't give you the information you want. It wasn't easy to get it, you know.'

Raza put out a hand, caught his cousin by the elbow.

'Sorry. Please tell me. What did you discover?'

The name and telephone number of a man in Kabul; that was all Sajjad had for him. In 1983, this man had been the Commander at the camp where Raza had spent that terrible afternoon.

'I was only able to find out which camp it was because the ISI have a record of Raza Ashraf from Karachi who the Americans sent to that camp,' Sajjad said, grudging in his admiration for the wild adventure of Raza's youth.

'Does the ISI have a record of whether anyone in the camp was told anything about me? My name, what the ISI believed I was doing there?'

Sajjad shook his head.

'It's unlikely. The ISI doesn't give out information to anyone unless it's necessary. Certainly not to the Afghans. But I wouldn't get too hopeful about this man in Kabul. Even if he remembers your friend Abdullah – Raza bhai, what are the chances he's alive?'

And even if he is, then what? Raza thought as he drove back to base. What if he's become one of them – the black-turbanned men who banned everything of joy, blasted ancient prophets out of mountain-faces. Abdullah, he couldn't help remember, had talked of the carvings along the road to Peshawar as the work of infidels. And women – Abdullah at fourteen knew exactly what a woman's place in the world was, and it was nothing that Hiroko's son could understand. Then it hadn't really mattered, to be honest – but now, just two weeks in this country and the sight of women shrouded as though they were the walking dead made him want to scream. In Miami as in Dubai it was women who kept his life from becoming that of a drone – sex the habitat in which he was most at home, its balance of intimacy and transience perfectly suited to his temperament. He fell in love, briefly but intensely, with all the women who invited him into their beds, never seeing that what he truly loved was the version of himself which manifested itself in their company – a version comprised of his father's lightness and his mother's boldness.

At sunset, he was driving past a mosque, and the sky-blue beauty of its dome made him get out of his Humvee and prostrate himself on the ground as the muezzin's call wheeled across the plain. The sound was drowned out by the whup-whup of a chopper, which swooped closer to the ground to investigate the stationary Humvee. Raza jumped up, waved at the pilot, and stepped back into the vehicle just as a group of elderly men came out of the mosque to see what was happening.

'Sorry for the interruption,' Raza said in Pashto, leaning out of the window, but the men only looked accusingly from the American vehicle to the man whose features suggested tribes unfriendly to the Pashtuns. One of the men unslung a Kalashnikov from his shoulder – Raza remembered Abdullah lifting a piece of cloth like a magician to reveal the gleaming gun beneath – and another said, 'Go away from here.'

Last time I'm travelling in this beast, Raza thought as he drew up to the compound, waving away the warnings of the Sri Lankan guard who had witnessed Harry's fury when he discovered the Humvee was missing.

'Who came in the chopper?' he asked.

'American.' The man shrugged, as if to say anyone else would have travelled by road.

29

'Did I ever tell you I was so determined when I arrived in New York to cast off the shackles and constraints of life as Mrs Burton that I swore to myself I wouldn't be shocked by anything in my cousin Willie's life – even though he kept sending me letters before my arrival warning me that his social circle was not what I was used to?' Ilse burrowed down into the sofa cushions, arms wrapped around a cushion resting on her stomach.

So many late nights in Delhi had unfolded just like this: Ilse in this very position on the living-room sofa, Hiroko sitting in an armchair beside her sipping a cup of jasmine tea, chatter going back and forth between them. Then, as now, Hiroko always pretended the stories she'd already heard were new to her because she enjoyed the animation with which Ilse retold her favourite anecdotes.

'So my very second day in New York I walked into the kitchen in Willie's flat in the middle of the night to get some water, and there he was with this beautiful young man – naked! – doing something I had never seen done before, not even in a photograph. And I had so steeled myself to take everything in my stride that I said, "Don't mind me," and walked right past them to the fridge. Poor Willie almost fainted with embarrassment, and the young man caught a bus back home to Iowa the next morning and never returned!'

'Well, no wonder I stopped getting your letters in Karachi all those years ago,' Hiroko laughed. 'If you were writing things like that the censors must have been framing them on their office walls!'

'Oh I was so desperately in need of all that liberation,' Ilse said, kicking her foot up in the air. 'New York after the war. It was the most wonderful madness. I kept wishing you were here with me.'

'I was where I wanted to be,' Hiroko said quietly.

Ilse reached out her arm and caught Hiroko's wrist.

'I do know that. I used to wish it for my sake, not yours.' She paused for a moment. 'Well, all right. Maybe a little for yours. I place much too high a premium on material comforts, always have. I don't have your stoical Japanese spirit.'

'You talk such incredible nonsense,' Hiroko said, with as much affection as asperity.

The flung-open front door, the sound of Kim's voice shouting out Ilse's name, sucked all tranquillity from the room.

'Dad, have you heard from Dad? I can't get hold of him.'

'Kim, what's the matter?' Ilse tried to sit up, but her body was too ensconced in the sofa cushions and she only managed to raise her head a little before it, too, fell back, to her sharp cry of impatience.

'Haven't you heard the news? A man tried to light a bomb inside his shoe on a flight. To Miami. And I can't get hold of Dad.' She pulled Ilse upright as she spoke, and thought senility might have finally caught up with her grandmother when Ilse's only response was to pat her cheek as if she was a child who had just lost her favourite toy.

'There are hundreds of flights to Miami every day, and your father is almost never on any of them,' she said.

'And everyone on the plane is fine,' Hiroko added. 'Other than that stupid man. Was he still wearing the shoe while trying to set it on fire? The news report didn't make that clear.'

Kim looked from Ilse to Hiroko, not believing how unconcerned they were.

'It was a plane,' she said. 'Another suicide attack on a plane.'

'Come here.' Ilse pulled her down on to the sofa, and put her arm around her. 'Stop doing what you're doing. Stop trying to imagine precisely what would happen to a plane mid-air if a bomb went off inside it.'

Kim closed her eyes.

'I'm not trying to imagine it, Gran. I can't help imagining it.' She had trained to be a structural engineer because she'd always wanted to know how to keep things from falling, from breaking apart. Only these last months had she seen how much she'd had to learn about falling, about breaking, in order to do it.

'Let's try getting hold of your father,' Ilse said, dialling Harry's satphone number. He answered almost immediately.

'Have you been in the vicinity of any flammable loafers today?' Ilse asked.

'What?' Harry shouted over the roar of something that sounded like helicopters. 'You mean that shoe guy on the flight? No, of course not. Is that why Kim called? I've just got to my phone and seen three missed calls from her.'

Ilse passed the phone to Kim, who shouted into it, 'When you see three missed calls, you might want to try calling right back.'

'I was about to!'

And there they went, Ilse thought, exchanging an exasperated glance with Hiroko who just said, 'Love to him and Raza,' before slipping away to the kitchen.

'I hate this,' Kim said, after hanging up the phone. She rested her head on Ilse's shoulder, but lightly, aware how frail the old woman's bones were. 'I hate that it felt familiar, trying to get hold of him. Those hours I couldn't get through to you on 9/11 . . .'

'It was minutes, not hours,' Ilse said. 'Look, your skin is so young compared to mine we could be creatures from different species.' She rested her hand on Kim's, gently patting it.

'I just want the world to be as it was.' Ilse said nothing, just carried on patting her hand. Only with Gran was it possible to be this way, to feel herself sinking into peace. Her father would have responded with some CIA-style political analysis about shifting geopolitical trends. And – worse – her mother with her cod psychology would be saying, 'Now, Kim, darling, you know this is bringing up those suppressed feelings of loss and vulnerability around your father and my divorce. I know you chose this profession of yours because in some way you're trying to atone for what you see as your own inability to hold our marriage together. So when anything threatens to collapse or crumble it

265

brings back that sense of personal failure you felt when the marriage broke up.' And she always emphasised the words 'broke up' as though they conclusively proved her point that Kim's passion for engineering was really all about her.

'I've lived through Hitler, Stalin, the Cold War, the British Empire, segregation, apartheid, God knows what. The world will survive this, and with just a tiny bit of luck so will everyone you love. But it is entirely possible you'll need some kind of holiday before that happens.' Ilse rapped Kim's hand firmly at the final sentence. Kim had said she was only coming to New York for a meeting about ironing out details of her relocation and would be on vacation after that until the Christmas holidays ended, but somehow she'd ended up working on a project out of the New York office instead.

Kim made a non-committal noise deep in her throat.

'I don't know how I managed to never worry about Dad all those years he was with the CIA. But now—' She stopped as Ilse pinched her and gestured her head towards the kitchen where their voices might easily travel. They had never spoken of it, but silently both had agreed on a pact to allow Hiroko to continue believing Raza and Harry's euphemisms about administrative work in security. Lowering her voice she said, 'Everything in the world is so scary, nothing more than the thought of where he might be, what he's doing. I'm frightened all the time, all the time. And I hate it. It must make me so amazingly tedious to be around.'

'Your conversation has been somewhat limited of late,' Ilse said. 'Sometimes I wish I had been in London during the war simply so I could pull you up with stories of the spirit of the Blitz.'

'Oh, don't beat yourself up over it. It wouldn't have worked.' She gave her grandmother a resounding kiss on the cheek.

'I mean what I said about the holiday.' Ilse spoke with that voice of gravity which she only brought out when she was very seriously concerned about Kim.

'I know you mean it. But right now, I need some place to go at least five days a week where I feel a sense of control.'

Ilse, who knew her granddaughter far better than either of Kim's parents did, had long ago recognised it was the need for control

266

rather than atonement for her inability to hold together a marriage at the age of four which had drawn her into the profession she'd chosen. She still remembered the expression of fierce accomplishment – almost defiance – on Kim's face the day she came home from university for her winter holidays and said, 'I know how to make a building earthquake-proof.' Earthquake-proof! As if there was anything to be done in defence if the world opened up beneath you.

Poor Gary! Ilse found herself thinking in unexpectedly sympathetic terms about the man who she'd never thought good enough for her granddaughter. Kim had only chosen him to begin with because she knew he'd never make her feel uncontrolled. She had enough of that around her father – had always wanted to summon up indifference to both his absences and his presence, and grew so enraged when everything but indifference was what she felt. And, of course, she'd always ultimately break up with the Garys of the world simply because her basic nature was too passionate to settle for someone towards whom she could feel so completely lukewarm. One day, Ilse thought, one day someone will come along and knock her sideways. It will either be the best or the worst thing of her life.

'What were you and Hiroko talking about before I whirled in like a banshee?' Kim had kicked off her boots and curled up on the sofa, her body pliant with relief now that Harry was OK.

'The "Willie in the kitchen" story.' Ilse laughed.

'If there is a heaven, Uncle Willie will be glaring down at you from it,' Kim said, shaking her head as if disapproving, though Ilse knew Kim loved this bawdy side to her, and would often encourage her to say the most outrageous things with a single smile or glimmer of the eye.

'Nonsense. If there is a heaven, Willie is doing exactly what he was doing in the kitchen. Otherwise it's not heaven. Not for Willie.' Suddenly she cackled. 'Imagine if those suicide bombers end up in Willie's heaven. Imagine the looks on their faces.'

'Gran, that isn't funny.'

'It's hilarious! Hiroko, isn't it hilarious?'

Hiroko, re-entering the room, handed Kim a cup of something steaming-hot.

'When I knew her first, she was very well behaved. I promise you, she was.'

Ilse's laughter was clear and unconstrained – the laugh of a woman who knew how fortunate she had been to get a second life.

It was this laughter that Hiroko thought of some days later, when Kim was back in Seattle packing up her life to move it to New York, and Ilse didn't respond when Hiroko rapped sharply on her bedroom door and asked her how long she was going to go on sleeping. She thought of the laughter even before she opened the door to receive confirmation of what she already knew to be true.

Pushing the hair away from her old friend's tranquil face, she thought, It can happen like this, too. Not just scales and shadows and bullet wounds, but peace is also possible at the end.

She picked up the phone from Ilse's bedside and called Raza's satphone. When he answered, his voice distracted at first but instantly snapping into concern as he heard the tone of her voice, she said, 'Raza-chan, you need to be Harry's support today. Ilse has died in her sleep.' When he was finally assured that she was not about to fall apart and didn't need him to phone anyone in New York to come over and hold her hand she hung up and sat with Ilse for a few minutes more, crying with sorrow but not despair.

Then she drew a deep breath, asked any part of Ilse's spirit still lingering in the room to give her strength to do the unbearable, and called Kim to say her grandmother was dead.

30

H arry Burton walked through the bright winter morning, jet lag and sorrow colliding to make everything in New York seem a little off-kilter. He had expected to come back and find the city as he'd last seen it near the end of September with a great pall downtown, survivor's unease uptown, but instead he found an ongoing collision between the city's forward-strutting nature and the demands of tragedy which insisted grief must be held on to like a dying lover.

He wanted to be done with it, his own grief. It was unbearable, seeping into everything. Her ghost everywhere along these SoHo streets. Did Kim feel it too? He glanced sideways at his daughter, easily keeping pace with his long strides, everything about her appearance a warning: combat pants, steel-toed boots and a bomber jacket half unzipped to reveal the black T-shirt beneath, freshly shorn copper hair sleeked against her cheetah-skull, tipped with the black dye which still hadn't entirely grown out.

'Penny for your thoughts, panther,' he said, wincing at his own inability to exit cliché.

'Gran was half the reason I'm moving to New York.' She glanced up at him. 'You didn't know I'm moving to New York, did you?'

'No. But that's great. I mean, I always picture you here. I know you've been in Seattle a while but . . . the hills, the grunge, the self-conscious coffee drinking! No, no, not my daughter. It's always seemed like one of those short-term flings, you know?'

'I know short-term flings, Dad. Just not as well as you do.' She grinned, and put her arm through his.

Surprised, but far from displeased, he squeezed her arm and tried to think what a father should say in such a moment, his daughter's eyes still red with weeping as they had been ever since he arrived yesterday just in time to bury Ilse.

'Sweetheart, she died as she would have wanted to. In her sleep, at peace, after what Hiroko tells me was a raucous dinner with her closest friend. We should all be so lucky.'

'Doesn't make me miss her less,' Kim said, resting her head against her father's shoulder.

They walked that way for a while, though the posture was slightly awkward. The SoHo crowds were thinned in the post-Christmas doldrums, for which Harry was grateful. Too much time in narrow mountain passes these past weeks, and his body was still primed for danger. The fire escapes running in zigzags along the length of cast-iron buildings looked like misshapen spines, deliberately twisted out of shape, and on either side of the street buildings loomed, their windows reflecting sunlight as the barrel of a gun might do.

'What's the other half,' he said, 'of the reason why you're moving to New York?'

'This.' Kim waved her hands in the direction of the flags flying from every edifice, then gestured to the emptied skyline. 'The thing about structural engineers, Dad, is that we knew right away. Switched on the television, saw the flames, and knew the building would fall. The rest of the country had a few minutes' grace but we were the Cassandras standing in front of the first images, saying it's coming down, all of it. And then the second one. From that moment, I haven't wanted to be anywhere except back here.' She looked around fiercely. 'We'll keep building.'

The Cassandras! Harry thought. Because you predicted total disaster an hour before it happened? Just one hour.

'If you slow down construction the terrorists have won,' Harry said, and felt her arm slip out of his.

'I suppose this is all very mundane to you,' she said. 'Death and destruction. Good for business and entirely unsurprising.' She knelt down by a lamp post and buried her hands in the thick fur of the collie leashed to it, furious at how much she had wanted his understanding. The cold seeped from the sidewalk through her combat pants.

Harry held his hand out and the collie, who had accepted Kim's attention with the air of an aristocrat receiving nothing more than what's due, nuzzled at his palm.

Traitor, Kim thought.

'Unsurprising, yes,' Harry said. It's true, he was entirely unsurprised by 9/11 – had, in fact, assumed a jihadi connection to the Oklahoma City bombing in 1995 – but he was also stunned by his reaction to it, the depth of his fury, the wish for all the world to stop and weep with him for the city which had adopted him when he was eleven. He was in the Democratic Republic of the Congo at the time, overseeing the setting up of Arkwright and Glenn's operation to provide security for a Belgian diamond-export company, and was well aware of how disproportionate his attitude must seem in a country which had lost more than two and a half million people in a war which seemed to have pauses rather than an end. He sat down with a calculator on 12 September, and worked it out to more than two thousand deaths a day, each day, for over three years – but he couldn't find any way to connect those numbers to his emotions. 'And good for business, very definitely.'

'Well, that's honest,' Kim said, standing up and swatting at her combat pants with far greater vigour than was necessary to brush off the dust.

'It's only part of the story. We only ever hear part of each other's story, panther.'

'We?' She stared at him and shook her head. 'You're the one who keeps leaving.'

'I'm here now.'

'How long?'

He looked away.

'Thought so.' Despite the disappointment there was a satisfaction about being right.

'Kim, you and I – we're going to spend a lot of time together soon. More than you want. Take that as a threat or a promise.'

'Sure,' she said, her voice tight with disbelief. 'When the abstract noun is defeated . . . or will you be going after horror and misery next?'

He couldn't help laughing.

'Your father's an old man. I'll be sixty-five in June. Retirement time, sweetheart.'

Kim snorted.

'You'll never retire.'

'Well, OK,' he admitted. 'But I'll take a holiday. How about we go to Delhi together? I'll show you my childhood.'

It was an old promise, but she couldn't help being drawn in by it. That was the thing about Harry Burton which made his smiles so impossible to resist – when he said a thing, he meant it. For that moment.

As they walked down the street there was a strangled sound behind them – Kim turned to see the collie straining at his leash, eyes fixed on Harry. *Pathetic*, Kim thought, even as she allowed Harry to take her arm and loop it through his own again.

'Mom sends her condolences,' she said. 'She offered to fly across, but I'm not sure I can handle dealing with both of you at the same time.'

Harry's laugh was an acknowledgement of the truth behind that lightly uttered comment.

'How is she? Still masterfully hiding the heart I broke behind a veneer of total happiness with what's-his-name?'

'Yes, Dad, she's still very happily married. Desperately worried about me, though. She thinks the fact that I've been single for over three months is some kind of curse. Last time we spoke she said when I meet men I shouldn't tell them what I do for a living. Apparently, engineering is too macho. It scares off the boys. I think she's trying to tell me I come across as a lesbian.'

'You come across as you,' Harry said. 'And if the boys think that puts you out of their league, they're probably right!'

She knew he wasn't just trying to win her over with cheap compliments. Whatever else could be said about Harry as a father, he left no doubt about his belief that his daughter was the best thing his life had ever produced. She took his hand in hers, as she used to when she was still young enough to pretend she needed his help crossing the road.

Further down the street, a woman – elegantly dressed in camel-coloured winter coat with a beret jauntily angled on her head – was staring intently at a store window.

'What is she looking at?' Harry whispered, horrified, and Kim laughed and let go of his arm to rush forward to Hiroko.

The window was dominated by a male mannequin dressed in skintight leather, an improbable bulge below his waist. Kim put her arms around Hiroko's shoulders and they stood there – half laughter, half tears – recalling Ilse stopping in front of the mannequin on her ninetieth birthday, saying, 'I wonder what this decade will be like? My eighties were not what I anticipated – Viagra, you know. All those old lovers crawled out of the woodwork.'

Harry cleared his throat uncertainly behind the two women and Kim winked at Hiroko.

'He's so not ready to hear it,' she said.

Hiroko stood on tiptoes, as tall as her sensible old-lady shoes would allow, and kissed Harry's cheek, watching the blush spread across it to reveal just how rare such gestures of affection were in his life.

'Come to China with me,' she said, taking his arm.

Kim watched Harry carefully modulate his gait to keep time with Hiroko's without making it evident that she was slowing him down and suddenly she knew that they would go to Delhi. Harry, Hiroko and she – and Raza.

Kim had never met Raza Konrad Ashraf – his blink-and-you'll-miss-it trips to see Hiroko never coincided with her more frequent sojourns in New York – but he was framed on the mantel of the Mercer Street apartment and in every third sentence out of both Hiroko and Harry's mouths, so perhaps it wasn't so surprising that he sometimes made his way into her dreams. He would appear in the strangest situations, his presence never a surprise.

They'd probably drive each other crazy when they met, she thought. It was clear that Raza was just another version of Harry himself. Their two personalities a collision waiting to happen. She found herself smiling at the prospect, lagging behind Harry and Kim as they neared Chinatown, her mind in Delhi already.

Harry was glad for the distance between his daughter and him, so he didn't have to feel her bristling disapproval as he said firmly, in response to Hiroko's question, 'Of course Raza's not in India or Pakistan. I promised you I'd keep him out of danger, didn't I?' Harry made many promises but that one to Hiroko was among the few he had tried his utmost to keep. As far as possible he ensured Raza stayed in the sterile world of Arkwright and Glenn's Miami head office, translating his way through client meetings and contracts and emails and wire-tapped conversations. But Afghanistan was different – the first time A and G had been contracted by the US military, an opportunity that had the shareholders giddy with prospects both short-term and long. And Raza Konrad Ashraf, the translating genius who had once passed himself off as an Afghan, was an asset too great to be left behind.

Hiroko was unsure how to raise her next question. It concerned a matter they'd never discussed since the day they stood together over Sajjad's corpse. To allow herself a moment to decide how best to broach the subject she slowed and looked at the faded poster pasted on to the heavily graffitied wall of a loft building. It consisted of a picture of a young man and the words: MISSING SINCE 9/11. IF YOU HAVE ANY INFORMATION ABOUT LUIS RIVERA PLEASE CALL . . .

Hiroko thought of the train station at Nagasaki, the day Yoshi had taken her to Tokyo. The walls plastered with signs asking for news of missing people. She stepped closer to take in the smile of Luis Rivera, its unfettered optimism. In moments such as these it seemed entirely wrong to feel oneself living in a different history to the people of this city.

'You must still have friends in the CIA.' The question tumbled out of her mouth.

'Everyone's doing their best to make sure both sides back down, Hiroko,' he said, understanding precisely why she had asked the question.

It was an answer she trusted more than any assurance that there wouldn't be nuclear war. She patted his arm and turned away from Luis Rivera, though Kim who had come up to stand next to her remained staring at him.

As she entered the higgledy-piggledy streets of Chinatown, pushy and cantankerous in a way that made the 'attitude' of the rest of Manhattan appear amateurish, Hiroko recalled the thrill of coming here for the first time and discovering so many vegetables she hadn't seen since Nagasaki. She still remembered some of the Chinese names for produce her mother used to buy in the Chinese quarter – and recalled, also, Konrad Weiss's invented names for the vegetables he didn't know: pak choi was 'windswept cabbage', a lotus root sliced down the centre was 'fossilised flower'. And ginger, which Sajjad used to eat copiously, dipping sticks of it into achaar as a snack, was 'knots of earth'.

Harry stopped beside a squatting man moving three dead fish around on the sidewalk while other men around him gesticulated and called out. Some magic trick, some betting game – he was determined to work it out. It gave Hiroko the opportunity to look at the cardboard boxes filled with fruit and vegetables in front of a cramped store. She pointed at the green-yellow spheres in a box and found herself saying, 'Hong xao,' – a word she hadn't uttered since Nagasaki. In Urdu it was 'bair'. She had no idea what the English name was.

Nagasaki. She touched her back.

'Is that bair?' Harry said, making her smile at this nephew of Konrad's.

He had disappeared from her life for years after Sajjad's death before arriving at her home in Abbottabad in the early nineties to say he had quit his previous job (even then he didn't utter the name of his former employers), now he was in private security – a glorified bodyguard, really – but the business needed translators, so he was wondering how Raza might feel about coming to work with him. It didn't occur to her whether she should forgive him or not for lying to her and Sajjad – he was a Weiss and he was offering Raza a chance to escape the soulless pit that was Dubai. And of course, he said, of course Raza wouldn't be in the path of bullets.

A few minutes later, Kim, Hiroko and Harry were settled on a bench in Columbus Park, Kim uncertainly twirling between her fingers the fruit with unappealing scent which her father and Hiroko were eating with the relish of nostalgia.

'If you're moving to New York you should live around here,' Harry said.

'Here? Why?' She looked around, trying to imagine what about this neighbourhood made her father picture her in it: was it the wrinkled twins in baseball caps playing Chinese chess on the bench opposite? The women pulling coats closer to their bodies as they bent over mah-jong pieces? The blind man caressing in long-slow strokes the air between him and the woman who was looking straight at him as she sang, high-pitched and mournful, accompanied by men with weeping stringed instruments?

'Just,' Harry said. If he told her that anyone wanting to strike America again was unlikely to do so in Chinatown she'd just say his line of work made him paranoid. But she turned to look at him, and confusion left her expression, replaced by understanding. There was a tiny smile – acknowledging his concern – and then, a nod.

It bothered him, the nod. She shouldn't understand fear sufficiently to know what he was thinking. He recalled how she had stiffened, earlier on their walk, at the sight of a dark-haired man doing something with his shoes. He had laughed then, said, 'He's tying his laces, Kim, not detonating a bomb,' but now he couldn't see it as amusing. In the valleys of Afghanistan, fear was necessary; he'd been trained how to use it. But what did Kim know of moving through the world with fear at your back? Weapons in the hands of the uninitiated, he thought, understanding now what it was about this new New York that made him so uneasy.

'I told Hiroko we'll stay together in Gran's apartment until I decide where I want to live,' Kim said. She bit into the green-yellow fruit and tried to pretend she enjoyed its bitter taste.

'We both think the other one needs looking after,' Hiroko explained. She looked at the half-eaten fruit in Kim's hand. 'That's not ripe,' she said. 'It must taste horrible. Why are you eating it?'

Kim spat the fruit out into the tissue Hiroko handed her.

'I didn't want to offend you by saying it's disgusting,' she said.

'Oh dear,' Hiroko sighed. 'You're going to be a nightmare to live with if you insist on cultural sensitivity.'

'It's a smelly little fruit, and you've got to be crazy to like it,' Kim said.

276

'Excellent.' Hiroko smiled. 'Thank you. And you need to vary your wardrobe. How many black T-shirts do you own?'

Harry watched with satisfaction. Whatever might be happening in the wider world, at least the Weiss-Burtons and the Tanaka-Ashrafs had finally found spaces to cohabit in, complicated shared history giving nothing but depth to the reservoir of their friendships.

31

I n the green world, Harry Burton stepped on a dark clod and watched it break open, revealing an interior of phosphorescence. He took off his night-vision goggles and pointed at the glowing ember while his eyes adjusted to the dimness of the cave.

'Someone was here, not so long ago.' He ran his fingers along the cave wall and encountered a groove beneath the soot, which his fingers followed to reveal a carving of a falcon.

'Arabs?' asked his ex-colleague Steve, who had long since moved to the CIA paramilitary. He meant 'al-Qaeda'.

Harry shrugged.

'Portraiture doesn't fit with their brand of Islam.'

'Yeah. But mass murder, that's OK.' Steve gestured wearily at the contractor who walked in from the connecting cave. 'Tell the guys we're heading back. Nothing here. Again.'

'It's like they know we're coming,' the contractor said before returning to the adjoining cave.

Harry doubted there had ever been anyone here worth coming for. If he were an Afghan he'd light and extinguish fires in every cave of these mountains before running to claim an informant's reward from the Americans, who were acting as though they owned a rainforest of money-growing trees. He spat on his sleeve and wiped around the falcon. It was a creature of exquisite artistry – one talon raised in imperious command. He wondered how long ago it had been perched in the mustiness of the cave, listening to battles roar and recede outside. Perhaps an Arab mujahideen of the eighties had placed it here.

He had always been uneasy about the introduction of 'foreign fighters' into the Afghans' war against the Soviets. It wasn't, he'd be the first to concede, because he had any inkling of how history would unravel over the next two decades – it was simply that some lingering idealism in him had found a nobility in the struggle of a people to win back their land from a superpower, and he could find no corresponding nobility in the men who arrived to fight infidels who had overtaken a Muslim land. It seemed so medieval.

He stepped out of the cave on to a mountain ledge, pulling binoculars out of his pack to see the land beyond the dried riverbed and barren gullies. In the plains of the Gomal district the sky and ground were in different centuries – one cut open by the blades of a Huey chopper, the other smothered by a collapsed fort and the remnants of mud houses. After two decades of war, barely anything lived here other than juniper bushes and small groups of villagers.

'We make a desolation and call it peace,' he said, not for the first time, placing his M4 rifle on the ground and sitting down heavily next to it, the mountain sharp against his back. The rest of his team – all younger and fitter than him – were already scrambling down, singing some song they'd made up which rhymed 'Arkwright and Glenn' with 'dark fighting men', while the Afghans who had come with them followed more quietly.

'You want to get shot?' Steve said, picking up the M4 and holding it out to Harry. 'Come on, move.'

'If they shoot me, we'll know where they are. I'm not such a prize.'

'When did you become such a moaner?' Steve said, tossing the rifle into Harry's lap and lighting a cigarette. 'People keep asking me what the hell happened to Harry.'

'People around me got stupid. It made me cranky.'

'The Great Seer, Lala Buksh, speaks.' Steve bowed from the waist.

Harry didn't bother to respond. He had long suspected that it was Steve who had tipped off the CIA at the start of the nineties about the identity of the 'insider' who wrote a blistering article in an influential defence journal about the CIA's decision to turn its back on Afghanistan after the Soviet withdrawal. Steve was one of the few people to know that 'Lala Buksh' – the pseudonym of the writer – was also Harry's Pathan alias. Harry had never taken it personally; he'd been planning to quit the CIA in any case and being forced to move up the date by a few months really made little difference to his life.

'So I guess you must feel pretty smug now. You were right. Everyone else was wrong. Jihadi blowback, that was your phrase, wasn't it?' Steve made a whistling noise between his teeth, which Harry recalled as the sound of disgust he made at the end of every meeting with the ISI.

'I didn't say "blowback" – and I never thought we'd be back here. Violent revolution in Saudi Arabia, that was my forecast. Being here . . . there's no smugness. Just failure.'

'We shredded the Iron Curtain. That's a failure I can live with.' Steve took the binoculars from Harry before a reflection off its lenses drew unnecessary attention to their location. Harry resisted telling him that his obviously dyed blond hair was just as likely to provide a target.

'But I do owe you an apology,' Steve said. In the twenty or so years Harry had known Steve it was the first time the other man had truly surprised him. 'Not for unmasking you. No regrets there. But I remember saying there was no future in private military corpora- tions. I was wrong. PMCs are the future of warfare – fighting and reconstruction both. And you, Harry Burton, are a pioneer.'

'I see the compliment – now where's the backhand?' There was something to be said for knowing someone as well as he knew Steve. Even when you didn't like each other your awareness of the other's temperament brought a familiarity to interactions that almost made the relationship seem intimate.

'You're an idiot to hire all these Third Country Nationals. Economically, sure, I see the sense. But stop recruiting them from Pakistan and Bangladesh. You're acting like this is a territorial war and they're neutral parties. Go with guys from Sri Lanka, Nepal, the Philippines. Indians are OK, so long as they're not Muslim.'

'I've worked with these men for years,' Harry said, standing up and pulling his binoculars out of Steve's hand. It wasn't restraint, simply a lack of energy that kept him from reminding Steve that fifteen years ago he loved to joke that the difference between Vietnam and Afghanistan was 'there we just had GI – here we have jee-had'.

'Harry, Harry, Harry. Wake up and smell the burning buildings. You think I don't know you well enough after all that time in Islamabad? There's too much nostalgia in you. You look at those men and you see your childhood. The cook, the gardener, the driver. The Urdu teacher.'

'If this speech is about Raza you need to seriously reconsider continuing it,' he said, looking casually from Steve to the drop off the ledge.

'No need to start performing Quietly Menacing Man,' Steve said, stepping away from the edge. 'It really doesn't bother you – in this time, in this place – that he's found religion?' In response to Harry's look of bafflement he added, 'I saw him prostrating himself in front of a mosque the first time I flew in. He thought there was no one around to see him.'

'Maybe he had his nose to the ground for the scent of a woman. God knows you're not going to find one here using your eyes.'

'You know his skill at deception. Come on, Harry. A seventeen-year-old boy from Karachi convinces the Afghans he's one of them to the point that they take him to a muj camp. Better than that! They take a Hazara to a Pashtun camp. Unbelievable! And even now, no one except us knows, do they? Surrounded by Paks and no one knows he's one of them.'

Steve was right – Raza Konrad had dinner every night with the Third Country Nationals, translating between them from Urdu to Bengali to Tamil, but never revealing that one of those languages contained in it the memory of his father and all his childhood friends. The men had privately decided his name was an alias – Raza Konrad. It made no sense.

In the pass beneath there grew a single tree, shaped by the wind that raced between the mountains – trunk bent, leafy branches streamlined in a flamelike formation, it was curiously frozen in the act of animation. Hiroko, Sajjad, Konrad, Ilse, Harry: history had blown all of them off course, no one ending – or even middling – where they had begun, but it was only in Raza that Harry saw reshaping as a reflexive act rather than an adaptive response.

'What gives you the arrogance to think you alone see his true face? This is the guy who held you responsible for his father's death twenty years ago. Hell, Harry, I hated my dad but if I thought anyone . . .'

Harry raised a hand.

'Enough.'

Steve made a gesture of surrender.

'Just giving some friendly advice before I go.'

'You're leaving?'

'The United States will play no part in your *private* incursions into Pakistani territory tomorrow.' He grinned, extinguishing his cigarette on his arm where an old injury had left him without nerves. 'Make sure you get the bastards, Burton. Uncle Sam is getting so bored of failure.'

'Yes, sir,' Harry said, saluting with a sneer. 'But could you tell Uncle Sam to step up his efforts to cool temperatures in the neighbourhood. I had an uncle in Nagasaki – that's one piece of family history I don't want to relive.'

'I'll pass the word along.' Steve gestured to Harry to lead the way down, hoping that when he was sixty-five he'd have enough of a life beyond work that he'd be content to retire instead of climbing mountains in war zones.

The sky was thick with stars by the time the convoy returned to the compound, and the temperature had plunged vertiginously. Raza was sitting in the doorway of the one-room structure he shared with Harry, huddled in a blanket.

'Handprints getting to you tonight?' Harry asked.

The interior walls of their room were covered in the grease-stained fingerprints of a child, level with Raza's waist. More than once Harry had woken to see Raza walking around the room in the early morning, following the trail of prints, his fingertips skimming the grease stains. The compound had been deserted when the Americans arrived, its dust disturbed only by bird claws, and the locals were quick to relate the tale of the family who used to live here before the attack on this compound by a feuding tribe – the tribe had broken in to find one dead child and no one else. Some form of black magic had made the rest of the family disappear, the locals said – powerful black magic, conjured up with the blood of a child.

Raza shook his head.

'Just felt claustrophobic in there, Uncle Harry.'

The last time he'd said 'Uncle Harry' was over two years ago in Kosovo, when the jeep taking them to a meeting with KLA commanders at a 'secure location' had driven past a mass grave.

Harry sat down, a hand on the younger man's shoulder. Raza unwound the blanket and offered its warmth to Harry, who moved closer, his shoulder pressed against Raza's, and pulled one half of the blanket tight around himself. It had been a long time since he had felt awkward around the Pakistani's casualness with physical intimacy. Steve, stalking across the compound ground, thought sourly that they looked like a two-headed creature examining the world from the safety of a patterned cocoon.

'One of your local stooges brought in a guy he claimed was Taliban,' Raza said. 'Two of the new A and G guys interrogated him. They wanted me to act as interpreter.'

'Which two guys?' Harry's voice iced over.

'Don't worry. I told them I don't take orders from the hired help. Anyway, they let him go. Eventually. He was just some guy with a long-standing enmity with your stooge. You ever interrogated anyone, Harry?'

'Yes. But rarely in the way you mean. It's largely ineffective.'

'Is there anything you wouldn't do if you thought it was effective?' He recalled the day Harry had come to Dubai in search of him – Raza had asked if the CIA had ever even tried to find the man who shot his father. 'I found him. And then I killed him,' Harry had said, and even though Raza knew his father would have been appalled and his mother furious he couldn't help but feel grateful to Uncle Harry for doing what he wanted done but would never have been able to accomplish himself.

'What wouldn't I do if it was effective?' Harry said thoughtfully. 'Almost nothing. Children are out of bounds, rape is out of bounds, but otherwise . . . what works, works. When I'm dead, Raza, and my daughter asks you what kind of man her father really was, don't tell her I said that.'

Kim Burton. The much imagined Burton who he was now accustomed to thinking he'd seen every time a red-haired woman entered his field of vision. Somewhere, in a world very distant from this one, she was living with Hiroko. Raza crossed his arms on his knees and rested his head there. Heaven lies at the feet of the mother, his Islamiyat teacher in school once said, and Raza came home and searched between his mother's toes with a magnifying glass, laughing. 'This carpet is heaven? This ant?' until his mother hauled him up by his collar and turned the magnifying glass on him saying, No here, here – she held the glass against her eye and looked at his smiling face. Here's heaven.

Harry knew Raza's silences well enough to know he was thinking of Hiroko. The adored and neglected mother. He rested his hand on Raza's wrist. Impossible to believe Ilse was dead. Even in her very old age, she had seemed more alive to him than anyone else in the world. He wanted to tell Raza that one day he'd regret spending so little time with his mother simply because he didn't want her to fully understand how devalued a being he had become, but he knew Raza would only hear Harry's own regret in the words rather than understanding any wisdom in the advice. And perhaps there wasn't any wisdom there.

'I haven't been able to find Abdullah,' Raza said abruptly.

'Who?'

'Abdullah. The boy I went to the camps with in '83. My cousin got me in touch with his old commander.'

Harry frowned, and shook his head.

'Why are you . . . Whose side is his old commander on now?'

'Could you please stop being an employee of A and G for a minute. I don't know which side he's on. I didn't ask. But I didn't tell him what I'm doing either. He thinks I'm with a relief organisation based in the Gulf.'

'Hold on, Raza. Hold on. You really think it's smart to call Afghans whose allegiance you know nothing about and announce you're in the country?'

'It's a big country and I didn't say which part of it I'm in.' It had occurred to him that the Commander might remember him as the boy who worked with the CIA, but when he spoke to the man he discovered he was remembered quite differently: *You're the fainting Hazara who fooled a Pashtun boy into thinking you were important to the CIA just because a man who looked American held out a pair of shoes to you.*

'What else did he say?' Harry asked.

Raza looked up towards the sky, while his fingers traced constellations in the sand.

'That the last he heard of Abdullah he was at a camp in Afghanistan which the Russians decimated.'

Harry tried to put aside his feelings of hurt that Raza had sought out this boy without telling him he was doing so.

'I'm sorry. I know you once considered him a friend. But that was a long time ago.'

'After my father died, I went to my mother and begged her forgiveness. She said it wasn't my fault. I could not have known anything like that would happen, there was no part of me that was responsible. And then she said but if you know of any way to get that boy Abdullah out of the camps, you must do it. What happens to him there, that is your responsibility. You made him go when you could have told him not to.'

'You're not the reason he became a mujahideen,' Harry said.

'Yes, I am. If it hadn't been for me he would have been driving a truck instead of standing in the path of Russian bombs. And, whatever my mother might have said to the contrary, my father would still be alive.' In the sand he connected the stars of Orion – belt, bow, knees.

Harry leaned his weight slightly against Raza. He wished more than anything that he had not been the one to tell Raza that Sajjad had gone to the docks looking for him. He would have been willing

285

to live with the blame Raza had cast at him the day they stood over Sajjad's body if that had spared the younger man – but years ago Raza had decided the responsibility for his father's death was his alone.

'Abdullah's brothers were all mujahideen – he grew up knowing it was his next step the way you knew tenth grade follows ninth grade.'

'Yes, yes.' Raza's voice was tough with anger. 'I convinced myself of that, too. And I did nothing for Abdullah. I didn't even stop to think if there was anything I could do for him. Twenty years, I've hardly even thought of him.'

'And you were right to put it out of your mind. God knows I adore your mother, but she doesn't know the realities of war.' As soon as the words were out, he stopped, red with shame at what he'd said.

'When you don't know the realities of war, that's when you can put things like this out of your head. But coming here, being in this place, seeing all the young men who have been old men almost their entire lives, it does something to you. It must do something to you, Harry. Don't you feel any responsibility at all?'

'Sometimes I listen to these liberals in America and marvel at their ability to trace back all the world's ills to something America did, or something America didn't do. You've got the disease on a personal rather than a national level. You're not responsible for Abdullah. And as for your father—'

'As for my father, he would have wept to know the kind of men you and I have become.' Raza swept the palm of his hand across the ground and buried the Hunter. 'How long ago was it that you decided to justify your life by transforming responsibility into a disease?' He stood up gracefully, the blanket a cast-off chrysalis, and walked away in the direction of the radio broadcasting music from a Pakistani channel.

Good, Harry thought, picking up the blanket and trudging inside. Feeling superior to Harry was Raza's way of quietening his own conscience. Now he'd stop staring at handprints and searching out a past he'd ignored for twenty years, and get his head back in the game.

32

When Hiroko Ashraf had arrived in New York three summers ago, the immigration official – a man with a peace sign tattooed on his forearm – looked quizzically from her face to her Pakistani passport, then heaved a great sigh as he opened the passport and saw her place of birth scrawled beneath her husband's name.

'It's OK,' he said, stamping her passport without asking a single question. 'You'll be safe here.'

What surprised her even more than his hand reaching out to squeeze hers was his obliviousness to irony. She did not share it. A week after India's nuclear tests, with Pakistan's response in kind looming, she didn't see the ache in her back as a result of the long plane ride but rather a sign of her birds' displeasure that she should have chosen this, of all countries, as her place of refuge from a nuclear world.

When she stood in line at the taxi rank, aware that everything was familiar from the movies except the tactile quality of the early-summer air and the run-down look of everything from terminal to taxis to travellers, it occurred to her that Pakistan might have tested its bomb while she was flying from continent to continent. So when the cab drew up and a young man who could have been either Indian or Pakistani got out of the driver's seat to help her load her luggage, she blurted out instantly, in Urdu, 'Has Pakistan tested yet?'

The man drew back in surprise, and then started laughing.

'You speak Urdu!' he said. 'No, no. We haven't tested yet. Not yet. How do you know Urdu?'

'I've lived in Pakistan since '47,' she replied, feeling strangely flirtatious. 'I am Pakistani.'

'Amazing!' He held the door open for her. 'You're Pakistani, and I'm American. Became a citizen just last week.' He switched to English to say, 'Welcome to my country, aunty.'

His name was Omar. He was from Gujranwala, but he'd once been to visit distant relatives in Karachi, in Nazimabad.

'It's a good thing you didn't arrive yesterday,' he told Hiroko as they drove past boys playing cricket near a large silver globe – a sight enormously cheering to Hiroko. 'Major cab strike. 98 per cent of yellow-cab drivers took part. 98 per cent!'

She smiled at his tone of voice – she had heard it from many of her former students in 1988 when boys who had once sat at the back of the class were out on the streets, waving the flags of their political party and singing songs of victory. The details of the cab strike remained slightly mysterious to her but through her jet lag, and attempts to keep up with Omar's rapid-fire delivery, one thing struck her.

'Many of the cab drivers are Indian, aren't they?' Omar nodded at her in the rear-view mirror. 'And many are Pakistani?'

'No, no, please,' Omar said. 'Don't ask how it's possible that we can strike together when our countries are in the middle of planning for the Day of Judgement. It's what all the journalists ask. Aunty, we are taxi drivers, and we're protesting unjust new rules. Why should we let those governments who long ago let us down stop us from successfully doing that?'

Hiroko opened the window and let in the New York air, laughing as if she were part of a victory when a turbanned cabbie drew up alongside and reached out to clasp Omar's hand.

Omar of Gujranwala was the first New Yorker whose number she wrote down in her address book. 'I work the day shift,' he said. 'Any time you know in advance that you need a cab between 6 a.m. and 6 p.m., just call me.' And his smiling 'Welcome to my country, aunty' marked the start of her love affair with New York.

A city in which she could hear Urdu, English, Japanese, German all in the space of a few minutes. The miracle of it! Sometimes she rode the subways, overheard conversations her only destination. It was the young Japanese women who intrigued her most of all – their unabashed laughter, their vocabulary peppered with words she didn't understand, forcing her to recognise that her own Japanese belonged to 'Grandmother's generation'. Nothing foreign about foreignness in this city. 'Like Mary Poppins' handbag', Ilse had said to explain how much the little island of Manhattan could hold within it. She felt she had been waiting all her life to arrive here.

And when the buildings fell, she found herself caught up in a feeling of solidarity quite unfamiliar, utterly overwhelming. She stood beside Kim – who had driven across from Seattle – in the early-morning hours, handing out food to emergency workers; later, she demanded to be allowed to give blood – what did it matter if she was old? She didn't need so much blood – and retreated only when told firmly she was from a malarial country, her blood was unacceptable regardless of age. She didn't take that personally – was touched to be given a badge announcing she'd donated blood, 'because intention matters', the exhausted Red Cross woman had told her. When Hiroko said the Prophet Mohammad made exactly that point – surprising herself by the need to say such a thing – the woman smiled and said, 'I'm sure he did.'

But then, things shifted. The island seemed tiny, people's views shrunken. How could a place so filled with immigrants take the idea of 'patriotism' so seriously? Ilse had laughed and said, 'The zeal of the convert.' And that phrase spoken by a smiling young man in Tokyo kept returning to her: 'American lives.' It was a talisman, that phrase, the second part of it given weight by the first part.

All this she had thought and uncomfortably felt for weeks, but today, finally, mid-January in New York, the world felt different as Hiroko sat with a cup of jasmine tea and the morning crossword at a West Village bistro in that rare space of time between the breakfast and lunch crowd when lingering at a table didn't feel uncivic. She looked up as the bistro's only other customer opened the door to depart; cold air and voices rushed in – a man irritable on his cell phone, a dog's bark, a truck trundling past on the cobblestones – then the door closed and she was once more sealed into the silence disrupted only by the waitress tapping her pencil on a counter top.

It would be overstating things to say this felt like peace; but at least it felt like space in which to exhale. For the first time in over a month there seemed a movement away from, rather than towards, nuclear war and Hiroko felt a swoop of affection towards everything in the world – from New York and its inhabitants to a dictator half a world away. Not that she'd ever had faith in leaders – not in Pakistan any more than in Japan. She remembered lying on her stomach on the floor of a Nagasaki hospital, watching a young boy use a pair of chopsticks to lift maggots out of the pulsating redness that was his mother's breast – he was the only one not riveted by the sound of the Emperor's voice, heard by his public for the first time, announcing Japan's surrender on the radio. Despite all the iconoclasm she'd learnt from her father, she was dismayed by how high-pitched and feeble the Emperor's voice was. She felt betrayed by that voice more than by anything it said.

'Seven across?' The waitress held up her copy of the crossword. ' "QWEET" isn't a word, is it?'

'Honey, it should be.' The waitress pointed to the door. 'I'm stepping out for a smoke. You'll be OK in here.' It was an assertion rather than a question.

Once more, there was the open door, the rush of winter and sound – and again, silence.

Hiroko took her cell phone out of her handbag. She knew who she had to call to celebrate this step back from the nuclear brink. For a moment she wondered if she should get home first and make a cheap call using the landline – largely she retained her frugal habits despite the vast sums of money Raza kept depositing into her account – but then a feeling of wild glee ran through her, and she punched the necessary buttons.

At first she didn't recognise Yoshi Watanabe's voice. He sounded nothing like the man who had arrived in Pakistan three years ago with a group of hibakusha, determined to say what he could to turn Pakistan away from the idea of nuclear tests. Hiroko had translated the words of the hibakusha into Urdu through the press conference, spent an afternoon filled with tears and laughter with Yoshi afterwards, and then boarded the plane to New York.

'It is me,' he said. 'My voice . . . that's the cancer you're hearing.'

'Yoshi-san!'

'It's everywhere. There's nothing anyone can do.'

She was surprised by the tears burning her eyes. In Nagasaki he had only been someone she knew very vaguely, Konrad's friend who betrayed Konrad. And then she became, to him, atonement. Following that, through all the years of letters exchanged, he was her one remaining link to Nagasaki.

'You're calling to celebrate, I suppose,' he said, his voice slightly peevish. 'About that mad country of yours. It will survive incineration, it seems.'

'You don't think this is cause for celebration?'

He lowered his voice.

'Hear my confession, Hiroko-san. I was diagnosed a month ago, and in my brain there was a mad logic which said if there is nuclear war in the sub-continent then I'll survive. Them or me. Them or me. And every day these last weeks I've turned on the television wanting so much to see mushroom clouds in the news.' Her exclamation of horror only made him raise his voice. 'Between the dead cells mushrooming inside my body and those out there, annihilating a section of the world, there is no choice. There is not even a question of a choice.'

There was the sound of a small struggle, and a woman came on to the phone.

'The cancer has reached his brain,' she said. 'He doesn't mean any of this.'

In the background, Yoshi was shouting, 'I mean every word!'

Hiroko ended the call, hands shaking. Throwing money down on the table, she left the bistro in a hurry. The wind cut through her. She had forgotten her hat and gloves inside. Never mind. She couldn't go back to that funerary atmosphere.

She walked, half blind with tears, towards the West Side Highway unable to keep herself from imagining the congestion of Karachi manifest in a post-bomb landscape by shadows overlying shadows overlying shadows. She needed to stand at the edge of the island and look towards the water. She needed room to breathe. *Sajjad*, she kept repeating, trying to invoke something of his presence, his ability to make her feel everything could be borne. His optimism.

When the phone rang, she almost didn't answer it, but it was Kim, so she did. Within ten minutes of hearing the tone of her voice, Kim was slamming a cab door behind her, hurrying towards Hiroko – the lone figure at the edge of a pier, white hair whipping around her face. Her bare hands were resting on the railing and Kim said nothing until she had peeled her own gloves off her hands and eased Hiroko's stiff fingers into them.

Then she said, 'No one should get pneumonia looking at New Jersey,' as she wrapped her scarf around Hiroko's head.

'I want the world to stop being such a terrible place,' Hiroko said.

Kim didn't know what to say in response. She was feeling so weighed down by it herself – the terribleness of the world. Every morning she'd read the newspaper, word leaking through of casualties in Afghanistan, and think of Harry. Then to work – always before a place of refuge for her. The psychology of structural engineers! She often used to laugh about it with her friends at university. We anticipate disasters, calculate stress with mathematical precision. The messier our personal lives the better we are at designing structures that withstand the pressure they'll inevitably – or potentially – endure. Bring on your storms, bring on your earthquakes. We've done our calculations. And lovers, take note – here the joke which was not a joke reached its climax – when we break up with you it's because we've modelled the situation, run the simulations, we know which way things are headed.

But now even work was smeared by what was happening in the world. Earthquakes and floods were one thing – but to start having to calculate the effect of a bomb or an aeroplane, that was something else entirely. What size of plane? What weight of a bomb? If a man walked into a lobby with dynamite strapped to his chest? If chemical gas was released into the ventilation system?

'It is not part of my job to imagine this!' she had shouted yesterday at the architect she was working with.

'The world won't get more or less terrible if we're indoors somewhere with a mug of hot chocolate,' Kim said. 'Though it's possible it will seem slightly less terrible if there are marshmallows in the hot chocolate.'

'I'll go indoors soon,' Hiroko said, patting her hand. 'I'm sorry – I didn't know you were going to run out of work to come here. I feel quite foolish now.'

'Tell me what you're thinking,' Kim said, burrowing her hands into the pockets of her winter coat.

'Fairy tales,' Hiroko replied, watching the river rush past. A few degrees colder and it would freeze. Were there lovers or artists standing by ready to paint a beloved's name under the ice? Hana. Her lost daughter. She glanced sideways at the woman standing next to her. 'When Raza was young I didn't want him to know what I had lived through but I wanted him to understand the awfulness of it. Does that make sense? So I invented all these stories, terrible stories. Too terrible to tell my son, in the end. I keep thinking of them these days.'

Kim nodded.

'My father told me about them once. You don't mind, do you?'

'No. I wish now I'd told Raza. Told everyone. Written it down and put a copy in every school, every library, every public meeting place.' She frowned, as though trying to unpick some minor knot of confusion. 'But you see, then I'd read the history books. Truman, Churchill, Stalin, the Emperor. My stories seemed so small, so tiny a fragment in the big picture. Even Nagasaki – seventy-five thousand dead; it's just a fraction of the seventy-two million who died in the war. A tiny fraction. Just over .001 per cent. Why all this fuss about .001 per cent?'

'You lived it,' Kim said. 'Your father died in it. Your fiancé died in it. There's no shame in putting all the weight in the world on that.'

It was the wrong answer.

Hiroko turned to her, face bright with anger.

293

'Is that why? That's why Nagasaki was such a monstrous crime? Because it happened to me?' She pulled the gloves off and threw them at Kim. 'I don't want your hot chocolate,' she said and stalked away.

Kim picked a glove off the ground and slapped herself with it. Hard.

33

'Raza Hazara?'

Raza spun away from the group of Afghan men whose words he'd been translating, satellite phone pressed to his ear.

'Raza Hazara?' the voice on the other end said again.

Steve snapped his fingers in Raza's direction.

'I said, tell whoever it is you'll call back.'

'Who is this?' Raza said in Pashto.

'Are you Raza Hazara?'

'Yes, yes. Who is this?'

Steve caught Raza by the arm.

'You're on company time here.' He gestured towards the delegation of Afghan men who had come to pledge allegiance to the Americans. 'Now tell them I'll need some proof of their loyalty.'

'Do any of you speak Urdu?' Harry cut in. One of the men raised his hand quickly as if he were a student trying to curry favour. 'Finish your call, Raza. I've got this.'

'Make sure you get a percentage of his pay cheque,' Steve grumbled.

'Who is this?' Raza said again, walking quickly away from the Americans and Afghans.

'Ismail. Abdullah's brother. Do you still have the pattusi I gave you twenty years ago at the camp?'

Raza leaned his weight against the trunk of the broad-leafed tree which grew in the compound.

'Is Abdullah alive?'

'Yes.'

Raza put one arm around the trunk and rested his head against it.

'He said to tell you first that he's sorry.'

For nearly twenty years Raza had imagined Abdullah felt betrayed by him – he had never returned to Sohrab Goth, never attempted to contact Abdullah through Afridi or any of the other Afghans he knew there. And it seemed inevitable that, when the reality of war made itself known to him, Abdullah would have seen that Raza's greatest betrayal was in pushing him towards the camp instead of agreeing he should stay in Karachi. But here was Abdullah's brother saying, 'He knows that, whether or not you had a connection to the CIA, you came to the camp with him as a brother; and for twenty years he's lived with the shame of knowing that in a moment of anger he told the Commander you were an American spy and had you sent away.'

Raza shook his head, hardly believing.

'Why are you calling me? Why isn't Abdullah calling?'

'The Commander told me you had called, looking for Abdullah. He had your number. Raza Hazara, is it true? Did you work with the CIA?'

'Why would any Afghan today admit having worked with the CIA?' Something was wrong, he knew, but he didn't know what answer he should be giving, how much of the truth he should reveal.

'It was a different time before,' Ismail said. 'We believed they were helping us.' Raza made a noise that could have meant agreement. 'Please, I need to know. Do you have friends in America?'

'Why are you calling me? Where's Abdullah?'

There was a long pause. Neither man wanted to give anything away before seeing the other one's hand – but Raza knew he had the advantage.

'I'll tell you,' Ismail said. 'Because my brother said I should. He said you would help.'

A few minutes later, Raza was sitting beneath the tree, satphone by his side. *This country, this country*. He looked up into the distant

296

hills – already darkened into silhouettes in the early part of the long winter night – memory rather than sight providing him with images of coloured strips of cloth tied to the ends of long poles. Some bleached to whiteness, some bright as fresh blood, each marking the burial place of those who had died in some version of the war which had rolled across Afghanistan for over twenty years. Raza had thought he was one of the hundreds of thousands of people from around the world whose conscience had been buried in Afghanistan – his reaction had been to decide if he was numbered among the damned he might as well get paid for it. But here was his conscience, tapping him on the shoulder, offering him one more chance.

Seized with resolution, he sprang up and ran into the room he shared with Harry, plucked Harry's satphone off his bed, and dialled a number stored in its memory.

'Dad!' Kim Burton answered.

It might have been all those times he'd heard her voice on the answering machine in Harry's apartment; it might have been something else. But her voice was so familiar there was no question of addressing her as he would a stranger.

'Hey, Kim. It's Raza.'

'Has something happened to my father?'

'No, no, Harry's fine,' Raza said, stepping out of the room and looking towards Harry embracing the Urdu-speaking Afghan and the tribal chief just before escorting America's new allies to the front gate of the compound.

He could hear her exhale in relief.

'You guys really need another line of work.'

He smiled at the familiarity of the 'you guys'.

'How's my mother?'

'You should call and ask her that yourself.' She walked away from the construction site, removing her hard hat so she could hear him better. There were traces of both Harry and Hiroko in his unplaceable accent. She'd always assumed he'd sound arrogant – instead there was something in his voice which said please like me!

'I will. How's the cohabiting going?'

'We have a bump or two now and again. But it smoothes itself over.' Between her and Hiroko 'I don't want your hot chocolate' had become a line to laugh hysterically about within just a few hours of Hiroko throwing the glove at Kim. *As if I was challenging you to a duel!* Hiroko had said that evening over the dinner Kim had cooked as a peace offering. 'I'm moving out into my own place next month, but it's close to her.'

'Uh huh.' She could tell he wasn't really interested.

'I need to ask you a favour,' he said. 'It's about an Afghan I used to know. A boy called Abdullah.'

'Abdullah?' Kim repeated. 'That boy you went to the training camps with? Where exactly in Afghanistan are you?' She looked around her at the tall buildings, the woman walking past in miniskirt and thigh-high boots, the men with yarmulkes stopped in front of a hot-dog stand with a *HALAL* sign painted across it, and thought he might as well be calling from another planet.

'You know I can't tell you that. Listen, Kim. You have to help Abdullah. He's in America. In New York.'

'What's he doing in New York?' Kim said, looking around sharply.

'Cab driver.'

'Of course.'

'He's illegal there.'

'Again, of course.'

'Some FBI guys came around to his apartment building a couple of days ago. He jumped out of the window when they knocked on the door.' Across the compound a game of night cricket was about to commence on a makeshift pitch lit up with the headlights from the Humvees. Harry the only non-TCN involved, though some of the contractors were standing by, watching in bemusement as Harry called out to the other players in Urdu as he dragged over the wooden chair which served as wicket.

'How do you know all this?' She crouched to see into the driver's-side window of the cab that had stopped across the street, as if it would be possible to recognise Abdullah the Afghan.

Raza had long ago learnt from Harry to reveal as little as

necessary in any operation. As with Harry, the lesson had spilled over into his private life.

'That's beside the point. The point is, he's terrified. He's an Afghan who ran from the FBI. These days that's the kind of thing your paranoid nation thinks is evidence of terrorism.'

She stood up straight, moved the phone from her ear and held it in front of her eyes, face scrunched in disappointment and outrage. Paranoid? The whole country was jangling with fear, and all the Raza Ashrafs of the world could do was sneer about it. And how did it become 'your nation' after he'd lived in Miami for a decade and was a green-card holder in the process of applying for citizenship?

'Why did the idiot run? The FBI isn't the INS. They don't care if he's legal or not. Tell him to just turn himself in and say he's sorry he panicked.'

'Say he's sorry?' He mimicked her tone and accent with disconcerting accuracy. 'Did you really just say that? Have you read the Patriot Act? Of course they care if he's legal or not. They can indefinitely detain someone with just minor visa violations if they have even the vaguest suspicions about them.' In the pause that followed he said quietly, 'OK, you haven't read the Patriot Act.'

'Why are we even having this conversation?'

'He can't stay in America now. And there is a way for him to get back to Afghanistan from Canada. So you need to get him across the border. They'll never search a car driven by someone who looks like you. None of his friends in New York look like you.'

'This is where I hang up.' She ended the call, and then switched off the phone to prevent further conversational insanity before hurrying back to work. She was made uneasy about the idea of an Afghan who ran from the FBI, and made more uneasy to know she found such a thing suspicious. Damn Raza Ashraf. What right did he have to call her up and make her feel . . . caught out. Yes, he was just like Harry. Passing the buck and making you feel guilty for noticing it was counterfeit.

Part-way across the world, Raza was disappointed but unsurprised. Plan B then, he thought, as he watched the lazy shuffle that was Harry's bowling run-up. He knew exactly what would happen when he told Harry he had to leave for New York – right away – to get Abdullah out. Harry would say he was being sentimental and idiotic. He'd also curse the ineffectiveness of the FBI, the ineptitude of politicians, the stupidity of stupid laws – but follow up by pointing out that Abdullah's innocence would do nothing to help Raza's case if he was found attempting to help a suspected terrorist. And then, when Raza refused to back down, he would say fine, he was going along, too – Raza didn't look nearly all-American enough to cross the border without being stopped. Raza smiled, and stretched contentedly. It would be good to be back in America, no matter how briefly. He thought longingly of a high-pressure shower, and wondered if he owed Kim Burton some kind of apology.

Harry bowled an off-break, short of a length, followed by an exaggerated cry of pain when the batsman hit him for a four. Steve stepped out of his room to see what the noise was about. The ball landed near Raza, who held up a hand to the fielders to signal he'd retrieve it.

He was bending down to pick up the ball when he saw the movement up in the guard tower.

Harry was turned towards Raza, holding his hands out for the ball with a smile that anyone who had been loved by Konrad Weiss would have recognised, when the stranger in the guard tower swept his Kalashnikov from right to left as though it was his partner in a dance, and Harry fell in synchronised response, his shirt incarnadine in the bright lights of the Humvee.

34

R aza watched the mud lift off the ground in concentric circles, earth flattening around it. He was huddled in a crouch, arms raised against the rush of air, refusing to look any higher than the walls of mud rising an inch or so before collapsing back down as the chopper pulled itself away from earth, carrying two wounded contractors and the body of Harry Burton.

As the noise of the chopper muted in the distance, Raza heard the sound of a revving engine. The jeep carrying the bodies of three Pakistani Third Country Nationals was about to leave the compound, unescorted, headed for the border; the other jeep, with the unwashed corpse of the Afghan gunman tied to its bumper by his feet, would wait until sunrise before departing to drive around the surrounding terrain as a warning. The corpses of the two Bangladeshi TCNs were in a storage room, awaiting a decision on what was to be done with them in the absence of an embassy in Kabul to which they could be sent. And somewhere out of sight two men were digging a grave – Raza could hear the flump! of earth being turned over by shovels – for the Sri Lankan man without identity papers.

Raza stood, his clothes so stiff with dried blood they were resistant to the unfurling of his body. He made his way slowly to the jeep which had the Afghan tied to it, and raised his foot to feel the satisfaction of bone snapping beneath his heavy boots. But instead, he pirouetted to retch on the ground.

No one recalled seeing the Afghan before. In all likelihood he was part of the group of men who had come to pledge their allegiance to the Americans. He must have slipped away from the group and made his way to the watchtower where he garrotted the Sri Lankan guard. The tribal chief who had led the group of men into the compound insisted he had never seen the man – but he would say that, wouldn't he, Steve had pointed out.

Raza unzipped his bloodied jacket and let it fall to the ground as he made his way to the room he shared with Harry. Had shared with Harry. The gunman seemed most intent on killing Americans – the TCNs who died were simply in the way as the bullets sprayed an arc from Harry to the other two contractors in the yard. But the other two had survived because of their body armour. Harry should have been wearing it, too – A and G's policy specifically stated that all its employees who were provided with body armour should keep it on at all times. But it wasn't cost-effective to provide body armour for the TCNs, so they had none – and Raza said he felt ridiculous sitting down with them for dinner around their firelit campsite if he was the only one bent over under the weight of protection, so he refused to wear it. And Harry said if Raza wasn't wearing it, he wasn't wearing it either.

Indoors, Raza sat on Harry's camp bed, and picked up the book Harry had been reading. *Mother Goose's Nursery Rhymes*. He'd said it was the only thing that could keep a man sane. Raza closed his eyes and leaned back into the scent of Harry Burton. He wanted to be home. Not in Miami – but in a Karachi of twenty years ago, which had long since disappeared as civic violence turned Nazimabad into a battleground and all Raza's closest friends moved to other parts of the city or away to the Gulf or Canada or America. The house which Sajjad and Hiroko had bought with Ilse Weiss's necklace had been torn down to make room for a more 'modern' construction.

'You should change out of those clothes. They reek.'

Raza looked up at Steve, who had stepped inside, flinging Raza's jacket on to the bed.

'What's the quickest way for me to get to New York?' Raza asked. 'Kim said they'd delay the funeral until I get there.' Kim hadn't said it – he had phoned his mother instead and told her what happened.

– But why are you in Afghanistan? – Ma, I'm sorry. I'll tell you everything when I get there. – Raza, are you involved with this war? – I'm sorry, I'm sorry. – Shh, stop crying. No, cry. Cry all you need to. And come quickly. We'll wait for you, of course. It's what Harry would want. Oh Raza, how can he be dead? How will I tell Kim?

'Don't be ridiculous. You're not going anywhere. We're going to interrogate every Afghan who entered this compound in the last twenty-four hours to find out who helped Harry Burton's killer – and you're going to sit there and translate every word that comes out of their diseased mouths.'

'I'm an employee of A and G,' Raza said, carefully placing *Mother Goose* on the bedside, next to Harry's reading glasses. 'You can't tell me what to do. Come to think of it, I may be in charge of operations here now. I'm the seniormost employee.'

'You may want to reconsider your attitude.' Steve sat down on Raza's bed. 'I employ your employers. I've just been on the phone with them, in fact. They've given me operational control until they fly in a replacement. It's really a dry run for them and me – if things work out well I'll be taking over Harry Burton's office soon. Next door to yours, I understand?'

'I'll draft my letter of resignation right away.'

'That's nice. But don't forget the ninety-day waiting period before it comes into effect. If Kim Burton is putting Harry on ice until you get to New York, check she has enough ice to make it through to April.'

Raza closed his eyes and leaned back against the wall.

'Please. You have other people here who can translate. Just let me go for the funeral. Harry was . . .' His voice refused to continue.

Steve stretched himself out on Raza's bed, adjusting the flame on the lantern in the space between them so that shadows flung themselves across the walls and on to the ceiling.

'Harry was the man I admired above all men,' he said. 'He never knew that. A visionary. And now what is he? A piece of rotting meat.'

'Please let me go for Harry's funeral.'

'But the one thing he wasn't a visionary about was the TCNs. I tried telling him. Sure, they're cheap. And no one in their own countries cares what's being done with them. But what do you do about the question of allegiance?' He played with the flame control, shadows alternating between lurking and leaping. Raza could feel the sweat spread under his armpits, wetting the blood on his shirt into pungency. Steve turned to look at Raza. 'That's not a rhetorical question. I'm asking your opinion.'

'They're desperate for money,' Raza said, pulling his legs up against his chest. What was Steve trying to suggest? That one of the TCNs had smuggled in an Afghan? 'Their allegiance comes from their need to keep getting the pay-cheque. And their sense of brotherhood to each other.' He closed his eyes. He could see himself behind the till of one of Hussein and Altamash's super-markets – scanning the barcode on a packet of milk, opening the cash register, answering customers' queries about where to find the flour. It was an image of peace. He knew then he wasn't just going to quit A and G; he was going to walk away from this whole life. It was nothing without Harry.

'But you don't need the pay-cheque, Raza Ashraf of Karachi and Hazara. You're not one of the grunts who know their positions can be filled by a million other desperate rats if they mis-step even slightly. You're the ageing boy wonder – the translation genius. You can name your salary in corporations around the world. And you certainly have no sense of brotherhood with anyone.'

'My allegiance was to Harry. His family and mine—' Again his voice cut out. When he had told Hiroko she had to break the news of Harry's death to his daughter he thought of the American woman he had never met as his family, closer in some ways than Hussein and Altamash of Ashraf Stores, Dubai.

'I was there, Raza. In Pakistan, nearly twenty years ago. When you sent Harry Burton from your house accusing him of being the cause of your father's death.'

'I loved Harry.' He said it quietly, simply, the stark truth of it never evident to him until that moment.

'Is that why you signalled the gunman to fire?'

'I . . . what?'

Steve reached into the pocket of his jacket and pulled out Raza's satphone.

304

'And is that why you made a call a few days ago to a known supporter of the Taliban in Kabul?'

Blood and shadows everywhere. The Commander?

'I didn't know . . .'

'And am I really going to have to track down whoever called you from that PCO in Kandahar – Taliban HQ – just a few minutes before Harry died, or are you going to spare us some time and just tell me, Raza Hazara?'

'I haven't used that name in twenty years. I was a boy then.'

'I was standing next to you, you lying filth. Just a few hours ago when the call came. I could hear the man on the other end of the phone. Raza Hazara. That's what he said.' Steve stood up, picking up the copy of *Mother Goose* as he did so, along with Harry's satphone and the handgun from the bedside-table drawer. 'Humpty Dumpty,' he said conversationally and walked towards the door, book in hand. Opening the door, he pointed to the two contractors standing guard outside – they were the ones Raza had dismissed as 'hired help' just a few days earlier.

'Could you give me my phone,' Raza said, holding out a hand and then quickly withdrawing it as he noticed its tremble. 'I need to call A and G – their lawyers should probably know you seem to be accusing me of something.'

Steve shut the door and walked back to Raza, vastly amused.

'Do you really think A and G is going to get into a legal tussle with the CIA just when they've finally got what they've wanted for the last decade – a slice of government action? And over you?'

'You have no evidence. I can explain the phone calls.'

'Oh, you can explain anything, I'm sure. But here's the bad news for you: I saw you signal the gunman and I saw you duck just before he opened fire. That's sufficient evidence in my world.' He put a hand on Raza's shoulder. 'I know what you're all about. And I'm counting on your cowardice – tell me who else was involved before this gets unpleasant.' He stepped back. 'I'll give you time to think it over. You'll see sense.'

He left, quietly closing the door behind him.

There was a place in Raza's mind where nothing existed but the practical application of selected facts – it was the part of his brain

305

he used when reading reports or sitting in on A and G meetings in which it was manifest that his company was in business with murderers and thugs. That part of his brain had once allowed him to sit through a meeting in which a new client of A and G's extolled the effectiveness of rape as a tool of war. Raza impassively translated every word he said. Afterwards, Harry had found him in the A and G Olympic-sized pool, swimming furious laps, and said, 'I've made it clear I'm not getting involved with this contract.' Raza replied, 'Even so, I'm really quitting this time. Don't think a raise will change my mind.' Harry crouched by the side of the pool and placed his hand on Raza's slicked-down hair. 'I don't know what I'd do without you, son,' he said, and Raza stayed.

As Raza changed into a shalwar kameez, first wiping blood methodically off his body with a wash cloth and the water from Harry's bedside flask, he retreated to that purely practical section of his mind. Harry had chosen this structure for himself and Raza rather than any of the more spacious ones for a very particular reason – Raza moved his camp bed away from the wall and tapped on the floor until he heard the hollow sound which had confirmed to Harry the theory he'd constructed around the locals' tales of the vanishing family who had lived here. ('What about the dead boy?' Raza had asked. 'He was just a dead boy,' Harry replied.)

Raza made his way around the room, picking up whichever items would be of use – a large knapsack, a bottle of mineral water, a torch, granola bars, a key, his Pakistani passport and US green card. What considerable space was left in the knapsack he filled with the vast sums of money Harry kept on hand to buy Afghan loyalty. He hesitated a moment over the photograph of Hiroko, Ilse and Kim in New York, and then decided against it. He wanted nothing on him which would tie him to anyone else. But he took Harry's bomber jacket – his own was too stained, and the smell might attract wild animals.

The tunnel was narrow and musty, its roof too low for upright walking. Raza thought of Harry in here just weeks earlier, hunched over with his body angled sideways to ease his progress. 'I feel like Alice in Wonderland stuck in that house,' he'd groaned and Raza, slight enough to walk through with minimal discomfort, had laughed and said that if ever they really needed to use this tunnel as an escape route he'd go first because there was every likelihood that Harry would get stuck. 'What then? You'd leave me?' Harry said, turning to smile at Raza and tripping on a stone – here, here, the torch-light shining on the tunnel wall showed Raza the smear of dried blood from Harry's temple. Raza wiped tears off his face and pressed them against Harry's blood. Then, awkwardly – it required him to crane his neck uncomfortably – he pressed his mouth against the moist blood. But it still didn't seem quite real to him.

It was almost an hour later that he finally emerged on the other side of the tunnel into a roofless structure which smelt faintly of livestock, no sign of habitation around. The scent came from the dun-coloured tarpaulin which Harry had found in a barn filled with goat droppings. Beneath it was a jeep.

Raza pulled off the tarpaulin, unlocked the jeep with the key from Harry's bedside, and drove out of the derelict barn. Through the darkness he made out the faint outlines of mountains – the border, and Pakistan. He stopped the jeep, consulted his GPS. Pakistan was the obvious destination. Obvious to him, and to Steve. He might just be able to convince the Army guards at the border to phone Captain Sajjad Ashraf and receive assurances that Raza was just another Pakistani who the Americans had turned against after extracting all that was useful from him, but the bigger problem was the bounty hunters who prowled the border area, on the lookout for 'enemy combatants'.

Raza stepped out of the jeep and unbuttoned the soft top. The stars glittered malevolently. One phone call from Steve – perhaps that call had already been made – and he would enter data banks the world over as a suspected terrorist. His bank accounts frozen. His mother's phone tapped. His emails and phone logs, his Internet traffic, his credit-card receipts: no longer the markers of his daily life allowing him to wind a path back through a thicket of lovers to the specificity of the 3.13 a.m. call with Margo, the poem forwarded to Aliya, the box of Miami sand couriered to Natalie, but a different kind of evidence entirely. That nothing in the world could possibly show him to be Harry Burton's murderer seemed barely to matter in the face of all that could be done to his life before that conclusion. If anyone even bothered with a conclusion. He had never felt so sharply the powerlessness of being merely Pakistani.

Perhaps he should go back, back through the tunnel to Steve. Back where he could explain about the cricket ball and Abdullah's brother, and the Commander – and Kim Burton could verify he had called her to discuss Abdullah. And what would that prove? Only that he wanted to help a man he hadn't seen in twenty years who ran from the FBI. If Steve was looking for confirmation that Raza's allegiance belonged to some brotherhood of jihadis he would find it right there, right from Kim Burton's mouth. He leaned his head against the doorframe with a small pathetic cry.

No, there could be no going back – not to the compound, not to his life. He unzipped the knapsack, tossed out his passport and green card and watched the wind sift fine particles of sand on to the documents that made him legal. For an instant longer he breathed in deeply the desert air, everything around him vast and indifferent, and felt the terror of unbecoming.

Then he returned to the jeep, and plotted his course on the GPS navigation system.

35

I n New York taxi cabs Hiroko always made sure she sat behind the passenger-side seat so the cabbies could turn to look at her as she talked to them about their lives – discussing everything from the disconnection between their families back home and their all-male New York world to every component that went into strike action: leasing and medallions, the TLC and the TWA, the brokers and the garage-owners. Through these conversations she began to understand a great many things about this varied group of migrant workers, including their network of communication – via CB radios, cell-phone networks, holding-lot conversations, driver-welfare organisations, the Taxi Workers' Alliance.

It was the effectiveness of this network of communication – and Omar from Gujranwala's willingness to put it in motion on her behalf – which had her walking into the reading room of the New York Public Library four days after Harry Burton died.

As she entered the cavernous reading room made cosy by its many desk lamps, Hiroko found the teacher in her beaming at the sight of all those heads bent over books, some thrum of energy and the turning of pages slipping the room out of the grasp of silence into the comfort of quiet. She walked down the aisle between desks, the chandeliers reflecting their light off the floor, turning it into a bronze river.

Halfway down the room, a broad-shouldered, dark-haired man wearing a thick green sweater was sitting straight-backed in his chair, his fingers resting very lightly on the page of a book. The electric-blue tape which held together the frame of his glasses identified him as the man Hiroko had come to meet.

. She sat down in the empty seat beside him. The expectancy of his glance towards her quickly shifted into discomfort, and he stood up, taking the book with him, and moved down to another chair which had empty seats on either side of it.

The old man with crumpled features sitting opposite Hiroko raised his eyebrows at her.

'Afghan. They don't like women,' he said.

Hiroko smiled politely and made her way down the table to one of the empty seats beside the Afghan man with the hazel eyes and the chin several shades lighter than the rest of his face. He ignored her, and carried on looking down at the photograph of lush orchards against a backdrop of mountains in his oversized book.

'Abdullah. I'm Raza's mother.'

His instant reaction was to push his chair back from the table with a loud scraping sound his expression one of disbelief. She put her hand on his arm, and he paused, seeing Raza in her features.

'Raza's not Hazara. I'm Japanese. And his father was Pakistani. Originally from Delhi. He and I moved to Karachi in '47.'

Her accent – Karachi mingled with something else – countered the improbability of what she was saying. Also, Abdullah had heard what the other man said about Afghans and women and now he saw the hand resting on his arm as a refusal to accept that analysis.

He moved his chair forward once more.

'But Raza's in Afghanistan.'

'Yes.'

'Why?'

She shook her head, made a gesture which didn't only imply a lack of understanding but also failure. It had never occurred to her that her son would enter wars.

When Abdullah continued to look at her with a suspicion that obviously wanted itself overturned she pointed at the double-paged photograph he had been looking at.

'Beautiful,' she said.

'Kandahar. Before the wars.' He ran his palm across the photograph, as though he could feel the texture of the ripening pomegranates pushing up against his skin. 'First they cut down the trees. Then they put landmines everywhere. Now–' He bunched his fingers together and then sprang them apart. 'Cluster bombs.'

He turned the page to a picture of a very old couple, the woman vibrant in multicoloured clothes, the man resting his hand on her shoulder as they walked across sand dunes as if he knew his drabness would become part of the desert floor if he didn't stay moored to the woman's column of brightness. The sky was impossibly blue.

'Light,' Abdullah said. 'The light in Afghanistan. Like nowhere else.'

Hiroko nodded, touching the page as reverently as Abdullah had. It was difficult to find photographs of Nagasaki that preceded the bomb, but Kim had presented her with what remained in the Burton family of George Burton's old pictures – Azalea Manor, the bund, Megane-Bashi when the river was high – and when she looked at them she was surprised by how strong a grip childhood had on her ageing mind.

Abdullah continued to turn the pages of the book, stopping briefly on some pictures, lingering over others. Occasionally he'd point out a detail to Hiroko – a goat rearing on its hind legs in the corner of one photograph with the poise of a dancer, a kite flying high above a dome painted an identical green which made the kite appear an escaping roof tile. Sometimes he'd point to an object and identify it in Pashto – she'd repeat the word, pleased when she found any overlap with Urdu and delighted when she found resemblance to the Hindko words she had learnt while in Abbottabad.

When they came to the end of the book, Abdullah closed it and said, 'That's where I want to live.'

'Afghanistan?'

'Afghanistan then.'

He said very little beyond that until he and Hiroko exited the library into the dull light of late afternoon. The cold had nothing of the savageness of which it was capable at this time of year, but even so Abdullah pulled a wool hat low over his eyes and wrapped a broad scarf around his neck.

'He was not even an Afghan and he came to fight with us. Not a Pashtun, and he knew our language. And I had him sent away.' Hiroko didn't know who he was talking about. 'But instead of hating me, he still tries to help me.'

Understanding, Hiroko turned her face away, wishing she had raised a son who could fit such a glorified image. She didn't know whether or not to tell Abdullah the truth – her son was a mercenary, all he had done to help Abdullah was make one phone call to a woman he'd never met to try and pass all responsibility on to her, and despite his promises to the contrary he hadn't returned for Harry's funeral and hadn't even bothered to explain why. That final failure was the one which most convinced her that her relationship with her son was entirely comprised of lies – she still felt betrayed as she recalled her final conversation with him, just hours after Harry's death, when he said in a tone of voice she believed completely, 'Ma, I have to come to bury him. I have to see you. I have to see you.' But when Kim called his satphone to find out when he was flying in, and if he'd agree to read something at the funeral, a man called Steve had answered the phone and said Raza wouldn't be coming back to New York for the funeral, or at any time in the near future; for security reasons, he couldn't say anything more.

Kim had ended the call, shaking her head.

'Dad really moulded Raza in his image, didn't he?' When Hiroko tried to protest, there must be some other explanation, Raza had insisted he'd come for the funeral, Kim sat Hiroko down in front of the computer and explained to her, with the aid of the Internet, the real business of A and G. While Hiroko was still struggling to overlay the world of private military contractors on to her image of her son's life, Kim added, as if it were a matter of little consequence, 'And on top of all that, he wanted me to smuggle some Afghan across the border.'

'When I asked my brother to see if Raza – his name is really Raza? – knew someone who could get me across the border I didn't mean he should tell his mother,' Abdullah said, patting a stone lion's paw with the familiarity of ritual as he walked down the library steps. 'I don't want to get you into any trouble.'

'You won't,' Hiroko said, longing to be back in the sanctuary of books. She spent so much of her life in and around the Village that the regimented yet frenzied intersections of midtown made her feel as though she were stuck in a deranged crossword grid. 'Do you know if your brother has spoken to Raza since—' She almost said 'since Harry died'. 'Again, I mean. Has he spoken to him again?'

'I don't know. I will call him in three days.' Almost apologetically he added, 'He doesn't have a phone. Once a week he goes to the call office.' He took a cell phone out of his pocket and looked wistfully at it. 'So many things you promise yourself you won't get used to, and then you do.'

'How long have you been in New York?' She had come here not knowing what kind of man she would find, certain only that she had to see this mysterious piece of her son's life. But now she couldn't see the boy who drew Raza into a life of violence but only a man who understood lost homelands and the impossibility of return. He had looked at the photographs of Kandahar's orchards as Sajjad used to look at pictures of his old moholla in Dilli.

'I was with the mujahideen until the Soviets left. But then, peace never happened. And Afghan fighting Afghan, Pashtun against Hazara . . . no. So I went back to Karachi. Yes, for four years.' He switched to Urdu. 'I was a truck driver. Every time I went to the fish harbour I'd have one eye watching for Raza Hazara. But my brothers said one of us had to go to America where you can earn a real living. I was the youngest, the most fit – I had the best chance of making the journey across. And I was just married, so there was only a wife to leave behind and no children.'

'You have a wife?'

'Yes,' he said, taking a long stride forward and bodily lifting up a drunk who was weaving towards Hiroko and setting him down again, out of her path, with a quick pat on the shoulder. He was unaware she had seen his entire character in that gesture. 'It wasn't easy to leave her, but my brothers were all fighting or trying to farm between the landmines and I couldn't earn enough in Karachi for

313

everyone. So '93 I came here. And I haven't seen any of them since. My brothers, my wife. She had a son six months after I said goodbye to her. She knew it was happening before I left, but she didn't want to make it harder for me to go. So it's not so bad, leaving. I'll see my son, my wife. The light of Afghanistan. It's not so bad?'

He looked uncertainly at Hiroko, who found herself wanting to cry.

36

Three days earlier, just outside Kandahar, two Pathan men stepped out of a jeep, reaching for the guns beneath its seats before their feet had touched the ground. To the passenger in the back seat, head moving side to side, the men appeared sectioned into many pieces – the effect as disorienting as it was disturbing.

One of the men looked around the compound into which they'd driven, silent in the mid-afternoon sun.

'It's safe,' he called out to the figure in the back seat.

The cloaked figure stumbled out, attempting to pull off the giant blue shuttlecock while disembarking, an endeavour which resulted in a sprawl on the mud floor and a cry of pain.

'Slow down,' one of the men laughed. 'You've had it on for nearly ten hours. Another thirty seconds won't kill you.'

Still in the dust, Raza pulled off the burkha – tugging furiously at its constricting grip around his head – and threw it to one side. Lying back on his elbows, he breathed in the air, choking slightly on it, but smiling all the same as his eyes swivelled this way and that and the slight breeze touched his skin.

'Come. Have some tea,' the taller of the men said, walking to one of the mud houses.

'No, no. I don't have time.' He stood up, holding out the burkha to the shorter man. 'Thanks for the disguise.'

'Thanks for the lift,' the man said. He gestured at the burkha. 'Keep it. You may still need it.'

'Thank you.' Raza slung the cloth – so innocuous now – over his shoulder. 'Though I'm not sure I wouldn't rather be captured by the Americans.'

A woman dressed as Raza had been a few minutes ago stepped out of one of the houses, her head angled in Raza's direction. He looked at her, imagined her chequered view of him, wondered if she had been watching from the window when he wrenched off the burkha and threw it into the dust – had there been an instant when she imagined it was the act of a woman? He looked quickly away before his glance could be misconstrued. Or correctly construed. He felt he might go mad if he didn't soon see a woman's face, or hear a woman's voice.

'After you've had some tea, I can drive with you to the shrine,' the man beside him was saying. 'Hazaras aren't popular here, not even those who speak Pashto as beautifully as you.'

It was the first time the word 'Hazara' had entered the conversation. Near the start of his journey he had found the two men walking away from a car which had snapped its axle in a ditch and offered them a ride to their homes on the outskirts of Kandahar. After just a few minutes in their company he knew that he need only reveal he was hiding from the Americans in order to make allies of them.

'You've been travelling long enough,' Raza said. 'But I'll be back to take advantage of your offer of dinner.'

A few minutes later – after gulping down a cup of green tea; a quicker process than refusing a Pathan's hospitality – he was driving out of the compound, tongue and throat burning, away from Kandahar. Twenty years ago, in Sohrab Goth, in highway restaurants, in the cab of the truck decorated with the dead Soviet, Raza had listened to Abdullah rhapsodise about the beauties of his city – the emerald in the desert whose fruit trees bore poems, whose language was the sweetness of ripe figs. But Raza's brief glimpse of Kandahar had shown him only dust, fierceness and – a month after the Taliban's defeat – not a single unshrouded woman.

The drive to the Baba Wali shrine was even more tortuous than the drive to Kandahar's outskirts had been. Given a choice between seeing a woman and seeing an American-style highway Raza wasn't sure which he would choose. Everywhere, remnants of the American bombing campaign – a door standing unsupported in a field of bricks as though it were a miracle crop; craters in the road, indiscriminate as a meteorite shower; black metal shaped like a jeep in a headstand. He wondered if a burkha-clad woman standing near the jeep when it scorched might have a mesh tattooed on her face. In these ways he had been thinking of his mother almost constantly on the road to Kandahar. For some reason she had become part of the ache of losing Harry, though he really couldn't understand what one thing had to do with the other.

When he finally reached the shrine his first act, on getting out of the jeep, was to throw himself down on the ground and roll around. Grass! Actual green, tickling grass. He pulled a fistful out of the ground and rubbed it on his face, his arms, along the back of his neck before stepping on to the marble terrace which surrounded the airy shrine with its turquoise domes. Here, at last, a tiny glimpse of the world Abdullah held on to, the lost beauty which had allowed him to contemplate grotesque violence. It was not the shrine with the many-coloured tiles to which Raza paid attention – or of which Abdullah had talked when he spoke of coming here each Friday with his family before the Soviets cleft them from the body of the saint they had venerated for generations. Instead, Abdullah had talked about the surrounding orchards, the fleet river and the mountains beyond, which, his brothers used to tell him, were the ridged backs of slumbering monsters.

Raza removed his shoes and socks, and walked across the marble tiles, the shrine at his back and the Arghandab River before him. As opposed to Kandahar, there was still enough here to suggest what it might once have been. A chequerboard of green-and-brown fields, the green sharp and rich; beyond, the sunstruck river and, further, through the haze of the afternoon, mountains carved into a cloudless sky.

A policeman was the first to come up to Raza and ask who he was and what he was doing there.

'The mujahideen who taught me how to fire a gun venerated Baba Wali,' Raza said.

The policeman nodded, and left him alone.

A few minutes later, another man – half his face caved in – approached Raza.

'You knew a mujahideen who came here?'

'Yes. Can you help me find his family? I owe him a debt I must repay.'

The man scratched the cheek which still remained.

'Perhaps. You're Hazara?'

'No. I'm not Afghan.'

The man stood waiting for more. Raza turned away from him and continued looking at the view.

'His family were farmers near here. They came every Friday to this shrine. He was Abdullah Durrani, son of Haji Mohammed Durrani. There were five brothers, all of them mujahideen. The eldest became a martyr in the first year of the Soviet occupation when a MiG fired on the convoy of arms he was transporting.' He knew how discourteous he was being in refusing to reveal anything about himself, but his mind was past sifting out what could and couldn't be safely said.

The man went away, and Raza sat down on the cool tiles, shaded by the shrine, and thought of Harry.

The policeman came back to give him a cup of water.

He was watching a spider crawl across the floor – recalling Harry asking him about the story of the spider in Islam which Sajjad had told Konrad and Konrad had told Hiroko and Hiroko had told Ilse who told Harry – when someone called his name. It was a man with a hooked nose, steely hair and a full beard down to his chest.

'Raza Hazara,' the man said again, and Raza remembered the unexpected youthfulness of his smile the day he'd driven the two boys to the mujahideen camp. Now everything about him was old. 'Why did you tell that man you're not an Afghan?'

'The Americans will be looking for you,' Raza said, standing up to feel less intimidated. He was surprised to find he was taller than Abdullah's brother. What was his name? 'I mean, they're looking for the man who called me . . . yesterday.' It seemed much longer ago than that. 'They think he – you, they think you are involved with the murder of an American.'

318

The man laughed.

'The Americans aren't very good at finding people they're looking for in Afghanistan. Why do they think this? Were you involved with the murder of an American?'

Raza thought of Harry laughing with him at the contractors in their body armour, which they only took off to sunbathe – at which vulnerable time the guards on the watchtower were doubled.

'Yes,' he said.

'Well done. You came to find me to tell me this? That they're looking for me? It's no problem. I used a public call office – the man who runs it is an old friend. We bear scars from the same battle. Besides, this is Kandahar. No one here will help the Americans. We aren't like you Hazara.'

'You're Taliban?' It came out blunt and – to Raza's ears – accusing.

The man shrugged, something in the gesture calling Abdullah to mind.

'I'm twenty years too old for them. I'm a farmer. Wait here—' He entered the shrine, and Raza watched him pray by the grave of the Sufi – a sight that made him lower his own head and mumble 'Surah Fateha', though not for anyone who'd been dead hundreds of years.

'You know who loves to come here?' said Abdullah's brother – Ismail, that was his name! 'Abdullah's son.'

'He has a son?'

'His name is Raza.' Ismail nodded at Raza's look of confusion. 'Yes, named after the friend who Abdullah betrayed when he was just a boy. Raza – our Raza – has never met his father, but when they speak on the phone once a month Abdullah says tell me when your hand is big enough to fit around the largest Baba Wali pomegranate.' He gestured towards the grove of pomegranate trees alongside the terrace. 'So every week our Raza comes here, sometimes sneaks off on his own – though now that the bastards are back in power he's forbidden to leave the house without being accompanied. He's a very beautiful boy, praise be to Allah, though in these days perhaps that's a curse.'

'Why a curse?'

'Our new governor and his men. These are the ones who were in power before the Taliban came and saved us from them. Neither women nor young boys were safe in those days – then the Taliban came, they rescued the kidnapped women, drove away the warlords who were fighting in the bazaar over a young boy.'

'So you did support them? The Taliban?' He was trying to find the man Abdullah might have grown into through this brother who he had once idolised.

'I told you. I'm a farmer. I want to plant crops and harvest them. Do you understand? I need peace for this. I need security. In exchange for that, there's much that I'll give up.' He rested his hand against the wall of the shrine. 'This is what I fought for. The right to come back here with my family, to farm in the shadow of Baba Wali, and visit his shrine every Friday as my family has done for generations. To watch my sons measure hand-span against a pomegranate, not a grenade. But the Taliban – they don't know Sufis or orchards. They grew up in refugee camps, with no memory of this land, no attachment to anything except the idea of fighting infidels and heretics. So when they came they brought laws different to the laws I grew up with. So what? Football is banned! I can live without football. Music is banned! This is painful, yes, but when I watch the crops growing or my sons walking down the street without fear at least there's music in my heart.'

'And what about your daughters?'

'Hazara, my daughters are none of your concern.'

Raza looked impassively at Ismail for a moment, then turned and stalked away. The Taliban – saviour of women's honour! Well, he had done what he came here for – he had warned Ismail, and now it wasn't his responsibility any more if Steve were to find him. Now he could head back, with a clear conscience, towards his two new Pathan friends who had promised they'd get him across the border without any hassle, via an unpatrolled route used by many of the Taliban fighters. Though what he'd do once inside Pakistan he still didn't know.

He would visit his father's grave. At least he could do that.

'Raza Hazara!' Ismail caught Raza by the hand. 'Please don't go. Tell me about my brother. Have you found a way to get him to Canada?' When Raza said nothing, Ismail stepped back, holding himself up very straight in the manner of a man who finds he's about to beg, and can't quite bring himself to do so.

'You said he had to be in Canada by the tenth of February. Why?'

'That's the day the ship leaves.'

'The ship?'

'Yes. For Europe. From there he'll go overland to Iran, across the desert, and then he's home. Usually it's my poppy crop travelling in one direction; this time it's my brother coming home in the other direction.'

'Could you . . . ?' Raza stopped. *Think it through*, he heard Harry say. When the two Pathans said they could get him into Pakistan the offer had seemed too enticing to refuse, overthrowing all his earlier concerns. But his earlier thinking had been correct. Steve would expect him to go to Pakistan, expect him in Karachi at his father's grave, in Lahore at his uncle's house. The ISI would be asked to find him to prove their recemented friendship with the Americans and he was of no strategic value to the ISI – there was no reason why they shouldn't find him. And they would. They were the ISI – of course they would find him (in all his dealings with A and G he'd never met anyone who terrified him as much as the man with the pink tissue paper).

He pressed his head against a pillar of grey-and-white spirals, wishing Harry were here to separate the practical from the paranoid, the unexpected move from the ridiculous one.

Ismail's hand was on his back.

'Are you unwell?'

Raza held up a hand, asking only for a moment to think. His schoolfriend, Bilal, was in Canada. In Toronto, working as an engineer. His parents were there, too, living with Bilal and his wife and children – and when Hiroko needed to have her visa restamped to maintain her legal status in America, she would cross the border to visit Bilal's mother, her old friend and neighbour. Every six months she crossed the border. There would be nothing suspicious, nothing unexpected, in her doing so again. And Bilal would welcome him in, he knew that. They'd met in Miami a few years ago, and their friendship was reaffirmed when Bilal threw an arm around Raza and said, 'My sister told me how badly she treated you all those years ago. I wish she'd married you instead of that drummer in Prague with his tattoos.' There was nothing in that sentence Raza could imagine with any degree of credibility.

Raza turned to Ismail.

'Can you get me into Canada?'

'Why?'

Why? How could he put in words this ache to see his mother? It was as if everything in his world had disappeared in a flash of light and only she remained – a beacon, a talisman, a reason to run somewhere instead of just running.

'There's only one person left in this world who I love. She can come to see me if I'm there.' After that, after he'd seen her, he could decide what else, what next. But first he just needed to see her. There was nothing else. There was no one else.

Ismail drew him into an unexpected embrace.

'Everyone dead, except one? Allah, what have we Afghans done to deserve such sorrows?'

Raza rested his head on Ismail's shoulder, knowing that of all the embraces he had ever received this was the one he least deserved.

37

I n one corner of the penthouse on Brickell Avenue, amidst boxes and more boxes, Kim Burton sat on the ground, head resting against the wall, glass of Scotch balanced on her knee. She never drank Scotch, certainly not in the middle of the morning, but the rare phone calls her father made to her from here almost always started with his salutation, 'Keep me company while I have a drink?' so there was a necessary pain in holding on to the glass on this her first visit to the apartment where her father had lived for a decade.

Soon the movers would be here, to transport all Harry's possessions into a storage facility. One day perhaps she'd be able to look through them, decide what was worth retaining, what could be discarded of her father's possessions. Not now. Now all she was taking with her was his laptop, the largest single folder on its hard drive filled with photographs of Kim, videos of Kim, scanned copies of Kim's letters, her high-school reports, her university thesis. The most recent photograph of Kim and Harry together was nearly eight years old, and had been taken at Ilse's insistence.

The apartment was not as she had imagined. She didn't think her father a man interested in interior design, expected an ordered efficiency of bookcases filled with non-fiction, furniture that was upmarket and entirely without character, bare walls, an empty fridge. Instead, there were floor cushions with paisleyed covers, thick Persian carpets, a beautiful antique sword mounted on the wall, a fridge stacked with sauces and condiments and capers and peppercorns, and bookshelves everywhere with poetry and fiction in English, German, Urdu. There were also at least eight copies of *Mother Goose's Nursery Rhymes*.

Which is to say, there had been these things when she arrived. Now there were boxes.

Kim wondered what part of her would be lost now that her father was dead. With Ilse, it had been obvious; she knew precisely that version of herself – unreserved, slightly petulant, protective – which existed only in Ilse's company, knew the conversations she could have with Ilse and no one else. But everything around her grief for Harry was nebulous – and crushing. She kicked at the laptop lying at her feet; how like him to accumulate evidence that he'd been paying attention rather than simply paying attention.

A man's footsteps, precise and measured, made their way through the tunnel between stacked boxes towards her and she found herself tensing, an image of a bearded man with a Kalashnikov springing from her imagination.

'Ms Burton?' It was Tom – the doorman. 'I tried calling up.' He looked over to the entryphone, its receiver dangling abjectly just inches above the ground, and then turned back to her, trying to pretend he hadn't noticed the glass of Scotch. 'The movers are here. Should I send them up?'

'Sure.' She stood up, wiping dust off her tank top and cargo pants. 'Sorry, Tom.'

'That's no problem. Ms Burton, my brother works at A and G – Mr Burton got him a job there. He said your dad died in Afghanistan, looking for Osama. You should be proud.'

Was pride supposed to temper grief? She wanted him alive. Why was this man standing here, talking as though there were ways of dying that rendered death bearable.

'If your brother works at A and G maybe he could get one of the suits there to return my call.' In the five days since Harry's death there had been no further word from Raza – he got like this after Sajjad died, Hiroko had said. Running. It's what he's always done. He learnt it from me. But ever since Kim had walked into her father's Miami flat she'd felt a powerful compulsion to talk to Raza.

He was the only one who could tell her about the last few minutes of Harry's life. Perhaps he was the only one who could tell her about Harry's life, period. She had called on his satphone all day yesterday, all day today, and the lack of response was making her uneasy. Who was Steve and why had he answered Raza's phone? She wasn't about to say anything to Hiroko, but she'd called A and G repeatedly and left three messages about Raza for the men who'd pressed her hand and spoken with such feeling about Harry at his funeral.

Tom looked as if she'd slapped him.

'He's just a driver. He doesn't have that kind of pull.'

'I'm sorry. Really, Tom. I'm just . . . you know? Angry.'

'We're all angry, Ms Burton.'

While the movers removed Harry's presence from the apartment, Kim stood out on the balcony from where it was possible to see the offices of A and G, just a few blocks away. Harry had once told her he hated this location. 'Millionaires' Row' – the snobbery of James Burton's son recoiled at the ostentation. But the CEO had urged him to live as near the office as possible, explaining that when you only had an hour or two between work days you didn't want any kind of commute. And then Raza had moved in to the second-floor apartment and loved everything about the location – after that it was clear Harry never even considered moving.

Kim had used the key marked 'R' in Harry's cutlery drawer to enter Raza's apartment. She didn't ask herself why, she just did it. There she found the atmosphere she had expected of her father's penthouse – lots of technology, no personality – though when she thought of Hiroko's room with nothing adorning it except a faded painting of two foxes she wondered if Raza was just displaying a Japanese aesthetic. She didn't know if that thought was racist and was too drained to work it out. She slid open his wardrobe door and the first thing she saw hanging from its railings was a beautiful cashmere jacket. She ran her fingers along its softness, and slipped it on to her own frame. It fitted almost perfectly – the sleeves only a little too long. When she slid her fingers inside the pockets the texture of desiccation made her jerk them out immediately. Gingerly, she reached in again and scooped out a handful of dried

325

rose petals. She imagined Raza filling his pockets with the petals weeks or months earlier when roses were in bloom, enjoying the sensuous, velvety feeling each time his hands entered his pockets. Suddenly aware of how strange her behaviour was, she returned the jacket to its hanger and hurried out.

Now she looked out towards the water and Miami Beach beyond, linked to downtown by the slab-and-girder MacArthur Causeway. Its foundations: eighty-four-inch drilled shafts in the water, forty-eight inches on land. And if a plane were to nose-dive into it? If men with dynamite on their chests overlaying the madness in their hearts . . . ? If one Afghan man with an AK-47 were to climb on to it and spray bullets? No, he could do no harm. Surely, he couldn't send the world crumbling.

One of the movers came out on to the balcony to say they were done.

'You drink whisky? There's a couple of bottles under the sink. I don't want them.'

The mover took two steps back and waved his hands in the air.

'No, no. No.'

She looked closer at him. She'd assumed he was Mediterranean, but now she saw he might be Arab.

'You Muslim?' She said it in a tone that wanted to convey it was OK, she wouldn't hold that against him, she was sorry if anyone had these last crazy months.

The man laughed, a short bark.

'No, don't say that. Don't say that. We're not allowed to take anything from the homes we're working, not even when we're offered. That's why we can't. Do I look Arab? I'm Italian.'

'My mistake,' she said.

'No one else had better make that mistake.'

'There's nothing wrong with most Arabs,' she found herself saying, and then wondered how that 'most' had slipped into the sentence.

'Hey, I'm not being racist. It's crazy enough being mistaken for a Cuban, but Arab! God help me. And Gitmo just across the water.'

That thought hadn't even crossed her mind all the while she'd been in Miami.

What she needed, she decided on the flight back to New York, was to retreat. And she knew just where to do it – her mother's cabin in the Adirondacks, a place without memories of Harry, where disputes over ownership of a moose carcass could push almost everything else off the front page of the newspaper. She had spent some part of every summer of her youth there, could point to the spot where she danced with a boy for the first time, saw the world from the top of a mountain for the first time, smoked a joint for the first time, ran a half-marathon for the first time, thought she'd lost her virginity for the first time. Her mother wasn't there now – it was only during the summers or the height of fall that she thought to leave Paris for upstate New York's mountains – but that only added to the appeal. To live alone, in the mountains, watching the snow fall on silent valleys while the fireplace roared, the local news channel filled with familiar faces . . . Her mother used to tell her she'd find such a life comforting by the time she was sixty and she'd always laughed; now here she was at thirty-five, desperate to sink into that world and be lost in it like a tear in a lake.

Hiroko could come to visit, she thought, when she was in the elevator headed up to the Mercer Street apartment. Hiroko was about the one person in the world whose presence there wouldn't be an intrusion.

Her mood was almost cheerful when she opened the door to the apartment to announce her new plan to Hiroko.

A man – hazel-eyed and broad-shouldered – sprang up from the sofa when Kim walked in.

'It's all right,' Hiroko said. 'It's just Kim. Kim, this is Abdullah.'

Kim looked from the man to Hiroko and back again. Through the haze of shock, habit took over and extended her hand to the Afghan man. He looked at it, and hesitated just long enough in responding to make Kim snatch it back.

'Why is he here?' she said to Hiroko.

'I'm very sorry about your father,' the Afghan man said. 'But he is with Allah now.'

'Does Allah accept unbelievers?' she said, and the man lowered his eyes.

'I wasn't expecting you back yet,' Hiroko said quietly. She added something in Urdu, and the Afghan nodded, said something in return, and let himself out of the apartment without looking at Kim again.

'What?' Kim said. 'What are you doing? What did you say to him?'

'There's no need for you to get involved,' Hiroko replied, picking up the book she'd been reading.

'You've found someone to drive him to Canada, haven't you?'

Hiroko didn't look up from her book. Kim threw her hands up in the air. If one of Hiroko's friends was willing to get involved with such lunacy it was none of her business. She needed a long bath, and a glass of wine.

Seconds later, she was pulling the book out of Hiroko's grasp, standing in front of her with a car key dangling from her fingers.

'What's this?'

'I have no idea.'

Kim held up the other hand which was grasping the paperwork from the car-rental company.

'Your signature is on here. Who rents out a car to a seventy-seven-year-old woman with a Pakistani driver's licence?'

'This is New York,' Hiroko answered with great satisfaction. 'Everything's available for a price.'

'Oh Christ, Hiroko. You can't be thinking of taking him yourself.'

'Stay out of this, Kim.'

'You have a Pakistani passport. They're not going to just wave you over the border.' She could hear the rising panic in her voice. 'You've never driven on the right-hand side of the road and you've no experience with highway driving. Exactly how much craziness are you capable of?'

'You Americans have very timorous notions of craziness.'

'Timorous!' Kim stuffed the keys into the pocket of her jacket. 'If you were anyone but you I'd suspect you of manipulation.'

'What manipulation? Give me those keys, Kim Burton.'

'No. I'll drive him across. You stay here. And don't – do not, Hiroko Ashraf, start arguing with me. Raza was right. They won't search a car driven by anyone who looks like me.'

Hiroko looked at Kim with an expression which pulled together all her life's experience at conveying scepticism.

'You think he should be smuggled across the border?' Kim was the first person Hiroko had ever known with an unshakeable faith that she lived in a world that allowed all protests, all acts of discontentment, to take place within a legal framework. Moving out of that framework was simply grandstanding.

'If I promise you I'll take him, that means I'll take him. Why should anything else matter?'

'I won't be the reason for you to go against things you believe in.' She felt about people who believed in the morality of their nations exactly as she felt about those who believed in religion: it was baffling, it seemed to defy all reason, and yet she would never be the one to attempt to wrestle the comfort of illusory order away from someone else.

'You're not,' Kim lied. 'Now, do you want him to have the best chance of being safe or not?' Though the argument continued on for a while that was the moment she knew she'd won – though, of course, she had no way of knowing Hiroko would wake up the next morning, too late, remembering with a sense of unease that James Burton used almost exactly the same words to convince Sajjad Ali Ashraf to leave Delhi for Istanbul.

38

B y the time he was in Muscat, Raza decided the man with blood in his eye had been right: he didn't have the mental strength for this journey; his mind had broken apart

'Like this,' the man with blood in his eye said, smashing a pomegranate against a table-top. He delicately plucked out one ruby-encased seed from the fractured fruit and held it out to Raza, winking as he did so – the red tear in his cornea disappearing from Raza's vision just as the ruby seed entered it.

'He's going to help Abdullah get into Canada,' Ismail said. He had clearly been uneasy since bringing Raza to this spartan room near the central bazaar in Kandahar.

The ruby-eyed man waved his hand dismissively.

'I'm not interested in that. Abdullah made the journey once; if he's lucky he'll make it again. This one, this one is a different matter. Leave me alone with him.'

When Ismail was gone, Ruby Eye motioned for Raza to sit down.

'The way you're clutching that bag of yours it either contains love letters or money. For your sake, I hope it's the second. You're not nearly desperate enough to survive the journey of the desti-tute.'

Raza relaxed. Now he was in a world he understood – where anything was possible for the right price.

'From Iran to Muscat, though, you have to travel as they do—'

Many cups of tea later Ruby Eye waved his hand in the direction of the man who was traversing the room on his haunches, picking up, one by one, the pomegranate seeds which Ruby Eye had been flicking off the walls while he and Raza haggled over price. 'You just missed the first-class trip out of Iran. Though if you wait a few weeks—'

'No,' Raza said, standing up, his knapsack considerably lighter than it had been when he entered, though he could see Ruby Eye's look of amazement at the extent to which it was still weighed down. 'I'll leave now. It's not so far from Iran to Muscat.'

Ruby Eye smiled.

'The sea crossing alone will seem the furthest distance any man has ever been asked to travel.'

Raza left Kandahar at sunrise in a pickup truck, squeezed between the driver and an armed guard. His own jeep he left with Ismail, along with a promise – only partially believed by both him and Ismail – that he'd find a way to bring Abdullah into Canada. Ismail had offered him hospitality for the night, but he'd stayed with the two Pathan men instead; Ruby Eye had laughingly warned him that Ismail had not even a blanket to spare after he'd sold everything to raise the money for Abdullah's voyage back to Afghanistan. In the glove compartment of the jeep Raza placed a thousand dollars. It felt generous, but it made no discernible difference to the weight of his knapsack.

The guard and driver in the pickup were taciturn, showing no more interest in Raza's attempts to engage them in conversation than they did in the NATO convoys that hulked past as they made their way out of Kandahar. He slept, and when he woke there was no road, only sand and at least a dozen pickups – each one identical in its tinted glass, its gleaming blue paint. More armed guards had appeared from somewhere and had taken position at the back of the pickup. The vehicles raced across the desert at unnerving speeds – a pack of animals evolved in a world where nothing mattered but chase and escape.

'All this for me?' Raza said to the guard beside him.

The men gestured to the back where the other guards sat on gunny sacks piled on top of each other, and Raza thought of the effete quantities of heroin which he used to deliver personally to the most valued hotel guests in Dubai as part of his duty to give them whatever it took to ensure they returned.

331

At a certain point, when it seemed to Raza that his eyes would never see anything but sand outside the window, something extraordinary happened. The convoy passed a group of nomads making their way across the desert on foot. And there they were – finally, miraculously: women.

Faces uncovered, arms laden with bangles, clothes bright. He always thought they had to be beautiful – those women of fairy tale who distracted princes on mythic quests with a single smile. Now he saw it was enough for them to simply be.

'Stop,' he said to the driver, but of course no one did, and within seconds the landscape was sand again.

But just that glimpse moved Raza into a profound melancholy – no, not melancholy. It was uljhan he was feeling. His emotions were in Urdu now, melancholy and disquiet abutting each other like the two syllables of a single word. He thought of the man whose name he was still unable to consider entirely as his own: his mother's German fiancé who entered a new country, its language alien to him, and set about knowing it. That Konrad, he knew, would have found a way to make the convoy stop. He would have seen the desert as something other than a shore without a sea. He would not have spent more than a month in Afghanistan and remained so entirely separate from it.

Raza didn't know that even as he was thinking this he was nearing the edge of Afghanistan. The pickup climbed a sand dune, and on the other side there was a habitation of sand-coloured structures.

'You'll get out here,' the guard said. He pointed to the men who were watching the convoy approach. 'They'll take you now.' The guard had answered all Raza's questions with monosyllables and shrugs but now he looked at him with compassion. 'Just remember, it will end. And the next stage will end.'

By early morning the next day, Raza was repeating those words to himself as though they were a prayer to ward off insanity.

He was in another pickup – one with a covered rear compartment – though this one was decades and several evolutionary steps behind the gleaming blue desert racers; it bore a comforting resemblance to the pickup in which the Pathan driver had ferried

Raza and the other neighbourhood boys to and from school. Then he used to laugh at the other boys squeezed together on the two parallel benches that ran the length of the rear compartment while he was in the front learning Pashto from the driver, a tiny window between the driver and passenger seat allowing him to look back at the other boys, who made obscene gestures in his direction without malice. If he'd only stayed in the back of the pickup with them, he now thought, he would never have learnt Pashto, never have talked to Abdullah, never set off everything that led him to be sitting in a cardboard box at the back of a pickup while young Pathan boys bowled cabbages towards him.

'Vegetables can cross the border without paperwork, so you must become a vegetable,' one of the men from the sand-coloured houses had explained to Raza. So here he was trying to contain his panic as the cabbages piled up in the back of the pickup, reaching his knees, his chest, his eyes . . .

'I'll suffocate in here,' he called out.

'You'll be the first,' replied a voice that seemed to find this notion intriguing.

For most of the journey he stood, stooped beneath the canopy, hemmed in by chest-high cabbages. But as the border approached the driver rapped sharply on the partition that divided them and with long, deep breaths Raza lowered himself into the cardboard box. Within seconds, with the motion of the pickup, the cabbages had rolled over him, cutting off light and air. And so, in the company of cabbages – breathing in cabbage air, pressed in by cabbage weight – Raza reached Iran.

Time had never moved so slowly as in the dark dankness of cabbages. The pickup seemed to stop for a long time before the border guards approached. The cabbages muffled all sound except that of his heart.

When the pickup moved again, Raza still dared not stand up. He had been firmly instructed to wait for the driver to signal an all-clear. But there was so little air.

Finally the driver stopped the pickup and rapped again on the partition. Raza burst out of the cabbages, displacing the ones that were covering him with such energy they went thud-thudding against the canopy, and gulped in great mouthfuls of air. While the driver watched him, laughing, he clambered into the space between the cabbages and the canopy and, like a swimmer, propelled himself outwards.

'Had fun?' the driver asked, taking Raza's hand and helping him down to the ground. 'Cabbage soup for dinner!'

After Ruby Eye's guards, Ahmed the driver was a joy to sit with. His family were nomads, he explained, as he drove Raza south towards the coast. But drought and war had brought an end to the lifestyle his family had known for centuries, and now they had grudgingly settled near the border and become drivers if they were lucky, stone-pickers if they weren't.

'The landmines are the worst,' he said, while Raza was still trying to work out whether 'stone-pickers' was a Pashto euphamism. 'Once we used to travel in large groups for protection. Then we started to move in groups of three or four so if anyone steps on a powerful mine it can only have so much impact and others following behind will see the bodies – or the birds swarming around – and know to avoid that place.' He smiled jauntily as he said this, and Raza didn't know whether to believe him or not, but was glad just for the camaraderie.

He wanted to ask Ahmed the driver, Where – or what – is home for your people? But though he knew how to ask where someone was from, or where they lived, the word for 'home' in Pashto eluded him. As he tried to think of ways to explain it, the meaning receded.

He was so caught up in talking to Ahmed that it took him a while to understand why Iran felt so strange, despite its topographic similarity to Afghanistan.

'No war,' he said near sunset to Ahmed, when he finally understood.

Ahmed nodded, for once forbearing from jokes. He didn't need to ask what this statement was doing in the middle of a conversation about poisonous snakes in Dasht-e-Margo – the Desert of Death – which Raza had travelled across in the pickup truck without knowing its name.

They stopped for the night in a hotel, where Raza amazed Ahmed with his command of Farsi, and set off again the next morning. They'd hardly gone any distance when a car drew up alongside them filled with women wearing headscarves and dark glasses, calling to Raza's mind all those Hollywood actresses of the fifties who Harry had loved. For a few seconds the car and pickup travelled alongside, Ahmed shouting out questions to the women, which Raza translated with a disarming smile: 'Which of you will marry me, which will marry my friend?' 'Why are you travelling by road, don't angels fly?' The women shouting back in response, 'We don't want husbands who smell of cabbages. Women are superior to angels, why are you insulting us!', all the while looking at Raza. All too soon they turned off the road with waves and air-kisses, leaving Ahmed to clutch his heart while Raza mumbled, 'I think I love Iran.'

He had begun to think the worst part of the journey was over, was already starting to think of the cabbages as his test of fire, and for the first time since Harry died he felt a certain lightening within. They'd left the desert behind by now, and at his first glimpse of the sea Raza hollered in delight. Karachi, Dubai, Miami – all seaside cities, though until he saw the Iran coast he didn't know that had any meaning for him.

But the closer they drew to the coast, the quieter Ahmed became.

'Why don't you just stay here,' he said, by the time they were close enough to the docks to smell the sea air. 'If you're running from the Americans, Iran is a good place to be. You even speak the language. And the women are beautiful – and Shia, like you Hazara.'

He didn't understand quite what it was that made Ahmed worry so much until after he'd embraced the nomad goodbye and promised that in happier times he'd return and together they would traverse Asia in a pickup without cabbages. Then the ship's captain into whose charge Ahmed had delivered him took him to a wooden boat with a tiny motor, and when Raza asked if there was anywhere in particular he should sit the captain pointed to the wooden planks underfoot and said, 'Beneath there.'

Raza laughed, but the captain didn't join in.

'Have you pissed?' he said.

'What?'

'Go on. Over the side of the boat. You're not coming out until Muscat. And there's no room for your bag down there.'

Raza clutched his knapsack.

'There are holy artefacts in here. I swore to my mother—'

The captain made a dismissive gesture.

'Just hurry up.'

While Raza emptied his bladder into the sea, the captain pulled up a section of the floorboards. Raza could hear voices beneath. How many people were down there?

Many. Too many. Raza looked into the bowels of the ship and all he saw were prone men looking up at him, more than one crying out – in Farsi and in Pashto – 'Not another one. There's no room.'

'Go on.' The captain pushed at his shoulder blades. 'Get in. We're late already because of you.'

Raza peered down. There was no space between one body and the next, the men laid out like something familiar, but what? What did they remind him of? Something that made him back up into the ship captain, who cursed and pushed him forward, into the hold, on to the bodies which groaned in pain, pushed him this way and that until somehow, he didn't know how, he was squeezed into the tiny space between one man and the next and his voice was part of the sigh – of hopelessness, of resignation – that rippled through the hold. It was only when the captain slammed down the hatch, extinguishing all light, that he knew what the line of bodies made him think of – the mass grave in Kosovo.

In the darkness, the man to his left clutched Raza's hand.

'How much longer?' the man said, and his voice revealed him to be a child.

Raza didn't answer. He was afraid if he opened his mouth he would gag from the stench – of the oil-slicked harbour, of damp wood, of men for whom bathing was a luxury they had long ago left behind. The boards he was resting on were slick, and he didn't want to know if anything other than seawater might have caused that.

When the boat set off, things got worse. The motion of the sea knocking beneath the men's heads was a minor irritant at first – but, when they left the harbour and headed into the open sea, the waves bounced their heads so violently the men all sat up on their elbows. It wasn't long before they started to suffer seasickness. Soon the stench of vomit overpowered everything else. The Afghan boy next to Raza was suffering the most, weeping and crying for his mother.

Raza closed his eyes. In all the years he had sat around campfires with the TCNs listening to their tales of escape from one place to another, in the holds of ships, beneath the floorboards of trucks, it had never occurred to him how much wretchedness they each had known. And Abdullah. Abdullah had made this voyage once, would make it again. Across the Atlantic like this – it wasn't possible. No one could endure this. What kind of world made men have to endure this?

He placed his knapsack beneath his head and, lying down, lifted up the boy who was weeping and retching next to him and placed him on top of his own body, buffering the boy from the rocking of the waves.

The boy sighed and rested his head on Raza's chest.

The hours inched past. No one spoke – conversation belonged to another world. By mid-afternoon, the hold felt like a furnace. Several of the men had fainted, including the boy, who was now a dead weight on Raza's chest. But Raza didn't attempt to move him. He thought, Harry would have done for me without question what I'm doing for the boy. Then he thought, Harry would have kept me from a place like this.

At a certain point it started to seem inevitable he would die in the hold. All he could think of was his mother. She'd never know he had died. No one would put a name to the dead piece of human cargo. So she'd keep waiting for news of him. For how long? How long before she understood that she'd lost one more person she loved? He whimpered softly, uncaring of what the other men might think of him.

When the boards lifted up and moonlight streamed in he didn't understand what it meant until the captain's head appeared.

'Quiet!' the captain warned in response to the ragged cheer that ran through the hold. 'Raza Hazara, where are you? Come out. The rest of you stay here. We haven't reached yet.'

Nothing in Raza's life had felt as shameful, as much of a betrayal, as the moment when he identified himself as the man who was leaving. The boy on his chest, conscious again, clutched his shirt and said, 'Take me with you,' and Raza could only whisper brokenly, 'I'm sorry.' He reached into his knapsack, lifted out a bundle of hundred-dollar bills, and pressed it into the boy's hand. 'Don't let anyone know you have this,' he said, before crawling over the other men and holding out a hand for the captain to lift him out. For a moment he considered dropping the knapsack in the hold, but he knew there was something else he needed the money for so he looked away from the men in the hold breathing in as much fresh air and moonlight as they could before the boards came down again.

A small rowing boat was alongside the ship, and a voice emerged from it saying, 'Raza Hazara? Hurry. The plane's been delayed already for you.'

Raza climbed into the boat, but before he could sit down the man rowing swung an oar and knocked him into the water. He had barely enough presence of mind to throw his knapsack into the boat as he fell.

He emerged spluttering and bone-cold. The man with the oar held up a bag.

'Clothes in here. Take those ones off. And use this—' He threw a bar of soap at Raza.

Despite the man's urgency to get going he allowed Raza a few moments to float, naked, in the cold cold water, looking up at the expanse of sky.

I will never be the same again, Raza thought. He watched his vomit-slimed clothes float away, holding on only to Harry's jacket, and changed that to, *I want never to be the same again.*

On the rowing boat there was water and food and a shalwar kameez only slightly too big for him. It was as much as he could bear – any further luxury would have been repellent.

Near dawn the boat reached shore. There, another blue and gleaming pickup truck was waiting. This time Raza didn't attempt to speak to the driver and armed guard inside. He kept thinking of the boy whose head had rested on his chest, and wished he'd given him Hussein and Altamash's number. Dubai was not so far from Muscat.

Beautifully paved roads lined with palm trees led to a private airstrip. A plane was on the runway.

One of the guards from the pickup accompanied Raza up the steps and grinned as he opened the plane door.

'Welcome to the zoo,' he said. The sounds issuing from the plane were extraordinary.

Raza stepped in, cautiously.

A blue heron unfurled its wings, a white peacock snap-closed its fantail, macaws squawked, a baby anteater fell off its mother's back and protested shrilly, African wild dogs bared their teeth, winged things flew about under a black sheet, meerkats sat up on their hind legs and watched. And to one side, a baby gorilla slept.

The guard pointed to the cage with the gorilla in it.

'You'll be travelling inside the monkey,' he said.

And that's when Raza realised Ruby Eye had been right. His mind had definitely broken apart.

39

As the rented SUV approached border control, Kim Burton allowed herself to imagine the consequences if the Afghan hiding beneath blankets in the trunk were discovered. She skipped over the question of what would happen to either him or her, and instead envisioned a world in which 'political profiling' became customary at the borders, with immigration officials trained to identify Americans suffering liberal guilt.

She rolled down her window and smiled at the Canadian official, handing him her driver's licence as she did so.

'Not the most flattering picture of you,' he said. 'Staying long?'

'Just a few hours.'

'Come on,' he said. 'We're worth more of your time than that.'

'Not in January, you aren't. I'll come back in the spring.'

'I'll look out for you,' he said, handing back the licence and waving her through with a wink.

She wasn't doing this because of liberal guilt, she reminded herself, though all along the journey she'd felt more than a pang of it as she found herself thinking about how she had always taken for granted her ability to enter and exit nations at will – those nations which required Americans to go through a visa-application process she'd simply never visited. It had come as a shock last year when she'd asked Hiroko and Ilse to go to Paris with her to discover how difficult it would be for Hiroko to get a visa – 'Not worth the hassle,' Hiroko had sadly concluded after looking at the list of requirements.

'You can come out now,' she said when the border was behind them and the surrounding landscape was snow-covered fields.

Abdullah clambered into the back seat.

'Should I stay here or come forward?' he asked with that careful politeness which disconcertingly blanketed his personality.

She pulled over on to the shoulder, so he could come around to the front in a dignified manner. He stepped out, walked a few steps to the field and bent to punch his fist through the snow. Kim gripped the wheel and considered pressing on the accelerator.

Abdullah got into the front seat, holding up his arm, which had snow clinging to it up to the elbow.

'It's deep,' he said. 'Last year in Central Park, my friends and I made snow angels.' He didn't look at her as he spoke.

'Have you been outside New York much?' she asked. It would take her approximately thirty minutes to get him to the fast-food restaurant near Montreal where he was due to meet the man who would take him onwards. Thirty minutes in a car with an Afghan. She glanced sideways as he carefully wiped snow off his black-gloved hand, and told herself there was no need to feel threatened.

'Once,' he said. He spoke slowly, choosing his words carefully – or perhaps he was conscious that his accent wasn't easy to follow. 'My friend Kemal rented a van and took a group of us to Massachusetts, to a mosque there, during Ramzan. We were seven of us. Two Turks, one Afghan, one Pakistani, two from Egypt, one from Morocco. All travelling together in America.'

'Just once? In nearly a decade.' Then she felt foolish for the incredulousness that revealed her inability to conceive of a life without holidays and travel.

'Yes. It was amazing, the way America drives when it isn't in New York city.' He smiled. 'The road signs! We laughed so much about the road signs.'

'What's so funny about road signs?' She could feel her mouth position itself into a smile, wanting very much to find some shared moment of humour but unable to see how 'road signs' might lead to levity.

'For everything, everything that is, everything that might happen, there's a road sign. DEER CROSSING. MOOSE CROSSING. OLD PEOPLE CROSSING. CHILDREN CROSSING. ROCK FALLING. Only one rock? That one I don't understand.'

At that, she did laugh, genuinely, relaxing her grip on the wheel slightly and becoming aware for the first time how stiff with tension her neck had become. She almost made some joke about Sisyphus.

Abdullah almost caught her eye as he smiled, and continued: 'BRIDGE AHEAD. COVERED BRIDGE AHEAD. SOFT SHOULDERS AHEAD. ROAD WIDENS. ROAD NARROWS. My friend Kemal – he's Turkish, very educated – he said what a thing it is, to live in a country where every possible happening is announced in bright glow-in-the-dark letters. We wondered what would happen if something unexpected happened in a country like this, without any warning.'

Kim glanced sharply at him, but he was leaning forward rotating his arm in front of the heating vents to dry off the sleeve of his grey winter coat and still not looking at her. She hadn't noticed any of the road signs while driving up I-87. But she'd noticed flags. Despite these months of seeing so many of them in the city she'd still been taken aback by their profusion. Flags stuck on back windows of cars; flags on bumper stickers; flags impaled on antennae; flags on little flag poles adhered to side mirrors; flags hanging out of windows; flags waving a welcome at service stations; flags painted on billboards (with some company's logo printed discreetly yet visibly at the bottom in a patriotically capitalistic gesture). They made her remember Ilse laughing that the phrase 'God Bless America' struck her as advertisement rather than imperative (STUDENTS – BUY SCHOOL SUPPLIES HERE. MOMS – GIVE YOUR KIDS THE GIFT OF LOVE WITH HEARTY™ SOUP. GOD BLESS AMERICA.) And yet, though she knew both Ilse and Harry would have rolled their eyes at the display of patriotism she saw something moving in it. But she kept wondering what her Afghan passenger made of it.

'Then we got our answer,' he said. 'To what America would do if something unexpected happened.'

'Yes, you certainly did,' she said, discovering all the tension in her body seemed to have moved to her jaw, making it difficult to get the words out.

This time he looked directly at her.

342

'No, I didn't mean . . .' He shook his head, looked offended, made her feel apologetic, then irritated for being made to feel apologetic. 'That night, on the way back to New York, I was half asleep when I realised that up ahead all cars were slowing, swerving around something. I woke up fully, and imagined someone dead in the middle of the highway. Then I heard Kemal laugh. There, in front of us, lit up by headlights, was a big pile of blue and pink toy animals – rabbits and bears.'

Kim saw it as he spoke in his soft voice, envisioned something almost reverential about the way all cars slowed and swerved, not daring to run over a little blue tail or a soft pink ear. It would have been a moment of silence, of wonder, she knew, uniting everyone on that dark dark highway.

'And Kemal also swerved,' she said.

It wasn't a question, until Abdullah didn't respond, turning instead to look out of the window at the unblemished whiteness.

He had cut right through the stuffed toys. Kim found the image grotesque, and knew she couldn't indicate as much without appearing to suffer from misguided American empathy – cluster bomb the Afghans but for God's sake don't drive over the pink bunny rabbits!

Could he tell her, Abdullah wondered? Could he say he had asked Kemal to drive as close to the toys as possible and each of the men inside had taken armloads of rabbits and bears – their fur softer than anything the men had touched in years. Each of them had a child or a nephew or niece or young sibling to whom they would send the toys as a gift the next time one of the lucky ones with legal paperwork left New York and headed to whichever part of the world he had left behind. Abdullah's son now slept with the soft blue bunny the father he'd never met had sent to him via a cabbie from Peshawar.

But if he told Kim Burton this she might think he was a thief – all of them, thieves – stealing fallen cargo.

'Your English,' Kim said, after a short silence. 'It's very good. Where did you learn?'

'When I first arrived in America I only knew what I remembered from Raza's classes. But my first week in Jersey City I went to the mosque there and asked the Imam to tell me where I could learn English. And he found a retired teacher, from Afghanistan, who said it would be his farz – you understand the word? No? It means religious obligation. It's a very important word to us. He said it was his farz to teach a mujahideen. Not everyone forgot. What we had done, for Afghanistan, for the world. Not everyone forgot.'

'I can't really imagine what it was like,' Kim said, carefully, mentally testing her own sentences before she spoke them for anything that might give offence. 'All those years of fighting the Soviets.'

'No. No one can. War is like disease. Until you've had it, you don't know it. But no. That's a bad comparison. At least with disease everyone thinks it might happen to them one day. You have a pain here, swelling there, a cold which stays and stays. You start to think maybe this is something really bad. But war – countries like yours they always fight wars, but always somewhere else. The disease always happens somewhere else. It's why you fight more wars than anyone else; because you understand war least of all. You need to understand it better.'

In the silence of the SUV, with the heating on a fraction too high, she realised just how uncomfortable he was making her feel when she found herself unwilling to retort: 'So what you're saying is . . . the way to end wars is to have everyone fight them?'

But why should she feel uncomfortable? She was the one making all the effort. Abdullah seemed to feel he owed her nothing. This morning when she met him at the street corner he and Hiroko had picked the evening before he had thanked her, very politely, and insisted that he would stay hidden under blankets as long as they were in America; if the car were searched at the border he would say he climbed into the back at a service station on I-87 when he discovered the SUV unlocked. But beyond that he had offered nothing, hadn't even acknowledged she was breaking her nation's laws for someone whose innocence she had no reason to take for granted.

The snow from his jacket had melted into a stain of water, which he was attempting to dry, very carefully, with a handkerchief. What reason was there to believe the story his brother told Raza? How

344

did they know the FBI knocked on his door for no reason except that he was an Afghan? How did they know he had run for no reason except panic about his migration status? That he was an Afghan didn't make him a liar or a terrorist, of course not; but wasn't it just as absurd – condescending almost – to assume that because an Afghan he couldn't be a liar or a terrorist? If his story were true he should just have gone to the FBI. No matter how bad things had become in the name of security no one – no one – was going to be detained indefinitely for just being an illegal migrant worker. Come on! New York would shut down if that become a crime anyone cared about. And if the FBI did turn him over to the INS, what of it? He'd be deported. To Afghanistan. In the comfort of a plane!

She cracked open the window, and let the racing wind whistle through, though Abdullah huddled into his coat and put his hands over his ears – whether to cut off the sound or the cold she didn't know.

It had all happened so fast. Less than ten hours between the time she met him and the time they left the city.

'What's the point of waiting?' Hiroko had said when Kim queried the need for such haste. 'The FBI's already been to the garage from where he leases the cab, and to the home of the man who takes the cab on its night shift to ask if they know where he is. This afternoon he called this person in Canada who's arranging things to say he'll meet him tomorrow, so tomorrow he's going. I told you, I'll take him.'

Hiroko made everything seem inevitable – this journey, the timing of it, his innocence. And so Kim had gone against everything in her training, hadn't even considered the points of stress under which Abdullah's story might buckle, and had simply curled up in her bed and fallen asleep as soon as Hiroko had agreed to let her drive the car. The truth, she now realised, was that she was so busy looking at ways of keeping Hiroko from smuggling an Afghan across the border that no other threats had been visible.

'Hiroko's an amazing woman, isn't she?' Kim said, rolling up the window, trying one last time to establish common ground.

'Raza has a place in heaven because of her,' Abdullah replied. 'Imagine knowing your whole life you have a place in heaven.'

'I don't understand.'

'She converted to Islam. The one who converts another is guaranteed a place in heaven for himself and his children and grandchildren and so on down for seven generations. I think it's wrong only to honour Raza's father – the man who did the converting. The convert should also be honoured. It's because of Raza's mother also – not only his father – that he's going to heaven. And his children and grandchildren after him. Even martyrs who die in jihad can't do so much for their family. It's written in the Quran.'

'Have you read the Quran?'

'Of course I have.'

'Have you read it in any language you understand?' Suddenly the traffic seemed to have thickened; a reassuring number of people were driving alongside, and no fear of giving offence could possibly match her indignation at listening to Hiroko being reduced to a launch pad for her husband and son's journey to a paradise in which she didn't appear to have secured a place for herself in this Afghan's mad system of belief.

'I understand Islam,' he said, tensing.

'I'll take that to mean no. I've read it – in English. Believe me, the Quran says nothing of the sort. And frankly, what kind of heaven is heaven if you can find shortcuts into it? Seven generations!'

'Please do not speak this way.'

'Tell me one thing. One thing.' Unexpectedly, such a rage within her, overpowering everything. 'If an Afghan dies in the act of killing infidels in his country does he go straight to heaven?'

'If the people he kills come as invaders or occupiers, yes. He is shaheed. Martyr.'

How slowly, unwillingly, her fist had opened to drop the first clod of earth on to Harry's coffin. It was the moment when her heart truly understood that all the imagined tomorrows of their relationship – Delhi, conversations without recrimination, days of hearing the other's stories in full – would never come. Because of just one man with a gun. She had always thought it would take so

346

much more than that to bring Harry down. But it was just one Afghan with a gun who never stopped to think of Harry Burton as anything but an infidel invader whose death opened up a path to Paradise.

'He is a murderer. And your heaven is an abomination.'

'We should not speak any more.'

'No, we should not.'

There was not another word between them – the tension almost suffocating – until she pulled into the parking lot of the fast-food restaurant. But as he opened the car door to leave he said something in Arabic in which she only caught the word 'Allah' and followed it up with, 'I won't forget what you've done.'

What had she done? She watched him walk across the parking lot, his stride that of a man walking into freedom, a family with two children entering the restaurant behind him.

40

The sleeping gorilla was a work of artistry; a button beneath its matted hair controlled the machinery that surged its chest, a lever concealed beneath its armpit unhinged the animal and revealed the cavity within. It was only during refuelling stops and on landing near Montreal that Raza needed to hide within the animal; during the rest of the journey he sat with the Kuwaiti pilots in the cockpit, incredulous at their tales of ferrying the whims of their Saudi employer from one corner of the globe to the other.

When the plane reached the airstrip near Montreal, a forklift was waiting to lower the gorilla cage on to yet another pickup. Raza heard the animals and birds chittering and shrieking and squawking as the cage was lifted out; but there were no sounds of human protest.

A thirteen-year-old boy hiding in a barn to escape his father's drunken rage was the only one to see the pickup drive into the barn, where the driver got out and opened the cage at the back, resting one hand on the steadily moving chest of the beast within and then reaching under its arm to split the creature in two. The boy ducked his head into the straw, more afraid of the sight of entrails than of being discovered by the man of inhuman strength; when he looked up again, the gorilla was intact but lifeless, a second man standing beside the first, shaking his hand. The boy never spoke of this to anyone.

'You owe me the remaining ten per cent,' the driver, John, said to Raza as he drove the pickup away from the barn, Raza now more comfortably seated beside him.

'I can give you just the ten per cent,' Raza said, reaching into the knapsack, which was looking considerably more battered than it had at the start of his journey. He pulled out the requisite amount of money, then tipped the knapsack on to its side, so John could see the wads of notes that remained within. 'Or I can give you everything that's here.'

'Keep talking.'

'My friend Abdullah is supposed to leave Canada on a ship next month. Ruby Eye arranged it.'

'Ruby Eye collected the money from his family in Afghanistan,' John corrected. 'I'm the one who arranged it.'

'Good,' Raza said calmly. 'So you can arrange for him to fly back in the gorilla instead.'

John glanced down again at the knapsack.

'I suppose I could. I'll tell him tomorrow when I meet him. Or you could go in my place and break the news yourself.' He looked over at Raza and smiled. 'Yeah, surprised you there, didn't I, Taliban?'

So it was Raza seated in the orange bucket chair, beside a Formica tabletop, who Abdullah saw when he walked into the fast-food restaurant near Montreal.

'Raza Hazara!' He spoke softly so as not to alarm any of the other diners, but his voice was warm as he pulled Raza to his feet and embraced him. When they drew apart neither of them spoke, each smiling and narrowing his eyes, tilting his head this way and that to find familiarity in the stranger across from him, and then Abdullah caught Raza's ear and tugged on it.

'I had no idea you would be here. Neither of them let on.'

'Neither of who?' His voice had deepened, Raza thought, but the eyes and smile were unchanged.

'Your mother. And Kim Burton. You didn't know? She just dropped me here.' He took a step towards the window, and shook his head. 'She's gone. You really didn't know?'

Kim Burton? Raza shook his head. For the last six days he'd been wondering what she'd been told, what she believed.

'She has a phone with her. You could call her.' He held out his cell phone.

349

'You have her number?' Raza said.

Kim Burton! Whatever they had told her, she would never believe Raza was involved with Harry's death. He knew this. He thought again of the story of the spider. When the Prophet was on the run from Mecca to Medina, he stopped in a cave for the night because his friend and travelling companion, Abu Bakr, had been bitten by a snake and needed to rest. As he sat in the cave, knowing his pursuers would follow his tracks across the moonlit desert, all the way to the base of the rocky slopes, he saw a spider scuttling frantically across the mouth of the cave. Then he heard his pursuers' footsteps outside and a voice said, 'No, he's not here. No one's been here for a long time. Look . . .' and as the moon emerged from behind a cloud the Prophet saw the cave mouth was entirely covered by the gleaming web of a spider.

This story had passed hands between their two families for three generations. In Afghanistan, Harry had pointed this out and said, 'You need to tell it to Kim. Weiss-Burtons and Tanaka-Ashrafs – we are each other's spiders.'

Then he and Harry placed side by side the stories each knew of their families. Stories of opportunities received (Sajjad found, through Konrad, a way out of the constraining world of his family business), loyalty offered (Hiroko refused to back away from Konrad when her world turned him into an enemy), shelter provided (three times Ilse gave Hiroko a home: in Delhi, Karachi, New York), strength transferred (Ilse would never have left the life she hated if not for Hiroko), disaster elided (James and Ilse ensured Sajjad and Hiroko were well away from Partition's bloodletting). And – this part Raza and Harry didn't have to say aloud – second chances (at being a better father, a better son). Now Kim, too, was part of the stories. Whatever happened to him, Raza knew she would watch over his ageing mother as the spider dance proceeded.

But Abdullah said, 'Her number? No. I don't have it.'

Raza tried to hide his disappointment as he caught Abdullah's sleeve and pulled him down into a chair.

'You've met my mother?'

'Yes, Raza Ashraf. She found me. You have her eyes. Now that I've met her I look at you and wonder how I ever saw a Hazara.'

'I'm sorry I lied to you. I'm sorry I pretended to be an Afghan. It's only very recently I realised how wrong it was to claim that.'

Abdullah waved his hand in the air, not dismissing the matter so much as putting it to one side for the moment.

'Before anything else, explain to me how we're both here at the same time. This can't be coincidence.'

Raza told him everything, in as truncated a version as he could manage without confusing the narrative. When he finished, Abdullah laughed.

'Your mother told me something of your life – your real life. So. Your mother lost her family and home to war; your father was torn away from the city whose poetry and history had nurtured his family for generations; your second father was shot dead in Afghanistan; the CIA thinks you're a terrorist; you've travelled in the hold of a ship, knowing that if you died no one would ever know; home is something you remember, not some place you live; and your first thought when you reach safety is how to help a friend you haven't seen in twenty years, and this is the part of your story you say the least about. Raza, my brother, truly now you are an Afghan.'

Raza touched Abdullah's hand lightly.

'The Abdullah I knew twenty years ago would not have been so forgiving.'

'That Abdullah was very young, and very foolish. He thought corpses spouting blood were decorations for the sides of trucks.' He looked out towards the parking lot again. 'I feel very bad, Raza. Your friend Kim – she did so much to help me, and I was . . . ungracious.'

'My friend Kim.' Raza shook his head. 'We've never met. We've just been presences in each other's lives for a very long time. What did you say to her? What's she like?'

'She has short hair. Like a boy,' Abdullah said, his index fingers knocking against his jawline, just beneath the ear.

'And we all know how much you Pathans like your pretty boys, walnut,' Raza laughed.

Abdullah cuffed him lightly.

'Still the same Raza. I don't know what I said to her. There's something – don't laugh at me when I say this – there is something open in her face. Some Americans have it, that openness. You think you could say anything to them. And we were both sitting in the front seat. Ten years of driving cabs every day, twelve hours a day, and this was something new.'

'You hit on her?' Raza switched to English.

Abdullah drew back.

'What kind of man do you think I am?'

'The kind of man I am. Go on, what did you do?'

'I spoke to her. As I have never spoken to an American woman before. I wanted her to understand something, I don't know what, about being an Afghan here. About war. Again and again war, Raza. And then. Then, I don't know. She started attacking Islam. They're all, everyone, everywhere you go now – television, radio, passengers in your cab, everywhere – everyone just wants to tell you what they know about Islam, how they know so much more than you do, what do you know, you've just been a Muslim your whole life, how does that make you know anything?'

Raza put an arm on Abdullah's.

'Quiet, quiet. People are looking. Abdullah, Kim's not like that. I know. She can't be like that.'

'She said heaven is an abomination because my brother is in it.' He covered his face with his hands. 'You hear them now all the time. Talking about how they won the Cold War, now they'll win this war. My brother died winning their Cold War. Now they say he makes heaven an abomination.'

'You're tired,' Raza said, holding Abdullah's hands between his own. 'Come with me. The car's outside. You can sleep on the plane. Today, Abdullah, you make the journey home to your family.'

'New York is home,' he said brokenly. 'New York is my home. The taxi drivers are my family.'

Raza felt a curious sense of envy amidst his pity.

'I know things are bad, but perhaps there wasn't any need to run. Even now, it might not be too late. Kim and my mother will help. They'll find you a lawyer. These things still matter, they must.'

'You're living in another world. My friend Kemal – he was

picked up ten days ago. No one has heard from him since. New York now is nets cast to the wind, seeking for any Muslim to ensnare.'

His words made Raza turn reflexively to look out of the window. No nets, but there was a police car in the parking lot which hadn't been there a few seconds ago, and two policemen talking to a redhead whose hair reached her jawline. The woman turned towards the window, her finger pointing—

Raza grabbed Abdullah's shirt and yanked hard, ducking at the same time so neither of them could be seen from outside. He pressed his keys into Abdullah's palm.

'Go from the back door. The silver Mazda. Take it. Run. Trust me.' He pushed Abdullah from his chair.

'Raza, what—?'

'For your son's sake. Go quickly. Please.' He picked up the baseball cap that had been resting next to his elbow and put it firmly on Abdullah's head, handing him his jacket – Harry's jacket – at the same time, and reached across to take the coat Abdullah had slung over his chair.

'Allah protect you,' Abdullah said, squeezing his hand, before walking very rapidly to the back door.

But not rapidly enough. The policemen had entered; one pointed towards Abdullah, the other shrugged and called out, 'Sir?' in his direction.

Raza stood up, wearing Abdullah's grey coat, said 'Allah-o-Akbar' loudly enough to be heard. The diners seated next to him shrank into their seats; a man standing by the utensils picked up his child and held her protectively in his arms; someone called out to the policemen.

Kim Burton crouched beside a car in the parking lot, the side-view mirror allowing her to see the door to the restaurant without being seen. She didn't want him caught, she didn't want him to escape, she didn't want to be responsible either way. When the policemen exited, Abdullah in his grey winter coat handcuffed between them, she felt both sickened and relieved.

And then she saw his shoulders, far too slight for the great bulk of the winter coat.

41

The policemen had identical grips. Each had hold of his upper arm with a pressure that was merely professional. One was left-handed, one right-handed, and Raza wondered if this had been a consideration in pairing them up. Did policemen, like opening batsmen, work well with a left-right combination?

Pellets of ice were falling out of the grey sky. Raza was glad to be outside, away from the atmosphere of terror replaced by thrill – the diners had witnessed something, it would be on the evening news, they would tell all their friends to watch.

A car in the parking lot was covered in snow; it would have been here since the previous night. He wondered if its owner had spent the night in the restaurant, hiding in the bathroom stalls until the closing-up shift departed, scavenging through the kitchens in the dregs of night, finding everything locked up save for condiments. Or perhaps someone was in that car – had been there for days, would stay there until the first spring thaw revealed the corpse of a man so defined by absence that no one noticed he was missing.

His head was down so she wouldn't see his face. He wasn't actually looking at the car, was only recalling he had seen it as he entered the restaurant and had paid it no attention then. All he was looking at now was ice melting at every moment of impact – with paving, with shoes, with the soil in the otherwise empty flowerbeds near the restaurant door. Annihilated by contact, any contact.

'Wait!' he heard her shout. The policemen stopped, angled their bodies towards her.

There was the spider, and there was its shadow. Two families, two versions of the spider dance. The Ashraf-Tanakas, the Weiss-Burtons – their story together the story of a bomb, the story of a lost homeland, the story of a man shot dead by the docks, the story of body armour ignored, of running alone from the world's greatest power.

Still he didn't look up, but the space between one footfall and the next told him she was walking towards him in large strides. No other sound in the parking lot; the zip of cars on the highway was backdrop – and hope. Abdullah should have left through the exit around the back, he would be on the highway now, using his phone to call John and set up another meeting place. But it wasn't enough to be out of the parking lot, he needed time to get away, time in which no one would know they should be looking out for a broad-shouldered, hazel-eyed Afghan.

'I need to make sure that's him,' he heard Kim say.

Raza raised his head and bellowed, 'Chup!', the end of the word half-strangled with pain as the policemen's hands pressed down on his head, forced him to his knees.

He saw Kim Burton's eyes refuse to believe what they were seeing. Blood rushed to her face and for a moment she looked angry, furious – Harry's quick temper manifest in her – as though the world was attempting to play a trick on her which she didn't find even remotely entertaining. Then she was reaching a hand out to him, and Raza's body jerked away from her touch.

'Stand back,' he heard one of the policemen say.

Raza wasn't sure she'd heard. She was staring at him as a child might stare at a unicorn or some other creature of legend whose existence she'd always believed in yet never expected to receive proof of.

In any other circumstance he'd be reflecting her expression back at her. In the twenty years since Harry had handed him marsh-mallows on the beach and said Kim was asking if he had a girlfriend he'd been imagining and re-imagining their first meeting. Now his mouth twisted at how far his imagination had fallen short.

His grimace brought her back to the moment. He saw her looking up towards the restaurant window, then at the winter

355

coat . . . she took a step back. She would be wondering, he guessed correctly, if he had set her up from the beginning, from that first phone call from Afghanistan. Why had he recoiled from her touch and why had he said, 'Chup!' It was one of the Urdu words with which Harry most liberally seasoned his language – Raza would be aware she knew it meant 'Be quiet.' What did he think she was going to say? He saw Harry's careful intelligence in her – looking at the pieces, trying to understand the picture.

The ice was falling into her auburn hair, splinters winking as they dissolved. For a moment, he wavered. All he needed to do was allow her to say what she had been about to say when he stopped her. She had only to say, 'That's not him,' and they would let him go. And then – a bead of melted ice trailed down her face, following the route a tear might take – he and Kim Burton would finally sit down face to face, to talk about Harry, to talk about Hiroko, to talk about everything.

But he would not do that to Abdullah. Not this Raza Konrad Ashraf – not the one who had lain in the hold of a ship bearing the weight of an Afghan boy, not the one who had floated in the dagger-cold sea looking up at Orion, promising himself he would not be as he was before. Every chance, every second, he could give Abdullah he would.

He looked once more at the snow-covered car, the desolation of it, and wryly considered this new heroic persona he was trying to take on. Truth was, he didn't have the temperament for this kind of running anyway; they'd catch him soon enough. Perhaps arrest Bilal, or his mother, or anyone else who might be termed accomplice. Kim Burton, too, if she walked with him out of this parking lot. What a gift, then, what a surprising gift, to be able to say the moment when freedom ended had counted for something. Finally, he counted for something.

'Is it him?' one of the policemen said.

He looked straight at Kim.

'Hanh,' he said very softly. Hanh. Yes. Say yes.

He saw her decision, though he didn't know how or why she had come to it.

'Yes,' she said.

356

The men nodded and lifted Raza to his feet. Her expression became frantic as she heard the jangle of his handcuffs.

'I don't know that he's done anything wrong. He just looked suspicious. My father died in Afghanistan a few days ago. I'm not coping very well. There's nothing he's done wrong. Please let him go.'

'Don't worry,' the policeman said in the tone of voice men reserve for women they decide are hysterical. 'We're just going to ask him a few questions. And I'm sorry about your father.'

They walked Raza past Kim as they headed to the car. The look on her face was one he knew he'd never forget. No matter what happened to him, what anyone did now, what they said, how they tried to break him, he would remember – as if it were a promise of the world that awaited if he survived – Kim Burton's expression, which said, clearer than the words of any language, 'Forgive me.'

He would have. If it were in his power he would have taken her mistake from her and flung all the points of its gleaming sharpness into the heavens. But he knew it didn't work that way. He could only try to convey, in that final instant before they dragged him away – in the dip of his head, the sorrow of his smile – that he still saw the spider as well as its shadow.

42

By the time she was speeding down the West Side Highway – every traffic light turning green at her approach, the river lit up with Manhattan's liquid reflection, the sky that glowing orange which passed for darkness on cloudy nights – Kim Burton was no closer than she had been six hours earlier in the parking lot to understanding what had transpired that afternoon, both in the restaurant and in her own mind.

In one moment she saw Abdullah as the innocent. What had he said after all to warrant sending the law after an illegal Afghan? That he had sat in a car which might have driven over teddy bears? That Hiroko was to be honoured for assuring her son a place in heaven? That those who defended their nation against attack were heroes? In the next moment he was a threat, seeing virtue only through the narrow prism of his religious belief, conferring martyrdom on those who attacked Americans. It was necessary to allow the experts – those involved with threat assessment of a kind that was not part of her experience – to speak to him, to make the decision she wasn't competent to make.

In that first moment, she was grateful beyond measure to Raza, that deus ex machina, long waiting in the wings of her life for the moment when he could enter with a flourish and interpose himself between her misguided intentions and their fulfilment. He would be fine, of course. She had concluded this before she even reached the border, once she was able to brush away the awful tension of the parking lot and consider the plain facts. Of course he would be fine. There wasn't any question of that. However bizarre his behaviour, there was nothing illegal about it, or about his presence in Canada. The policemen need never know he had helped Abdullah escape; they'd merely conclude that the American woman was paranoid, seeing a threat in every Muslim.

But in the next moment she was so angry she had to pull over – more than once – to collect herself. He had allowed Abdullah to escape. And now there was nothing she could do without exposing Raza as an accomplice. And how had that become the line she couldn't cross? This was the part that confounded her the most, made her want to rip the windpipe from Raza's throat. There had been such a surprising gravitas to him, such an urgency and knowing in his eyes, that she had done what she never otherwise did – suspended her own judgement, and complied.

She missed Harry. She missed Ilse. She missed the world as it had been. Abdullah's voice in her head said it had never been.

When she entered the Mercer Street apartment the total darkness within told her Hiroko was asleep already. Kim had driven all the way back to the city instead of stopping in the Adirondacks as had been her original plan purely so she could tell Hiroko what had happened, but now it felt like a reprieve to be spared that tonight.

She switched on the floor lamp, and Hiroko was sitting upright on the sofa, looking at her.

'Where's my son, Kim?'

'God, Hiroko. You scared me.'

'I called you. Many times.'

'My battery died.' For some reason it seemed necessary to extract her phone from her pocket and hold it out as proof.

'Such a strange thing happened this afternoon.' Hiroko stood up and walked over to the window. 'Omar called and asked me to come downstairs.'

'Who's Omar?'

'Omar!' Hiroko snapped, turning to glare at Kim. 'You've been in his cab at least a dozen times.'

'Sorry. Of course.'

Hiroko continued to look at her for a moment, and then resumed staring down at the lights strung across the Williamsburg

Bridge like stars too curious about the life of New York to keep their distance, her voice returning to its tone of neutrality.

'When I went downstairs he handed me his phone and said it was Abdullah. I thought he must have lost my number. Why else would he call Omar? But it was because he thought my phone might be tapped. By the CIA. As part of their investigations into your father's death.'

'What does Abdullah know about my father's death?' Her mouth had some trouble forming the words.

'Only what Raza told him.' She opened the side window, breathed in the slicing wind. 'He is running, Kim. Just as I said he was. He's been running since Harry's death. But not for the reason I thought. He's running from the CIA. They think he was involved, that he planned it.'

'Planned what?'

'Harry's death.' The wind rattled the pane, blew in a light scattering of snow.

'Is that supposed to be a joke?' When Hiroko didn't respond, Kim raised her voice. 'Does your friend Abdullah think my father's death is something to joke about?'

'He was calling to ask if it would help Raza or hurt him if he turned himself in. He said he saw you talking to the policemen before they took Raza away. Why was that, Kim Burton?' She closed the window, sealing the two of them into a dimly lit room. 'Could you explain?'

Kim had thought the world was strange and wrong a few hours earlier. Now she understood she had only been approaching the precipice.

'I didn't know Raza was there. I called the police – yes, I did that; I had reasons – I called them because of Abdullah.'

'What reasons?' She still had her back to Kim, but both women could see each other captured, inches apart, in the window.

The van he was in drove over a pile of teddy bears. There was no way to explain the terror in the silence of the Afghan which conveyed that image to her. Kim waved a hand imploringly and it passed through Hiroko's reflection.

'I trusted my training. Don't you understand? If you suspect a threat you can't just ignore it because you wish – and I really really wish this – you lived in a world where all suspicion of Muslims is just prejudice, nothing more.'

'And there it is,' said Hiroko, finally turning to look at her.

'No, there it is not. How can you? Over three years we've been constant in each other's lives, and you think I'm a bigot? I'm sorry, but it wasn't Buddhists flying those planes, there is no video footage of Jews celebrating the deaths of three thousand Americans, it wasn't a Catholic who shot my father. You think it makes me a bigot to recognise this?'

'I think you're too scared and too angry to be allowed to make a judgement. What did you talk to him about? The orchards of Kandahar? The exaltation of being part of a successful cab strike and knowing this is how fights can be won, this is how they should be won? The fear of being a disappointment to his wife and son?'

Kim sat down where she was, all the way across the room, back pressed to the wall. The only light in the room was directed at Hiroko, standing up against an empty orange sky.

'I've seen you angry, but never like this,' she said in a small voice.

'I don't remember ever being like this. I don't like it. I don't like it at all.' She clenched her fists and shook them in front of her – a strange gesture that only stopped short of being foolish by its surprising venom. 'Ilse once accused Sajjad of being a rapist. For all of two minutes she thought he was a rapist. She told me afterwards, those were two minutes in which she was lost. And look at you now, Ilse's granddaughter. You don't even know you're lost.'

'You can't possibly compare! She'd known him for years.'

'You'd known him for five minutes. That's how long he said you spoke to each other for. Was he lying about that? No, he wasn't, was he? You condemn a man based on five minutes of conversation. In its own way, that's as much of a crime as what Ilse did. Five minutes! I spent one evening and almost all the next day talking to him. Do you think I would have let you get into a car with him if I thought . . .' She pulled short, her voice strange to her in its rage.

Kim stood up, and walked a few steps towards Hiroko.

'If I did look at him and see the man who killed my father, isn't that understandable? I'm not saying it's OK, but you have to say you understand.'

'Should I look at you and see Harry Truman?'

Kim's eyes first widened, then narrowed. Was that supposed to be a trump card? Ridiculous, and insulting. Her own family had lost one of its own in Nagasaki; Konrad's death was the most vivid story of terror she had grown up with.

'Raza will be fine,' she said, turning her back on Hiroko. 'He's got A and G's lawyers on his side; there's nothing he can't get away with.'

'Not even Harry's murder?'

'Hiroko, I'm too tired for this,' she threw over her shoulder as she poured herself a glass of Scotch. Bath, drink, bed. Exactly what she'd wanted twenty-four hours ago before Hiroko had drawn her into this mad plan. Bath, drink, bed – and tomorrow she'd call the estate agents and find if there was any way to bring forward the start of her tenancy. 'No one could think Raza is involved with Harry's murder. Your Afghan is a liar, and I don't know what besides.'

'Come back here and sit down.'

'I'm not one of your ten-year-old students, Mrs Ashraf.'

She was almost all the way to her bedroom when Hiroko spoke again.

'When Konrad first heard of the concentration camps he said you have to deny people their humanity in order to decimate them. You don't.'

Walk on, Kim told herself. Get into your bedroom and close the door. But she stayed where she was, cradling the glass of Scotch that put Harry in the room with her.

'You just have to put them in a little corner of the big picture. In the big picture of the Second World War, what was seventy-five thousand more Japanese dead? Acceptable, that's what it was. In the big picture of threats to America, what is one Afghan? Expendable. Maybe he's guilty, maybe not. Why risk it? Kim, you are the kindest, most generous woman I know. But right now, because of you, I understand for the first time how nations can applaud when their governments drop a second nuclear bomb.'

The silence that followed was the silence of intimates who find themselves strangers. The dark birds were between them, their burnt feathers everywhere.

Kim was the first to speak. Not to Hiroko, though. She picked up the phone and dialled Canada. She spoke to someone, then someone else, insisted, pleaded, held on a very long time. Finally she was asked to leave her number and wait by the phone.

She and Hiroko sat on a sofa, side by side, unspeaking.

Within a few seconds one of the policemen from the parking lot called. Kim put the call on speaker phone.

'I'm glad you called,' he said. 'I wanted you to know you did absolutely the right thing today.'

'No,' she said. 'No, he did nothing wrong. I'm the one who broke the law.' She would turn herself in. She would say the man she reported was a man she had smuggled across the border. She would say that after she reported him she started to worry he would reveal her complicity if arrested and so she identified the wrong man in the parking lot. She would say could she please speak to the arrested man and apologise in person.

'There's no law against reporting someone on a hunch. And he did a lot wrong,' the policeman said. 'I probably shouldn't be telling you this. But I think you deserve to know. Your government has been searching for that man. They're very glad to have him in their custody now. Miss, your father would be proud of you.'

Hiroko stood up and walked slowly over to the window. Outside, at least, the world went on.

Acknowledgements

Thanks to: Omar Rahim, Samina Mishra, Jaya Bhattacharji, Ruchir Joshi, for accompanying me 'on location' in Karachi and Delhi; Aamer Hussein, Mohammed Hanif, Elizabeth Porto, for comments on various drafts; David Mitchell, for his generosity in suggesting avenues of research to a stranger; Beatrice Monti della Corte, for the haven that is Santa Maddalena; Victoria Hobbs and Alexandra Pringle, for continuing to be my dream team; Gillian Stern, for her sharp editorial eye; Ali Mir, for Sahir Ludhianvi and walks through New York City; Bobby Banerjee, for introducing me to the world of private military contractors; Karin Gosselink and Rachel Holmes, for their intellectual and political rigour; Biju Mathew, for allowing me to pick his brain; the dinner group in Galle, for the title; my parents and sister, for continuing to be my greatest support; numerous friends – particularly Maha Khan-Phillips and Janelle Schwartz – for listening to me talk about this book, or pulling me away from my desk when I needed it; everyone at Bloomsbury and A. M. Heath; Frances Coady; Mark Pringle; finally, and most of all, the writers, journalists, film-makers and photographers whose works helped me imagine the worlds I've written about in this book.

The translation of Sahir Ludhianvi's poem in the epigraph is my own; the title of the novel's final section is from Michael Ondaatje's *The English Patient*.

Further Reading

Eqbal Ahmed, *The Selected Writings*

Steve Coll, *Ghost Warriors*

John Hersey, *Hiroshima*

Biju Mathew, *TAXI*

Takashi Nagai, *The Bells of Nagasaki*

Keiji Nakazawa, *Barefoot Gen*

B. K. Zahrah Nasir, *The Gun Tree*

P. W. Singer, *Corporate Warriors*

Mohammad Yousaf and Mark Adkin, *Afghanistan – The Bear Trap*

Robert Pelton Young, *Licensed to Kill*

A NOTE ON THE TYPE

The text of this book is set in Berling roman. A modern face designed by K. E. Forsberg between 1951–58. In spite of its youth it does carry the characteristics of an old face. The serifs are inclined and blunt, and the g has a straight ear.

ALSO AVAILABLE KAMILA SHAMSIE
IN THE CITY BY THE SEA

Shortlisted for the John Llewellyn Rhys/Mail on Sunday Prize

Hasan is eleven years old. He loves cricket, pomegranates, the night sky, his clever, vibrant artistic mother and his etymologically obsessed lawyer father, and he adores his next-door neighbour Zehra. One early summer morning, while lazing happily on the roof, Hasan watches a young boy flying a yellow kite fall to his death. Soon after, Hasan's idyllic, sheltered family life is shattered when his beloved uncle Salman, a dissenting politician, is arrested and charged with treason. Set in a land ruled by an oppressive military regime, this eloquent, charming and quietly political novel vividly recreates the confusing world of a young boy on the edge of adulthood, and beautifully illustrates the transformative power of the imagination.

*

'Full of fun, longing and wit ... a debut of spirit and imagination, loaded with intelligent charm'
ALI SMITH, SCOTSMAN

'Lively, playful, provocative'
ANITA DESAI

'A touching and engrossing story ... an assured debut'
THE TIMES

*

ISBN 978 0 7475 7164 3 · PAPERBACK · £7.99

BLOOMSBURY

SALT AND SAFFRON

The Dard-e-Dils are known for their clavicles and love of stories. Aliya may not have inherited her family's patrician looks, but she is just as much a prey to their legends. They have plenty of stories to tell and secrets to hide, particularly the curse of 'not-quite' twins, and soon after Aliya falls for a boy from the wrong side of the tracks she begins to believe she is another 'not-quite twin', cosmically connected with her romantic, scandalous Aunt Mariam, in a way that hardly bodes well.

*

'Beautifully written in cunning, punning, glancing prose ... this book provides some delicious recipes for living and loving'
INDEPENDENT

'A funny, clever and romantic story ... perhaps Kamila Shamsie is our new multi-culti Nancy Mitford; a global girl who does love in both hot and cold climates'
BARBARA TRAPIDO

'Shamsie has created a rich, bright world'
TIMES LITERARY SUPPLEMENT

*

ISBN 978 0 7475 5395 3 · PAPERBACK · £7.99

B L O O M S B U R Y

KARTOGRAPHY

What is the moment, that exact moment when everything changes and the friends you have been, become the lovers you might be? Soul mates from birth Karim and Raheen finish one another's sentences, speak in anagrams and lie spine to spine as children. They are irrevocably bound to one another and to Karachi, Pakistan. It beats in their hearts – violent, polluted, corrupt, vibrant, brave and ultimately, home. However, Raheen is fiercely loyal and naively blinkered and she resents Karim's need to map their city, his need to name its streets and to expand the privileged world they know. When Karim is forced to leave for London their differences of opinion become a painful quarrel. As the years go by they let a barrier of silence build between them until, finally, they are brought together during a dry summer of strikes and ethnic violence and their relationship is poised between strained friendship and fated love.

Impassioned and touching, *Kartography* is a love song to Karachi. In her extraordinary new novel, Kamila Shamsie shows us that whatever happens in the world, we must never forget the complicated war in our own hearts.

*

'A boisterous tribute to her home town that crackles with the chaos of Pakistani political life'
THE TIMES

'Deftly woven, provocative ... blistering humour'
OBSERVER

'Perceptive, funny and poignant ... Kamila Shamsie has a sharp but sympathetic understanding of adolescent restlessness, boredom, and the anxious fantasies about an unknown future that are part of growing up ... memorable, and at moments deeply moving'
TIMES LITERARY SUPPLEMENT

*

ISBN 978 0 7475 6150 7 · PAPERBACK · £7.99

BLOOMSBURY

BROKEN VERSES

Fourteen years ago Aasmaani's mother Samina, a blazing beauty and fearless activist, walked out of her house and was never seen again. Aasmaani refuses to believe she is dead and still dreams of her glorious return. Now grown up and living in Karachi, Aasmaani receives what could be the longed-for proof that her mother is still alive. As she comes closer to the truth she is also irresistibly drawn to Ed, her ally and sparring partner, and the only person who can understand the profound hurt – and the profound love – that drives her.

*

'The delight in words and all their shades of meaning, characteristic of all her writing, is here used as the linchpin of the plot ... The voice that guides us around this world darts with wit and lightness in a way that is unique and often lovely'
GUARDIAN

'Her characters are all highly articulate, juggling, twisting and subverting language with breathtaking ease'
DAILY TELEGRAPH

'A gripping read'
INDEPENDENT

*

ISBN 978 0 74757 893 2 · PAPERBACK · £7.99

ORDER YOUR COPY: BY PHONE +44 (0)1256 302 699; BY EMAIL: DIRECT@MACMILLAN.CO.UK
DELIVERY IS USUALLY 3–5 WORKING DAYS. FREE POSTAGE AND PACKAGING FOR ORDERS OVER £20.

ONLINE: WWW.BLOOMSBURY.COM/BOOKSHOP
PRICES AND AVAILABILITY SUBJECT TO CHANGE WITHOUT NOTICE.

WWW.BLOOMSBURY.COM/KAMILASHAMSIE
TO DOWNLOAD A READING GROUP GUIDE FOR THIS AND OTHER BLOOMSBURY
BOOKS VISIT OUR READING CLUB AT WWW.BLOOMSBURY.COM/READINGCLUB

BLOOMSBURY